CRIMES OF

Passion

NANCY MEANS WRIGHT

MAGGIE PRICE

JONATHAN HARRINGTON

B.J. DANIELS

W🌐RLDWIDE.

TORONTO • NEW YORK • LONDON
AMSTERDAM • PARIS • SYDNEY • HAMBURG
STOCKHOLM • ATHENS • TOKYO • MILAN
MADRID • WARSAW • BUDAPEST • AUCKLAND

CRIMES OF PASSION

A Worldwide Mystery/January 2002

ISBN 0-373-26407-0

Printed in U.S.A.

CONTENTS

FIRE AND ICE
by Nancy Means Wright

For my extended family,
a support through the fire and ice of my life.

Acknowledgments

Grateful thanks to the following: my ecologist son-in-law, Marc Lapin, for his expertise on forests and ice storms; my daughter-in-law, Lesley Wright, for an insightful critique of this manuscript; the Addison *Independent* of Middlebury, Vermont, for its comprehensive coverage of the '98 ice storm; my perceptive editor, Feroze Mohammed, for his confidence in my muse.

Also Eric Neil, Joe Schatzle, Joan Payne, Doris Severy, Dr. Paul Morrow, Vermont State Medical Examiner, and the late Robert Frost for use of the title of his famous poem (not to mention a certain celebrated Vermont restaurant).

MONDAY

LINEMAN ERNIE HILAND had never seen such a storm in his thirty-nine years. It was still raging Monday evening, a day after the rains had begun and already the whole world was turning to ice. The trees he was clearing away from the downed wires were thickly coated. Branches crashed around him, as though somebody had swept off a table full of crockery, a hundred cups and glasses smashed to bits. Each wire he fixed took a good hour. And thousands still to splice. Even then the splicing didn't always work. He'd cut away the broken limbs, repair the wire—then the ice would melt a little in the fluctuating temperatures and the tree would snap back up, hit the wire. A man couldn't win.

Ernie hadn't had a decent meal in hours either, not since Crystal went directly from work to a friend's house, and then to a planning board meeting. He couldn't believe they were still holding that meeting in the middle of a storm. But there was some big deal pending, she'd said, and they were fighting against a deadline. Now the phone lines were down in East Branbury, so she couldn't call home.

There was something about bad weather that seemed to coincide with Crystal's disappearances. Ernie was beginning to see a pattern. The last big snow storm—end of January it was—she was gone twenty-three hours, came home all kisses and excuses. The car was stuck in a snowbank, she said, and no phone in sight. He'd wondered about that.

He spliced the wires together with a sleeve. Ernie was a slow worker, but careful; he wanted it done right. His workclothes were soaked through, and he was half-starved. The other linemen had suppers with them; Ernie had only a couple of black bananas he'd found in the kitchen, saltines with peanut butter their daughter Gracie made up—not enough to keep a working man alive. At least Gracie would have a meal with the kids she baby-sat, though the parents were vegetarian—nothing he'd ever want to be. Ernie was a meat and potatoes man, and Crystal knew it.

When Crystal came home, he'd give her a piece of his mind, all right. He'd like to throttle her right now! He'd make her realize her man and kid were more important than any damned planning board.

Who was on that board anyway? What man that might interest Crystal? He thought of Pete Willmarth, big football player she'd gone out with in high school—left his wife for some fool actress. Ernie couldn't condone that; a man should stick with his wife for better or worse. Willmarth was here in Branbury now, staying across the street at his kooky daughter Sharon's—a "visit" he called it, according to Gracie, but was there more to it? Why, just this afternoon Ernie had caught Crystal with him, looking more than chummy. He didn't like that. Not a bit.

And there'd been others. He saw the way men looked at his wife. Not that he could blame them. Crystal was a looker, all right: all curves, dimples, hair. The way she permed the hair, it looked like she'd been hit by lightning, black frizz shooting up all over her head—like she was all excitement. And men wanted to be part of that excitement. One of these nights Ernie would go and cut off that hair.

Ernie was no Romeo, he knew that. He hadn't gone to college like she did for a year, getting big ideas. But he was steady; he brought in the paycheck. He loved her. By Christ, he loved her, he loved that woman. She wouldn't leave him for any other man.

Over his dead body she would!

He wrung the wires together so they'd stay put. It was, like, he'd strangle them, if they didn't.

THE STORM WAS WORSE than Crystal had anticipated when she'd planned the forest rendezvous. The world had frozen solid, it seemed, just in the half hour it took to walk up from the old schoolhouse where she'd left her car. Icicles dazzled on the tree limbs as she swung her flashlight in a slow arc above and beyond the bridge she stood on. A freezing drizzle was soaking her sweater, her red tights and boots, turning her mane of dark hair into frosty ringlets. She tossed her head and they tinkled. Lifting her chin, she let the sleet trickle down her throat. Crystal was an outdoor girl: she loved to hike, she loved to hunt—it was Crystal, not Ernie, who brought down the deer each fall, the wild turkey. Once she'd stalked and shot at a moose! He'd gotten away, but that was all right; it was all part of the game.

Tonight she'd bring down human prey. Not to kill him, oh, no. She'd lead him to a warm bed, at Betty's place. Old Betty was gone for the winter, and she'd left Crystal the key. A twist of the thermostat and the apartment would vibrate with heat. They'd have a couple of drinks, munch on his favorite Paul Newman pretzels and make slow, passionate love while the storm pounded on the windows. How she loved a wild night of love! This time she'd make him stay the whole night. After all, it was Valentine's Day. If he loved her he'd do it—face the home front in the morning.

It was after she'd read the weather report that she'd planned the meeting. Weather was a stimulus, as well as an excuse—Ernie would think she'd stayed overnight with a girlfriend. "It was so-o bad outside," she'd say when she came home the next day. "Would you want me to catch my death?" There would be finger pointings, recriminations, but finally he'd give in. He worshipped her, Ernie did. He always gave in.

But tonight topped all the weather she and her lover had ever met in. She was getting chilled, she had a cold coming on. She should have worn her parka, but it was ripped, not suitable for a romantic liaison. And hey, where was he, anyway? Her watch read 9:14. Fourteen minutes late! Crystal didn't like to be kept waiting—not in this weather. She jogged up and down on the log bridge to keep warm. She'd give him ten more minutes, then go on home. Or maybe to Alibi bar. See who was there to talk to.

Oops! She'd almost slipped off the bridge. There was no railing, only the frozen water six feet below. The locals called the place Molly's Crotch because of the way two streams flowed together in a V. She liked that name; it was why she'd chosen the site years ago for a meeting place. Though that same Molly had drowned here—back at the turn of the century it was—she didn't like *that* thought.

She heard a car below on the road, the sound of a sputtering engine. It would be him. She recognized the way the gears shifted, the motor reverberating even after it was shut off. She started down the path toward the car, then turned back. She wasn't going to let him think he could keep *her* waiting—not Crystal Hiland. She stood at the edge of the embankment; she would give him her backside.

"You're late," she hollered at the sound of the crunching footsteps. "You'll have to find somebody else to make love to tonight. Not Crystal—nunh-uh." She folded her arms across her chest.

He didn't answer, he just kept coming. She'd let him try to make it up to her, embrace her. She'd resist for a while and then give in—she liked a reconciliation. She did love him, she really did. Besides, she needed what he was bringing her. She had to be careful, she didn't want to alienate him. She waited until he got closer. He was unhappy with her, sure, for being perverse. She heard him running now, she heard the heavy breathing, the crack of breaking ice. Suddenly alarmed, she half turned—and something struck her head, stunned.... An icy point invaded her neck—aahh! She stood a moment, dazed—then lurched toward the assailant.

And fell, with the second blow, down toward the frozen water, her flashlight falling, rolling down the ice, the world reeling black...then stopping altogether.

TUESDAY

WHEN RUTH WILLMARTH opened the barn door for the morning milking it was still raining, freezing as soon as the drops hit the ground. Maple limbs hunched over like old men in wheelchairs; the roofline of her house was layered with raggedy icicles. A downed electrical wire swung dangerously in midair. A tall poplar had fallen against a high-tension wire and killed the electricity. The air was filled with the creak and groan of trees under the weight of the ice; limbs were cracking like toothpicks.

The whole town of Branbury, Vermont, was in a blackout. Thousands, she'd heard from the Agri-Mark driver who came to collect the milk, were without power. Even the radio was down. Thank God for the generator, she told herself. But the words were hardly out of her mouth when her hired man, Tim, came running up with the news that their twelve-year-old generator wouldn't start, and just before milking.

"I tried everything. We gotta use rain water from now on. And Ruth, the cows are full and bawling," he shouted over the pulsing of the rain. "Branbury Farm Supply is out of new machines. They've had a run on them."

"Call the National Guard," she hollered back.

"I already did. They said they could send us a military tank, but no generator."

"The power company?"

"They got a couple of Vermont Railway workers with some 50-amp generators, but I don't think it's enough to milk on."

"Let them try anyway. And call around to the other farmers. Try the LaFramboises, the Pomainvilles. Try the Audets over in Bridport. See if they have a generator they can do without just to get us through a couple of milkings anyway."

Her words were running one into the next, like water rushing over stones, and Tim was shaking his head. He'd start hand-milking, he hollered.

"Good lord," she cried. Hand-milking thirty-three cows was all she needed at this point. And now a neighboring couple, Dawn and Noah Hemphill, were about to invade her home. People with woodstoves, it seemed, were taking in strangers. With Emily in college and only herself and young Vic in the house, she had an empty room. When she'd heard that the Hemphills, who lived down the road in a brand-new electrified house, had no heat and no water, her nagging sense of hospitality made her invite them to stay until power was restored.

Here they were already, skidding to a stop, even on the sand Tim had thrown down on the driveway. Not that the sand was much help when the rain kept falling and new ice built up on top of the sand. She thought about her daughter Sharon and the grandchildren as she picked her way across the icy grass to greet the couple; she hadn't heard a word lately about their welfare. Sharon had an extra burden on her own woodstove: Ruth's ex-husband Pete and his paramour were visiting—most likely an extended stay because of the ice storm. Ruth was dying to hear how things were going, but when she'd tried to call late last night, the line was dead.

"Hello there. Hang on, I'm coming. Just throw your stuff on the porch and I'll give you a hand," she called out to the young couple.

Though they aren't so terribly young, are they? she thought as she struggled up to the porch and they all shook gloved hands. The husband might be in his mid-forties, and the wife in her thirties at least. Ruth could see the crow's feet when Dawn smiled. She was still clinging to Noah as they moved, amoeba like, through the kitchen door. Though even forty was young to Ruth, who was forty-nine and not exactly happy about that! Already her bones were aching with this cold weather; she felt weighted down, like one of those ice-laden trees.

"It won't be long, just a few days," said Noah, gently disengaging his wife's arm from his so he could follow Ruth upstairs with their suitcases. A middle school English teacher, he'd brought along a battery-operated laptop as well, and a briefcase full of books. "At least I can get ahead with my lesson plans. Although," he added, "I want to help out around here, so put me to work."

"I might do that, sooner than you think," she said. "Our barn generator is down. The cows are stressed, they've a bellyful of milk and no way to get it out except by hand-milking. But with thirty-three cows…"

It was Noah's turn to look stressed now. He didn't know anything about milking, he allowed. But he'd give it a try. "I'll be there. As soon as we settle in."

Ruth ran up ahead to show them their room. Behind her Dawn warned, "Be careful now, sweetheart. Those cows can kick. Be careful of you know where."

And Noah gave an embarrassed laugh.

SHARON WILLMARTH WAS in a bad mood. She wanted to talk to her mother, but the phone lines were down. She wanted to talk about her father's girlfriend, Violet. The woman was driving her up a wall. Sharon had served a tofu stroganoff the night the couple arrived; she'd spent two hours, chopping up vegetables. And Violet just gave her dragon-tooth smile and said pointedly to Sharon's father, "Let's go out to dinner, get out of Sharon's way, shall we, honey?"

Sharon poured herself a teeny glass of red wine and threw together a pile of tofu salad sandwiches. Pete and Dragon Lady were lunching at the local diner and Gracie Hiland was upstairs with the children. Sharon had to take a lunch to her ecologist husband who was in the Green Mountain Forest "experiencing" the storm; and then she'd drive him home. Jack both loved and hated the ice. The broken limbs could bring on fungi that, in turn, could cause infections that would rot the trees. It tortured him to see a beautiful tree lose its limbs. On the other hand, he insisted, ice storms and fires were natural processes, like human life and death, making way for new life, new trees.

Sharon loved and feared for the trees, too. It was some of the people around here who were driving her bananas.

Like yesterday afternoon: the freezing rain, the kids raising merry hell, and there was her father, slurping a glass of beer, telling old tales in the living room with that hairy Crystal from across the street. Crystal crooning in a honey voice how it'd been "all downhill since you, Petey-sweet"—and her father looking like a lamb just dying to be led to the slaughter. Then down comes Violet from her beauty nap, and walks in just as Crystal is giving Sharon's dad a big hug—"for old times' sake"—and her father hugging back.

Then Violet, furious, slamming out the door into the storm and Crystal laughing her head off. Violet running back in again with an umbrella, like an Amazon on the attack, and Crystal shrieking and dodging and racing out of the house—and smack into her husband's jealous arms. Afterward, Violet lacing Dad up and down like he's a goose she's getting ready to hurl into the oven. "I hate that woman! If I see her around here once more, I'll stab her with this!" she'd said, brandishing the umbrella.

It would have been a funny scene, Sharon thought, if it hadn't happened in her own house. Even the two kids, Willa and Robbie, had stopped fighting over a stuffed Valentine bear their grandfather brought them and were hushed for once, awed by the violence in the living room.

This was why Sharon needed to talk to her mother. She wanted to see if Ruth would let Pete and Violet stay at the farm. Just for a few days, she'd argue, until the roads improved and the couple could drive back to New York City. Her mother would be in the barn most of the day anyhow; she could ignore her ex-husband and his girlfriend. Whereas Sharon was right in the middle with no place to escape to.

Now Sharon would have to drive way across town and out to Cow Hill Road in order to talk to her mother. Well, she would do that, she resolved, as soon as she brought Jack home.

Her red-haired, freckle-nosed husband was so engaged with his endangered trees that he hardly glanced at the lunch Sharon had prepared. He'd eat it later, he said, when it got dark. The great naturalist, John Muir, he reminded her, had even climbed trees at the height of a lightning storm to "feel" what it was like; to "become" the tree. Himself, Jack said, he wanted to "hear the universe crashing around him."

"Uh-huh," she said. "But I can't wait till dark to drive you home." It was still raining, a fine, cold drizzle that turned the tips of her mittened fingers to icicles. The rain penetrated even her green slicker and the long blue striped underwear she wore under her purple cotton pants. It seeped into her lime green rubber boots and down between her toes. "Gracie has to go home to get supper for Ernie—it seems Crystal got stuck somewhere after last night's meeting and can't phone home. Though if you ask me, she's off at some tryst. This weather's a great excuse for it."

Sharon didn't have to wait, he told her as he examined a fractured pine limb and made a note in a small damp journal. "Dan Murphy'll come and pick me up. I didn't know that when we made our plans earlier."

"So you got me here in all this weather for nothing."

"I wouldn't say that," he said, and he gave her a frosty hug, one that she returned with gusto. She didn't really mind, after all. It felt good to be out here in the woods; it was like Christmas again the way the icy limbs were tinkling and jingling against one another, a chorus of bells.

She left the lunch in his backpack and picked her way carefully down the forest path toward the road where she'd left the car. A slippery quarter of a mile later she reached the bridge that overhung the V of mountain streams at Molly's Crotch. Always when she came here she thought of poor Molly, who'd drowned in the swirling waters.

"Whoa!" She slipped herself on the edge of the icy bridge, sliding halfway down the embankment to the frozen stream. Just in time she caught herself on a limb.

Though it wasn't a limb but a hand she'd grabbed. "Omigod!"

The hand didn't respond to her grasp. It was frozen solid, like the rest of the flesh it was attached to: rigid legs clad in red wool tights, thighs and buttocks raised like the victim had been trying to push herself upright. In the neck—"Oh!"—a mammoth icicle, sticking out like an ice pick. No tree could have hurled it in so deep, Sharon thought. It was as solid as an ice pick, too. There had been no melting up here on the mountain, not like in town where the temperature had actually shot up to 33 degrees this noon. Tonight though, it would drop again, refreezing the world.

But could an icicle kill? "Jack!" she screamed, "Jack, come see. Help! Jack!"

The corpse's hair was caught on a briar bush: this was why the body hadn't slid all the way down into the stream the way the killer had doubtless hoped it would. It was as if the killer had heard someone coming and then fled in a hurry. Whoever had come later—if anyone—hadn't noticed the body that was quickly, quietly freezing in the sub-zero temperature.

She knew who the dead person was, of course, by the hair. That head of wild black frizzy hair—though almost white now with frost; hair so tangled in the briars that it seemed to be growing out of the bush.

"Jack!" she yelled again, and softened her voice when she saw him jogging down the path. "It's Crystal. She's dead. Stabbed with an icicle!"

"Dead? My God! But not from an icicle."

"Yes. Look! Stay here, I'll call the police." She scrambled back toward the road. The police would have to deal with the body. Who was she to tell Ernie Hiland that his wife was now one with the icy universe?

Though Ernie himself could be the killer. The awful possibility struck her, like that sweep of icy snow cascading down on her head from a stand of pine trees. She swept it out of her face with a wet mitten; still, the ice shards froze her nose and cheeks.

She thought of her father—Crystal was an old girl-friend of his. Would the police suspect him? And what about jealous Violet, who hated Crystal with a passion? And oh, dear Lord, what was she to say to Gracie, up-stairs this very minute, babysitting her children: "Gracie, dear, I just ran into your mother—she's turned into an icicle…."

Sharon needed her mother for advice, for comfort. The world was closing in on her, freezing her out of the mainstream. She'd call the police from home, she decided as she got into her car. Then she'd load the children into the pickup, Gracie, too—let the girl have a few more contented hours before she learned about her mother. After all, Ernie didn't know yet. Let *him* break the awful news to his daughter.

But all Sharon's mother could do when Sharon got there with Gracie and the children was talk about her fretful cows. There were two Vermont Railway men outside the barn with 50-amp generators; they didn't produce enough power, Ruth told her daughter. "Send the kids in the house with Gracie and roll up your sleeves, girl. I need your help hand-milking."

This was not why Sharon had come. A neighbor woman was dead and her mother was telling her to milk a cow? "You don't understand," she hissed in her mother's ear, waving Gracie into the house with the children. "I found something. Someone! And Dad might be mixed up in it."

That got her mother's attention. Anything to do with her father, who'd run off with that so-called actress, sent sparks flying out of her mother's mouth.

"I'm sorry he landed in your house, Sharon. The motels were full up, I heard." When Sharon opened her mouth to speak: "But don't think for one minute I'm going to have him here—with that female. You'll have to deal with them till they can go home. And that's final. Tim," Ruth hollered, "did you call the Pomainvilles yet? Can they lend us a generator?"

"Yep. Just what I was coming in to tell you." Tim was standing in the barn doorway, his cowboy hat shoved way back on his head. The hat must be taped there, Sharon figured; it never seemed to fall off. "You take over here, Ruth, and Noah and I'll go after it in the truck, right, Noah?"

A tall man with a shock of light-brown hair, a wide mouth, and a lopsided reddish-brown mustache rose up from under a cow. "I can't get a drop out of her," he said, looking chagrined. "Sorry. I don't have the right hands for it, I guess."

Ruth introduced him as Noah Hemphill; she explained his presence, his willingness to help out. She flung the keys to the pick-up at Tim. "Hurry," she said. "Zelda's been kicking in the side of the barn, she's so antsy to be milked."

Zelda was Ruth's most ornery cow. Too bad, Sharon thought, it wasn't Zelda who'd frozen out there in the stream. "Mother," she said, after Tim and Noah had left, "I've been trying to tell you. I found a dead woman up at Molly's Crotch. It was my neighbor, Crystal Hiland. Someone stabbed her with an icicle."

She had her mother's full attention now. "They'll want to talk to me—the police, I mean. They'll want to talk to Dad. Everybody in town knows Dad was her old boyfriend—Ernie will tell them. They had a little run in yesterday, you see. Violet chased Crystal out of our house and then Ernie came over in a jealous fit. And it wasn't the first time the pair had got together."

She told the story while Ruth listened, half amused by the scene, half aghast. The cows complained in their stanchions. Outside she heard the rumble of men's voices. The railway workers were leaving with their useless generators.

"Hurry!" Ruth called to the two men, who were sprinkling sand on a spot under the pick-up's wheels to get it moving on the icy drive.

Sharon was at her wit's end. Her neighbor had been stabbed with an icicle and her mother was more worried about a generator. Why couldn't they just hand-milk the cows for a couple of days till the electricity came back on? Sharon had done it as a child. It wasn't that hard. You just grab the teat between thumb and forefinger, relax the grip and push up, then pull down as you squeeze. Nothing to it. Though she wouldn't want to do thirty cows twice a day; no, definitely not.

Her mother had other ideas. Sharon found herself squatting on an upended pail, under a cow. Which one was it? Jane Eyre? Esmeralda? Oprah? Her mother named her cows after famous women, living, dead, or fictional. Sharon hardly knew which was which now; she had her own busy life with two kids and a part-time job at the counseling service.

"Someone killed her, Mother. They've probably thawed her out by now. They'll be looking for Ernie. We'll have to tell Gracie. Poor little shy Gracie."

"How sad. How awful," Ruth said. "But, Sharon, you can't kill someone with an icicle. Not unless it falls from a great height—like a roof. And there's no roof near Molly's Crotch."

"I saw it, Mother," Sharon said stubbornly. "It was in the side of her neck. It must've struck the carotid artery." She turned to the black and white Holstein she was milking. "What do *you* care, anyway, about a dead woman?" But the cow only turned an indifferent eye on her and bellowed out its reproach as if she was some interloper who didn't have half the finesse of a milking machine.

WEDNESDAY

By MID-MORNING, just when Ruth had her own world in semi order—the borrowed generator working and the cows back on schedule, though still nervous—she walked into the madhouse on Bristol Street where Sharon lived. She'd made sure, of course, that Pete and Violet were out: they were having brunch at the Branbury Inn. The police had ordered them to stay in town.

"You can bet Violet was in a tizzy about that," Sharon said, sweeping her mother into the house. "Who do they think they are anyway," she said, mimicking Violet's husky contralto. "They must think their feces are ice cream!"

Ruth smiled; she loved to hear stories about Violet's hangups. Just so she didn't hear them from Violet herself.

But upstairs in the two-hundred-year-old house where the chair you sat on in the living room (when there was a chair) slid slowly down the rickety floor to the kitchen, there was only a prolonged wailing. "It's Gracie. You go up this time, Mom," Sharon said. "I've been trying all morning to comfort the poor kid ever since Ernie left her here."

"She needs her father. Why isn't he home? Surely they'd let him off work."

"He won't quit. It keeps his mind off things, he says.

He brought her here at eleven o'clock last night after the police broke the news, and then he went back on a new twelve-hour shift.''

Ruth wondered exactly what "things" Ernie needed to get his mind off. Could he have killed his wife? It happened all too often in the domestic triangles she read about in the papers. It had been a blow to the head that killed Crystal, according to Ruth's friend Colm who was a part-time cop; it wasn't just the icicle they'd found in her neck. Had Ernie done it in a fit of jealousy? If a triangle though, who was the third party? Should she try to find out? But it wasn't her business. She'd hardly known Crystal, who was four or five years younger than herself. She had only seen her once or twice in recent years when the woman popped over to Sharon's house to borrow a cupful of sugar or something. The home cupboards were poorly stocked, according to Gracie.

She found the trio in Sharon and Jack's room, where toddler Willa still shared a bed with her parents. Gracie was facedown on the bed, sobbing. She was a tall, skinny girl of fourteen—the word anorexic came to mind. She had her mother's heavy dark hair—uncombed it looked like, though Sharon said she'd done her best with it. "It's like cruising through stalagmites," she'd confided to Ruth.

"Her mama's dead," Robbie reported to his grandmother. "She turned into an icicle."

"Shhh," said Ruth when Gracie only sobbed harder, her thin shoulders convulsing.

"She did, too," Willa piped up. "Some bad witch turned her into one."

"That's ridiculous," Sharon snapped, "and you know it. Come downstairs now, and leave poor Gracie alone."

Ruth put a hand on the girl's heaving back. "It's all

right to cry, child. Get it all out. There now.'' She massaged Gracie's back and shoulders.

Gradually the wailing subsided and Gracie sat up, her face smudged with snot and tears. ''It's my father who's to blame,'' she said. ''He was always mad at Mom. All the time. He kept accusing her of doing things.''

''What things?'' Ruth asked softly.

Gracie let out a snort, and snuffed it back. ''Like other men. He thinks—he thinks I'm not his kid. I heard him say that one time. He called me a little—a little—'' She couldn't say the word.

''He didn't mean that,'' Ruth soothed. ''They were probably just having a tiff. Married people do sometimes.''

There was an outcry downstairs and Gracie jumped up off the bed. ''I'm supposed to help out. Dad said so. He said I'm to stay here till we get power, till school starts.'' She paused by the window that was lashed with icy drizzle for the fourth day in a row. A branch snapped off a big maple and struck the roof gutter. The girl flinched. Then she turned and ran downstairs.

In the living room the grandchildren were hanging on to Sharon and weeping. ''Don't let them turn you into an icicle, Mommy,'' Robbie cried, while Willa sniveled and clung to her mother's pantleg.

All business now, a stoic Gracie took them firmly by the arms: ''Stop bothering your mother. She's not going to turn into an icicle. Neither did *my* mother. So stop saying that. Stop it! Now let's go back up and play hide-and-seek.''

''I'm it,'' Robbie cried as the children clattered upstairs.

Ruth told Sharon what Gracie had said about not being her father's child. "Do you suppose that's true? Have you heard any scuttlebutt?"

"Oh, sure. But nobody really knows." Sharon dropped down on a brown meditation pillow. She waved an arm at a pine rocker, the only chair in the spare living room; then she gazed out the window that in lieu of curtains was hung with Jack's grandmother's wedding dress. "I hate this ice. I hate it! Ice is creeping into our psyches, too—everybody fighting and weeping and complaining. That miserable Violet," she cried. She flung up off the pillow to hurl a log into the woodstove, as if it were Violet she was heaving into the fire.

"It's hard," Ruth sympathized.

"Mother, you've got to help us clear up this mess so the police will let them go. It's hard enough having Gracie here. I mean, I'm trying, but I can't bring her mother back. And look at that madness outside, will you? There's not a candle or kerosene lamp in the stores now. I'm miffed at Jack for persuading me to buy an electric stove instead of gas. It takes forever to cook on this woodstove!" She waved a hand at a pot of squash soup that was slowly, laboriously heating.

Ruth pulled aside a sleeve of the wedding dress to peer through the frosty window. She'd heard a car slowing down—not that anyone dared speed on this ice. "Oh, no," she cried. "It's them already. I thought you said they were having brunch. Well, I'm out of here." She flung an arm into her parka sleeve. "I'll go out the back door. You'll have to visit at *my* place till they can leave town."

"You can't get out the back door, Mother, it's frozen solid. Jack will have to saw through it when he comes home. Be brave. Face them down."

Ruth realized it was too late anyway; they were parking the car, cutting off her escape. Besides, Pete would have recognized the green pick-up. Ruth sat back down in the rocker, arms folded over her chest—a defensive position. Violet was the first to enter. She dropped her coat on a hall table, shuffled off her giant boots—Violet was a b-i-g woman. Seeing Ruth in the rocking chair, she coughed loudly and clomped upstairs.

"Well, hi there," Pete said, coming up behind Ruth, always the good guy as if he hadn't knocked the family into a cocked hat by running off with Violet. Ruth had never gone to see the film the woman had made in town. Anyway, she had only two lines in it, according to a neighbor. Couldn't Pete see what a fake she was?

"How're the cows making out?" he asked in his loud genial voice. "Generator not working, Sharon says. You try the National Guard?"

"They offered to bring a tank," Ruth said, getting up. With Violet upstairs, it was safe to take her leave. "Would you mind moving your car so I can get out?"

"Come on, Ruthie. Sit down and have a cup of coffee. I brought some hot from the inn. It takes too long to heat on the woodstove."

Ruth was going to stay with Violet eavesdropping on every word? She guessed not! She zipped up her parka, pulled on her gloves.

Too late again, she saw. A police car was pulling into the driveway; two men were getting out. One of them was Colm Hanna. Now the fur would fly.

They wanted to talk with Pete, Detective Plotkin informed them. "Oh, just routine questions," he added, smiling a slow-burner smile. Behind him, Colm grimaced at Ruth, then glanced away when Pete scowled at him. Colm and Pete had been rivals ever since junior year in high school when Ruth dropped Colm to take up with Pete, the big football star. It was in senior year that Pete, Ruth found out later, had met Crystal, who was then a precocious ninth grader. Obviously Ruth had had blinders on.

Did Pete know about Crystal's death? the detective asked. He did, Pete allowed, in his big booming voice, his eyes appropriately cast down. Colm winked at Ruth. She coughed, glanced away, rocked in her chair. This might be amusing, she thought—just so long as Violet stayed upstairs. There was a small crash in the room above where the couple was staying. Were the children playing hide-and-seek with Violet? Probably not. More likely Violet had dropped one of her long dangly gold earrings.

"We understand that you and the deceased," the detective began delicately, "had a relationship...."

"Had had," Pete corrected, looking poised, sitting down in one of the chairs Sharon had brought from the kitchen.

"Could you—would you mind..." Detective Plotkin was obviously new at this game of diplomacy; he was struggling with the proper words.

"Tell us where you were Monday evening?" Colm finished for the detective, his eyes fixed on a watercolor of a dense forest hanging on the wall beyond Pete's left ear. He couldn't look *at* Pete, Ruth knew. He was terribly jealous, poor Colm. After all, she and Pete had had three children together. Colm couldn't overcome that mountain.

"It's just routine, please understand," the detective said. "We have to ask everyone. That is," he amended, "everyone who might have been, uh, involved with the victim."

Pete had stopped smiling now. He didn't like the

wording. "I was never *involved,* officer. I had a relationship with the deceased before I was married. If I've seen her more recently, well, it's because she happens to live across the street from my daughter here. Lived..." He nodded at Sharon for support, and Sharon smiled back. Of course Sharon loved her father, Ruth had to remember that. "Her daughter babysits my grandchildren. It was only natural for Crystal to come over. I couldn't exactly run out of the house."

"Now wait a minute here." It was Violet, appearing in the doorway like a big breasted genie oozing out of a bottle; most likely she'd been sitting on the stairs, listening. A tidal wave of perfume hit the room. "She didn't come over just to see Gracie. Tell the truth now, Peter. It was to see *you.* And you damn well know it. She still has the hots for him, officer—had. Tell him, Peter. Tell us both. The who-ole truth." She folded her arms across her expansive front.

"For chrissake, Violet." Pete was flustered now. "What truth? That she came over, yes, that she flung herself at me, yes. That was Crystal. She liked men, period. You just happened to come in, Vi, when—"

"When what?" the officer asked. Colm caught Ruth's eye. He was enjoying the scene. Any minute she feared, he'd break out in a giggle; his bony shoulders were already quivering. At least he wasn't dazzled by Violet and her perfume. Ruth was grateful for that.

But what about this Crystal relationship? Ruth wanted to know, too. Had it been going on while she and Pete were married? She stopped rocking, waited for his response.

"When she'd thrown herself at me. I was caught, for chrissake. It was nothing, Vi. I'd liked to have killed her for coming on to me like that!" He hesitated, the blood creeping into his cheeks. "I didn't mean that the way it came out. But I was pissed." He glanced at his girlfriend. "You know that damn well, Vi. I wasn't having any bloody relationship with her." His cheeks were red hot now.

"She seemed to know you awfully well," Violet said, towering over him, where he sat hunched in his chair. If Pete was six feet, she was a good six-two. One hulking foot shoved the tiger cat aside when it rubbed against her leg. Violet hated cats. Domestic cats, that is—she'd worked with big cats in the circus, Ruth knew, before she went into the theater.

"We were on the planning board together, that's all," he said. "We saw each other now and then. Nothing out of the way. And I didn't see her Monday night, if that's what you're leading up to."

The planning board, Ruth thought. All those Monday nights when Pete left early to attend meetings. And came home late.

"Can you account for your movements, then, that night? Both of you?" the detective asked, blinking at Violet, as if intimidated by her size.

"*I* was here," Violet said. "I can't tell you where Peter was. He went out for an hour."

"Now wait a minute," Sharon cried. "You were gone for an hour, too. You went out looking for *him*, you said. It was between nine and ten. I remember because I was putting the kids to bed and Robbie asked for Grampa and I heard the door close and Dad had just walked in. He was at Poppy's Pizza, right, Dad?" She smiled at her father and he nodded self-righteously.

Upstairs there was a giant crash, a high-pitched scream. Sharon said "Oh no," and took off. The detective stood. "We'll talk again later," he told Pete.

"Maybe you'll both remember by then where you were that evening and what you were doing."

"See you tonight?" Colm hissed in Ruth's ear as he got up to follow his colleague. "I'll bring in some Chinese."

"They're closed," she said. "I've tried. They don't have a generator."

"Cheese and crackers then."

"We'll see. I've houseguests, you know."

"And tell your daughter and her husband to stick around," Detective Plotkin called from the open doorway. "Yourself too, Ms. Willmarth. We'll want to talk to all of you again."

"Who's going anywhere in this weather?" Ruth said, following the policemen outside. She ducked as a branch cracked off a tree and splintered at her feet. Flying ice shards struck her cheek and neck, and strangely, made her feel like crying.

Behind her, Pete laughed. He'd come out to move his car so Ruth could get out. He brushed the ice shards off her sleeve. Ruth was glad Colm couldn't see that intimate gesture.

"I'm fine," she said. "I can deal with a little ice."

"A little fire, too, Ruth? *You* getting any of that in your life? You know what I mean. Oh, and I'd like a private word with you. Maybe this afternoon for a couple of minutes while Violet has her hair done? She's found a place with a generator."

"Oh, all right. One-thirty." She sighed. "But leave the fire in the woodstove, please."

DAWN HAD A LIGHT LUNCH on the table, a pleasant surprise, when Ruth arrived. "It's only tuna fish sandwiches," she said, "but I found some celery in your fridge that's still alive."

"A little limp maybe," Ruth said, cozying up to the woodstove. The temperature had dropped today after a relatively warm night—well, in the twenties. But warm for February. Though a freezing rain was still falling.

"I didn't dare use the mayonnaise, though. It smelled a teeny bit rancid. So I added some yogurt I had in our cooler. And there's hot tea, courtesy of the woodstove."

"You're wonderful," Ruth said. "What about your husband?"

"Oh, he's upstairs on the laptop. He has all these people to e-mail. Other teachers, mostly. They exchange ideas about students, lesson plans, that sort of thing. Anyway, I'll bring him up a lunch." She nodded at a tray set with a flowered tea towel and a china vase with a single rose in it.

"Where on earth did you get that rose?" It was a brilliant red, perhaps a bit past full bloom, but still lovely. Ruth couldn't take her eyes off it.

Dawn looked triumphant. For a moment her pale heart-shaped face took on a shade of red from the rose. "From my sweetie," she said. "Even an ice storm couldn't keep Noah from bringing me a dozen Valentine roses. He knows I love red ones. He bought them Monday morning. He drove home in the freezing rain with them. Most of them died when our heat went off. But this one hung on."

Dawn bent to smell the rose. Her face, when she stood upright again, appeared worshipful. Ruth couldn't imagine ever feeling that way about a rose. Or a man. Though she had at one point, hadn't she? She'd sat in the bleachers at the high school football stadium and felt her heart go bang in her chest, her temperature soar as Pete ran out on the field in his blue and white uniform. Captain Pete Willmarth he was then; the name thrilled on her lips.

Colm had brought her chocolates for Valentine's Day. Each year she would say, "No chocolates, please, I don't want to be tempted." And each Valentine's Day there'd be another box. Of course Pete never even remembered their wedding anniversary, much less a minor event like Valentine's Day. It might be nice, she thought wistfully, to have a sweet considerate man like Noah Hemphill hanging around.

Dawn said, "I've been lucky. I've been blessed. Noah is all I ever wanted."

The young woman had a degree from some New Jersey college, Ruth knew, and like Noah, had taught school for several years—some subject she'd mentioned but Ruth had forgotten. Noah was Dawn's vocation now. Besides, she confided in Ruth, "I'm pregnant. I just found out last week and told Noah."

"How nice for you," Ruth said. "How lovely. And great sandwiches."

"Noah's crazy about tuna fish," Dawn said.

RUTH WAS IN THE BARN when Pete arrived. The borrowed generator worked for the milking but wasn't enough to keep the milk refrigerated. The way the temperature kept fluctuating, they'd had to throw out gallons of it; it made Ruth ill to think of the waste. "You were the one who wanted to keep that old generator when we modernized," she accused Pete. When he looked chagrined, she softened her voice. "Well, I know at the time we were trying to cut back. We didn't anticipate a storm like this. When's it going to quit?"

"They say tomorrow," Pete said. "But the temperature's going down. It may be a couple more days before you get power.'' She noticed he said "you," not "we." Pete was a New Yorker now, not a Vermont farmer. "Got a few minutes to talk?" he asked softly, so the hired man wouldn't hear. "In the house?"

"I'll give you twenty. Then I have a sick calf to tend to, some restless cows. They're still stressed from the long wait between milkings. Call me in the house if there's an emergency," she shouted at Tim.

"When isn't it an emergency?" Tim called back, but then he laughed and said, "Go ahead," and less warmly, "Hello, Pete." Ruth knew that Tim was on her side.

Before she could even pour her ex-husband a cup of coffee he started in on his problems. Elbows planted on the table, he stared into the scarred wood as though he'd see his own face there. Pete had always been a narcissist. He hadn't uttered a word of sympathy for her problems, just concentrated on his own.

"The storm will quit but we have to stay," he complained. "And Violet's got auditions. She has a chance for a choice part in a new off-Broadway show. They're looking for a tall woman, she fits the part."

"She certainly does," Ruth said. "She must be one handful of female for you."

Pete took the remark as a compliment. "I can handle it," he said, spooning sugar into the coffee. He was looking quite dapper this afternoon, in a tweedy jacket and gray wool pants under his rain gear. Ruth supposed Violet picked out his clothes—Pete never used to worry about what he wore. "Coffee's not very hot," he observed.

"The woodstove runs on logs, not electricity." She sat down across from him. "So what did you want to talk about? Not the coffee, I'm sure."

"It's Crystal," he said. "I need your help. About what to say to the police."

"The whole story, I'd imagine. The whole truth. So what about Crystal? You have a post-high school relationship with her? Post-marriage?"

"We were on the planning board together, you know."

"When you and I were still together, you mean."

"Yeah, but like I told the cops—there wasn't anything going on, really."

"Not 'really' but just a little bit? A little flirtation?"

"You could call it that. She'd kind of, come on to me, you know. For old times sake. I mean, we went together a couple of years, Ruth, before you and I got serious."

"Uh-huh." She bit into a doughnut, offered him one. He took two. Good old Pete. One doughnut was never enough for him. One woman.

"We never did anything—any real sex," he said, looking closely at her. "I mean, back then while you and I were still married."

"Well, thanks, very loyal of you."

He nodded, he wasn't getting the innuendo. Pete was never much on reading signs. He'd failed psychology at the university. "But when I came back to visit last summer—Vi and I were staying at the Inn—Crystal suddenly appeared at lunch. She said she was between meetings, didn't like to eat by herself, you know."

"And Violet jumped for joy."

"Well, Violet's an up-front kind of gal. Wears her feelings on her sleeve."

"I've noticed that."

"But she was civil. That time. Then Crystal showed up at a movie we were at. Next thing I knew she was sitting next to me. There I was between Violet and Crystal...."

"What was a fellow to do in a terrifying situation like that?"

It was awful, he agreed. "Violet got up and walked out."

"Uh-oh. So get to the present. I have to get back to work."

"Nothing more happened that visit. I told Crystal I had a new woman."

"As if she didn't know. Violet's such a petite little thing."

"But last week when we got to Sharon's, she showed up again."

"Ah."

"Well, Sunday evening I was coming back from Poppy's Pizza—Violet's crazy about pizzas—and just as I'm walking up the path to the house, there's Crystal, yanking me off the path, down into the trees. It's raining, but that's nothing to her. She's all dolled up, she smells—you know, like lilacs or something."

"Lilacs in February. Who can resist? So you succumbed to her charms? The ice hadn't put out the fire yet?"

Pete looked up, a hunk of sugar doughnut in his cheek. His eyes clouded over. "Don't ever tell Violet. I'm only telling you because I need advice. Violet, well, I guess she smelled the perfume on me; she suspected. We had a terrible row the next day—Monday afternoon, it was. She came in on us in the living room, you see."

"So I heard, from Sharon."

"By then I was thoroughly pissed. At Crystal, I mean. I wanted her to leave me alone. I didn't want her coming between me and Violet. Violet gets so anxious—it's a physical drain on her. You know how that is."

"A bit, yes." Though Ruth had trusted Pete all those years. She'd never suspected anything until she got the note, after the fact. The taxi cab disappearing down the driveway, the numbing shock of it. She'd wanted to run after it, shoot the tires, shoot Pete. She could kill. Oh, yes, she could, driven to the extreme.

So could Pete, she bet. Kill. Under the right circumstances.

"So you made a rendezvous with her at Molly's Crotch? After her meeting? There was an argument and you pushed her down toward the creek, hit her with something? Stabbed her with an icicle? Is that what you wanted to tell me?"

"No, Ruth, no! You know I wouldn't kill the woman. It's Violet I'm worried about, you see. She had this part in a play back in drama school where she played Medea? And Medea kills her children? Well, Violet—she's a method actress—got so rolled up into the part that she *wanted* to kill them, she said. She was a hit. It got her a part in an off-Broadway show."

Ruth sat frozen, her cup halfway to her lips. "Do you have any proof that Violet might have done it? I guess you can't leave fingerprints on an icicle. Or an icy branch, or whatever hit Crystal."

He held up his palms. "She was gone for an hour Monday night—wouldn't talk to anyone afterward." He dropped his head in his hands, looking as if he were ready to break down. "She'd have done it for me. *Because* of me. Because she *loved* me," he said, his voice hoarse.

What could Ruth say to that note of passion? She stood. She had to get back to the barn. The cows needed her. Elizabeth was still spooked from the time Violet had stuck a knife in her, out of anger at Ruth. Anger at Ruth's having been married to Pete for all those years and she wasn't. What wouldn't Violet do in a jealous rage?

"What shall I do, Ruth?" Pete jumped up, knocking over the chair, his big rugged face close to hers. "I can't let anything happen to Violet. I love her, Ruth."

For a moment he looked like their adolescent son Vic, after he'd gone to school with manure on his boots, and the kids taunted him. She put a hand on his arm. He was Vic's father, after all. "Like I said, tell the truth about yourself and Crystal. Let Violet tell her own story."

She wouldn't mind being rid of Violet, would she? But did she want Pete back? Sometimes. Sometimes at night she did. Lying alone and cold in bed....

The phone rang and it was Colm. He had a free hour, he said. Could he come over?

Pete was waving his arms. "Don't tell *him* anything I said!"

Dawn was coming down the stairs, looking pert and pretty in a long blue flowered skirt. A silk skirt, on a day like this? Ruth saw Pete look at her appreciatively and her heart cooled. But Dawn wasn't a Crystal. Dawn was a one-man woman. Upstairs Noah was clacking away on his laptop. He would have complimented his tuna fish sandwich, smelled the red rose. Neither Hemphill knew yet about Crystal's death. The radio was still out, the newspaper was a weekly. And it was just as well; Ruth didn't want to upset the lovers.

"Okay," she told Colm, "but you'll have to share me with the cows."

"By the way," Colm said, "Plotkin found a pair of bootprints on the top of the slope near the bridge. They were iced in under today's melting stuff. Size twelve. Ask Sharon to do some measuring, okay? Of her guests' boots?'' And he hung up.

Pete gave Ruth an insinuating glance. He wanted her to have someone, even if it was his ex-rival; it lessened his guilt. She ignored the glance, and told him about the bootprint. He said, ''What does that prove? Could be one of the linemen.''

''No electrical lines that far up, are there?'' she asked, knowing the answer, and Pete grunted.

She introduced Dawn to Pete. Pete gave the young woman the old football captain's grin. ''I want to make Noah a cup of hot chocolate,'' Dawn said, giving Pete a cursory nod as though he might be the plumber or maybe an itinerant salesman. ''Is there enough hot water?''

Pete's smile faded; he left the house with a pleading glance at Ruth, his shoulders slumped, as though he'd just lost the big game.

Ruth didn't have to look at his boots to know the size. She'd lived with them long enough. They were a size twelve.

THE FOOTPRINTS WEREN'T Jack's, Sharon was glad about that. After all, it was Jack who was there with the body when the police showed up. But Jack wore a size ten boot. He'd always wished he were taller than his five-nine height, but that didn't bother Sharon. She was only five-three herself; her head fit nicely in the hollow of his neck.

''So that more or less absolves Jack,'' she told her mother on the phone. The phone lines had been restored on Bristol Street minutes before, and Sharon was making full use of them: calling neighbors, checking in with the counseling service, calling the local co-op to see if they had any fresh parsley and wheat germ; she wanted to make a chick pea loaf. "Violet hates chick peas," she said, grinning into the mouthpiece.

"Don't be nasty," her mother said. "She's your father's darling. Oh, and speaking of Violet, you might check the size of her boots."

"I hadn't thought of that. Hang on a minute, will you? Oh damn, she's wearing them. She went to get her hair done."

"Look at her shoes then."

"Right. You want to come over and help?"

"You're sure she won't be there?"

"Dad's going to pick her up at the hairdresser's. Then they're going shopping and then to Dog Team Tavern for dinner. I told her about those big gooey sticky buns."

"Smart girl. Well, all right. I'll be over after milking. But Sharon—"

"Uh-huh?"

"Your dad's boots are a size twelve, too, you know. The police will find that out soon enough."

"Oh, dear," said Sharon.

"OH, DEAR," said Ruth when she and Sharon had rummaged through Violet's things and pulled out a whole suitcase full of red, purple, green and black shoes. They were all size eleven and a half. The cat was playing with the laces on the purple ones.

"But boots usually run a half size larger, right?" said Sharon. So they'd have to wait for the woman herself to appear—at least Sharon would. Ruth hugged the children and talked with Gracie, who was pouring out her grievances against her late mother, who was never home.

"Mom never baked a pie, not a single one. And all

my friends would bring brownies and stuff to school and what would I get? A peanut butter and jelly sandwich. Mom was always on the phone with somebody or getting her hair frizzed—jeezum, she looked like—like an orangutan!''

The girl burst into tears then. ''And now she's gone dead,'' she wailed, as if her mother had played one last trick on her for which she could never be forgiven.

''You loved her though,'' Ruth said.

''She was my mother. What do you think!'' The tears rolled down her cheeks.

Ruth and Sharon had just diverted Gracie into the kitchen to make a package of no-cook fudge when someone banged on the front door. A man's voice called, ''Hello?'' Gracie screamed, ''Dad!'' and raced through the living room to let him in.

Ernie stood there in the hallway, his big knobby hands turning his hard hat over and over, his booted feet—size twelve, Ruth bet—dribbling melted ice on the pine floor. He looked down on them apologetically. Sharon had tacked a sign on the door that said PLEASE REMOVE YOUR SHOES but he made no effort to comply. Gracie lunged at him, her arms circling his neck. ''You're never home!'' she shrieked. ''You don't have to work. They'd give you time off. I need you, Dad. I'll cook your supper....''

He peeled her arms carefully off his neck as if she was a spray of icy snow that had come flying at him. ''You run along home now, girl, and fix that supper then. I brought us some spaghetti and hamburg. I'm done with my shift. Go along now, I'll be over.'' Obedient, her eyes bright with tears, Gracie pulled on a parka and dashed out into a cold wind.

''I heard about you,'' Ernie said, taking a step toward

Ruth. "You help folks out. Well, I'm here to tell you I didn't kill my wife if that's what you're thinking. The police think so, though. They came to North Road to talk to me. While I'm at work! Like they don't know I'm trying to get this town going again. And that's what I done. Folks on North Road got lights now."

"What about our street?" asked Sharon hopefully.

"Two days most likely. Three. Substation for this part of town's still out."

"The shoemaker's kids never get shoes," Ruth reminded Sharon, and smiled at Ernie. "I'm glad you're taking Gracie home. She needs you. It's hard to lose a mother."

"What about a wife?" His lower lip quivering, he folded his arms and leaned against the stair banister. If he and Ruth were going to talk, it would have to be here. Ruth picked her own spot on the wall to lean against. She was conscious of her smelly boots—did she see his nose twitch? Well, she couldn't help it, she'd come straight from the barn.

"I know," she soothed. "It's a terrible thing. It must be awful for you."

They were silent a moment. His thin lips were trembling with something they wanted to say. She waited for him to get it out.

Finally he said, "Gracie's not mine. Crystal was pregnant with her when we married. Sometimes I think— well, that's why she married me. I'd been trying for years, you see, I was always crazy about Crystal. She was smart you know, smarter'n me. Went to college for a year. Then dropped out to marry that fellow."

"What fellow was that?"

"Oh, he's gone now. Gone west somewhere. It didn't

last, he beat her up, you know. She was lucky to get free. It was after that she met this other one.''

''The one who got her pregnant?''

''Oh, yeah, he was crazy after her, she said, wanted to marry her. But it wasn't him she wanted, you see. She wanted *me*. She did, you can bet she did! I'd give her everything she asked for. Nice house, nice clothes; she didn't have to work in that office. She just wanted to, that's all. That's where she met *him*.''

''What office was that?'' Ruth shifted position. The wall was ungiving to her aching spine; it was damp where there had been a leak in the roof. She could feel the wet spot in the back of her denim shirt.

Ernie didn't answer. He straightened up, looked her in the eye. ''She was a beautiful woman. Men looked at her—they liked to talk to her.'' He seemed dazed, as if he were in a trance, back in some confrontational past.

The phone rang and Sharon said, ''It's Gracie. She says your supervisor called. He wants you to call back. Your supper's about ready.''

Ernie jumped away from the banister then. ''Tell her I'm on my way. Been twelve hours since I ate. I brought the girl a surprise. Chocolate eclairs, her favorite.''

''Ernie,'' Ruth asked, as he turned toward the door. ''What was his name—this man who wanted to marry her, who got her pregnant?''

But Ernie had his mind on other things. The door shut. Then it opened again. ''Funeral service tomorrow,'' he said. ''Seven o'clock at Hanna's Funeral Home. Maybe he'll come. If he does—'' His face clouded over. He didn't say what he might do. He turned to go, and then spun. ''You talk to that fellow if you see him. You ask him what he done.'' This time he took off, running.

''Shall we attend?'' Ruth asked Sharon, who'd just

been assailed by two hungry children. She wondered how she would know which fellow was Gracie's father. Did Gracie know?

"Meet you there at ten of seven." Sharon struggled into the kitchen, like a mother cat with kittens clinging to her tail. The last words Ruth heard were "Chocolate milkshake, Momma, with whip cream." But when Sharon told him, "No chocolate, it hypes him up too much," Robbie whined that his daddy always let them have it.

Ruth shut the door on that familiar argument. She was greeted by a shower of stinging sleet. Ice covered the kitty litter Sharon had sprinkled on the walk, kitty litter that the children carried on their boots into the house. Ruth remembered it well.

THURSDAY

IT WAS A STRANGE NIGHT. Arrows of electricity arced through the air where some streets had power and some didn't. Fortunately, Hanna's Funeral Home had a generator—how otherwise could it deal with the bodies that came to it, regardless of weather? Ruth remembered hearing about some ancient general coming home packed in honey to keep him from rotting; another one, pickled in brandy. Centuries of folk with imagination but no electricity, and they'd coped. Who was she to complain about a loss of milk?

"Violet's not coming," Sharon said when she and Jack came crunching up the sanded walk behind Ruth.

"She's upset that Dad wants to go." Sharon was wearing purple polka dot tights under a green rayon skirt, her honey-colored hair heaped up on one side of her head and hanging loose on the other. Jack was neatly dressed in khaki pants and jacket, with a ginger-colored bow tie that matched his hair. He didn't seem at all embarrassed by his wife's attire. Just as well, Ruth thought.

"Pete told Violet she should come," Jack said, grinning. "Or they'll think she did it."

"Which might not be far from the truth," Sharon said, and Ruth said "We-ell, now."

They were greeted inside by Colm's father, an el-

derly, pink-cheeked man, his shoulders stooped with
arthritis. He winked at Ruth and squeezed her hand. He
called her his surrogate daughter-in-law—wishful
thinking, of course, on his part. His employee, a short
squat man in black with a sad waterfall of a face ush-
ered them into the parlor. The place was dimly lit with
candles. The air was close, the perfume from Crystal's
women friends cloying. Ernie had spent a small fortune
on flowers, along with a polished oak casket. Although
Ruth didn't care for open caskets, she joined the line
of mourners. She was curious to see this Helen who'd
sunk a thousand erections.

And here she was: Crystal Hiland, looking as icy
cold as her name with her white marbly skin. She was
beautiful—not because of her features, which were
marked by overly full lips and a rather sharp nose—
but because of the shiny hair that filled the coffin with
its opulence. The hair seemed to grow even as Ruth
watched, ebony tendrils curling to the elbows that were
sheathed in red satin. Medusa, Ruth thought, Medusa
with the snaky locks that turned men to stone. The figure, too, was voluptuous, the dress tight over the full
breasts that revealed the pointy nipples. Was it Ernie
who had chosen that red satin dress? Ruth wondered
what Gracie thought of it.

"My God," someone breathed behind Ruth, and she
turned to see her boarder, Noah Hemphill. She'd forgotten he was coming—he had Gracie in class, he'd
told her that afternoon; he'd known Crystal slightly
from teacher's conferences. Now though, he seemed
awed, entranced, as he gazed at the dead woman, his
eyes luminous in the white candles that glowed on either side of the bier. Like Ruth, he was breathing in the
subtle odor of incense that emanated from the coffin.

"It's like any minute she'll open her eyes," he whispered—more to himself than to Ruth, and she murmured assent.

She joined Sharon and Jack in one of the back rows. The room was full. Crystal had a lot of friends, Gracie had told Sharon, both men and women. Ruth saw Pete come in, breathless, bits of ice in his hair. She watched him take a seat by a man who'd served with him several years before on the planning board. Finally the family shuffled in. Ernie, looking distraught and uncomfortable in an ill-fitting black suit and maroon necktie, slightly askew; anorexic Gracie in a black skirt and white blouse, clinging to his hand, her cheeks working in and out; then an elderly woman who might be Crystal's mother, or grandmother, judging by the white hair that haloed her head like a fresh snowfall. The woman's blue print dress hung awkwardly on her thin bones; her ankles were swollen over the black broken shoes. Crystal, according to Sharon, had been brought up in a trailer park. It was not surprising that she'd found Ernie and his offer of a white clapboard house and nice clothes highly attractive.

The minister stammered out a eulogy that made it clear he'd not known Crystal. "They say," he would murmur, or "according to her husband…." Crystal had not been a churchgoer, but Ernie, it was obvious, wanted things done right. Crystal would have the best, right down to the shiny casket. Ernie kept turning his head slightly, as if looking for someone. Maybe the man who'd made Crystal pregnant? Had there still been a liaison there? A motive for killing? Though why would a man, if he were in love with Crystal, kill?

Ernie's eyes rested on Pete, and Ruth wondered if it had been Pete who'd gotten the woman pregnant. Pete had been known to cover up, to prevaricate. Fourteen years ago, though, he was still married to Ruth. She glared at the back of his balding head. She was glad they were no longer married. She wished Colm were here to hold her hand. But it was Colm's night for police duty; Ruth was to be his eyes and ears.

There was a rustle in the chair behind her; Ruth turned to see Noah getting to his feet. He didn't want to leave his wife alone, he whispered—she wasn't feeling well. Though Dawn had been zealously cutting up onions and turnips, making a "woodstove stew" when Ruth left, looking perfectly healthy. Noah was a good husband, but an anxious one.

The minister droned on, uttering platitudes, ending with the Ecclesiastes that Ruth liked: "For everything there is a season...a time to be born, and a time to die...;" then the familiar: "In my father's house are many mansions... I go to prepare a place for you." Poor Crystal, Ruth thought: it was not a place she'd have chosen. The group struggled up to sing "Abide with Me," and the service was over. A churchwoman announced that refreshments would be served in the "blue parlor" and the mourners straggled into an adjoining room.

"Mom, we're leaving," Sharon said. "We have a ten-year-old watching the kids and Robbie will take advantage. He's at that stage. Tell Gracie we'll see her tomorrow."

"You assume I'm staying?"

"You said you wanted to observe. All the die-hards will be in the refreshment room."

"Except Violet, of course."

"Oh, Lord, I forgot her. She'll be drinking up our wine."

"Let's hope it'll put her to sleep."

"It just gets her going. She'll do a scene from Romeo and Juliet."

"I'll try to send your father along then."

Ruth saw Pete moving toward the parlor, a head taller than the three men who preceded him. The candlelit room made Ruth think of a medieval hall; it lacked only torches flaring from the walls. She caught up with Pete, suggested he leave soon to see to Violet.

"Before the wine gets to her," she told him and he frowned.

"I don't need to hear your criticism, Ruth. I think I should stay. For Gracie's sake."

There was a lineup of family against a far wall. Ernie was there with the elderly relative on one side, and Gracie on the other. The black skirt hung long and loose on the girl, a make-down most likely of her mother's. When women clucked over her she would gaze at the floor and squeeze her lips together. Ruth resisted the urge to pluck her up and run her home to Sharon's. But the girl should be with her father tonight. If there was any warmth between Gracie and the grandmother, it wasn't apparent.

Ruth bit into a tired-looking egg sandwich with its crusts cut off. She decided she would forgo the line, she could observe better that way. Which one was this lover who'd gotten Crystal pregnant but then was spurned? She eyed several possibilities: a gangly blonde-haired man with a tattoo on the side of his narrow face; an overweight man with red, scaly skin; a gray-haired, rather distinguished looking fellow who might be the man she'd worked for. None of them, she decided, would have pleased Crystal enough to let him sire a child. Perhaps the child's father hadn't come after all, not wanting to risk Ernie Hiland's temper on such an emotional night.

Pete was closing in on the family trio, looking all innocence, compassion. He took the old woman's hands in his and squeezed them. He hugged Gracie, who gave in to his embrace like a rag doll and then, flushing, ran a hand through her hair that was tamed with something sticky to lie flat. The girl would not want to lead her mother's life. Ernie was still talking with the tattooed blonde man; she caught a few words about ice, wires, voltage.

Pete waited his turn, his hand already stuck out. Ernie turned. Saw him. "Son of a bitch," Ernie said. "You got a nerve coming here." He swung, a hard punch to the groin. Pete went down on his knees. Instinctively, Ruth cried out. Pete struggled up slowly, looking astonished, as if, a good Samaritan, he'd been repulsed in the act of offering succor. His face reddened; surprise turned to anger. He took a stance, his fists clenched. He was pulled away, protesting, by the blonde man and another fellow who sprang out from the crowd, and hustled out of the room.

Gracie was crying, the mother shrieking at her son-in-law. Feeling an old tug of loyalty, Ruth followed after Pete, elbowing her way through the crowd.

"He belong to you?" the blonde man asked, and not knowing how to answer, she said, "More or less," and hurried her ex out of the funeral home. The professional mourner at the door waved them peremptorily through, like uninvited guests; the night chill struck her face like the flat of a knife.

"Bastard," Pete said. "She never loved the guy. You can see why. He was never good enough for her."

"Pete," she said, as they walked back to Sharon's

house where she'd left her truck, "tell the whole truth now. Did you have a fling with Crystal? Did you get her pregnant?" It would have been when she herself was carrying Vic. She felt her blood come to a boil. "If you did, you deserved to have him hit you." She punched his arm.

"Wait a minute now," he said, fending her off. "I didn't get her pregnant. I swear I didn't. I told you, we'd have a little drink now and then at Alibi. She'd tell me how boring it was to be married to Ernie. She needed an old buddy's ear. That's all, I swear it, Ruth."

He slipped on an icy patch and she helped him up. He was so vulnerable. So weak. She realized that now. The big clunky football shoes had hid the Achilles heel.

They turned into Bristol Street in silence. Sharon met them at the door. "Dad, Violet's gone. I called the police. She took your car. She took her stuff, too, and the rest of that box of chocolates you gave her. That's when I noticed—I was looking for one of those caramel ones."

Pete stood absolutely still, in the doorway. It was as if he'd been hit one too many times and his mind was fuzzy.

"What?" he said.

COLM HANNA and a rookie cop named Bernadette Hammer were on the Northway in pursuit of Violet Jones. Hammer was driving. They'd started out as soon as Sharon made the call about her disappearance. Violet would have had an hour's start on them, according to Sharon. She wouldn't have bothered to call the police, Sharon added, except that she knew her father would worry.

"Do you think Jones is her real name?" Hammer

asked. Bernadette Hammer preferred, she said, to be called by her surname.

Colm smiled. "It's an alias, I bet. She's probably wanted in ten states for murder."

"You think so?" Hammer was a naive young woman with a warbly soprano voice (it tortured Colm to hear her high-pitched humming), but a body built, it seemed, of steel wire. Ever since the first handshake, Colm had vowed he wouldn't try to cross her.

"You never know. Can you step on it, Hammer? She's probably through her ice cream sundae by now." A cop in Saratoga had seen Violet's car outside a Friendly's. The man was supposed to keep watch, then stop her when she came out. Though Colm had hoped to be the one to intercept her, with Hammer as a backup, of course. Colm wasn't cut out to be a cop— he'd only blundered into the job because of his deceased grandfather, who was something of a legend down at police headquarters. Colm, unfortunately, was made of flesh and blood. Soft flesh for all that—his belly was definitely expanding from the Otter Creek Ale he had a particular fondness for.

Hammer reached over to turn on the siren and Colm told her to cool it. "She hears that she'll make a run for it into the woods."

"Suspect leaving restaurant. I'll go in for the snatch," the Saratoga cop grunted over the staticky radio. And then, "Holy moley—she's a big one!"

"There'd better be two of you," Colm responded. "Take her to headquarters. We'll meet you there."

The cop said, "Here we go," and signed off.

Colm pictured the scene at Friendly's: the cops intercepting, Violet yelling and pummeling, a crowd gathering; and finally Violet restrained, handcuffed, squeezed into the cop car. A second cop holding her down in back while the first guy drove like hell to get her safe and subdued, into the cooler.

The scenario wasn't far off track, the first cop told him when they arrived at the precinct. "She gave us one hell of a fight, I'll tell ya! But we got her. She's yours, you want to take her back to Vermont. We can do without this baby."

Colm hadn't thought of that. Of their being the ones to take her back to Vermont. But that was the whole point, Hammer informed him. "Detective Plotkin wants to talk to her again about the Hiland woman's murder. She's got a motive all right. And Lieutenant Ashley's got her on a speeding fine from six months ago. She never paid it or showed up in court."

Surprisingly, a handcuffed Violet climbed docilely into the back of the Branbury cruiser, as if the play was over and this was just the curtain call.

"You can't think—you absolutely can't think I would kill some woman over a mere man. I mean, she wasn't any competition, really. She was just a small-town girl—no, I take that back. Not a girl—an older woman! You could see the wrinkles she covered with makeup. And that awful hair. It was like fur. Fur! A she-bear, that's what she was. Pete was trying to get rid of her, you see, get her off his back. My back! Not by killing her, oh no, God no, he just wanted her to stop coming over and harassing us. Harassing me! I didn't want to be here anyway, it's that ice storm keeps us trapped in this godawful wilderness. I just want to get home to New York. I've got an audition coming up. A big one."

"That's why you took off," Colm suggested, pulling onto the Northway. It was his turn to drive.

Violet took the bait. 'That's it, absolutely. I couldn't take one more minute of that ice. Every time I go out a branch breaks over my head. I'll be surprised if I don't have a bloody concussion.''

"So when Pete went to the funeral service without you, you were fed up. You thought you'd teach him a lesson."

"Yes. No! Well, yes. I begged him not to go. Even dead, she'd only make him miserable. And that boorish husband—Eddie, or Ernie, whatever his name is— wouldn't want him there either, the man is insanely jealous. Insanely! Turn your searchlight on *him*, officers. Don't look at this poor little female.''

Colm heard Hammer giggle beside him. He suppressed a laugh himself. Violet had done a stint in the circus, he'd heard; dancing, most likely, with lions and tigers.

"But you want to know something, officers? Do you? Hmm?'' Her voice was low, confidential, sexy; the perfume tickled his nose. She would have laid low the wild beasts, Colm thought. He turned slightly in his seat, seduced himself by the provocative question. There was a dramatic pause.

"I don't think it's the husband who did it," she said. "I really don't. There's something, well, sweet about him, for all that bravado and jealousy. Sweet men don't kill. I was in a murder mystery once. It turned out *I* was the killer.''

"Really?'' said Colm.

"It was a play, of course. I was the victim actually, the character abused me. And I killed him. It was self defense for *my* character. But they suspected this other guy, this sweet, secretly jealous guy. And it wasn't him. It was me! All the time it was me.'' She giggled.

"Goodness," said Hammer.

"But what did you want to tell us?" Colm coaxed. "You said there was something we ought to know."

"Did I? Oh, yes." The voice softened again, turned subtle, sly. Colm was impressed with her acting ability. "You can deduce something from that play I was in. There's truth in theater, you know. Deeper truths than in real life."

"Uh-huh."

"So you should look to the woman. To the woman with the mostest motive."

"The mostest motive," Colm repeated, intrigued by the superlative.

"You know who I mean," she said coyly.

Something leaped in Colm's chest. "I do?" he said, warily.

"Think of someone," she said, "who has a lot to gain if they pin the murder on Peter—someone who owes him money, right? For his share of the farm? A whole lot of money? (Colm's heart went cold.) Someone who hates me. Who wants to pin the murder on *me*. To get *me* out of the picture, oh yes. Someone who'd kill just to get back at me and Peter. Thinking Peter really had an affair with that creature—when he didn't! Oh, no. Why, there was never anything between them."

"So you told us," Hammer said dryly.

"And finally," Violet said, pulling out her trump card, "it wasn't Crystal Hiland that Ruth wanted to kill anyway, no, of course it wasn't."

Colm waited. He heard Hammer's high-pitched humming in the passenger seat.

"It was me. Me!" she shouted. "Ruth killed the wrong woman. Thinking it was *me*."

Colm's pulse was racing. "That's ridiculous," he said, choking on the words. They were turning onto Route 149, heading up into ice-land again; the car swerved on the slick road. "Your theory is full of holes. Why would she go to that place anyway? To Molly's Crotch? She was in the barn, milking."

"Killed her first!" Violet cried, thrilled with her theory. "Threw her in the truck and then dumped her in the Crotch when she thought no one would suspect. The perfect murder. Just like the theater."

"Ridiculous," Colm said again, glancing over at Hammer, but his colleague was deep in thought. Icicles blazed in the headlights like silver daggers. "No one who knows Ruth Willmarth would give that theory a second thought."

There was a triumphant laugh in the back seat. Hammer stopped humming. Violet had made her case and was resting it. "I'm exhausted," she said, lifting her handcuffed hands, then clanking them back into her lap. "I didn't mean to take off like this. I was just giving Pete a lesson. I would have come back on my own. I mean, it's his car, after all. I wouldn't leave him stranded."

"Of course not," Colm said. It wouldn't occur to her that now Pete would have to rent a car to retrieve his from Saratoga. Violet was out for Violet. She was more dangerous than any circus tiger.

They deserved each other, Pete and the tiger lady, Colm told himself. He took a wide curve, hit the brakes and the car shimmied. Violet squealed.

He was damned if he'd say he was sorry.

RUTH SLAMMED DOWN the phone. "It's crazy," she told Colm. "The police want to talk to me tomorrow morning. 'Be sure to be here,' the detective said. Like I'd be anywhere else but in the barn at eight in the morning.''

She picked up an overly ripe tomato and hurled it at the wastebucket. It missed, and squashed at Colm's feet. "Jeez, Ruthie," he said. "It's not my fault they might suspect you. It's Violet's theory, like I said. It's just a ploy on her part, right? To get the onus off her?''

"Maybe. Maybe not. I *could* kill, you know. Oh, not Crystal, but Violet. Yes, Violet! You'd better keep me away from her, Colm. Miss Seduction. She ripped my life apart, Colm. And Vic just a kid...."

Upstairs Vic gave a holler. "Mom, you're shouting. How can I sleep when you're shouting?"

"Sorry, love. Go back to sleep," she called upstairs. Vic's life was affected, too, by the ice storm. If her shouting kept him awake, so did Dawn's and Noah's constant traipsing up and down the stairs. And here was Dawn now, followed by a patient Noah.

"She can't sleep without a glass of warm milk and some of those carob peanuts I bought her," he said. He was wearing blue striped pajamas that needed washing—you could see the stains where he'd spilled tomato juice. But then, they all needed baths and clean clothes.

He turned to Dawn, who was clad in a pink nightie, a black shawl over her plump shoulders. "I told you I'd get it for you. You didn't have to get out of bed. Go back up now." His voice sounded long suffering. Ruth wondered how he was going to get through the nine months of Dawn's pregnancy. She was weeping off and on, too, he'd confided only that morning. He didn't know "how to handle it."

Dawn looked contrite. "I didn't want to bother you, sweetie. You've been getting up so early to help in the barn." She looked sternly at Ruth, the taskmaster, then at Noah. "Thank you, sweetheart. Just put the pan of milk on the woodstove. Don't let it boil over now." She trudged back upstairs in fuzzy pink slippers.

"Don't worry," Ruth told Noah. "There isn't enough dry wood in the stove to make it boil."

"I'll go down in the basement and get you some," Noah offered. But Ruth put out a hand.

"Wait till tomorrow. We've used two thirds of our winter supply already. We'll have to make do. Besides, it's warming up a little out there. We can cope. You have enough blankets?"

"Plenty." His voice sounded weary. He'd been dragging about the last two days, as though he were coming down with something. Ruth worried. He seemed a nice fellow, earnest, perhaps too intense. She tried to make small conversation while he warmed the milk. Colm wasn't much help, leaning back in his chair with a peevish look on his face. He'd come over to be with Ruth after the unexpected chase to Saratoga and here was an interloper.

"You knew Crystal then," she said to Noah, making conversation. Besides, he might be able to add something she didn't know about the dead woman.

A little milk spattered when Noah picked up the pan and he ran for a sponge. He explained again how he'd had Gracie in his class, met Crystal in parent conferences.

"Did you detect any home problems? I mean, child neglect or anything?"

"She was a good mother," he said, sponging up the milk. "I mean, so far as I could tell. She worried about Gracie's schoolwork. The girl wasn't doing too well. It wasn't Crystal's fault," he said again, turning to face

Ruth. "It was the situation at home. The husband always after her to stay home—be the angel in the house, you know. Crystal was a bright woman. She could have been somebody. It wasn't her fault she didn't finish college. The money ran out, she said." He poured the warmed milk into a glass, his hand shaking a little.

"You're tired," Ruth said. "Get some rest now. They think we might get electricity on this street tomorrow. Though I wouldn't bet on it."

Noah grinned. "Neither would I."

"I hear he's a good teacher," she said when Noah had gone upstairs with the milk. "Vic will have him next year. He'll know all about Vic's home life, that's for sure." She grimaced, wondering how much the couple upstairs had heard after the police called. She'd gone out of control for a minute.

"Okay, Ruthie. But the guy did know Crystal. So let's add him to the list of suspects, what do you say? Make the game more exciting. So now we've got Violet, Pete and Ernie, maybe Noah—and you," he added, with a snide smile.

She ignored the last. *She* hadn't done it! She knew that much, even if the police didn't. That sneaky, stinking Violet.... "And there's Mister X," she said, taking a bottle of ale from the refrigerator for herself.

"Mister X?"

"The guy who got Crystal pregnant. Ernie knows, I bet. But he doesn't want Gracie to know. I gather Crystal slept around before she married Ernie."

"Understatement of the year."

"But if Noah is right, there was more to Crystal than we thought. She was more than just a sleep-around girl." Ruth sipped the ale. It felt warm in her belly. She needed the warmth, the comfort. It was chilly here in the kitchen. She got up and threw the last dry log on the fire.

She wanted to go to bed now, curl up in the warm quilts. "Finish your drink, will you, Colm? I have to turn in. I need to be in control when the police come tomorrow. Then I want to go to the hospital, look up some old records."

"Birth records?" He stood up, looking put-upon. She knew what he wanted: a little smooching on the sofa. But she wasn't into it tonight. That police call had wrecked her libido.

"Right," she said. "If not at the hospital, the town hall. And if the father's name isn't on the records, I'll have to find out some other way. Pressure Ernie, for one thing."

"I forgot to tell you," Colm said, pulling on his coat. "Something I found out after we got Violet back to the station. They're not keeping her overnight, by the way. Pete's already bailed her out."

"Poor Sharon. But what didn't you tell me?" Colm had a habit of mentioning things and then not following through. Though she had to be patient. Patience was one of her New Year's resolutions.

"Oh, yeah. About Ernie, I mean. Seems he fell off a tree where he was working on the wires. Pretty good concussion. Seems nobody can talk to him till he comes round. Bummer, just when the chief wants more information. The husband's usually suspect number one, you know. He's *my* man anyway. Motive, opportunity—Ernie worked right up to the edge of the Green Mountain Forest. Means? Trees full of icicles. Rocks and heavy limbs. Ernie'd know they could kill. Or maybe he brought a weapon with him."

Colm might be right, she thought. Ernie's assault on

Pete at the funeral home proved he could be violent if provoked. She sighed deeply, let Colm hug her. She clung to him. "That accident's one more thing," she murmured. "One more thing keeping us in limbo. Trapping us in our houses. In our heads."

Outdoors something struck the roof; ice shards came crashing down the kitchen window, shattering on impact.

FRIDAY

SHARON HAD TO GET OUT of the house. She couldn't take this infighting one more minute. Her father and Violet were upstairs now: arguing, accusing, counter accusing. "You could have got us out of here sooner," Violet was shouting. "*I* had no trouble driving out of this hell hole."

"But Crystal died," Pete hollered. "We had to stay. Have to," he amended.

"I don't care, we could have gone," Violet shrieked. "I'm sick of it all. Sick of the police. Sick of this house. Sick of everyone yelling around here."

"Who's yelling now?" Sharon shouted up.

"Just flow with it," Jack had told her, on his way out the door. Sure, Sharon thought. For Jack it was easy. He had his trees to escape to. He was mourning every fissure, every cracked branch. "Twenty years," he'd said as he pulled on his boots and parka, "twenty years to recoup. I know it's part of life—like death. But I hate to see them go."

She accused him of caring more for the trees than for her. He just smiled, gave her a warm embrace and suggested she take Gracie to see her father in the hospital. Ernie's accident, she agreed, had been the last straw for Gracie. "I'm practically an orphan," the girl had wailed last night, and the children wept with her.

They would go see Ernie at once, Sharon decided—never mind that visiting hours were only in the afternoon. School was still out, so the ten-year-old babysitter was available; she came right over. Hearing the brouhaha upstairs, the sitter watched, awed, as Violet stomped down the steps, snatched up her coat, and slammed out the door. Sharon's father came down afterward, muttering to himself. He nodded at Sharon and the sitter and headed toward the kitchen to fix himself a drink. Sharon checked her watch. It was nine o'clock in the morning.

"I'll bet you wish you were still married to Mother," she said softly. Her father gave her a black look and uncorked a bottle.

Sharon and Gracie were halfway to the door when Robbie came flying down the stairs. "Give it back!" he screeched at Willa, who had taken his dump truck. "Mother—make her give it back."

"Good luck," Sharon told the sitter, and opened the front door. "Oh!" The glare struck her eyes like a powerful searchlight. Why, the sun was out! It bounced off the icy trees and shrubs, blinding her. It was like summer coming suddenly after winter, without spring. She ran back in to grab her sunglasses. She needed a rosy outlook on life.

Out on the porch she put her face up to the sun. But then a gush of melted ice dropped from a tree; it struck both lenses, dead center, and the world went dark again.

RUTH WAS IN THE COW BARN when the detective arrived. The man would get the full bovine treatment. The cows were all present, too, mooing, bellowing, chewing, voiding. She was treating Elizabeth, who was down with mastitis. Poor Elizabeth had been through the mill the year before when she was slashed with a hunting knife; her nerves had never recovered. Then the ice storm hit, unnerving the whole herd, poor beasts. The sun was out, yes, but so was the power. Still.

The detective was as nervous as the cows, perhaps because of the cows. He was a city man. As they talked, he'd stroke his thin gray mustache, then punch his fingers together. He'd stick them in his pockets, then pull them out again, like a pair of forgotten gloves. He was clearly embarrassed to be questioning her; the color squeezed slowly up and outward into his cheeks. He knew Colm Hanna, he knew Ruth's reputation for "helping to find a perpetrator. I never thought I'd be here questioning you in regard to, well, a murder. I mean, well…" He shoved his hands back in his pockets again.

"It's all right," she said, trying to put him at his ease. "I understand. I have a motive, I suppose, for killing Crystal Hiland. I'm not happy with the way my former husband has acted. I don't care for his girlfriend. I'm bitter about the whole thing, in fact. I might want to see one or both of them implicated."

"Ah," he said, and pulled out a small notepad, scribbled on it.

"But really, officer, not enough to kill for it. Pete is, after all, the father of my three children. They're in my care now—the two younger ones, anyway. What kind of mother would I be going out and killing some woman I barely know?"

The detective's nose was a carrot. He was shaking his head. He was married, she saw, a plain gold ring on his left hand. "Not Crystal Hiland, no," he said in a small voice. "But if you saw a woman, thinking it might be

Violet, um, Jones—and in a moment of outrage—you do have a reputation for a bit of a, well, temper...."

"Wait a minute," she said, "you haven't asked the Big Question. Where was I the night Crystal was killed? Well, I can tell you. I was right here in the barn. Here with my hired man. Both of us trying to get the old generator started after the lights went out, and me swearing up a storm. *At* the storm! You may've heard about my temper, officer, but you haven't seen it yet."

The detective's face was the purple-black of eggplant; he backed up a step. "With your hired man," he repeated. "He can vouch for you? Every minute of that evening?"

She considered. The cow she was tending gave a sickly bellow and let go with a stream of manure. The detective clapped a handkerchief to his nose and stepped back. "Mostly here. But he did go into town to bring back a little supper."

"You were alone then for—a half hour? An hour? Without—a witness?"

Now he'd gone too far. She stuck her hands on her jeaned hips, took a step toward him. "Thirty-three cows, detective. They were my witnesses. You think I'm going to leave them and drive up in an ice storm to some notch, or crotch, and stick an icicle in some woman's neck—even if I do think it might be Violet Jones? Oh, never mind. Just keep me on your list of suspects. It's a challenge. A challenge to find out who really did kill Crystal Hiland."

"Yes," he said. "That of course is what we want to find out. Yes, indeed." He was backing toward the barn door now. The cows bellowed in their stalls as if heckling him. He turned and opened the door wide. The sun struck her face; she blinked in its icy brightness.

"Come again, Detective," she said sweetly. "Any time."

SHARON AND GRACIE PAUSED at the nurses' station to see Ernie, who was to have—"absolutely"—no visitors beyond family. "I'm an aunt," Sharon said, swinging along, not waiting for a response. Besides, she couldn't *not* go, the way Gracie was clinging to her hand, practically strangling it. Inside Room 201 Gracie cried out. There was Ernie, trapped in tubes, done up like a mummy, but his eyes wide open.

"Daddy!" Gracie shrieked and rushed to his bedside. She buried her head in his blankets.

"I killed her," he moaned, "I killed Crystal. I told him I did."

"Told who?" Sharon said.

But Ernie was silent now, his mouth foaming, eyes dilated. Gracie looked up, suddenly panicked. "He's having a seizure," she cried. She held his tongue so he wouldn't swallow it. She seemed to know what to do. Even so, Sharon rang for the nurse.

"He's an epileptic. Nobody told me," said the nurse, a tidy brunette with a stentorian voice. "An epileptic has no business working heights like that."

"He does, too. He never has trouble in the trees," said Gracie, confronting the nurse. "He takes medicine for it."

"Sure, he does," Sharon said, putting an arm around Gracie, holding her close. The girl was trembling. She's so fragile, Sharon thought. And good Lord, she'd just heard her father say he'd killed her mother! They waited, clinging together, while Ernie worked his way out of the seizure.

"Killed her, my Crystal," Ernie moaned, his big homely face screwed up into a mask of pain.

The nurse glanced meaningfully at Sharon, and stuck a needle into him. He fell back on the pillow, his mouth opening and shutting without words; finally hanging open in his torpor. Beside his bed the tubes gurgled and glunked, feeding his inert body.

Gracie wept openly into Sharon's shoulder. "He's just delirious, that's all, he's imagining things," Sharon told the girl. "He didn't mean what he said."

But all Sharon could think was that it wasn't her dad. He was off the hook now. It was Ernie who did it. It was a crime of passion. Sharon had encountered those moments of violence herself, though she'd never acted on them—except to kick the cat one time, and she'd broken a toe when she missed and kicked the wall.

As they left the room she looked back once more at her slumbering neighbor. He seemed at peace now, the way Crystal had appeared at the funeral service. No more midnight liaisons for Crystal, no more trying to find excitement in her life, Sharon thought, no more trying to compensate for a dull marriage. Madame Bovary came to mind. Poor Emma Bovary with that dull bovine husband, loving, but never understanding her, never feeding the psyche.

Outside in the corridor Sharon hugged Gracie; she could feel the bones close to the surface of the girl's skin. If Ernie didn't pull through, or even if he did and went to prison, she might adopt the girl.

RUTH CAME OUT of the hospital records office and ran into Sharon and Gracie. "How is he?" she asked.

Seeing Gracie's weepy face she thought she knew.

Ernie was gone. Gracie was an orphan, poor dear girl. Did Ruth need a fourth child?

But Ernie seemed to be holding his own, Sharon told her mother. "I didn't know he was epileptic, though. He just had a seizure."

"That's because he didn't have his medicine," Gracie said. "I should have brought it with me." She seemed in control, but nevertheless, clung to Sharon's arm.

"We'll see he gets it," Sharon said. The girl wanted to go home now to her own house. "I just need to be there," she said, and when Ruth and Sharon looked worried: "I'm not going to off myself or anything. I'm going to make popovers to take to Dad. Dad loves popovers."

There was a life force in the girl, Ruth felt—not unlike the one that had been snuffed out in Crystal. They were mother and daughter all right. "We'll pick you up in an hour," Sharon told her when they dropped her off.

"He killed her," Sharon announced after the girl had run into her house, kicking aside a dead branch that had fallen onto the walk.

"What? Who?" Ruth's head was muddled. She'd spent an hour going over baby records in the hospital. Gracie had been born there, but Ernie was listed as the father, so it was a dead end. They sat down in the bakery café. The odors of baking and frosting were intense, making Ruth salivate. The ice storm had made her eat more than usual, compensation perhaps for the devastation outside. How she missed her own oven! She hadn't had a homemade doughnut in three days. There was still no power. They were just milking the cows and dumping the milk. It was like running and running and not getting anywhere.

"It's Ernie, I said. He confessed it. You're not listening, Mother. You're off in one of your daydreams."

It was a familiar complaint from both her daughters. But she did listen! She'd listened to tales of "I love him and he doesn't love me," or "He loves me and I can't stand him," or "You're not eating right, Mother, you should eat more soy." And then, "Soy's not that good for you the way they process it; try brewer's yeast." She listened, and tried to give back, but the daughters were on a new track before she could offer advice, and then what she had to say fell flat.

"Ernie said he told *him*. I asked who *him* was, and he fell into that seizure. But he confessed. He did it, Mother. He stabbed his own wife."

Ernie had confessed to killing Crystal. Ruth was listening hard now. "You're sure you heard right? He was probably delirious."

"That's what the nurse said. But that's when truth comes out, right? In delirium? In semi-consciousness? I suppose the *him* was a policeman. Though I don't know how a cop could get in to see him."

"I'll make a call," Ruth said. "Wait here."

She found out what she needed to know. No policeman had been to see Ernie Hiland. "Nuh-uh," Chief Fallon said. "We know better'n 'at. A sick man in a coma? We don't drill sick men. We wait. Anyhow, we talked to him yesterday before he, um, fell. He said he didn't do it. Sure. He said how could he, such a beautiful woman? Hey! I could relate. Ever seen her? All that hair? She didn't need another stitch on, right? A regular Lady Godiva." He laughed his chugalug laugh.

"Check on it anyway, to be sure no cop got in early, okay?"

She hung up and dialed Colm at his father's mortuary.

William Hanna answered. "What'd you think of her?" he asked before she could speak her piece.

"Think of whom?" she asked. Like Roy Fallon, Colm's father preferred pronouns to proper names.

"That Hiland woman. Crystal! I used my best makeup girl. She did her up A Number One, you think? Like a Mona Lisa? That mysterious half smile on the cold lips. The candlelight brought it out, you know?"

Mona Lisa, Ruth thought. Lady Godiva, Helen of Troy. Medusa. How many names could you call the woman? Was she some sort of goddess? She left a message for Colm to see if any of the other cops had been to visit Ernie—not mentioning what he'd allegedly confessed. That would never do. It would be like the betrayal of a sick man.

"I find it hard to believe he confessed to anyone," she told her daughter. "I mean, he could have done it, of course, but I still think we have to look elsewhere." She told Sharon about the man who'd gotten Crystal pregnant. "Keep your ears open, will you, Shar? Ask around—friends, neighbors—discreetly, that is. It's just a hunch, you know, but we have to keep searching. If a cop does visit Ernie and Ernie raves on about killing Crystal—well, he's caught."

"DNA evidence?"

"But she wasn't raped. They'd probably just find Ernie in the semen. Or some other poor fellow she went to bed with. There was only that bootprint, and that's not definitive, either. Three people with a size twelve: Violet, Ernie—oh yes, Colm found out when they searched his house for evidence. And your father."

This time it was Sharon off in her own abstract world. "I'll talk to Sibyl Moon," she said. "Sibyl knows everything that goes on in town. She was a friend of Crystal's, too."

"Good. Call me if you find out anything. I have to get back to the farm, and then I'll try the town clerk. See if anything pops up there."

She bought a bagful of doughnuts and a mug of hot coffee for the drive home. On the way out she saw Pete and Violet in front of Poppy's Pizza. They seemed to be having a spat about something. Ruth heard the word Crystal. Even dead, it seemed, Medusa-Helen-Godiva-Mona Lisa was wreaking her havoc.

She paused in the bakery doorway until the couple had stormed past.

SIBYL MOON WONDERED if Sharon wanted her palm read. Or would she prefer tarot cards? Sibyl was a psychic. Sharon had been to her as a client, but not this time, she told the woman. They were sitting in Sibyl's trailer, a space Sibyl barely fit into: the woman resembled a five-foot-square tent in her purple wool bathrobe. She had no heat, she complained, only a kerosene stove that "scares the pants off of me. I mean, you heard the Silvernails' stove blew up—burned the whole goddamn house down? The worst is, I knew it before it happened. I sensed it, I smelled it. I tried to warn Hazel. But my phone wasn't working. My mental telepathy, neither." She waggled her several chins.

"How awful. What about Hazel?" Sharon asked. "Was she badly burned?"

"Took off her whole face!" cried Sibyl. "Which wasn't a bad thing. I mean, she has to be the homeliest female in town. She'll have plastic surgery now. Big improvement coming up."

Sharon clucked her sympathy. She told Sibyl why

she'd come. "You and Crystal were good friends, I know."

"Sure. She used to be my best client. Sometimes she'd help with my sittings. She had a little of the sixth sense herself. But not enough to help her in the end. My senses failed me. Jesus, I didn't know what was going on with her till the last minute. I mean I knew where she was—I knew it was Molly's Crotch. But I didn't foresee any murder. Oh Lordy, I was sick about that. If I'd of told the police I knew *something* was going to happen, they'd've just laughed at me. They think I'm nuts, you know? Then one of them called afterward and asked if I'd any notion who killed her. Well, if I did, I wouldn't tell *them*. Want a cup of pomegranate juice? It's good for what ails you."

Sharon shook her head. "What I really need to know is who fathered Gracie. Not that he was the killer. But we're looking for any possible leads."

Sibyl leaned back in a huge purple plush chair. Purple was her color. Almost everything in the room was purple: footstool, vase, loveseat, carpet. She had a coy expression on her face. If she knew the father, she wasn't about to say.

"I'm a psychic," she said. "I know things other people don't. That gives me a responsibility. To keep secrets."

"But Crystal's dead," Sharon argued. "We want to find who did it. So that person won't kill again. It's a terrible thing, Sibyl, to kill somebody. If you know something you have to tell. That's your responsibility, too."

Sibyl considered. She cradled her chins in her plump white hands. "We-ell," she said, "I don't know for sure myself, you see. Jesus, I mean I don't know everything that happens to everybody! I'm not your ordinary person, no. But I'm not your ultimate seer neither. Crystal was a popular girl. She slept around a little, you know. Looking for Mister Right. Always looking, dreaming, right? There were two or three at that time. Let's see, would have been back in eighty-eight?''

Sharon guessed so. "And who would those two or three be?''

Sibyl glanced around for her tarot cards, then realized she wouldn't need them. She'd have to rely on memory. She was sometimes short on that attribute, she allowed. "We-ell," she said again. "There was Georgie Lozario. But no, he sweated, she said. Crystal couldn't stand a sweaty man. He used some stinky aftershave stuff and that only made it worse.''

"Count him out then.''

"Yup. Then there was, uh, Patrick O'Neil.''

"Irish," Sharon said.

"No, black. He was only in town a year, his father taught at the college. The token black professor, you know. She was interested in him *because* he was black.''

"Very black—or light skinned?''

"Very black.''

"He wasn't Gracie's father then.''

"No, right. Then, uh, lemme see now. If it was in the future, why I could tell you more. But in the past, well, it's hard to recollect.'' She stuck a wad of Juicy Fruit gum in her mouth, chewed thoughtfully. Sharon waited.

"Teddy Snow. Yup, he could have been the one.''

"Tell me about him. Where is he now? Does Gracie look like him?''

"Dead," Sibyl said. "Very dead. Died half way down Bread Loaf Mountain. First time he'd ever skied and he took the expert trail. Met a tree. A hardhack to be exact." Sibyl was pleased with her recall.

"That's it then?" Sharon was disappointed. Sibyl hadn't turned up a single suspect.

"We-ell. There *was* someone else. Good-looking fella. She met him in the doctor's office where she worked. I recall her talking about him. He looked her right in the eye and she looked back, that's what she said. Looked right into her gut, she said. And they made it right off."

"In the doctor's office?"

"No, no—in bed. His bed."

"What happened that they split up? He didn't like what he saw in her gut?"

"He loved what he saw! It was her turned *him* off. She got bored, you know? He was too lovey-dovey, she said. When they were too easy to land she'd get bored. But he hung on even after she was married. Then she was bored with her husband, you know, earnest Ernie, and she was interested in Delbert again."

"Delbert was his name? Delbert who?"

"Honey, I can't remember that. You got the first name, that's enough for now. Be satisfied."

Sharon got up off the stool. It was getting hard anyway; her bottom stung from the round cracked wood. "You remember the last name, you give me a ring, okay? He's still alive, this Delbert?"

"Far's I know, honey. I saw him a year or so ago. Coming out of the doctor's office where she worked. Something chronically wrong with him, I guess."

"Or he went just to meet Crystal?"

"Maybe. Now if you'll 'scuse me, honey, I got some real work to do. Fellow up in Monkton wants to know what his wife does when she leaves the Grange Hall

Tuesday nights. A full hour he says, till she gets home. Offering some real money, too.''

"Delbert," Sharon said aloud. She'd never in her life known anyone named Delbert. She put on her sunglasses and went out into the bright inferno. Bristol Street still wasn't electrified. She might try cooking the kids an egg, though, on the sunny sidewalk.

"DELBERT?" Ruth said when she'd snatched up the phone with damp dishpan hands. "I don't know any Delbert. Did you look in the phone book?"

Sharon had checked the local book. She said, "It took me an hour to go through the whole town. And I found two. There's a Delbert E. Basebaum on North Street and a Delbert Fink on Hardscrabble Road. I don't know anything about either one, to tell the truth."

"Good girl," said Ruth. "That narrows it down. I'll look up Fink and you look up Basebaum."

"Suppose they're both in the nursing home?"

"Then we search the neighboring towns. Look, baby, Colm's coming over with the latest on the police findings. He's rattling into the drive right now, in fact. I'll call you back."

"Oh, and Mother? I forgot to mention that Crystal met him in the doctor's office where she worked. That's where the affair began. They both had high blood pressure right off."

Ruth laughed aloud and Clara Barton, a new heifer calf she was treating, mewled with her. She threw a shovelful of feed in front of the calf. At least there was a grain of humor in all this madness.

Colm, it turned out, had big news. "Definitive," he said as they moved out into the sunny afternoon.

"Whoops," he said, and grabbed her elbow. Blinded by the sun, she'd slipped on an icy patch.

"Nothing ever is," she said. "Definitive, that is. Life is too ambivalent."

"Yes, preacher. Well, listen up. We've got our killer. He confessed. In his right mind, too, more or less. And guess who?" He had a self-satisfied look on his face as though he'd bet on the horse of his choice and it won.

"Not Ernie Hiland. Nuh-uh. I won't believe it. I saw him this morning. He was delirious."

"Not so. He was raving earlier the nurse said, but by noon he'd settled down. Plotkin quizzed him and he spilled out the details. He'd gone up to Molly's Crotch; he was so incensed he didn't know what he was doing. The blood up in his head, you know. He picked up a stick and whacked her with it." When Ruth looked dubious, he said, "He was in a rage, right? A little out of his gourd?"

"A little out of his gourd *now,* I think," she said, ushering Colm into the kitchen. "Well, maybe he did it. That lets *me* off the hook anyway. But don't close this case yet. I'm working on another angle. You know a fellow in town named Delbert Fink—or Basebaum?"

"Basebaum? No. But I know a guy named Del Football."

"Oh, quit it, Colm, you're not even funny. You try too hard."

"I know," he said, his arm circling her waist, "and where does it get me?"

She laughed anyway, let him kiss her. Actually, he told her afterward, he did know a Delbert Fink. "He's in Dad's arthritis support group. He's ninety if he's a day."

So much for that Delbert, she told herself. Upstairs

she heard Dawn humming as she carpet-swept the rooms. Dawn had been maniacal lately, sweeping and cleaning, as if already she was building a nest for the baby. But it wouldn't happen in Ruth's house, would it? Surely they'd have electricity restored before nine months!

Suddenly a pile of shoes and boots came tumbling down the stairs.

"Sorry," Dawn called from the upstairs hall. "Noah always leaves things around. He's the spacey type, I'm afraid."

"I'll get them. And stop all that work," Ruth called up. "Take a lunch break. Where is Noah anyway?"

"He's gone to the house. He figures we'll move back tomorrow, electricity or no. It's a balmy thirty-four degrees out, he says. But I told him I'm not moving till the power's back on. You don't mind, do you?"

"Of course not." Ruth picked up a pair of boots. She checked the size, why not? They looked like twelves at least.

They were.

But what did that mean, anyway? Now there were four men all wearing size twelves. Maybe it was a gang killing, she told Colm. "Four of them. All after that one goddess. That's what happened, you know, back in Greek days. The whole city of Troy destroyed because of sexy Helen. I'm sure Crystal's a direct descendant."

She carried the boots and shoes upstairs. Dawn was upended, cleaning out under a bed in the guest room. "I'm going out," she told Dawn. "If anyone calls, I'll be back in an hour or so." Dawn's rear end wiggled in reply.

A moment later Ruth heard the sound of weeping. "Don't mind me," Dawn blubbered. "I'm just wondering if I can cope. All that's been going on, you know...."

Ruth murmured her sympathy, waited in the hall until the crying stopped, and then went downstairs.

"You're leaving?" Colm said. "And I just got here? I thought we'd take a cruise around town, see who's got power and who hasn't. I mean, jeez, we just got it back at Dad's, but the people across the street don't have it yet. They're furious. We might come to blows. Street fighting in Branbury, Vermont."

"I'm on my way to the town clerk's office."

"What now?" he asked, but was interrupted by the phone.

It was Sharon. "Delbert Basebaum is a twenty-year-old college student, living off campus. I don't think he got Crystal pregnant."

"No, not at six years old," Ruth said.

"Search the county phone book for Delberts, would you?" she asked a skeptical Colm after she'd hung up. She blew him a kiss, tossed a bag of doughnuts at him, and ran out into a cold wind.

THE TOWN CLERK'S OFFICE was in the town hall, a generic-looking white building opposite the white congregational church—founded 1802, according to a prominent plaque. Ruth found Jan Pearl behind her desk, listening patiently while Harry Bushey, one of the town's good ole boys, argued his case about "Why'n hell I need a goddamn permit just to burn some stinkin' garbage? Jeezum crow, it's all ice out there! What'm I goin' to burn up?"

"Your barn?" Jan suggested, and stood smiling at him until he gave up the argument and stomped off with his "fuggin" permit.

"He's not going to keep his match lit anyway in this wind," Jan told Ruth, and the pair laughed. Jan was a handsome, gray haired Branbury native in her late fifties who sang a sweet soprano in the church choir. She was the perfect town clerk—accommodating, but quietly standing her own in the face of opposition. Ruth explained her mission.

Jan asked no questions. She went to her filing case and got out the record of Gracie Hiland's birth. She stared at it for a long moment while Ruth held her breath. Of course she didn't expect to hear the name Delbert read out. But just in case....

"The father is listed as Ernest Hiland," Jan said in her matter-of-fact voice. "But—"

"But?" Ruth leaned against the counter. She didn't want to compromise Jan. Like psychiatrists and other doctors, town clerks must keep their counsel. "Off the record," Ruth said, reminding Jan that they were old friends. They'd sung a church duet once upon a time before Ruth decided she'd better look to the barn for spiritual guidance.

"Well, there was some scuttlebutt around town," Jan said with an embarrassed laugh. "I don't know exactly who...."

"Sure you do," said a husky voice behind her, and a woman with fading blonde hair emerged, looking something like Ruth's Sharon with her green woolly tights, long cotton print skirt and sensible boots. She had a pile of used paperback mysteries in her arms. It was Dolly Sweeney, one of Ruth's favorite people, who more or less ran the town as lister, head librarian (the library was housed in the town hall), and voice of the people. As town lister, Ruth figured, Dolly knew everybody in town, how many kids they had, what they hid in their closets, and what they paid for taxes.

And in this case, who might have fathered the kids.

"Everybody knows," said Dolly, one hand on her jutting hip. "It was Delbert Hemphill, sure. He was Crystal's shadow for a couple years."

"Well, I did hear that," said Jan, smiling down at her blunt fingernails. "But I wouldn't go around repeating it."

Ruth's heart gave a little lurch. Delbert was a Hemphill? Was he related to Noah Hemphill? The brother maybe, or a cousin—was that the real reason Noah was acquainted with Crystal? Was he trying to hide his brother's—or cousin's, folly? Noah seemed a forthright fellow, not the kind who would want to be connected with that sort of secret. After all, he's a schoolteacher, she thought; he has to walk the straight and narrow.

"Delbert?" she said. "Is he related to Noah Hemphill? I mean, Noah and his wife are staying with us till we get our power back."

"Ask Noah," Dolly said with a broad grin. "But don't say you heard it from us."

Beside her, Jan blushed and busied herself with a pile of papers. The interview was over.

COLM WAS IN HER KITCHEN gobbling doughnuts. "Don't you have anything else to do?" she demanded.

"Mmm," he said, his mouth full, pointing at some real estate correspondence. Dawn had gone out with her husband, he mumbled. "Seems their basement's flooded. Dawn insisted on helping to bail out."

"Glad to hear it. I don't suppose you found any Delberts for us?"

He was just about to look, he said. "Been busy, you

know.'' He waved at his open briefcase. He blew the sugar off a pile of correspondence.

''Well, I've found him, so you're off the hook.'' She outlined the scene in the town clerk's office. ''That is, I might have found him. I was hoping Noah would be here to set us straight. I guess we'll have to wait till he comes back. Meanwhile,'' she said pointedly, ''I've barn work to do.''

''Go on ahead. I'll just hang out here and finish up a few letters. One I got to get in the mail. Couple interested in that general store in Bridport. Nice profit if I can get it.''

She waved at her ancient typewriter; it was sitting on the living room table. ''Use it if you're brave.''

''No thanks. It doesn't have a working A or E. And it smudges. I'll have to write longhand. So go ahead. Give old Zelda a hug for me.''

Zelda had knocked Colm down once into a pile of manure. She giggled, remembering. Colm had been furious, of course. ''I'll tell her you're coming to visit,'' she said. Patting him on the head, she struck out across the melting ice.

A half hour later she saw Colm, face-to-face with Zelda, stroking her bony flank. She swung her head around, surprised.

''You do care,'' Ruth said, where she was cleaning the stalls. Tim was late for work; his foster boy Joey had come down with bronchitis. ''Don't just stand there.'' She handed Colm a broom. ''Sweep up, would you?''

''Me?'' he said, gazing into Zelda's savage eye. ''Look, I've got news for you. I borrowed Noah's lap computer—I mean, it was just sitting there on the table, and, well, I decided I'd write a couple letters on it. I didn't think he'd mind.''

"Uh-huh," she said, waving off a cluster fly. And then, "Tim! I'm glad to see you. How's Joey?"

"Pretty good," said Tim, running into the barn. "Sorry I'm late. I had to wait in line at the pharmacy."

"Anyway, what do I see when I turn it on," Colm said, "but his name, right there on the opening screen. Where it says 'Licensed to—'''

"I'm late myself," Ruth told Tim. "I had to go down to the town clerk's office."

"Forgot to pay your taxes?" Tim said, grinning.

"D. Noah Hemphill," Colm said. "I think, now that's interesting. I wonder what the D stands for?"

"I'm overdue myself," Tim said. "They'll be adding on interest. Whoa now, Zelda! Quit that leg action. Hook on some feed, will ya, Ruth? Keep the beast occupied?"

"So I rummage around in this little notebook he's got next to the computer with his e-mail addresses. I find his password, it's—wait'll you hear this. 'RobertFrost.' Ha! Must think he is. So I get into his e-mail."

"What? Colm, you have no right doing that. Invading Noah's privacy? Why, he could sue."

He waved away her protests. "There's nothing in the inbox but some letters from his schoolteacher friends. So I check the deleted mail."

"Tim, take a look at this calf, would you? She's looking pretty frail. Maybe we should call the vet?" Ruth knelt beside the calf, looked into its watery eyes.

"And I find a message he's deleted. That is, Delbert Noah Hemphill deleted, or thought he had. It was from crys@shoreham.net. It said 'Desperate to see you. Our mountain rendezvous. Monday after my meeting, 9 sharp. Bring Gracie's youknowwhat.'''

"She'll be all right. I'll keep an eye on her," Tim said.

"It was signed XXX, Crys," Colm said. "I printed it out."

"What, Crystal? Omigod," said Ruth, catching the echo. "But wait—what about Delbert?" Now she was confused. Who *was* Delbert anyway? Had he been using Noah's lap computer? She hadn't seen any strangers around lately.

"Same guy," Colm said. "I told you, if you'd only listen. Owner's user name is DelNoah. Delbert Noah. We're probably the only ones in town who don't know he goes by his middle name."

"Omigod," she said again. "It was Noah? But what went wrong? Why would he kill her?"

"Why'd who kill who?" said Tim. "There's times I'd like to kill Zelda here but she's still pumpin' out the white stuff. Besides, I'm kinda fond of the old gal."

"Tim," Ruth said, "can you take over? Prep the cows? Something's come up. It has to be taken care of right off."

Tim groaned, the cowboy hat tilted back on his thatch of graying hair. "You in the dairy business, Ruth—or police? If police, you gotta hire another guy to help out around here. Want I should tell you what needs fixing? The John Deere needs a new clutch. We need a bigger vacuum pump. That generator we borrowed—"

"Enough," she cried. "I'll be back, and so will the power. They're practically at Cow Hill Road now. Just hang on, Tim, please? You know I can't afford another fellow." Placing her palms together, Zen-like, she bowed, then ran to the door.

"Why would he want to kill Crystal if he was Gracie's father?'' she asked again as she walked with Colm across the slushy lawn.

''Found her with another guy? The heart hath reasons—and all that,'' Colm misquoted. ''But it's not him, Ruthie, I told you, even if he did go meet her. Ernie confessed. The motive's obvious in his case. Jealousy, revenge, anger—your classic crime of passion. He probably suspected she was there to meet somebody. Got there before this Noah fellow and—unh!—he gave it to her.''

''What about Dawn?'' she said, ignoring his hypothesis. ''What will happen to her if Noah's guilty? Do you suppose she'd heard any rumors about his liaison with Crystal?''

Noah, she thought, seems genuinely concerned about Dawn's pregnancy. She'd heard him only last night creaking downstairs to hunt for pickles or peanuts for his capricious wife. Was this solicitous Noah the killer of Crystal Hiland?

''If he really did kill her, what was his motive?'' she asked Colm.

''That's just it,'' Colm said. ''What was it? Whereas, Ernie—''

''Colm, get off Ernie and think Noah for now. Oh, you cops. You get on one horse and ride it to the end.''

''Part-time cop,'' he amended. ''Okay, then. Here's another thought on your Noah-as-killer theory. Dawn said he's spacey; he probably didn't know you have to delete messages twice. She may be clingy, but she's not stupid. She was a teacher, too, you said, before she married?''

''Didn't teach an academic subject,'' Ruth said, ''I mean like English or math. She worked in computers at some big regional high school.'' Then, ''Oh,'' she said, turning to face him on the sloppy drive, the water seeping into her boots. "So she might have looked into his deleted mail? You're suggesting they had a confrontation, right? She was pregnant, upset—and so she insisted he end it with Medusa—and when Medusa wouldn't, he killed her?"

"That's the idea. But I'm still for Ernie. He had the most to lose."

"But Ernie doted on his wife! I mean, Sharon's seen him with Crystal. He couldn't take his eyes off her."

"No. If he did, she'd be off with another guy. My theory is he killed her so no one else could have her." Colm took the porch steps in a leap. "I'd do it myself for you, Ruthie. Kill 'em all off. All the suitors."

"What suitors?" She paused to empty out a soaked boot. "So you really don't think it was Noah? After all this new evidence? Knowing she'd arranged a meeting at Molly's Crotch?"

"Okay," he conceded, "we'll bring him in. Just in case." He plodded in behind her to make the call. His boots dribbled a puddle on the floor. Ruth handed him a mop.

NOAH WAS IN THE BARN with Ruth when Colm arrived an hour later with Detective Plotkin and a female officer. She felt guilty to see Noah on his hands and knees, swabbing the smelly floor, unaware of what was to come. She wanted to shout, "Go away! It's all a mistake. It's somebody else you want."

"Me? What for?" Noah protested when the detective placed him under arrest. Then realizing: "Crystal? Why would you want me? What did I have to do with her death?"

Colm handed him the e-mail printout. Noah stared at

it with glazed eyes. He sank down on a pail. Behind him the cows stood chewing in their stalls, like a bovine jury. Now and then one of them would lift a black nose and bellow a response.

"All right," Noah said. "I agreed I'd meet her that night. I mean it was crazy, all that ice. But *she* was crazy—unpredictable. I said I'd go because, well, I was going to tell her we had to break it off. Dawn was pregnant. It couldn't go on the way Crystal wanted."

"You see?" Ruth mouthed at Colm.

"You mean the way *you* wanted," the detective said.

"Yes—no! I really was going to end it. I was!" Noah dropped his chin into his chest. Behind him Oprah mooed in sympathy.

"She asked you to bring her something," Ruth said softly. "What was that, Noah?"

He turned toward Ruth, as if surprised to see her there. "Money," he said. "The girl needed money for a winter coat. Ernie was stingy that way, said she'd have to fix over the old one. When it was too small. I still have a responsibility for the girl!"

"Gracie's your daughter," Ruth said.

He nodded. "I never wanted her dead, believe me. Crystal was a fascinating woman. Sensitive. Smart. Misunderstood—because of the way she looked. I wanted to marry her back then, she wouldn't. I was still in grad school. I couldn't give her what she wanted. Ernie could. Then."

Detective Plotkin said, "Had an argument, did you? You hit her on the head? Ran something into her neck. Icicle, was it?"

"Icicle?" Noah seemed confused. He lifted a heavy head toward the detective, his mouth slightly open. Slowly he seemed to comprehend. "You think I—no, no, I didn't kill her. No!'' He jumped up. ''I never went to that place. I never! I mean, that is, I got halfway there, turned around. I decided I'd stop the affair, then and there. I'd *send* the money for Gracie. I know how it can be with Crystal. She's like a magnet. You see her and next thing you know she's got you headed for a—well, you know.''

''You didn't go then, to Molly's, um, Crotch,'' the detective said.

''I just told you I didn't!''

''Where then? You turned around, you said. And went straight home?''

''I guess. I can't think now. To the co-op, I think. To get some carob peanuts for Dawn. She loves carob peanuts. She gets these cravings. I wanted to get what she wanted. I wanted to be a good husband. I wanted to wipe temptation—Crystal—out of my life.''

''So that's what you did,'' said the detective, ''wiped her out of your life.'' Noah stared at him, but didn't respond.

Ruth stood frozen by the door of the milkroom. The buzz of the generator was hypnotic. Out of the corner of her eye she saw Tim getting ready to start the four-thirty milking. She couldn't feel her legs; it was as if she were one big beating heart. She was trying to process what she'd been hearing. Noah hadn't gone to see Crystal. He hadn't killed her. Was he telling the truth? If *he* hadn't killed her—then who had? Was Colm right—was it Ernie after all? And what about Violet?

They were handcuffing Noah, taking him away for a more formal questioning. He glanced back at her with smoldering eyes. She felt her face and neck burn. ''Tell Dawn I'll be back,'' he said. ''She's in the house. I don't want her to know about Crystal. I don't know what it would do to her. She's pregnant, for God's sake! Make up some story why I'm gone. Anything.''

"Tell her what?" Ruth wondered aloud after Noah was out of hearing.

"Tell her he's gone after more peanuts," said Colm, following the men. "Anyway, he didn't do it. Hiland confessed, I told you. Look, Ruthie, Noah will be back. Someone at the co-op will remember seeing him. He'll be back with the peanuts."

TOO LATE though for excuses, Ruth discovered when she entered the kitchen to look for Dawn. A kerosene lamp was burning in the window, although there was still another hour and a half of daylight. The young woman was standing behind it; she'd seen the police drive off with Noah, she was in a state of hysteria. "What are they doing with my husband?" she wailed. She ran at Ruth, grabbed her elbows. "He didn't do anything. He didn't kill anyone!"

It was routine, Ruth lied. "They're simply questioning everyone who knew her. Don't worry. He'll be back." She held the quivering body for a moment, then felt herself shoved aside.

"They'll ask him questions, they'll make him answer. About Crystal. About his affair." Dawn was pacing the floor now, she had a knife in her hand where she'd been chopping onions. Ruth's eyes filled with the onion juices. "Put down that knife now," she told Dawn. "Let's talk a little."

"I know all about it," Dawn moaned, the knife still clutched in her hand. "I know who Gracie is. He should have told me. I would have understood. That was before he married me. Before he even met me. But it didn't stop! Oh, it wasn't his fault, it was hers, that conniving, scheming, revolting Jezebel!''

Jezebel, Ruth thought, mentally adding one more name to the list. Noah was probably right: Crystal was a fascinating woman.

"I hate her, I want to kill her. Over and over!" Dawn cried, curling her fists around the knife.

"Someone already has," Ruth murmured. She put an arm around the woman's shoulders. Under the flesh they were hard shoulders; Ruth's fingers sprang back.

Dawn stared at Ruth, as though pondering the words. Finally she said, "Yes, yes, somebody did. She's dead. She won't bother my husband anymore. She won't bother me.'' Her knuckles were bone white in her pinkish hands. "He was going there to see her, you know. The night she died.''

"You read the deleted message."

There was the barest nod. "There was more than one. I'd suspected. I knew he gave her money. Every month. He has a separate bank account for Gracie. I discovered that six weeks ago.''

She sat down on a high stool, the knife in her lap; she turned slowly toward Ruth. "They think Noah killed her. It's not any routine questioning, oh no, you can't fool me.''

She leaped up again, backed against the refrigerator as if she needed something to hold her up. "He took my car that night. I saw him go. He said he was going to the school, he had a key. I knew he was going to see *her.*'' She took a step away from the wall.

"And then?" Ruth was beginning to suspect something; her feet froze to the floor.

"I wanted to catch them in the act. So I got out his car—it was still in our garage. It was bad weather, I didn't care. Though the car was beginning to skid when I got on the mountain road.''

Ruth held on to the top rung of a chair. It was becoming clear now. ''You went to the mountain. To Molly's Crotch.''

Dawn appeared not to hear her; she went on with her story, like a mechanical doll reeling out its pre-set tune: ''I knew she was there, waiting. I thought he'd be with her. I couldn't bear to think it. The two of them—together like that.''

''But he didn't go,'' Ruth said.

''He was on his way!'' she cried, irritated at being contradicted. ''But he wasn't there yet. I saw her. I suppose she'd walked up from town. She was planning to go to a motel or someplace with him, oh, yes, that's what she'd want! I parked the car below. Noah'd left a pair of his boots in the back seat—I pulled them on....''

''The bootprints,'' Ruth murmured.

''...I went on up with my lantern. She was waiting on the bridge with a flashlight. Waiting for him! I put out my light. She was wearing a sweater—she didn't have a coat on, like she was some goddess who wouldn't feel the cold. Those red high-heeled boots, even on the ice....''

Ruth felt out of breath, as if something heavy had fallen on her chest. Her hands were numb on the chair rung.

''She had her back to me—she thought I was Noah, she was playing cat and mouse with him. I was angry—furious! It was those red boots, that clingy sweater—all that hair. I wanted to strike her. But my hands weren't enough. I picked up a branch—''

Dawn was quiet a minute. Ruth felt she might fall down if she didn't hold on to the chair.

The woman gave a high-pitched laugh. "I hit her with it. I thought I heard her laugh. So I grabbed an icicle, plunged it in her neck. I couldn't stop myself! I didn't think an icicle would kill her—I didn't think that. I just had to show her she couldn't play with me—with my husband."

Ruth waited. The thrum of the refrigerator split her eardrums.

"She made a noise then, tried to get at me and I hit her again—with a chunk of ice. Or maybe it was an icy rock, I don't know—must've been. She—she fell over. The night went black, like the inside of a tomb. So cold and wet. I grabbed my lantern, ran back to the car. I didn't think she'd die. And now they have Noah. I can't let them have him! You see, he never saw Crystal that night. He was in the kitchen when I got back. He'd only gone to the store to buy those carob peanuts for me. I killed her for nothing...." She let out a high-pitched wail, like a woman keening.

Ruth made a move to take away the knife. Dawn dropped it, sprang forward and dashed out the kitchen door. "Dawn, wait!" Ruth cried, but already Dawn was in her car, revving it up, roaring out the driveway, careening left into the slushy road. Ruth jumped in her pick-up, and followed. What craziness would the woman do now?

Sand, slush and pebbles flew from the wheels of the red Toyota as it raced down Cow Hill Road and then left onto the paved highway that led to the town's center. There was a blinking light at the foot of a hill where Cider Mill crossed but Dawn didn't slow down. A horn honked where she'd narrowly missed one of Carrara's dump trucks. She drove, too fast, through town. A pair of cops were standing by the entrance to the police station. Dawn hesitated, then rode past, veered right on Merchant's Row, up toward East Branbury and the Green National Forest.

Where was she going? Ruth honked at her to stop, but the Toyota only picked up speed. Then it stopped where the road ended and turned into a foot path. Dawn jumped out and started running. Ruth cut her engine, and ran after her.

It had been years since she'd been up here. The path was still icy, only a thin layer of late sun squeezed through the thickness of trees. Her feet tripped on fallen twigs and limbs. Ruth knew where Dawn was heading. She was almost there. At Molly's Crotch.

Ruth seemed to be running in slow motion; she couldn't catch up. While Dawn, pregnant Dawn, was running like a deer, up onto the log bridge where she paused for a moment, gazing down into the stream where the waters came together in a miniature whirlpool. "No!" Ruth cried. "No, don't, Dawn. Come back. Noah needs you."

Hearing her husband's name, Dawn glanced back. Ruth kept moving forward. She had almost reached the bridge. Dawn was hesitating, as though she might give in, go back. Then just as Ruth stepped onto the bridge, Dawn gave a cry and leaped. Ruth screamed. The ice cracked with the weight of the woman's body. Ruth raced around to the embankment, slid down to the stream's edge; she thrust out a dead branch. Darkness was coming on quickly, she could hardly see the woman. "Grab it, Dawn. I'll pull. Your baby needs you, Dawn."

Dawn laughed, a shrill sound like breaking ice. "I'm not pregnant. I never was. I don't think—I can be...."

Ruth moved out on the ice, still holding out the branch. "Then think of Noah. Save yourself for Noah."

Ruth felt the ice cracking with her own weight. She was floundering in the icy water, feeling its pull. "Damn you, Dawn!" she cried.

"Hold on. Grab this." It was Jack, her son-in-law, dashing across the bridge with a stout limb, pitching it at her. She grabbed hold and scrambled out. "Get *her!*" she yelled, pointing at the icy water.

Only Dawn's face was visible now in the dim light, her mouth a round O where she was choking on the water, panicking. This time the woman reached for the stick. Together, Jack and Ruth pulled her slowly toward the water's edge.

SATURDAY

RUTH AND SHARON WERE in Ruth's house, celebrating the return of the electricity. It was on all over town now. Everywhere washing machines were grinding away, refrigerators and microwaves humming, computers buzzing, vacuum cleaners rumbling. In Ruth's barn the cows were contentedly chewing their cuds, their bags empty, bellies full. The milk at that very moment was being pumped into the Agri-Mark storage truck—a full load. The cows were blinking at the restored barn lights; they were bellowing to go out in the pasture. The month of March was only ten days away, along with the first crocuses.

Mother and daughter were sharing a cup of hot chocolate while the grandchildren played in the living room with some Duplo toys their grandfather had bought before he and Violet left for Saratoga in their rented car.

"It's like a brave new world in my house," Sharon said, pulling off her green rubber boots and rubbing life back into her stocking feet. There was a hole in each toe. Ruth made a mental note to buy her a new pair. "The minute they left, the kids stopped fighting, the radio and lights came on, and my mood soared. I mean, I love my father, but he hasn't been the same since he met Violet. He's gone a little nuts."

Ruth agreed with that, more than a little. Her guests

had departed, too, though separately. Jack and Ruth had rushed Dawn to the hospital emergency, wrapped in Ruth's parka, her lungs full of water; she was suffering from hypothermia. Afterward Ruth had gone to the police station to tell about Dawn's confession.

"At first," Ruth said, "before we told Noah about Dawn's accident, he was furious with her for killing Crystal. The woman still fascinated him, you see, it was obvious. He'd vowed to give her up, but he wanted that fantasy to cling to. I think he wanted to know she was there in town, yearning for him."

"The old ego trip," said Sharon, lapping up the last of the hot chocolate with her tongue.

"More or less, yes. But his feelings were ambivalent. You can imagine his confusion. Later, when Colm and I drove him to the hospital to see his wife, he kept moaning that he was to blame; it was his folly that had driven her to attack Crystal. 'You can't put her in prison,' he yelled at Colm. 'She's pregnant. She's having my child!'"

"*My* child," Sharon noted.

"Uh-huh. But wait till you hear this."

"What?" said Sharon, leaning forward in her lime green sweatshirt.

"She's not pregnant. She never was. She told me that before she jumped."

"No!"

"Yes. She'll tell Noah she lost the child, I'll bet, and I won't contradict. Personally, I think she only told Noah she was pregnant after she read his e-mail—to tie him to her, you know. An antidote to Crystal."

"Possibly, yes," said Sharon, who loved this sort of psychological conversation. "Or it's some kind of revenge. She gives him a toy and then takes it away. Screw you, she tells him. It's all your fault.''

"The fact remains, Dawn killed Crystal. It was a moment of uncontrollable anger. It was seemingly unpremeditated—that'll help a little, I guess.''

"Poor Dawn. You know, if it'd been Jack in Noah's place I might have done what she did.''

"Don't. Just don't. Ever.''

"Don't worry. Jack wouldn't cheat on me anyway. He's too enamored of his trees. He's up in the forest now, worrying. Wanting to replant already.''

"Thank God for Jack and his trees. I think we'd both have drowned if he hadn't come along.'' Ruth looked out at her grounds that were littered with broken limbs. "Speaking of falling limbs, what about Ernie Hiland? Is he still in the hospital?''

"He's home. Gracie's taking care of him. He has a physical therapist coming in. And he retracted that confession. It seems one of his fellow linemen vouched for him that night. He wasn't anywhere near Molly's Crotch.''

"He killed her in his mind, didn't he? All those years she gulled him? He knew. He knew about Noah. He was just denying when he said he couldn't remember the name.''

"Maybe. Or maybe he was in full denial about Crystal's shenanigans. Or blaming himself that she took on other men, thinking he wasn't *enough* for her. Who knows what went on in his heart? Probably he doesn't know, either.''

"But I'm sure he'll miss her. He loved her, didn't he?''

"You know he did. Maybe too much for his own good.''

Ruth gazed thoughtfully into her cup of chocolate. "Look, which do you think is greater—fire or ice?"

"The old riddle," Sharon said. "What did Robert Frost say in that poem about how the world might end? I think I memorized it once. Oh, yes.... 'From what I've tasted of desire/I hold with those who favor fire.' Those are the lines stuck in *my* head. So that's my answer. Fire's the strongest. He'll miss her, yes, he will. Every minute of every day."

"Wait a minute," Ruth said. "Didn't the poet say that ice, meaning hate, can destroy just as much as fire? In my view, that's what made Dawn plunge the icicle into Crystal's back. It was ice. It was hate."

"It was anger, too," Sharon argued. "It was passion. It was fire *and* ice. A killing combination."

Ruth nodded, then went to the stove to heat up her cooling cup of chocolate.

NIGHT FLAMES
by Maggie Price

To fire cops everywhere

Maggie Price turned to crime at the age of twenty-two. That's when she went to work at the Oklahoma City Police Department. As a civilian crime analyst, she evaluated suspects' methods of operation during the commission of robberies and sex crimes, and developed profiles on those suspects. During her tenure at the OCPD, Maggie stood in lineups, snagged special assignments to homicide task forces, established procedures for evidence submittal, even posed as the wife of an undercover officer in the investigation of a fortune teller.

While at OCPD, Maggie stored up enough tales of intrigue, murder and mayhem to keep her at the keyboard for years. The first of those tales won the Romance Writers of America's Golden Heart Award for romantic suspense.

Maggie invites the readers to contact her at 5208 W. Reno, Suite 350, Oklahoma City, OK 73127-6317.

ONE

CRIME HAD NO RESPECT for a holiday. Never had. Never would.

Because crime was her concern, homicide Sergeant Jennifer Weathers, still dressed in the traffic-stopping red dress and strappy heels she'd donned for the Valentine's Day party at a local cop club, nosed her unmarked detective's cruiser to a stop a few yards from a fire engine with its pumps thrumming. After clipping her badge to the breast pocket of her black trench coat, she pulled on her fleece-lined gloves, then climbed out into the snowy night air, thick with the acrid scent of smoke.

It was just as well her pager had gone off while the party was in full swing, she decided as she secured the top button on her coat. Despite the club's festive mood, she'd spent the entire evening thinking not about this holiday, but the one six weeks ago. New Year's Eve, one-half minute to midnight. Thirty seconds that had clung in her thoughts like an irritating, stubborn burr.

Shaking her head to ward off the memory, she narrowed her eyes against the wind-whipped snow, and took in the scene around her. She counted four fire engines and a dozen other fire department vehicles. A handful of police black and whites, all with emergency lights strobing. Trucks from several local utility companies. Two mobile press units. The M.E.'s wagon.

Beyond the vehicles, barricades and crime scene tape, banks of portable lights poured candlepower onto the smoldering ruins of what appeared to have been an expansive, two-story house sitting on the crest of a gently sloping lawn. The windows were glassless; the double-wide front door was charred and splintered by what Jennifer assumed had been a fire ax. Flames had eaten away half the roof, leaving a yawning hole into which fell furling snow mixed with bits of ash and pieces of pink fiberglass insulation.

The amount of devastation had Jennifer easing out a breath that turned foggy on the cold air. For her, there would be other holidays to celebrate. Valentine's Day had been the last for the victim believed to be the resident's owner.

Stepping over a bloated canvas hose that snaked across the pavement, she moved to the rear of her cruiser and popped the trunk. She knew hours—maybe days—might pass before an official determination was made on how long she would play a role in this incident. Policy between Oklahoma City's police and fire departments was that whenever OCFD found a dead body in a fire, they stopped everything as soon as the fire was contained and called Homicide. Police and fire inspectors worked the case together until someone proved the death was an accident, suicide or murder. If it was the former, Jennifer would turn her role in the investigation over to the insurance company. Either of the two latter determinations required her to stay on the case.

While she traded her strappy red heels for the pair of crew socks and jogging shoes she habitually carried in the trunk, she studied the knot of onlookers huddled together behind the barricades. Because this was one of Oklahoma City's most well-heeled neighborhoods, many of the spectators were bundled in fur. Jennifer wondered if any of them noticed the firefighter standing to one side of the lawn with the video camera aimed their way. The taping was standard operating procedure at any fire scene—in case arson came into play, the first place investigators looked for their suspect was in the crowd watching the blaze.

The wind rose, sneaking under her coat like icy hands grabbing at her flesh. Shivering, she chided herself for forgetting to stash her heavy parka in the cruiser before she'd left home for the party.

Hoping she'd soon find a spot out of the biting wind, she shut the trunk, picked her way back over the snaking hose, then headed up the driveway. Water used to douse the fire had already formed frozen pools on the cement. Soot and ash from the burned house turned the firehose ice into patches of black and gray.

Ducking under a stretch of crime scene tape, she nodded to the female cop who stepped her way. C. O. Jones wore a black insulated uniform jacket with a thick collar, a black muffler and hat, its earflaps tied in the up position. Her ears and nose were raspberry red.

"Evening, Sergeant," the cop said, her breath a cloud in the icy air.

"Evening, C.O." Jennifer slid her hands into her coat's pockets and hunched her shoulders against the cold. "You the first uniform on the call?"

"Ten-four." Angling a clipboard in the crook of her arm, Jones began jotting Jennifer's name, rank and the division she represented in the crime scene log. "A neighbor arriving home from a Valentine's party spotted the fire and phoned it in. My partner and I—a rookie I'm training—arrived right after the hose draggers. By then, most of the house's window glass had blown, and flames were shooting out of the roof. None of the neighbors knew for sure if the owner was home. The fire was so intense, it took a while before a crew could get inside." Jones used a gloved finger to shove up the cuff on her jacket to check her watch. "They found the body about an hour ago. I advised dispatch to call Homicide and the M.E."

"Still just one body so far?" Jennifer asked, repeating the information dispatch had given her while en route.

"That's the last word I got." Jones tilted her head; the wind whipped at the tendrils of blond hair that peeked from beneath her hat. "I expected Smith and Gianos to show up here," she said, referring to the team of homicide detectives pulling night shift for the month of February.

"They've got their hands full on the east side, working a home invasion with three DRTs," Jennifer said, using cop shorthand for victims who were *dead right there.* "My partner and I are next on the night call list this month. He's down with the flu, so I'm on my own." She inclined her head toward the charred house. "Who's the owner?"

"Man by the name of Spencer Fitzgerald. I imagine you've heard of him. He builds business complexes and those exclusive housing communities you see advertised all the time."

Jennifer pursed her mouth. She would have to earn triple her cop's salary to afford a Fitzgerald home. "What about relatives?"

"The neighbor who called in the fire says Fitzgerald's been divorced for years. He has a couple of grown kids who live out of state. He—the neighbor—thinks he has their names and phone numbers stuck in a drawer somewhere. The rookie's at his house now, waiting to see if he can find the information.''

''If he does, get it to me.''

''Will do. The neighbor said Fitzgerald was a real social sort, hosting parties and to-do's all the time. He also got around in local politics. Friends with the mayor and people like that.''

''Great.'' Jennifer knew it was inevitable she'd soon feel pressure from City Hall to find answers to what had occurred here tonight. She glanced across her shoulder at the mix of emergency vehicles. ''Where's fire's command post?''

''Once they got the flames out, they pulled it farther up the driveway,'' Jones said, gesturing a gloved hand toward a cherry-red van with its sliding side door open.

''Thanks.''

At the van, Jennifer found a stout captain clad in a yellow helmet and full turnout gear, talking into his handheld radio. She waited until he signed off, then introduced herself and asked if the number of victims had increased.

''Still just one,'' the captain responded, his breath gray on the frigid air. ''It's always possible we'll find more after we start sifting through the rubble, but that'll take a while. We do know that the victim lived alone. He could have had an overnight guest, though.''

''Any idea yet on what started the fire?''

''Too early to call. Our lead investigator arrived about forty-five minutes ago.'' The captain held up his radio. ''He's who I was talking to when you walked up. This place isn't exactly the size of a cracker box, so it's taken him and a couple of our people this long to do a three-sixty walk-around of the house's perimeter.''

Jennifer nodded. She knew the main purpose of a

walk-around inspection was for fire personnel to check the house's structural integrity. The inspection also gave the investigator a chance to spot irregularities, such as windows where the glass had been broken from an intruder on the outside instead of having been blown outward by an explosion or the fire's heat.

From beneath his helmet's brim, the captain's narrowed gaze settled on Jennifer's jogging shoes and socks. "I'll walk you up to the house so you can hook up with our investigator as soon as we do something about your footwear." He leaned into the van's open door and pulled out a heavy-soled pair of black rubber boots. "Slide your shoes into these. There're hot spots, glass, nails and debris everywhere. These babies have steel plates in the soles, so you don't have to worry about stepping on anything nasty."

"Thanks." The boots weighed a ton and their tops covered her legs almost to the knee. Jennifer didn't care how absurd they looked—the smoky-colored panty hose she wore provided no protection against the wind that slashed like a razor at her skin.

Her boots in place, she and the captain joined the mix of men and women swarming over the yard. Some were firefighters, colorful in their yellow turnout gear and helmets. A few wore oxygen tanks strapped to their backs. Uniformed cops and utility company workers joined in the mix. This was one scene where Jennifer didn't take time to search the faces of the patrol cops to see if her brother had also snagged the call. Just before leaving the Valentine's party, she'd spotted Cam with an oozing-sex redhead hanging on to him and his every word.

As Jennifer clomped across the lawn beside the captain, the portable lights aimed toward the house illuminated bright red patches that dotted the yard. She crouched beside one of the red blobs. "What is this stuff?"

"Balloons. A woman neighbor said there was a party here tonight—for Valentine's Day, is my guess. She said red, heart-shaped balloons were tied in bunches all over the lawn and front porch. Earlier, she'd seen the catering people taking more of the same helium-filled balloons into the house." The captain raised a brow. "Balloons don't last long against a fire's heat."

"I wouldn't think so." Jennifer straightened, making a mental note to get a copy of the party's guest list. "Who's your lead investigator on this case?" she asked as she and the firefighter continued toward the house's burnt remains.

"Ballard. Max Ballard. You know him?"

"I...." Her gloved hands fisted against her thighs. "I ran into him on New Year's Eve." In truth, she had done a hell of a lot more than just run into the man.

Chuckling, the captain shot her a knowing grin across his shoulder. "Had to have been at a party. From what I hear, nobody parties quite like Max."

Or kisses like him, either. The unbidden thought had Jennifer faltering in the heavy, oversized boots.

"Careful." The captain gripped her elbow. "There's all sorts of debris and equipment out here to trip over."

"Thanks." Knowing she'd be paired with Ballard on this case had her shivering teeth clamping together. The knee-bending kiss they'd shared on New Year's Eve during that dark half-moment to midnight had been unintended, accidental and a mistake. A huge one. During the days that followed, she had sidestepped Ballard's phone calls, tossed away messages he'd left with the Homicide secretary, disregarded his voice on her answering machine at home. She had resolved that ignoring the man was the most expedient way to deal with what to her had been a mortifying situation. It was no secret that the tall, off-the-chart-handsome fire investigator was OCFD's answer to Casanova. Just because he'd kissed her brainless didn't mean she'd lost her common sense—no way did she intend to get involved with a man who was rumored to have notches on his bedpost. Still, she was honest enough to admit to the hard prick she'd felt to her pride when Ballard's calls stopped two weeks into the new year.

"There's the man you want," the captain said, gesturing toward the porch where a knot of firefighters stood just outside the ax-shattered front door.

Squaring her shoulders, Jennifer followed her escort up a short flight of brick steps, then across the wide porch, awash in murky, soot-blackened water.

The captain raised a hand. "Hey, Ballard, the cops finally caught up with you."

Every firefighter within earshot looked their way. Max Ballard's dark gaze was the one that drew...and held Jennifer's.

He looked just as she remembered—a lanky six-footer with a thick mane of ebony hair that skimmed the collar of his yellow coat and appeared to have been finger-combed. Probably by some woman, Jennifer thought. Light coming from the house's exterior painted his firm jaw and the faint cleft in his chin in dim, shadowy hollows. Hollows that deepened when his mouth curved.

"Well, hello, New Year's." His voice was deep and rich as brandy.

"Sergeant Weathers," she countered, ignoring the bump that slow grin put in her pulse rate. It was a grin that could steal a woman's dreams. She should know— she'd seen it a few times in her own.

"OCPD Homicide," she added for the benefit of the other men in the group. When she looked back at Max, she kept her gaze cool and deliberate while whispers of awareness stirred her senses. "I'm assigned to work this case. The captain advises you have one dead body so far. Do you know what caused the fire?"

"Not yet," Max answered and cocked his head. Despite the rubber boots that hid what he knew were a pair of great legs, she looked just as good as she had six weeks ago. Better, he amended. Tall and slender, she had a classic oval face with wide-set eyes the color of a cold sea. Tonight, her honey-blond hair was scooped back in a simple twist. And that mouth—full and wet and red. The memory of the rich, sexy taste of those lips rolled through him on a wave of greedy lust.

Instantly, he tamped back the urge to take another sample. They both had jobs to do that involved at least one death. There would be time later to deal with the fact he'd made up his mind during the last half-minute of the previous year that Jennifer Weathers was a woman he intended to get to know. Well. Just because she'd so far given the cold shoulder to his attempts had not changed his mind, nor deterred him from his goal. She had simply made herself more of a challenge.

He was a man who enjoyed challenge. And he knew how to wait for the right moment to go after what he wanted.

Since fate had paired them on this investigation, Max figured that time wasn't far off.

Movement from behind had him glancing across his shoulder in time to see two firefighters carrying SCBA's draped across their arms emerge from the house's front door. One of the men gave Max a thumbs-up, a sign there were no toxic fumes inside that required anyone entering the burn site to wear a similar breathing apparatus.

From where he stood, Max could see into the still-smoldering entry hall and living room. A black goo covered every surface. He would soon be covered in it, too, since most of his work involved a shovel and scrounging around in ashes.

"We've got a lot of the second story and most of the roof all heaped on the ground floor." As he spoke, he remet Jennifer's waiting gaze. "We have to photograph and video everything, then start digging through the rubble. It'll be morning at least until I'll know anything for sure about the fire's cause."

A gust of icy wind slapped across the porch, tugging strands of her honey-blond hair from its efficient twist. Max frowned when he noted her shiver as she turned up her coat's collar. There was nothing bulky about the way the black trench fit her shoulders and thin waist—whatever she wore underneath the coat didn't provide much protection against the freezing temperature.

"A neighbor said that Spencer Fitzgerald—the home's owner—hosted a party tonight," she said. "After we're done here, I'll see what I can do about getting a copy of the guest list. Word is, Fitzgerald was tight with Mayor Hart. If that's the case, both of our chiefs will probably get pressure to wind up this case fast."

"And that pressure'll roll right downhill and land at our feet."

"That's the way it always works."

"Too bad. I do my job at the pace it takes to get the answers I need," Max said. "A couple of those answers won't come until morning when the M.E. gives us positive ID on the victim and cause of death." Max shrugged. "Since we know Fitzgerald's in town and he hasn't shown up by now to watch all the excitement, we've got to figure it's him inside, fried to a crisp. Any word yet on next of kin?''

"He has two grown kids who live out of state. A neighbor's trying to find us contact information.'' She glanced toward the house's shattered front door. "Have you seen the body?''

"No, heard about its condition, is all so far. I just finished doing a perimeter walk-around when you and the captain got here. The walls look like they'll stand on their own, so it's safe to go in.'' Max shot a hitch-hiker-like thumb toward the firefighter with a soot-blackened face standing to his right. "Roger was just giving me directions to the master bedroom where the victim's still tucked in bed.'' Max looked at Roger. "Sergeant Weathers needs a hard hat before she can go in.''

"Give me a minute and I'll be back with a spare.''

"Snag an extra coat while you're at it.''

"Will do,'' Roger said, his boots thudding heavily as he strode off.

Turning, Jennifer thanked the captain who'd escorted her from the command post.

"You're welcome, Sergeant. Just drop those boots off at the van before you leave.''

"I'll be sure to.''

Several of the firefighters headed down the steps behind the captain into the front yard where snow streaked down in the bright glow of the portable lights. Two men remained on the porch, huddled over a report form on a clipboard.

Max shrugged out of his coat, felt the instant knife-edged cold cut through his heavy sweater and jeans. "Where's your partner?''

"At home in bed. Half of Homicide's down with the flu. He's one of them."

"A lot of our people are out with the bug, too." Gripping the coat by its shoulders, Max held it out toward her. "Put this on."

"I'm fine."

"You're freezing. Do you always work night calls in snowstorms wearing a trench coat and what I figure is not much underneath?"

Her chin came up. "I wasn't scheduled to work tonight. The team on duty has their hands full working a triple homicide that came out the same time as this call. I'm one of the few left in Homicide who's not sick, or getting over being sick, so I snagged this assignment."

Max jiggled the coat. "Consider this my contribution to keeping you healthy."

"What about you?"

"I'll put on the coat Roger brings."

She hesitated for a split second. "All right. Thanks."

"You're welcome."

When she angled her back toward him, Max stepped forward, shifting the coat while she slid her arms into the bulky sleeves. Close now, he caught a whiff of her perfume, dark and tempting. Sexy. It was the same scent she'd worn New Year's Eve. The one that had seeped into his brain while they'd kissed. And had stayed there ever since.

He let his hands linger on her shoulders for a second longer than necessary while he studied the smooth arch of her throat. "Interesting, isn't it, that we're paired again?"

"Again?" When she turned, she jerked back to keep from bumping up against him. The quick move sent the message she was as elementally aware of him as he was of her. "You've got it wrong, Ballard. This is the first time we've worked together."

"I was talking about New Year's Eve. That was a pretty close pairing."

"*That* was a mistake."

"True," he agreed. "A pleasant one."

Max didn't need his investigator's sixth sense to tell him the color that rose in her cheeks had nothing to do with the cold.

"An unfortunate one," she amended. "The lights went out, everybody yelled 'Happy New Year' and reached for their partner. I got jostled into the arms of a man whom I assumed was my date. I was kissing *him,* Ballard, not you."

"It sure as hell felt like me." Max crossed his arms over his chest. He'd been on call New Year's Eve, so he'd gone stag to the party that had been an equal mix of fire and police personnel. He'd spent hours sipping tonic water while everyone around him made merry. When the lights went off and he'd wound up with a warm, sexy female in his arms, his knee-jerk reaction was to return the kiss she offered. So, he had.

That kiss had started slow, wound up frenzied, and had slammed a fierce, hungry need into him. Need that was as biting now as it had been that night.

He angled his chin. "If I remember right, your date was an assistant D.A. You still seeing Perry Mason?"

He caught the flash in her eyes when she pointed a gloved finger his way. "Before we get down to business, Slick, let's get something straight."

"Slick?"

"I doubt it will come as a surprise to hear that you're quite the talk among some women at the cop shop."

He lifted a brow. "Yeah?"

"Word is, when it comes to relationships you're like lightning—one bright flash, then you're gone. Fine, if that's how you play things, that's your business. It just happens to be a business I know all about."

Max narrowed his eyes. "Is that so?"

"That's so. My big brother is the original love 'em and leave 'em guy. If Cam put his mind to it, he could probably charm a mother superior out of her panties. I grew up watching all of his moves, and wound up with a lot of girls—and later, women—whose hearts he'd broken crying on my shoulder."

"Not a fun job for a little sis."

"No." Jennifer closed her eyes, opened them. "Look, don't get me wrong, I love my brother. Adore him. Cam never sets out to hurt any of the women he dates. He has no interest in settling into a relationship, so he doesn't make promises he has no intention of keeping. He's never led anyone on. It's just that he draws women like a magnet, enjoys their company for a time, then moves on and never looks back."

"Which, you're implying, is what I do."

"I'm not implying it. I'm saying it outright. So, now that you know a little about my background, I'm sure you can understand why I'm not interested in being any man's conquest."

"Any man, meaning me."

"You've got a sharp mind, Inspector."

"And you've got a closed one. Maybe I'm not looking for a conquest."

"And maybe you are. Either way, it doesn't matter." As she spoke, she pushed a stray wisp of blond hair off her cheek. "The bottom line is, Ballard, when the lights came on New Year's Eve and I saw it was you I'd been kissing, all I felt was…nothing."

Max's jaw set, then tightened. His mind scrolled back to that night, picturing her at the instant the lights flicked back on. She'd stood in stunned silence, staring up at him with blue eyes smoky with need while a mix of surprise and shock settled in her face. For the space of several heartbeats, she had clung to him, breathless and trembling. And while her body pressed against his, he'd sensed the hungry rush of desire inside her, as hot and edgy as his own.

Maybe what had happened between them that night made no difference to her now, but it sure as hell had meant something then. The hit she'd just delivered to his pride compelled him to remind her of that.

"You felt something that night, Jennifer," he countered softly. He took a step closer, dipped his head. "Desire." He acknowledged a surge of pure male satisfaction when he saw the pulse in her throat jump. "I know, because I felt it, too. And I felt *you* feel it."

She opened her mouth to respond, then snapped it shut when Roger tromped up the porch steps, toting the spare hard hat and turnout coat.

With Roger's return, Max shoved his personal thoughts to the background. He would deal with the woman later. Right now, it was time to work with the cop. He pulled on the spare coat Roger handed him, buckled it against the biting cold. Turning, Max grabbed his helmet, evidence kit and shovel off the edge of the porch where he'd left them when he'd arrived.

He watched while Jennifer settled the borrowed hard hat on her head. "You ever work a fire death, Sergeant Weathers?"

"One. It turned out to be accidental, caused by an overloaded electrical outlet." She raised a shoulder beneath the dwarfing coat. "Just in case you're wondering,

Inspector, I don't plan to get in your way. I know what I don't know—fire isn't my field. It's yours. I just need you to tell me if what happened here tonight was accidental or intentional. If it turns out we're dealing with arson, that translates to homicide. Which is my field.''

"Fair enough.''

Max decided he was going to have one hell of an easier time dealing with the cop than the woman. He inclined his head toward the charred front door. ''Let's get started.''

TWO

AT FIRST LIGHT the following morning, Jennifer pulled her cruiser to a halt at the fire site. She noted OCFD's red van still parked in the driveway, along with a mix of other fire department vehicles. Her gaze shifted to what had been Spencer Fitzgerald's spacious, two-story home. In the early morning gloom, the devastation looked even more horrendous than it had the previous night.

Yellow crime scene tape circled the house's blackened corpse. Fire had scorched the brick walls, charred wood. What had been the roof was a massive hole that yawned toward the gray sky. The front door now hung by one hinge. Window glass blown out by the fire's heat scattered over the sloping yard like oversize ice crystals. Skins of the red, heart-shaped balloons resembled bloodstains against the sodden winter grass.

Jennifer opened the cruiser's door and slid out into the frigid air. The smell of doused ash, sour and acrid, invaded her lungs. Still, the fire's lingering odor wasn't as foul as it had been last night when she'd followed Max Ballard into the house. The sickly sweet stench of a fire death—akin to spoiled steak on charcoals—had permeated the air.

Though violent death was her business, Jennifer had never grown immune to the sight of it. Standing in silence, she had watched the M.E.'s aide examine the scorched body while her stomach tightened and a hollow feeling built in her chest.

"Smoke," the aide had said, flicking a grim look between her and Max. "Around the nostrils, in the nose and probably the air passages. We won't know for sure until we get him on the table, but it looks like this guy was still breathing during the fire." The aide raised a shoulder. "Part of the fire, anyway."

Jennifer could think of few more horrific ways for a person to die than by burning to death.

Freezing wind slapped at her face, dashed her long blond hair into her eyes. Shivering, she eased up the hood of her insulated parka on which she'd clipped her badge. Beneath the parka she wore a heavy sweater and thick wool slacks. Thermal tights and sturdy shoes completed her outfit. Despite the layers of clothing, the icy wind seemed to slash at her flesh as she ducked beneath crime scene tape and headed up the driveway.

She stopped at the van, asked the lanky, redheaded firefighter on duty if the body count had increased.

"Nope. One victim, that's all she wrote."

Jennifer nodded. "Is Ballard still working in the house?"

"I took a cup of coffee in to him a few minutes ago," the man advised, his breath gray clouds in the cold air. "He's in the living room." The fireman reached into the van, handed Jennifer the same type of thick-soled rubber boots she'd worn last night. "You want a cup of coffee, Sergeant?"

"Thanks."

Wearing the steel-soled boots and carrying a foam cup of steaming coffee, Jennifer trudged up the house's front steps, crossed the porch, then moved into the blackened foyer. There, she nudged down the hood of her parka.

The air inside the house felt damp and smelled of charred wood, soggy plaster and burnt carpet. The stench of death hung heavy. A black paste formed by a mix of ash and water covered everything. From where she stood, she could hear the murmur of voices of the investigators who worked throughout the house.

At the far end of the foyer, a staircase rose to what was left of the second story. From having been there last night, she knew that the gaping hole to her right led to the remains of the dining room and kitchen. The black abyss to her left had been a hallway leading to an arched entrance to the living room. She headed that way.

Jennifer paused beside a bank of portable lights just inside the living room door. In the bright beams, particles of soot and dust danced on the wintry air. Charred boards lay everywhere, crisscrossing like matchsticks on top of the tangled frames of tables, chairs and a long sofa. Remnants of other furnishings and mementos lay in blackened heaps. Wires dangled from the walls and the section of the ceiling that remained.

A thin coat of frost filmed everything.

Max stood alone among the rubble in the center of the room, sealing a glass tube. He wore his turnout coat, jeans and rubber boots, all smeared with soot. His dark hair was mussed, his expression grim.

Sipping her coffee, Jennifer studied him through the steam.

Last night, having been so ill prepared for the cold, she had appreciated the use of his turnout coat. What she hadn't anticipated was that the heavy garment carried a trace of the same intensely masculine scent of the aftershave he'd worn New Year's Eve.

Her heart had started pumping harder the instant she'd pulled on the coat and caught a whiff of that scent.

She scowled into her coffee. So, fine, she thought—the man's aftershave made her knees weak. The man, too, she conceded. She had never before been so acutely aware of her own femininity than when she was in Max Ballard's vicinity. If he were another type of man, that might mean something. She might *let* it mean something. Not with the playboy hose jockey. Thanks to her brother, she'd seen first-hand the damage a man with a charmer's grin and short attention span for relationships could do to a woman's heart. She did not intend to become a casualty of some raging Don Juan.

Beneath her parka, she rotated her shoulders to try to ease the tension that had settled there. It didn't take a cop's sixth sense to know that the heat started by the one kiss they'd shared could spark into a fire that would flame hot and high, then die away to nothing. She wasn't one to delude herself—she knew her one hope at keeping that fire banked was to keep her distance from Max.

As if sensing her presence, he glanced across his shoulder. His mouth curved. "Morning, New Year's."

She took a steadying breath. "Good morning, Inspector."

"You've got great timing," he said, holding up the glass tube between latex-gloved fingers. "This is my last sample. While I get it labeled, why don't you tell me what you've found out since you left here last night?"

Jennifer hesitated, mindful that she might be in the middle of a crime scene. "Okay if I come in?"

"Yeah." Crouching, he retrieved a marker from his kit. "The techs finished photographing, videotaping and measuring a couple of hours ago." As he spoke, Max began jotting on the tube's label.

Glass and blackened debris crunched beneath her boots as Jennifer snaked her way between charred boards and burnt frames of furniture. She paused near where Max bent over the open evidence kit. Beside the kit sat a foam cup of coffee.

"Fitzgerald was divorced, in his late fifties and never at a loss for a date," she began. "He had the political connections we heard about. I talked to a neighbor who came to the party here last night, which wasn't just to celebrate Valentine's Day. It also kicked off Mayor Hart's run for the governor's office."

Max glanced up from the label. "That so?"

"According to the neighbor, the heart-shaped balloons in and outside the house had Hart's name on them."

"Name's a convenient tie-in with the holiday."

"Yes. I've also learned that Fitzgerald was an amateur photographer. A fairly good one, I understand."

"We found what was left of some cameras and darkroom equipment." Max sipped his coffee. "You get a copy of the guest list?"

"I'm working on that. Fitzgerald had a daytime housekeeper who said she knew about the party, but didn't help plan it. She referred me to Fitzgerald's secretary. I sent a patrol car by her apartment, but she didn't stay there last night. I'll drop by his office this morning and see if I can hook up with her."

"When's the autopsy scheduled?"

"Already started. I called the M.E. when I left here, briefed him on Fitzgerald's connections and told him we'd get pressured for answers. The M.E. agreed to go in early and do the prelim, and to push the tox reports. He'll call when he has something."

Jennifer paused, sipped her coffee. "The housekeeper gave me the name of Fitzgerald's dentist. I rousted him out of bed, talked him into going to his office and pulling Fitzgerald's records. A patrol cop took them by the M.E.'s office. We'll know soon if Fitzgerald's our victim.''

Max sat his cup aside. ''You've been busy.''

''Just doing my job, like you.'' Jennifer glanced around the charred room, trying to imagine what it had looked like before the fire. ''According to the neighbor, it sounds like every local politician and some state reps were here last night. There was also a caterer, bartenders and other service personnel.''

''That's a lot of people on the talk-to list.'' Max put the lid on the marker, tossed it into his kit. Rising, he pulled a blue plastic box from his coat and placed the tube inside.

Leaning in, Jennifer peered into the box, saw that it contained a row of tubes, identical to the one he'd just labeled.

''Test tubes?'' she asked, her gaze rising to meet his. In the glow of the bright lights, she could see the lines of fatigue at the corners of his eyes and mouth. She didn't envy the hours he'd spent in the soot, stench and freezing weather. In some ways, her job was easier than his. At most scenes, she didn't have to wonder if a crime had been committed—a dead body was a pretty good indication. During an arson, fire consumed most of the evidence. Max had to start his work at ground zero.

''Officially, they're known as sampling tubes.'' He held out the box so she could get a good look. ''They contain an absorbent that recovers petroleum hydrocarbons in fire debris.''

She pursed her lips. ''At the one fire scene I worked, the investigator sealed all his evidence in sterile cans.''

''My Bronco is stacked with cans full of evidence that

I'll submit to the lab." He slid the box into his coat's pocket. "The tubes are new technology, considered state-of-the-art. I just brought these back from Quantico."

"You were at the FBI Academy?"

"I attended a special course on serial arsonists." He kept his eyes on hers. "It lasted four weeks. I flew back here yesterday morning."

Four weeks, Jennifer thought. She couldn't help but wonder if that was why his phone calls to her had stopped a month ago.

As if reading her mind, he grinned. "You doing the time line, New Year's?" he asked. "One thing you'll learn about me is that I'm patient. Persistent, too. I didn't give up on you after two weeks just because you gave my messages the cold shoulder. I stopped calling because I left town."

She angled her chin. "I didn't plan to return your calls."

"I know. I decided to drop by your office after I got back to see if that landed me anywhere. Before I had time to unpack, I got called to this burn, and you showed up. That's fate." He dipped his head. "Want to go where it leads us?"

She arched a brow. "Which, in your mind, would be to bed."

He said nothing for a minute, only studied her, as if considering. "I'd be lying if I told you I hadn't thought about taking you to bed."

"I told you, I'm not interested."

"That's what you said." He kept his eyes locked on hers as he pulled off his latex gloves. "You handle yourself well. Some people probably think you're a woman of little emotion. I might think that, too, if it hadn't been for that kiss.'' He trailed a fingertip down the line of her cheek. ''The emotion's there, Jennifer. You just know how to control it.''

''Keep your hands to yourself, Slick,'' she said, even as her heart stuttered.

''All that cool control appeals to me,'' he continued softly. ''So does the idea of holding you in my arms and feeling it slip.''

''I....'' She looked away in case the heat that had surged into her face had transformed into a flush. She let out a shaky breath as a need she hadn't been aware of exploded into bloom. She knew now that no amount of common sense could outweigh her instant and primitive response to the man. A man who had the same effect on uncountable women, she reminded herself. She pictured Max's grinning photograph featured on the firefighter calendar that hung in the women's restroom next door to the Homicide detail. Some enterprising female had placed a red lipstick kiss on his broad-enough-to-be-called-impressive chest. ''Cutie Pie'' was scrawled across a corner of the photo.

An almost desperate sense of self-preservation had her squaring her shoulders. ''Don't forget, Inspector, your track record is well known,'' she said, keeping her voice as cool as her gaze. ''I've got a good idea what you'll do if I choose to crawl into bed with you.''

His eyes narrowed. ''Why don't you tell me?''

''At first, you'll be charming and attentive. After a couple of rolls in the sack you'll decide to move on. Then you'll disappear like smoke.''

With her stomach churning, Jennifer lost the desire for coffee. She sat her cup on the floor, then wrapped her arms around her waist. ''I refuse to get involved in a relationship that's nothing more than a couple of one-night stands. And I doubt fate put us on this investigation—more like bad luck. Speaking of work, let's get back to it. Do you know if this fire was set by accident, or was it intentional?''

In the artificial light, Max's dark eyes looked intense, direct, and, she thought, just a little angry. ''We'll get back to work after I've had my say. First, I've gotten wind of some of the rumors going on about me. I don't have a clue where a lot of them came from. All I know is if I'd been involved with that many women, I wouldn't be able to stand up. Second, do you conduct your investigations on assumptions, or solid proof?''

She speared him with a look. ''I wouldn't have lasted long as a detective if I tried to build cases on assumptions.''

''Then why the hell do you assume I'm the same type of man as your brother? *I* don't go through women like water. I've never walked away from a relationship without looking back. I've even had my heart nicked a time or two. Don't judge me on another man's merits, Jennifer.''

''Look....'' Furrowing her forehead, she conceded that she'd been wrong to take the rumors she'd heard at face value. And automatically comparing him to Cam hadn't exactly been fair. ''Okay, Ballard, maybe I—''

He held up a hand to stop her. ''Third, I've never wanted a woman so damn much in my whole life as I want you. If you think all I'm looking for from you is a couple of one-night stands, think again. I've got a hell of a lot more in mind. What we've got here is arson.''

Her mouth had gone bone dry, her pulse was scrambling and the air in her lungs clogged. He had knocked her off balance—as she was sure he'd intended. Closing her eyes, she struggled to catch up. Right now, her emotions were too jumbled for her to think logically about the personal angle. She would consider what he'd said later when she was alone. When he wasn't around to stir her senses and see the confusion his words had settled inside her.

"Arson." She eased back to give herself space. Needed space. "You can prove it?"

She wasn't questioning the determination Max had made—she knew he knew that. According to law, the fire investigator had to be able to prove arson had occurred before a fire death could be ruled a homicide.

"Yeah, I've got proof," Max confirmed. "The fire traveled from the top of the main staircase to the bottom, something fire rarely does without an accelerant trailer helping it along. Plus, flashpoint occurred almost simultaneously at different locations, which means we've got more than one point of origin. Someone torched the place, all right."

"How many different locations?"

"Three. One in here." He inclined his head toward a corner of the room where exposed two-by-fours were charcoal black, their surfaces crazed into dozens of shiny, tile-sized squares. From the one fire scene she'd worked, Jennifer knew "alligatoring" was the term the experts used for the phenomenon.

"Another blaze started at almost the same time in the kitchen," Max continued. "The third in an upstairs bedroom."

"Do you have any idea what time that was?"

"Not long before the neighbor drove by and saw the flames. I took a break last night to check some facts with him. He didn't see any vehicles leaving the scene, or unusual activity near the house. That's a good indication the firebug was gone when the fire started."

Max paused while his narrowed gaze slowly traced a path around the room. Jennifer sensed he was recreating in his mind the way the flames had worked, following them from the corner to the room's center, licking up the walls, consuming the furniture as it heated and grew.

"Our guy had to have used a delayed timing device to start each burn," he said after a moment.

"What sort of device?"

"Good question. Sometimes in the rubble we'll find the remains of an egg timer hooked to a couple of six-volt batteries. Or a phone that had matches soaked in accelerant taped to it."

"How does that work?"

"The firebug leaves a phone in a pool of accelerant, then goes off somewhere to establish an alibi. When the time's right he calls the phone. The ringer sparks the matches." Max shoved a hand through his dark hair. "So far, we have no idea what type of timing devices this guy used to spark the three separate blazes. Same goes for the accelerant. If it were gasoline, this place would have exploded. Kerosene by itself is too slow burning—once this fire got started, it burned hot and fast. Took high-pressure hoses nearly an hour to kill it."

"Could the suspect have mixed gasoline with kerosene?"

"Some torches do. This fire looks like it could have been caused just that way. It wasn't."

"How do you know?"

"Gasoline and kerosene both leave distinctive odors. Some of the accelerant used here seeped beneath baseboards, so it didn't burn since oxygen couldn't get to it. The stuff has an odor, but I can't tag what it is. The lab'll have to do that."

"What about point of entry? Any sign of forced entry to doors, locks or windows?"

"Nothing. Whoever did this was either let in by the victim or had access to the house on their own."

Footsteps crunched in the foyer. Jennifer turned in time to see the redheaded firefighter who'd manned the command van step into view. "Yo, Max, you and the sergeant better get outside."

Max raised a brow. "Why's that, Prescott?"

"A limo just glided up, carrying Mayor Hart and his wife. They want to chat with whoever's in charge." Prescott's mouth curved. "Glad that's not me."

"TOO DAMN EARLY FOR THIS," Max muttered. Leaning against his Bronco, he toed off his heavy boots. That done, he traded his soot-stained turnout coat for the scarred bomber jacket he'd been wearing when he arrived last night at the scene.

"Political pressure always hits fast," Jennifer commented while greedy fingers of wind snatched at her long hair.

The rays of sun stabbing through the clouds at her back turned her hair ten shades of gold. Max didn't have to wonder how it would feel to tangle his fingers in those waves. He'd had that pleasure New Year's Eve. What he did wonder about was her reaction to what he'd said about his intentions toward her. Intentions that were new to him. Intentions he wasn't totally sure he, himself, understood.

She gathered her hair in one gloved hand as they moved down the driveway. "Considering Fitzgerald's connections, I have a feeling we'd better get used to the pressure from higher ups."

"Well, let's hope the mayor and his wife don't mind

the smell of smoke,'' Max commented. It would take a long, hot shower to rid himself of the acrid scent.

Jennifer slid him a look as they neared the limo, its finish gleaming like black pearls. ''If they mind the smoke smell, this might be a short conversation.''

''Good point, New Year's.'' Max gave her a wink. ''I'll sit as close to His Honor as possible.''

Max didn't get a chance. When he pulled open the limo's door, the mayor waved them to the seat across an expanse of gray carpet.

After a round of introductions, Max settled back in the warm, buttery-soft leather. The limo's interior smelled of rich whiskey and expensive perfume; to his right was a row of crystal decanters with silver tags around their necks. He knew the mayor's city salary didn't fund the ride—Adam Hart's family owned the state's biggest oil-producing company.

''Sergeant Weathers, Inspector Ballard, we appreciate your taking time to talk to us,'' the mayor said.

As if they had a choice, Max thought, regarding the man whose name appeared on his paychecks. Hart was tall, whip-lean, in his early sixties. His crop of silver hair swept back from a sharp-featured face that sported a firm jaw and dark, alert eyes.

His hands were large, and when he'd clasped Max's on introduction, they'd felt smooth as a baby's. Still, looking at him, one thought of power and authority.

By Max's estimate, Hannah Hart was at least ten years her husband's junior. She was thin, sleek and perfectly groomed. Her features were delicate, close to elegant, with just a hint of steel in the line of her chin. Her hair was the color of mink, pulled back at her nape. Her face was ice pale.

''We do appreciate your time,'' she agreed in a

breathy voice. She seemed to shiver inside her black cashmere coat. "Adam and I didn't hear about the fire until this morning. I...can't absorb it." She glanced out at the house's charred skeleton. "We just saw Spence...."

Jennifer leaned forward. "I understand Mr. Fitzgerald hosted a party here for you last night."

"Right," the mayor said. "A kick off for my gubernatorial campaign. Hannah and I are opening my headquarters this morning. Spence was supposed to be there."

Jennifer nodded. "I need the names of all the people you remember seeing here last night."

The mayor frowned. "Why?"

"Inspector Ballard has determined the fire that killed Mr. Fitzgerald was set intentionally."

"God...." Hannah's dark eyes seemed huge against her skin's pallor. "How? Who would do such a thing?"

"I'm working out the how," Max commented. "The who might take Sergeant Weathers and myself a little longer."

"That's why you need to know who we saw here last night?" Hannah asked. "Because you think a guest started the fire?"

"We need to interview everyone to find out if they noticed anything not quite right," Jennifer commented. "Anyone hanging around who didn't belong. Things like that."

The cop was good, Max thought. A murder investigation didn't just start with a body. It started with a list of potential suspects. Everyone who attended the party was on that list, including the two people sitting across from them.

"Hannah has the guest list," Adam said, reaching for his wife's hand. "She planned the whole affair."

"When Spence offered to host the party, I insisted that he not go to any trouble," Hannah said. "I compiled the guest list and dealt with hiring the caterer, the florist and so on. I wanted everything perfect for Adam last night."

Jennifer angled her head. "Was it?"

"If you knew my wife, you wouldn't have to ask." Max noted the admiring glint in the mayor's eyes when he brought his wife's hand to his lips, lingered over it. "Hannah's a genius at details. She spent five years teaching high school—after herding rowdy teens, overseeing social functions is a snap. She's also in charge of my campaign headquarters."

"When can I get a copy of the guest list?" Jennifer asked.

"I'll have our housekeeper fax it to me at headquarters," Hannah answered. "You can pick it up there."

Jennifer slid a pad out of her pocket and jotted the address the mayor gave her. "Do either of you know of anyone who might have reason to harm Mr. Fitzgerald? Someone who had a business or personal grudge against him?"

"Spence was a land developer," Adam replied. "When you're in that business, it's standard to engage in bidding wars for real estate. Spence won a lot of those wars. But none, I think, that would get him killed."

Max cocked his head. "What about the personal angle? He get along with his kids? Was there a special lady on the scene? Maybe one he'd jilted who was giving him trouble?"

"He loved his children." As she spoke, Hannah rubbed her throat in long, soothing strokes. "I was busy last night making sure everything ran smoothly, so I didn't notice if he had a date.'' She met her husband's gaze. ''Adam?''

''He didn't have one specific woman hanging on his arm, so I guess not.'' The mayor pursed his lips. ''Spence went through a bitter divorce years ago. That soured him on marriage. On relationships overall. It was rare to see him more than twice, maybe three times with the same woman.''

''Yes,'' Hannah agreed quietly. ''I've heard some of the women he dated say that Spence wasn't a man you could count on for a permanent relationship.''

''I need you to add the names of those women and the firms you hired to work here to the list I'm picking up,'' Jennifer said, jotting on her notepad. ''What time did you leave last night?''

''I left around ten,'' the mayor stated. ''Hannah later.''

''You didn't arrive or leave together?''

''No,'' Hannah confirmed. ''I came early to see that the food and flowers were done right. After the party, I made sure the caterer left things spotless. Spence poked his head into the kitchen to say he thought the event had been a success.'' Her voice trembled as tears welled in her dark eyes. ''I walked out with the caterer a few minutes later.'' She sniffed, accepted the handkerchief her husband offered. ''I can't believe that's the last time.... I don't understand how anyone could have done this.''

Max studied the faces of the couple sitting across from him. He saw nothing other than genuine sadness and regret.

''Was Fitzgerald the only person in the house when you left?''

Hannah dabbed at her eyes. "Yes. Well, as far as I know."

A phone chimed; Jennifer reached into the pocket of her parka, pulled out her cell phone, answered. "Hold on."

She met Max's gaze as she reached for the door's handle. "It's the call I'm expecting. I'll take it in my car."

He nodded. The call, he knew, was from the M.E. "I'll finish up with Mayor and Mrs. Hart."

Five minutes later, Max left the limo after giving the mayor the standard "we'll let you know if anything develops" line.

When the limo glided away, he headed across the street and climbed into the idling cruiser beside Jennifer.

Her gloves were off; she held her phone clamped between one cheek and shoulder while her pencil flew across her pad. Draping an arm across the top of the seat, Max leaned in. He scowled when he saw her notes were in shorthand.

A moment later she said, "Thanks, Doc, I appreciate your speed on this and the tox reports." Mouth set, she clicked off the phone, laid it on the dash.

"You going to keep me in suspense?" Max asked.

She swiveled to face him. "Dental records confirm it's Fitzgerald. Cause of death is carbon monoxide poisoning."

"So, he was alive when the fire started." Max pursed his lips. "Too bad he didn't wake up in time to get out."

"That would have been impossible, due to the mix of alcohol and tranquilizer in his bloodstream. The M.E. says Fitzgerald had enough tranq in him that a siren going off under his pillow wouldn't have roused him."

"Any idea how long the drug had been in his system?"

"He swallowed it sometime during the to-do for the mayor."

"Strange time for the host to take downers."

"I agree." She frowned. "It could have happened that way, though. If Fitzgerald was suffering from some sort of anxiety, he could have taken the pills on his own. I'll check it out with his doctor."

"If that's not how things went down, then someone probably slipped the tranq into our guy's drink during the party."

"Someone being the person who planned to start the fire that would kill him a couple of hours later."

"Bingo." Max gazed out the cruiser's windshield at the house's charred ruins. "That fire took careful planning. The torch knew what he was doing."

"He had to also know that it wouldn't take long for fire investigators to tag it an arson."

"Yeah, he knew. For some reason, he didn't care."

"So, hypothetically, if the killer got close enough to Fitzgerald to drug his drink, why not just slip him some sort of slow-acting poison? Something that would kill him during the night. That might even make his death look natural?"

"Because, hypothetically, the torch needed to destroy something in the house. Something he couldn't get his hands on."

Jennifer met his gaze. "Was there a safe?"

"Yeah, we unearthed it this morning. It'd been set into one of the upstairs walls. It's already tagged to go to the lab."

"It's possible the killer didn't know about the safe.

Maybe he hoped whatever he needed to destroy was stuck in a drawer, or hidden in a book somewhere.''

"That's possible. I've got the name of a locksmith who can get the safe open."

"Maybe whatever's inside will lead to the killer."

"We can hope." Max checked the clock on the dash. "I need to log my evidence into the lab. That'll take time."

"While you're there, I'll go by Fitzgerald's office, call his doctor, then drop by Hart's campaign headquarters."

"Want to meet at my office in a couple of hours? I'll have the safe open by then, so we can go through whatever's inside. We can also go over the guest list, decide on a plan of action."

A guarded look slid into Jennifer's eyes. "Fine."

"You have a problem coming to my office?"

"Get real."

He shifted his arm on the car's seat, toyed with a lock of her hair. "You thinking about what I said in the house?"

"That we have an arson resulting in homicide? Yes, Inspector, that's on my mind."

"What I said about the *other* fire," he corrected. "The one between us."

"I got your message. You think we should jump into bed just because we share a basic animal lust."

"Lust." His mouth curved. "I knew you felt something when we kissed."

"I...." She closed her eyes, opened them. "I don't want to get burned—"

"You think I do?"

"I don't know what you think. All I know is that passion without genuine feeling behind it flames high, then fizzles out. Fast. All you've got left are ashes."

"That's a fact." He cupped his palm against the side of her throat, felt her pulse jump. "Here's another fact. I've been thinking about you for six long weeks. I'm not sure what I feel for you, or how deep those feelings go. But they're there. I don't expect them to go away. You shouldn't expect me to go away, either."

She let out a shaky breath. "Are you always this relentless?"

"When I see something I want, yes. But I draw the line at the caveman routine." He angled his head. "I'll make you a deal. All you have to do to get me to back off is tell me you haven't thought about me since New Year's Eve. That you've cleared that kiss out of your head."

She lifted a hand to his wrist but didn't push him aside. "I've tried to clear both out of my head."

"Not good enough." He leaned in, his mouth inches from hers. "Doesn't the fact that I've stuck tell you something? Aren't you curious where all this might take us?"

"I don't like surprises. I prefer to know where I'm going before I get there."

"Here's where."

He lowered his head just enough to catch her bottom lip lightly between his teeth. He felt her breath hitch, felt her pulse shimmy beneath his palm.

The need tethered tight inside him strained hard at the remembered taste of her. Fire flashed in his blood. He took her mouth, savoring, absorbing. He hadn't realized how much he wanted. Craved.

Her lips parted on a moan while her fingers dived into his hair. Her mouth moved restless and hungry under his. He realized that she, too, wanted. Craved.

He fought the urge to gather her up, take her someplace quiet and dark where it was only the two of them. To spend hours, days, where it would only be the two of them.

It cost Max to draw back, to force himself to remember where they were. Neither of them needed the hassle of being spotted in an official vehicle engaging in unofficial business.

Jennifer stared at him, her cheeks flushed, her blue eyes wide, smoky. As passion faded from them, wariness slid in. Her hands fisted against her thighs.

"I don't like that you can do this to me. Make me feel this way."

"I was pretty content with my life, too, before the lights went out and you wound up in my arms. What we did New Year's Eve changed things. What we did just now is convincing evidence that we've wasted a lot of time during the past six weeks."

He reached out, skimmed his fingertips across one of her fisted hands. "Whatever's between us isn't going to ease up."

She jerked from his touch, dragged her fingers through her hair. "I need to think. Dammit, I can't think around you." The words came out in a heated rush. "Get the hell out of my car."

He raised a brow. "First time I've been kicked out of a cop car."

She gave him a shove. "I've got work to do."

One look at the stubborn determination in her eyes and he knew it was best to give her space. She was, after all, armed.

He opened the door and climbed out saying, "See you at my office."

She pulled away from the curb with only the slightest screech of burning rubber.

THREE

THREE DAYS LATER, Jennifer handed her black trench coat to a stiff-spined housekeeper, then followed the woman across a granite-floored foyer into a plush living room. Overhead, the ceiling swept upward a story and a half to crisscrossing wooden beams.

"Mrs. Robertson will be with you in a moment."

"Thanks."

Jennifer settled her purse in a wing chair covered with needlepoint roses. As the double doors clicked shut behind her, she moved across the room, passing twin upholstered sofas edged by tables polished to an almost painful gloss. She paused a few feet from a fireplace of pale green stone where fragrant wood sizzled. Settling one hand on her waist beside her badge and holstered Glock, she studied the oil portrait hanging over the carved mantle.

Pamela Robertson, gowned in ice-blue silk, stared out at the world through eyes the color of jade. Raven-black hair framed a creamy smooth face with high, classic cheekbones. A choker of blazing diamonds circled her swanlike-throat.

Over the past days, Jennifer had discovered that Spencer Fitzgerald made a habit of involving himself with gorgeous, elegant women. And, that those involvements seemingly lasted only as long as it suited Fitzgerald.

A spark popped, logs shifted in the fireplace. Dropping her gaze from the portrait, Jennifer watched the flames lick and twist among the logs. She could smell the enticing scent of wood, hear the crackle, feel the warmth.

This fire had been kindled to provide atmosphere and comfort. The flames that had swept through Fitzgerald's home had been set with the cold, calculating intent to destroy and kill.

The knowledge that she and Max were no closer to finding out who had started that fire and why had Jennifer frowning at the leaping flames. In homicide investigations, the first twenty-four hours were critical. If by then a strong lead or suspect had not emerged, the likelihood of success diminished with each passing day. To solve a homicide, you needed witnesses, physical evidence and a confession. Without the first and second, the third was unlikely. So far, the Fitzgerald case had a glaring absence of all three.

She and Max had interviewed the caterer, service personnel and each guest who'd attended the reception that marked the kick off for the mayor's race for governor. Everyone had corroborated each other's statements. No one had seen or heard anything suspicious. If Fitzgerald had received threats or feared for his life, he hadn't mentioned it to anyone they'd interviewed. If he suffered from depression for which he'd obtained tranquilizers, he hadn't gone to his personal physician to get them. Nor had anyone noticed the man had acted depressed. And if the fire that killed him had been set to destroy something inside the house, Jennifer had no idea what that something was. All she knew was it hadn't been among the personal papers locked inside the victim's charred safe.

Suddenly weary, she rubbed her fingers between her brows. Three nights with little sleep had left her feeling slow and sluggish. Still, long hours on the job were a standard part of working Homicide, and she knew her problem wasn't lost sleep. Max was her problem. She'd never before had to work a case with her emotions so jumbled. Never before had to force her thoughts to stay on the job.

Never before craved one certain man.

She'd always made a point to be cautious in relationships. Always held a part of herself back so she would come through unscathed. Made sure she came through that way. Her searing response to Max's kisses told her he was a man with whom there would be no holding back.

She closed her eyes, felt the heat of the fire pulse against her face. If he weren't in court on another case, Max would be working at her side, as he'd done for the past days. During that time, he had made no mention of the kiss they'd shared in her cruiser, hadn't again brought up the possibility of a personal relationship between them.

He had backed off.

Since she had wanted that—*insisted* on it—she should feel relief. Instead, every hour she spent in his presence increased an ache of longing inside her. A longing that had tendrils of panic curling into her stomach. With this one man, she feared the fire, even as she edged closer to it.

The click of high heels against the foyer's granite floor had her turning. Pamela Robertson glided into the room, shutting the door at her back. As her portrait hinted, she was tall and elegant, clad in a jacket and trousers in a rich green wool that matched her eyes. Discreet daytime diamonds winked from her earlobes. "I apologize for keeping you waiting, Sergeant...."

"Weathers." Jennifer moved to the wing chair where she'd left her purse, pulled out a business card and handed it over.

"Would you like something to drink, Sergeant?" The woman's voice was as creamy as her skin.

"No, thanks."

Pamela settled onto the sofa while waving a manicured hand toward the wing chair. "You said on the phone you had questions about Spencer. Since we saw each other for only a short time, I can't imagine I can tell you anything you don't already know."

"Just covering the bases." Jennifer sat, pulled her notepad out of her purse. "What sort of relationship did you have with Mr. Fitzgerald?"

Pamela arched a brow. "We had an affair, Sergeant. Emotionally, I don't believe Spence was capable of having a relationship."

"How long did you see each other?"

"A few months. We met at a dinner party—it was the first social event I attended since my husband's death from cancer the year before. Spence was witty, charismatic and marvelously attentive. He made me feel...desirable. Alive. At the time, I needed that."

Jennifer nodded. Numerous women she and Max had talked to had mentioned how charmingly attentive Fitzgerald could be.

"Over time," Pamela continued, "I came to realize all that attention was only surface. In truth, Spence was totally self-absorbed."

This, too, jibed with what they had discovered about Fitzgerald. "When did your relationship end?"

"Just before Christmas. I had a problem come up with

one of my investments, so I dropped by Spence's office to ask his advice. I caught him unaware and too busy to turn on the charm. I realized immediately he considered my problem a troublesome trespass into his time. I ended our association right then."

"Did you see him after that?"

"Once, over the Christmas holidays at the country club. He was dining with his stockbroker. We didn't speak." Pamela tilted her head. "I received an invitation to the Valentine's Day reception for Mayor Hart." Her glossed mouth curved. "I'm sure someone other than Spence compiled the guest list."

Jennifer pursed her lips. Hannah Hart had stated she wanted things to be perfect for her husband's reception, yet she had invited three women whom she knew had been intimately involved with the host. The event had been a fund-raiser, Jennifer reminded herself. The other two women were as well off financially as Pamela Robertson. When compiling the guest list, Hannah had clearly had her eye on her husband's campaign chest.

"Mrs. Robertson, did Mr. Fitzgerald ever mention he'd received any kind of threat? Or that he was having a problem with a business dealing? Anything along those lines?"

"No, then again Spence wouldn't have discussed anything like that with me. Although we were intimate, he never shared his personal thoughts." Pamela paused, her green eyes softening. "I am sorry that he died so horribly. I know of no one who wished Spence harm. In some ways, he led a charmed life. He was one of those lucky people for whom most things he touched turned to gold."

"How so?"

"As an example, I overheard him on the phone one

evening, talking about a vote coming up before the City Council.'' She furrowed her brow. ''Something about re-zoning land on the city's fringes so it would be eligible for commercial development. Spence told whoever was on the phone that he stood to lose millions because the council was split down the middle on the re-zoning issue. He said that wasn't going to happen, that one of the opposing councilmen would for sure change his vote. Weeks later, I read in the paper that the re-zoning had passed. The councilman obviously changed his mind.''

Or got it changed for him.

Although she'd found nothing nefarious in Fitzgerald's background, Jennifer's thoughts automatically shifted toward the prospect of blackmail. She felt it then, just a sniff of the killer, a whiff of the track. If what Pamela Robertson said was true, millions of dollars of the land developer's money had hinged on one man's vote. What if Fitzgerald had started digging, found proof of some sort of indiscretion—or worse—by that councilman? Fitzgerald could have confronted the man, held that proof over his head to force the vote change Doing that could have saved Fitzgerald millions of dollars. 1. also could have gotten him killed. And his house burne to destroy that proof.

''Mrs. Robertson, did you hear Fitzgerald mention the councilman's name?''

''Yes, Thomas Davenport.''

Jennifer kept her expression neutral. Since he had attended the mayor's reception, she and Max had interviewed Davenport the previous day. The councilman had claimed he'd had no business or personal dealings with Spencer Fitzgerald.

LATE THAT AFTERNOON, Max strode out of the Oklahoma County Courthouse into air as brittle as glass.

Overhead, the sky hung like a curtain of gray velvet, threatening snow. Hunching his shoulders inside his overcoat, he jaywalked past cars jammed to a halt at a stoplight and headed for the lot where he'd parked his Bronco.

He had wasted most of the day cooling his heels, waiting to testify. When he finally took the stand, the public defender had grilled him for over an hour. Although the attorney had tried hard, Max could tell the jury hadn't bought the P.D.'s claim that firefighters battling a grease fire at the defendant's partially burned house had planted the charred packages of cocaine Max found hidden in the pantry.

Max unlocked the Bronco and slid in. While he waited for the idling engine to warm, he turned on his cell phone he'd shut off while in court. He listened to two messages from his secretary and one from the lab. The fourth was from Jennifer, asking him to call her mobile phone. Hers was the number he dialed.

"Hello?"

"Hey, New Year's, how'd the interview with the Robertson woman go?"

"It was enlightening," she replied, then ran down the information Pamela Robertson had given her.

Max gave a low whistle when Jennifer detailed Councilman Davenport's sudden change of position on the land development issue. "So, Robertson gave us a door to open, and there's a city councilman behind it."

"Exactly. I did some checking after I left her house. She was right—Davenport's vote made the difference. The council had been split on the re-zoning, and no one expected it to pass. The day it showed up on the agenda, Davenport did a turnaround and cast a yea vote."

"I guess when we talked to him yesterday, he just forgot to mention how *his* vote saved Spencer Fitzgerald a few million dollars." Max leaned toward the dash, flipped on the heater's fan. Warm air surged from the vents. "Sounds like we need to have another chat with Davenport."

"I already did," Jennifer said over a clatter of dishes.

Max narrowed his eyes. "Are you at a restaurant?"

"In my kitchen. Davenport didn't like it when I showed up at his office with more questions. He got indignant when I pressed him for reasons why he changed his mind on the vote."

"Did he stop being a jackass long enough to tell you?"

"No. He gave me the spin about how he'd decided his voting to re-zone the land for development was in the city's best interests. He refused to explain why he'd shifted his way of thinking. I let him get away with stonewalling me. For now."

"Sounds like we need to go at him from a different angle. If we can prove Fitzgerald paid Davenport to swing his vote—then threatened to go public with proof of the payoff—we'd have one hell of a motive for Davenport to have torched Fitzgerald."

"You're way behind me, Ballard." The rattle of pots and pans sounded over the line. "Head to my apartment if you want to play catch-up on our investigation."

"Your apartment?" Max's mouth curved. "Does all that kitchen noise mean you're inviting me to dinner?"

"I've invited another man to dinner, Slick. You show up, we'll find you a plate." She gave him her address before disconnecting.

Another man.

Max drove across town with his jaw set. It clamped

tight when he pulled into the lot outside her apartment and spotted the OCPD black and white parked in a slot.

The thought of Jennifer sharing dinner—and more—with some faceless cop scraped at Max like tiny claws. Sure, he'd backed off for the past two days, kept his hands to himself and his mind on business. He figured she needed time to get used to the idea there was something between them. And going to be a lot more between them, if he had his way.

The hell with backing off! He climbed out of the Bronco and stalked through the first soft flakes of snow toward the nearest breezeway. No woman had ever gotten inside him the way she had. He'd never wanted anyone inside him that way. If he had to get past some cop in order to make her his, by God he would.

Max pulled off his gloves, gave the apartment's front door a sharp rap. With territorial instinct, he took in the tall, sinewy-built cop who answered. He had thick, sandy hair and blue eyes that gazed with calm interest from a face with distinctive etched features. Max figured most women would consider the guy handsome. And built, seeing as how his sharp-pressed gray uniform shirt covered broad shoulders and a tapered waist that evidenced hard workouts. Max shifted his gaze from the silver lieutenant's bars on the shirt's collar points to the brass nameplate over one pocket. When he read Weathers, the tightness in his chest eased.

"I guess you're Jennifer's brother," he said and thrust out a hand. "Max Ballard."

"I guess you're the smoke eater. Cam Weathers." He swung the door open wide. "Come in."

Max glanced around the living room, noted the soft colors, tidy accessories. Bookshelves filled to capacity framed the fireplace where flames danced around gas-fed logs.

Cam gestured toward a wide-armed leather sofa where his quilted uniform jacket and Sam Browne belt with holstered weapon lay. "Toss your coat there."

"Thanks." As he pulled off his overcoat, then his suit coat, Max caught an inviting spicy scent. "Something smells great."

"Pizza. Homemade. Jen's a whiz in the kitchen."

"A super whiz," Jennifer amended from behind the gleaming white-tiled counter that separated the kitchen from the living room.

Max walked toward the kitchen, studying her while he loosened his tie and opened the top button on his dress shirt. She looked good. Damn good in the cherry-red sweater with a hem that skimmed the waistband of slim black jeans. The snug jeans showed off her long legs better than any mini-skirt ever could. Her honey-blond hair was swept up in an untidy bun from which wispy tendrils escaped. She had a dishtowel draped across one shoulder and a smear of flour on her right cheek.

"Make yourself at home, Ballard," she said while lifting the lid off a pot on the stove. "Cam, get Max whatever he wants to drink."

"Sure." Cam gestured for Max to settle at one of the long-legged stools on the opposite side of the counter from where Jennifer stood, stirring the pot's contents. "I'm on duty, so I'm drinking tea. There's beer and wine, too."

"Wine sounds good." Reaching across the counter, Max used his thumb to swipe the flour off her cheek.

"Hey—" She jerked her head back. The spoon clanged against the pot.

Grinning, he held up his thumb. "Flour." He settled onto a stool, pleased that his touch had shot a look of wariness—edged by heat—into her eyes. He nodded toward the pot of bubbling sauce. "I thought pizza only came in a cardboard box."

She reached for the stemmed glass sitting beside the stove, took a drink of straw-colored wine while eyeing him over the rim. "Not around here, it doesn't," she said. Replacing the pot's lid, she started spreading dough in a shallow round pan.

As she worked, Max studied her deft movements. The homicide cop looked as capable in the kitchen as she did at a crime scene. For a silent moment, he watched her long, tapered fingers work, spreading and stroking the dough into place. The need to feel those hands against his flesh jabbed a quick spear of heat into his mid-section.

"Ballard?"

Max shifted his gaze. Cam Weathers stood just behind his sister, holding a glass of wine. As if he'd read Max's thoughts, the cop's eyes had hardened, even though his expression remained neutral. Meeting his gaze head-on, Max accepted the wine. He intended to become a part of Jennifer's life, and her brother needed to get used to the idea.

Pursing his mouth, Cam slid open a drawer, retrieved a knife. "After you taste Jen's pizza, you'll agree it's special." He began slicing thin strips of pepperoni. "Just like my sister."

"I expect you're right." Max sipped the wine, felt its revitalizing heat slide through him. "What can I do to help?"

Jennifer looked up from the dough. "You any good in the kitchen, Ballard?"

"Maybe." He shrugged. "You don't live half your life at a fire station and not learn how to cook."

Her mouth curved as she finished patting the dough into place. "Or play volleyball."

Cam chuckled. "Two cops against one hose jockey." He helped himself to a slice of pepperoni. "Afraid you're outnumbered tonight."

"Looks that way."

Cam swiped the towel off Jennifer's shoulder and wiped his hands. "Since Jen and I have our routine down, you can just sit there and enjoy the fruit of our labors." He waited while she finished ladling sauce over the dough, then he took the pan and sat it near the cutting board. "We try to get together for dinner once a week."

"There any more brothers or sisters running around?"

"No," Jennifer answered. "Just Cam and myself."

Max sat back, observing brother and sister work as a team. Cam layered pepperoni slices and cheese over the sauce-covered dough while Jennifer dumped chopped tomatoes and celery into a bowl of lettuce. A silent camaraderie existed between them, a fondness in the way they interacted. Max had been prepared to dislike the love 'em and leave 'em brother whom Jennifer claimed had made her gun-shy of relationships. Seeing them together, Max decided there was more to her resistance than just Cam's short attention span toward each woman he dated.

Max set his wine aside. "So, New Year's, you said I need to catch up on our investigation. What happened after Councilman Davenport stonewalled you?"

"I called Cam." Her mouth curved into a self-satisfied smile. "Since he's acquainted with a certain female assistant in the council support staff office, I knew he could get to the truth a lot faster than you or I could.''

''Makes sense.'' Max looked at Cam. ''I take it you found out what swung Davenport's vote on the land re-zoning?''

''Not what, who.'' Cam slid the pizza into the oven, set the timer, then leaned a hip against the counter. ''Jen clued me in that she suspected your fire victim was the one who changed Davenport's mind. According to my source, it was the mayor who put on the pressure.''

''The mayor.'' Max folded his forearms on the counter. ''So, what was in it for Adam Hart?''

''Maybe Fitzgerald promised some hefty campaign money if Hart got Davenport to change his vote,'' Cam theorized.

''Could have happened that way.'' Max furrowed his brow. ''If the image Hart projects is to be believed, he's got a lot of his own money from the family oil business. And he pulled in an ocean of donations from the guests who attended the party on Valentine's Day that kicked off his campaign. On the surface, it doesn't look like he would need to risk taking under-the-table money.''

Jennifer nodded. ''We need to dig below the surface. See if the Harts have financial problems. Could be they've got heavy losses in the stock market. Maybe one or both of them spend half their time gambling. Who knows what we'll find?''

''Lucky for me, one of the tools of my trade is a shovel,'' Max commented. ''I'm good at digging.''

Cam refilled his tea glass. ''One thing for sure, Dav-enport got—or will get—something out of this. My source said that when he voted for the re-zoning, he angered a group of environmentalists. The group's mem-bers tied up his office phone for a week calling in protests. He's up for re-election this spring, so he took a big chance angering that many voters."

"No politician would have done that without a safety net," Max observed. "There's a payoff for him somewhere. Maybe a cabinet post if Hart makes gov."

Several dim beeps coming from the pager sitting on the counter had Cam groaning even before he checked its display. When he did, he muttered an oath, then reached for the phone.

Brow furrowed, Jennifer flicked Max a look while she used a wooden spoon and fork to toss the salad. "That call probably means it'll be just you and me for dinner."

He could read the nerves in her eyes as clearly as he could see their color. "In that case, I'll help with the dishes."

"I've got to go," Cam said when he hung up. "Some guy in a four-wheel-drive pickup hit an icy patch and slid through an intersection. He broadsided one of my troops."

"Is your man hurt?" Jennifer asked, following him into the living room.

"Woman. The EMTs on the scene think she has a broken wrist." Cam retrieved his Sam Browne belt, strapped it on, then shrugged into his heavy jacket. "They're en route to the hospital. That's where I'm headed."

Jennifer reached, squeezed his hand. "Sorry about dinner, bro."

"Me, too." Cam dropped a kiss on the top of her head, then looked at Max. "I get the feeling I'll be seeing you."

Max rose off the stool. "Count on it."

After closing the door, Jennifer headed back into the

kitchen and checked the oven's timer. "We've got a few minutes until the pizza's done."

"Time enough for me to catch you up on a detail about our case." Max moved around the counter to the kitchen's doorway and leaned a shoulder against the jamb. "The lab left me a message while I was in court. Our torch used pyrogallol as the accelerant to start the fire at Fitzgerald's house."

"Pyrogallol." Jennifer arched a brow. "Which is…?"

"A compound used as a developer in photography."

"Fitzgerald was an amateur photographer. Is pyrogallol something he would normally have on the premises?"

"Yes. We found the remains of a darkroom in the rubble—stainless steel developing trays, an enlarger, cameras, things like that."

Leaning a hip against the counter, Jennifer pulled her bottom lip between her teeth. "The killer had to have known Fitzgerald pretty well. Knew he had a darkroom in the house and that pyrogallol would work as an accelerant."

"We still haven't figured out what the torch used as a delayed timing device to ignite the accelerant. We've literally sifted through all of the rubble and haven't found evidence of a device at any of the three points of ignition. That's rare, and it's got me stumped."

"Getting stumped during a homicide investigation isn't a rare occurrence."

"Yeah, well, I don't like the feeling." Biting back frustration, he shoved a hand through his hair. "Dammit, someone fed Fitzgerald enough tranq so he'd be out when the fire started. Whoever did that knew he'd burn, along with whatever else was in the house he needed destroyed. That's cold. Stone cold. I want that torch in the worst kind of way.''

Eyeing him, Jennifer tilted her head as if to gain a new perspective. ''That's how I feel about my cases. It's like an almost obsessive need to find the killer. Each killer.''

''You surprised we have that in common?'' Max left the doorway, walked toward her. ''What did you think, New Year's? That I go from burn to burn without giving a thought for how a victim dies?''

''I...never considered how you felt about your job. What you thought.''

''Guess you were too busy thinking that I spend all my spare time hopping from one woman's bed to another.''

''Max, I—'' She looked away. ''There's a firefighter's calendar hanging in the women's restroom around the corner from Homicide. No matter what month it is, *your* picture's the one displayed. Someone planted a big red lipstick kiss across your chest. And wrote 'Cutie Pie' in one corner of the photo. Things like that tend to give the impression that you get around.''

He hooked a finger under her chin, nudged upward, forcing her to re-meet his gaze. ''My squad did that calendar for charity, to help make the wishes of dying kids come true.'' He stroked his thumb across her bottom lip. ''I can't help it if some woman likes the look of my chest. Or thinks I'm easier on the eyes than the eleven other guys.''

''I guess not.''

He leaned in. ''The only bed I want to hop into is yours, New Year's. I meant it when I told you I'm not interested in some short fling. You need time to think about that, fine. Take it.''

"I—" She glanced across her shoulder when the oven's timer buzzed, then shifted her gaze back to his. "The pizza's ready."

"Then let's eat."

They filled their plates with pizza and salad, and settled on the stools at the counter.

"Best pizza I ever tasted," Max said after the first bite.

"Thanks. I happen to be a killer cook."

"I believe it," Max said around another bite. "Your mom teach you?"

"My dad." A crease formed between her brows as she sipped her wine. "When I was barely two, my mother decided a husband and children weren't what she wanted. She took a walk. We never saw or heard from her again."

"That had to have been rough."

"I don't remember much about her. When she left, my parents' marriage was on the rocks, so dad handled her going away okay. Cam's the one who suffered. He was six and he adored her. He couldn't understand how she could leave. Why she never came back. My dad once told me Cam cried himself to sleep every night for a year after she left."

"And now your brother makes sure he walks away from a woman first before she has a chance to walk away from him."

Jennifer used her fork to nudge a chunk of tomato around her plate. "You're perceptive, Ballard."

"That trait comes in handy, me being an investigator and all." Max reached for the wine bottle, refilled their glasses. What she'd told him about her past had given him additional insight into her, too. He figured now wasn't the time to bring that up.

Jennifer nibbled her pizza. "So, what about you?"

"What about me?"

"Tell me about your family."

"I'm a third generation smoke eater. Both my grand-dad and dad were OCFD. I fought fires until five years ago when a wall fell on me at a burn. Broke my right leg in three places. When I came back on light duty, I helped out in the fire investigation office. The work suited me, so I requested a transfer."

"Now you go after the people who start fires instead of the fires themselves."

"That sums it up."

"Does your family live here?"

"Yeah. My parents and all six kids."

The fork on which she'd speared a bite of salad halted halfway to her mouth. "*Six* kids?"

"I've got four brothers and a sister. Three of my brothers are married and have kids. Family get-togethers at my parents' house are chaos."

"I can imagine."

"You don't have to just imagine it." When he swiveled his stool toward hers, their knees bumped. He adjusted by sliding his thighs on either side of hers. "We're all having dinner this Sunday at my parents' house. Come with me."

She laid her fork aside. "That's not a good idea."

Max reached for her hand, linked his fingers with hers. "You're the first woman I've ever invited home to meet my family. Come with me."

He watched her eyes lift slowly from their joined hands to his face. "I don't know what to say to you. I never know what to say."

It was intriguing, he thought, how the tough cop could so quickly transform into a vulnerable woman.

His thumb stroked the pulse point in her wrist. "Say yes." Keeping her hand tucked in his, he traced light kisses over her jawline.

The deep, breathless moan that slid up her throat went straight to his head like a potent drug. "Say yes, Jennifer."

Her hand trembled in his. "Are you still talking about my meeting your family?"

"Everything." He covered her mouth with his, drawing the kiss out until she leaned forward and swayed against him. "I'm talking about everything," he murmured. "Say yes."

"This is a mistake. A huge one," she added, even as she fisted her hands in his hair and dragged his mouth to hers.

"No, this is right." His words were a hoarse whisper against her lips. "We're right."

He rose off the stool, drawing her up with him. "And we're about to prove it."

FOUR

A MAN HAD NEVER WANTED her like this, Jennifer thought hazily as Max tugged her up off the long-legged stool. Heat, hunger, passion and promise surged through her. She hadn't known she could want so much, need a man so desperately.

He closed a strong hand over the nape of her neck; his other hand settled at the small of her back, pressing her against him, center to center.

"We're right," he repeated, then arched her head back to expose her throat to his mouth.

Desire clawed inside her as his teeth seared her flesh. Heat pulsed from his body into hers, an unspoken assent they would give each other the turbulent thrill and dark delight that came with speed. Slow would come later. Much later.

"I want to feel you." Her voice was a raw whisper as she fought off his tie, her fingers trembling with heady desperation when she fumbled open his shirt buttons. Shoving aside the starched material, her hands explored his chest, savoring the power of sinew and muscle. When she used a fingertip to trace the swirl of coarse, dark hair that circled one nipple, she felt his heart jolt.

"Christ." He pulled back just far enough to drag the red sweater over her head, fling it aside. His eyes narrowed, heated as he used his thumbs to trace her nipples through the thin silk of her black bra. "You're beautiful." He dipped his head, slicked his tongue along the swell of her breasts over the top of the black silk. "Gorgeous."

Her breath turned ragged as hot points of pleasure erupted beneath her skin. "So are you." She caught the lobe of his ear in her teeth while tugging his shirttail out of his slacks then shoving it off his shoulders.

Hot, hungry mouths locked, they staggered together toward the living room. She wound up facing him, the back of her legs bumping into the coffee table.

The heat of the flames in the fireplace washed over her bare flesh, a heat as searing as that burning inside her. She had not known such a barbed, edgy need could exist, hadn't realized she could hunger so intensely.

"Here." As a log broke apart in a shower of sparks, her greedy hands unhooked his belt, the button of his slacks. "Right here."

"You've got a bed." His dark eyes glimmered in the fire's golden light as he speared his fingers into the hair she'd piled on top of her head. Pins pinged against the brick hearth; her hair flowed over her shoulders, covered only by thin straps of black silk. "You need a bed."

"Later." She needed only him, the fierce intimacy of his body locked with hers.

"Here, then."

When he slid his palm down over her midriff to the waist of her jeans, lust clutched deep in her center. She felt the tug of his fingers on the zipper; his hands stroked over her hips, plunging beneath the loosened material as he skimmed denim down her legs.

His eyes stayed on hers as he toed off his shoes,

stepped out of his slacks and briefs. He peeled away the swatches of silk that covered her, then dragged her down with him before the blazing fire.

The crisp weave of the rug beneath her back registered in her dazed mind as Max leaned over her. His mouth began feasting on her flesh, his greedy hands racing over her quivering body in ruthless exploration. She felt herself going warm and soft, melting into his touch, becoming one.

Her mouth nipped his neck, his chest. Her nails bit into the hard ridge of his shoulders. She couldn't get enough of him, of his taste, his touch. He seeped into her, pore by pore.

Her breath caught when his palm cupped her, molding against her with intimate possession. His fingers moved, relentlessly driving her up. Pleasure built inside her like the rush of some wonderful, erotic drug.

His lips brushed her eyelids, her throat, the sweat-glistening valley between her breasts.

The shadows around them seemed to shift while his fingers stroked. The air turned thick. Sensation slid over sensation, building inside her in trembling, shuddering layers, then exploded. Her vision grayed; a half sob tore from her lips.

Pliant as softened wax, her hands slipped from his shoulders. She lay motionless, her skin on fire, her heartbeat raging.

"We're right for each other." He knotted his fingers in her hair and drew her face to his. His eyes looked as hard as copper in the fire's glow. "Just right."

"Yes...."

His mouth plundered hers as he thrust himself into her, heat into heat.

Her body opened to his, joined with his. Arching,

she brought him deeper inside her, moved with him, matching each urgent stroke.

In the next instant, time ceased. The world stopped. There was only the ragged hiss of the fire as they plunged together into pleasure.

THE HEADY AROMA OF COFFEE nudged Max out of sleep around dawn. Instantly, he sensed where he was. The big mahogany four-poster bed wasn't his, but he knew whose it was and why he was there.

He also sensed he was the only one lying beneath the cozy blankets. A sweep of his palm across the far side of the mattress confirmed that.

When he turned his face into the pillow, he smelled Jennifer's punch-in-the-gut scent. It brought back sultry, heated images of the hours they'd spent together in front of the fireplace, then later in this bed. He lay motionless, steeped in her fragrance, remembering the feel of her, the taste.

It came as no surprise that what he wanted, craved from her was on a far different level than anything that had come before with any other woman. The instant they'd shared that New Year's Eve kiss he'd known there had never been a woman who had made him want so badly. He just hadn't known exactly what it was he wanted from her.

More had happened to him last night than passion and release. Things had clicked inside him, settled into place. Now he knew exactly what he wanted.

Sitting up, he ran a hand over his stubbled jaw. With the first weak rays of morning light coming through the windows, he saw his suit, shirt and tie draped over the wooden rocking chair angled in one corner. Sliding out of bed, he pulled on his slacks, then his shirt, which he didn't bother buttoning. Now that he knew for sure what he wanted, it was time to go after it.

He found her in the kitchen, clad in a white terry robe cinched at the waist. A tortoiseshell clip bundled up her blond hair, leaving her nape bare. She stood scanning the newspaper spread open on the counter while she sipped coffee from a thick-handled mug.

He walked to her, cupped her cheek…and felt her jaw tighten.

"Morning, New Year's."

"Good morning." Though she didn't shift away, neither did she return the touch.

He glanced down. "Anything interesting in the paper?"

"The hijacker who threatens convenience store clerks with a syringe he claims is filled with a deadly virus hit again. Third time this month."

"Bet he's giving the Robbery guys fits."

"Yes."

When the silence drew out, she reached for the coffee pot, filled a mug. She turned back, offered it to him. Max noted her hand wasn't quite as steady as the gaze she'd locked with his.

"I've been thinking about Mayor Hart," she said.

"Have you?" Max leaned against the counter. So far this morning, he had thought of no one but her.

"Yes. We need to interview him as soon as possible, try to find out why he pressured Councilman Davenport to change his vote on the land re-zoning. You and I need to talk about how we're going to handle the interview."

"Agreed." Max studied her over the rim of his mug. The vulnerability he'd seen in her blue eyes last night was gone. The woman who had melted under his touch had seemingly vanished. She'd drawn into cop mode, slipped back behind a professional barrier.

He would let her stay there until they finished talking business.

"Hart has money," she continued. "Political power and prestige. He could end up as Oklahoma's next governor."

"*If* his image stays sparkling clean," Max said. "It would have tarnished real fast if Fitzgerald had something to hold over Hart's head. Something to blackmail him with. If that's the case, it's easy to picture His Honor scurrying around, realigning votes on the rezoning so the outcome would have gone Fitzgerald's way."

Jennifer nodded. "From what we've learned, Fitzgerald put on a good show, but the charm was skin deep. He was self-absorbed, concerned with his own interests. If he did blackmail Hart into changing that vote, then found out Hart planned to run for governor, Fitzgerald might have decided to hold on to whatever it was he used to coerce Hart."

"The unidentified blackmail material that we figure was hidden in Fitzgerald's house. The incriminating something that had to burn along with him."

"The pieces are falling into place. Get enough pieces, we've got a case." Jennifer pursed her mouth. "Hart won't like our questioning him."

"That's an understatement. The minute we leave his office, he'll have both our chiefs on the phone. I doubt those will be uplifting conversations."

"I agree. So, you and I need to talk to our bosses first. Get the interview cleared up the chain of command before we hit Hart's office. That way, no one has a problem, except maybe Hart."

Max set his mug aside. He had his own problem at the moment, which was standing a few inches away, gazing at him with cool, dispassionate eyes.

He angled his chin. "You ever have a relationship before, Jennifer?"

She blinked. "I think you would have figured that out last night."

"I didn't ask if you'd been with a man before me." With his eyes on hers, he closed the distance between them, laid his palms on the counter on either side of her. Caged her in. "I asked if you'd ever had a relationship."

Her chin rose as she sat her mug on top of the morning's headlines. "Fewer than you've had, I would guess."

"By the way you're acting, I would guess you've had none."

Her eyes frosted as she slapped a palm against his chest where his shirt hung open. "Listen, pal, I have no clue where you're going with this, but you can just back off."

Quick as a snake, one of his hands came up, settled against the back of her neck. "Is this how you treat all your lovers the morning after? As if the only thing you shared during the night was hot sex and a mattress?"

A flush crept into her cheeks. "That's not how I'm treating you."

"Isn't it?"

"No." She slicked her tongue over her lips. "We're involved in a homicide investigation. The mayor—our boss—might wind up a suspect in that homicide. I thought that might be of interest to you."

"Right now, you're my primary interest. You think

after what happened between us last night I'm going to let you push me away?''

"I'm not trying to push you away."

"That's news, seeing as how you crawled out of bed and switched into cop mode."

"We have business to take care of."

"Some of which is personal." He leaned in, pressing his body against hers. "You told me your brother suffered the most when your mother walked out. That you barely remember her."

"I don't see what she has to do with—"

"Maybe you can't picture her, but you sure as hell haven't forgotten what it felt like to be abandoned. Cam gets involved on some level with a variety of women, but he makes sure he's the one who walks away first. You just won't let yourself get involved. Period. That way, there's no risk you'll get left behind again."

Her face had gone pale. Against his chest, he felt the rise and fall of her breasts. "What is it you want from me, Max?" He heard vulnerability in every word, saw it in her eyes. "What?"

"I want you to take a chance. On me. On us." He cupped her face in his hands. "Do you honestly think after what we shared I could just take a hike?"

She closed her eyes, opened them. "I don't know."

"I know you don't," he agreed quietly. "That's the problem. An understandable one, since the first thing you ever learned about relationships is that people walk away from them." His fingertips stroked her cheeks. "Jennifer, the feelings I have for you, they're new to me, too. Probably will take some getting used to. All I know is, I want a hell of a lot more with you than just a body in the night."

She pulled her bottom lip between her teeth, eyeing him as if he'd asked her to jump off a cliff.

He wrapped his arms around her waist, tugged her against him. "Look, we can take things one step at a time. I meant it when I said you're the first woman I've invited home to a family dinner. What about it? Will you go with me on Sunday?"

"I don't know."

"We're a fit, New Year's. The right fit."

She stared up at him. "I've never let myself get in too deep with any man. Never risked that. Never wanted to. I'm not sure I can."

Dipping his head, Max nibbled her jaw. "Guess it's up to me to make you sure."

FOUR HOURS LATER, Jennifer still felt remnants of unease over what had happened between her and Max that morning. He had been right, she acknowledged as she strode through City Hall's main entrance in front of him. Where her heart was concerned, she had never risked. Never allowed herself to get in too deep. Never put herself in a position where it would matter if she were left behind. Again.

Because of Max, she had looked inward for the first time to find the reasons for that behavior. She had never before equated her mother's leaving with her refusal to involve herself in anything more than a surface-skimming relationship with a man. That sudden realization had left her feeling vulnerable. Off balance.

Side by side, she and Max walked up a short flight of stairs, the heels of their shoes sounding like gunshots against the polished marble floor. Around them, a mix of city workers and citizens went about business.

Jennifer stood back while Max pressed the elevator's

call button, then shrugged out of his overcoat. He'd gone home and changed into a pale gray sweater and black slacks. His dark hair was wind-rumpled, his narrow, rawboned face a compelling mix of planes and hollows.

She eased out a breath as they stepped onto an elevator. It had been wonderful last night to escape into the passion that flared so easily between them. Passion she had tried to lock away when the night ended. Passion that Max had refused to let her deny.

She genuinely believed he wanted her, accepted that his feelings for her dipped below the surface. Yet, he didn't know—couldn't know—how long the fire that blazed between them would burn. While the flames flashed and seared, the heat was exhilarating. The dying out of those flames was something else altogether. She should know—she'd spent her life witnessing the devastation people left when a fire died to cold ash.

Sliding her badge case out of her purse, she stared down at the gold shield encased in black leather. Putting her life on the line was something she did daily without pause. Yet, the thought of risking her heart put a faint, uncomfortable tug of panic in her stomach. She wasn't sure if she could ever completely lower the barriers and let Max in.

When the door slid open, she stepped off the elevator, Max a step behind her. They rounded a corner. A wide, airy reception area opened at the end of the long, marbled hallway.

There, a mahogany, marble-topped counter rose from a sea of coral-colored carpet. Jennifer showed her badge to the vividly pretty young blonde perched behind the counter. "I'm Sergeant Weathers, this is Inspector Ballard. We need to see Mayor Hart."

The receptionist gave the badge a guarded look. "Do you have an appointment?"

"We don't need one," Jennifer stated. "We're conducting an official investigation." The powers that be at both Police and Fire had agreed that, if Hart had been involved in Spencer Fitzgerald's murder, the less notice the mayor had of her and Max's visit, the better. "It's essential we talk to your boss. Now."

"I'm…just filling in. The regular receptionist is at lunch with the mayor's secretary. All I know is, I'm not supposed to let anybody see Mayor Hart without an appointment." A hopeful look crossed the blonde's face. "Can you wait until his secretary gets back and make one?"

Jennifer turned to Max. "Inspector, how do you want to handle this unnecessary delay in our official investigation?"

Max tugged on his bottom lip, as if giving the question due consideration. "I'll leave that to you, Sergeant. After all, I only have the authority to investigate. Not arrest."

"Arrest?" the blond squeaked. "For what?"

"Interfering With Official Process," Jennifer said solemnly.

"Better known as IWOP," Max added. Giving the young woman a sympathetic grin, he leaned an arm against the counter. "Look, all this fuss isn't worth it. A friend of the mayor died, and we're checking into it. Mayor Hart asked us to keep him informed." Max shrugged. "Trust me, he wants to see us."

Minutes, later Jennifer and Max were seated in plush visitor chairs angled in front of Adam Hart's expansive wooden desk, its top looking as smooth as satin.

"Thank you for seeing us, Mayor," Jennifer said. "We know your schedule's busy."

"Yes." Hart lifted a starched cuff to check his gold designer watch. "I have to leave in a few minutes for a meeting at the Chamber of Commerce."

"We'll be brief," Jennifer said. Beside her, Max rested one ankle on the opposite knee as he leaned back in his chair. His relaxed posture purposely displayed his tacit relinquish of control to her. They had agreed before they arrived that she would take the lead in the interview.

When Hart angled his chin, the overhead lights glinted off the thick silver hair that swept back from his sharp-featured face. "Do you know who killed Spence?"

"Not yet," Jennifer stated. "We understand Mr. Fitzgerald recently stood to lose millions of dollars on a re-zoning issue."

Hart flicked a look between her and Max. "Spence purchased land on the city's fringes in the hope it would be re-zoned for commercial development. He made the investment with the full knowledge there was no guarantee that kind of development would be allowed in the area."

"It was a risk," Jennifer agreed. "Especially since the City Council was split down the middle on the issue. I'm sure Mr. Fitzgerald was relieved when you persuaded Councilman Davenport to change his vote in favor of the re-zoning."

Hart's dark eyes turned to marble. "What makes you think I did that?"

Jennifer kept her gaze locked with his while hoping to hell Cam's source in the council support office knew what she was talking about. "We know you did that, Mr. Mayor. The question is why?"

A muscle worked in Hart's jaw as he linked his long fingers in front of him on the desk. "I felt developing that land for commercial use was in the city's best interest."

"Not to mention Fitzgerald's," Max added, his voice casual. "He might have taken a huge loss if the issue hadn't turned in his favor."

Jennifer leaned forward, drawing Hart's stony gaze back to her. "Being mayor gives you power. Having some sort of hold over you would have enabled Fitzgerald to use that to his advantage. Like he did on the re-zoning issue."

A look crossed Hart's face, a quick shadow. Jennifer's spine stiffened. She recognized the look, had seen it hundreds of times over her career as a cop. Hart knew something about Spencer Fitzgerald's death.

Her heart rate skipped, then picked up speed. "The land deal worked so well for Fitzgerald, it's logical to think he wouldn't have stopped there," she continued. "After all, he was a self-centered man who put his own needs at the top of his agenda. No doubt, he would have viewed the prospect of your being elected governor as a way to further his own interests."

The shadow disappeared as Hart schooled his expression. "You're insinuating Fitzgerald blackmailed me into persuading Davenport to change his vote."

"Did Fitzgerald do that?"

"No."

"Sir, we have a witness who heard him say that Councilman Davenport would for sure change his vote. Davenport did exactly that, because you—"

"I'm a careful man, Sergeant. There is nothing in

my past or present which anyone could use to blackmail
me.''

She would find that out for herself, Jennifer thought.
''You stated you and your wife arrived for the party at
Fitzgerald's house separately. And that Mrs. Hart
stayed late to make sure the caterer left the kitchen in
good shape.''

''Yes.'' Hart pulled his fingers apart, linked them
again. ''That's correct.''

''Did you use your limo that night?''

''My driver had taken the evening off to attend a
Valentine's party at his daughter's school. I drove myself.''

''Where did you go when you left Fitzgerald's?''

''Straight home.''

''Was anyone else there?''

''No.''

Home alone, Jennifer knew, was a pretty unbreakable
alibi. ''Do you remember any neighbors being outside?
Someone who might have seen you arrive?''

''It was snowing, Sergeant. My neighbors have the
good sense to stay indoors on nights like that.''

''What time did Mrs. Hart arrive home?''

''I'm not certain.'' Hart rose, his dark eyes on Jennifer, focused and cool. ''As I said, I have a meeting
with the chamber. You'll excuse me.''

Minutes later, Max turned to Jennifer on the steps
outside City Hall. ''Guess we can say that went well,
seeing as how he didn't fire us. Yet.''

''Hart knows something about Fitzgerald's death.''
She cinched the belt of her black trench coat against
the sharp wind. ''I couldn't swear to that in court, but
I'd be willing to bet on it in Vegas.''

''Yeah, he knows something,'' Max agreed, his

mouth going grim as he gazed down at her. "Problem is, we don't have a clue what that something is. Anymore than I know what the hell kind of delayed timing devices the torch used to spark the burns that roasted Fitzgerald and his house."

Jennifer frowned as they walked toward the reserved cop slot where she'd parked her cruiser. "This doesn't feel right, Max."

"What part?"

"All parts." She paused, turned to face him. "In my mind, it works that Fitzgerald blackmailed Hart to get the vote on the land changed. When Hart decided to run for governor, something happened that told him Fitzgerald would never back off. Hart waited until the Valentine's Day to-do, slipped Fitzgerald a tranq, then burned him and whatever it was he used for blackmail."

"Yeah, all that works."

"In my mind, it does. But it feels bad."

Max angled his chin. "When something about an investigation feels bad, that usually means it is bad."

"We need to go back, re-interview everyone who attended the party. This time, we ask people if they saw Hart hand Fitzgerald a drink. If they noticed him and the mayor having a private talk. We didn't have our eye on Hart before so we didn't know to focus on his actions that night. Now we do."

Max shoved a hand through his dark hair. "We started our interviews with the guy who catered the party. Guess we'd better start with him again."

"I SWEAR, Sergeant Weathers, I just can't get over that God-given bone structure of yours."

"Thank you."

Max sat beside Jennifer at a granite-topped work island, scowling at DeWayne Venters, who held a
stemmed wine glass up toward his kitchen's bright
fluorescent lights. The guy was tall and thin with dark
hair pulled into a ponytail. He had a prominent Adam's
apple that bobbed when he talked. When Max had first
seen the caterer a few days ago, the image of Ichabod
Crane had snapped into his head.

Apparently finding no water spots, Venters began
wrapping the glass in tissue paper.

"You're just blessed," Venters continued, giving
Jennifer a smile as bright as the yellow shirt tucked into
his black leather pants. "I happen to know women who
would kill to have all that gorgeous blonde hair of
yours."

Jennifer's mouth curved as she opened her notepad.
"Thank you, Mr. Venters."

"DeWayne. After you and the inspector left the other
day, I called my friend Kevin and told him I'd met a
goddess." Clucking his tongue, Venters lifted another
glass up to the light. "I hope you don't mind my saying
you're wasting all that gorgeousness being a police officer."

Max shoved a stack of cookbooks and glossy mag-
azines out of his way. "And I hope you don't mind my
saying you're wasting our time." Venters's gushing
over Jennifer's looks hadn't gotten to him nearly as
much during their first visit to the man's home with its
kitchen refitted with massive refrigerators, triple ovens
and shining stainless steel sinks. Now that Max considered Jennifer his, the man's comments shot a burning
blast of irritation through his blood.

"Here's the deal, *DeWayne*. We need to ask you a

couple more questions about the party you catered at Spencer Fitzgerald's.''

''I believe I told you all I know the other day.'' As he spoke, Venters packed the tissue-padded glass in a box. ''I'm not sure there's anything else to add.''

''That's what we're here to find out,'' Max said. ''You told us you spent the majority of the time in the kitchen while you were at Fitzgerald's house.''

''Correct.'' Venters checked another wine glass for spots. ''I made a very delicate hollandaise sauce to go over the fresh asparagus. The fire for the sauce had to be just the right temperature throughout the cooking process. If not, the sauce would have turned. It makes me shudder to think about that happening.''

''Right.'' Max resisted the urge to roll his eyes. If the guy ever tasted some of the food the squad cooked at the fire station, he would probably drop dead.

''So, the hollandaise kept me glued to the stove for a time,'' Venters continued. ''Then, I had to shift my attention to the chocolate tartlets with frozen ice cream hearts. Mrs. Hart gave me specific instructions that dessert was to be served immediately after her husband announced his intention to run for governor. The frozen hearts had to be removed from the freezer and placed on the tartlets. They all had to be ready—and un-melted—at the same time. To pull off that little miracle, my staff and I set up an assembly line on the kitchen counter.''

Max glanced at Jennifer before asking, ''Did you see Mayor Hart at all that night?''

''Who had time?''

Max leaned in. ''I'm asking if you did.''

Venters pursed his mouth. ''Once. The kitchen door was the kind that swings in and out. I caught a glimpse of the mayor when one of my servers came through the door, carrying a tray of empty champagne flutes.''

"Did you happen to notice if Hart was talking to anyone?''

"His wife. I remember hoping she would stay out of the kitchen.''

"Why?'' Max asked.

"The woman is so detail-oriented, I'm surprised she doesn't carry around a magnifying glass. She's very demanding. And picky. If she finds a water spot on a glass or utensil, everyone hears about it.'' Venters shook his head. "I'm not really complaining, though. If Hannah Hart becomes the state's next first lady, I'm hoping she'll use me exclusively to cater social affairs. For that kind of money, I'll put up with her breathing down my neck.''

Out of the corner of his eye, Max saw Jennifer check her notepad before saying, "You verified the other day that Mrs. Hart arrived at the house early. About an hour before the party began.''

"Right.'' Venters crammed a fist at his waist. "Here's another example of what I'm talking about. She'd given me a hundred red, heart-shaped balloons with 'Hart' printed in gold script across both sides. According to her instructions, I had my staff inflate the balloons with helium, then tie half of them to the trees and bushes in the front yard. The other half were distributed throughout the house's first level.''

Max raised a brow. "What do the balloons have to do with Hannah Hart arriving early?''

"She brought more balloons! Like, did she think I wouldn't do what she had paid me to do?''

Max felt a twinge at the base of his spine. "Tell me

about the balloons she brought. Were they already in-
flated?''

"Yes. She had them in some sort of net bag so they
wouldn't float off. When she got there, she said she'd
brought a couple of extra balloons, just in case. In case
of what, I don't have a clue.''

"Where did she put those balloons?''

Furrowing his forehead, Venters closed the lid on the
box filled with tissue-wrapped glasses. "I'm not sure.
When she arrived, I was busy unpacking the silver and
china, so I didn't pay attention.''

"What about after the party was over?'' Max asked.
"You confirmed she left Fitzgerald's house the same
time you did. Did she have the net bag of balloons with
her?''

"No, just her purse. I remember that, because my
arms were loaded with the last two boxes of dishes.
Mrs. Hart wasn't carrying anything except her purse,
so she opened the kitchen door for me.''

"And followed you out?'' Max asked.

"That's right.''

"Did you see her lock the door behind her?''

"No. It had started to snow, and I was watching to
make sure I didn't step on any icy patches on my way
to the van. If I'd fallen, I might have broken all the
china and crystal in the boxes.''

Max nodded. "Did you see Mrs. Hart leave? See her
drive away?''

"I saw her get into her car, but I drove off first.''

Rising off the stool, Max met Jennifer's gaze. He
jerked his head toward the door, sending the message
they needed to talk.

She scooped up her pad. "Thank you, Mr. Venters.
We'll be in contact if we have more questions.''

Venters winked. "Calls from goddesses are always welcome."

Minutes later, Max and Jennifer climbed into her cruiser. "What's going on?" she asked.

"I'll talk while you drive," he said, snapping his seatbelt into place.

"Fine." She started the engine. "To where am I driving?"

"Your place. I need to pick up my car, then go to the lab."

"What for?"

"It's those damn balloons."

She slid him a look as she eased into the noonday traffic. "What about them?"

"That's what Hart used as a delayed timing device to spark all three fires." He shoved his hand through his hair. "Dammit, I *knew* they had balloons all over the place, but things just didn't click into place."

Jennifer shook her head. "You said arsonists make delayed timing devices out of things like egg timers and telephones. How would you make one out of a balloon?"

"Remember I told you I spent a month at Quantico at a school on serial arsonists? That I got back the day Fitzgerald fried?"

"Yes."

"At the school, arson investigators presented cases they'd worked that had unique angles. A fire cop from Texas described a case about a torch who used condoms as delayed timing devices. The guy was long gone from the scene when each fire started."

"*Condoms?*" Jennifer's foot goosed the gas pedal, making the cruiser lurch. "How do you use a condom to start a fire?"

"This torch filled a condom with water, then red phosphorous, which ignites when it comes into contact with air. He pinned the condom over a pool of gasoline. Then he put a pinhole into the bottom of the condom. The water dripped slowly out of the hole until the phosphorous was exposed. It ignited when it hit the air, then dropped down into the pool of accelerant."

"Good lord."

"Right now, it's theory." But he was right. Max could feel it. "I won't know if I'm on target until I go to the lab."

"Why? You've already got their report on the evidence you collected at the scene. Doesn't it say anything about traces of red phosphorous?"

"No. The torch only has to use a minute amount to spark the fire. Most of the phosphorous burns away. Add the water used to put out the fire, and you've got evidence that's almost totally saturated before it even gets to the lab. Then the lab adds solvents to samples in order to analyze them."

"Right. So?"

"So, remember the glass sampling tubes I used to collect some evidence from Fitzgerald's?"

"Yes."

"They can be introduced directly into an injection port of a gas chromatograph. You don't have to add solvent, so the sensitivity of the sample is enhanced anywhere from one hundred to a thousand times."

"Didn't your lab already analyze the evidence you collected in the tubes?"

"They're such new technology, they couldn't. Our lab has ordered the type of injection port that works with the tubes. It won't be here for a month. The state crime lab has one of those ports. I've already booked the tubes into evidence there. Their gas chromatograph can process each tube in minutes. I need to get them to move on it.''

"Dream on, Max. There's a six-month wait on getting results back from the state lab. What makes you think you can walk in and get instant action?''

"Because of the last name of our suspect. All it'll take is my chief making a call to the head of the state lab.''

"Suspects, plural. We're not just talking about the mayor now. Hannah brought the balloons to the scene.''

"Yeah.'' Max scrubbed a hand across his face. He'd been so focused on the balloons he hadn't thought any further. "The mayor could have doubled back and snuck into Fitzgerald's house after Venters's catering van drove off. He and Hannah could have both rigged the balloons.''

"Could have.'' Jennifer frowned. "The mayor knows we're suspicious. But he has to figure we don't have any solid evidence, or he'd be in a cell by now. He's at a meeting at the Chamber of Commerce, so he won't have had time yet to get with Hannah. I want to talk to her face-to-face before he does.'' As she talked, Jennifer switched lanes, then turned into the parking lot outside her apartment. "We know from what the Harts said the morning after the fire that Hannah's running his campaign headquarters. I'll go there now. Since you won't know for sure if your theory is fact until after the lab runs what's in those tubes, all Hannah and I will do is have a chat. That is, unless she wants to make my job easy by confessing.''

"Yeah.'' Max paused. "You be careful, okay?''

Shifting the cruiser into Park, Jennifer turned and looked at him. "I'm a cop, Max. Trained.''

He cupped his hand to her cheek. "You're also the woman I care about. A lot. I figure that gives me the right to worry about you. That okay with you?"

She hesitated, then placed her palm over his hand. "That's okay with me." Her mouth curved up at the edges. "You be careful at the lab, Ballard."

He grinned. "You've got a deal, New Year's."

FIVE

HALF AN HOUR LATER, Jennifer walked into the headquarters of the Hart for Governor Campaign. When she'd arrived there days before to pick up a copy of the guest list for Spencer Fitzgerald's Valentine's evening reception, she had been struck by how surprisingly simply the work areas were furnished. Still, the sturdy but utilitarian desks, chairs and office equipment evidenced Hannah Hart's organizational skills that her husband had boasted about.

"Help you?"

Jennifer turned in the direction of the baritone voice. Sitting behind the desk nearest the front door was a balding, bearded man who peered up at her through wire-rim glasses. Red, heart-shaped campaign flyers littered the desk, reminding Jennifer of the balloons that had been scattered throughout Fitzgerald's yard and house. Balloons used to kill him.

"I'm here to see Mrs. Hart."

"Yeah, I know." He shoved up the sleeves on his thick sweater. "We tried to call your pager to tell you an emergency came up. Mrs. Hart can't make the interview. Guess you didn't get the message?"

"You've got me confused with someone else."

"You're not the graduate journalism student?"

Jennifer pulled her badge out of her purse. "Sergeant

Weathers, OCPD. It's important I speak with Mrs. Hart.''

The man leaned back in his chair. "Sorry, Sergeant, I can't help you. She left with the mayor two hours ago."

Jennifer went still. Adam Hart had come here instead of going to the Chamber of Commerce for his meeting. "Do you know where the Harts went?"

"Nope. Usually Hannah tells someone where she's going when she leaves. She didn't this time. The mayor rushed in, went straight to Hannah's office, and a few minutes later they were both out the door like the place was on fire." The man scrubbed a hand along one side of his beard. "That journalism student is going to be disappointed. She's got some editor at a science magazine all excited about running an interview with Hannah."

"Why is a science magazine interested in Hannah Hart?"

"When she and Adam met, Hannah taught science at Casady High School."

"Science." Jennifer kept her face carefully blank as she slid a business card out of her purse. "If either of the Harts come back this afternoon, please give me a call."

"You got it."

The instant she walked out the door, Jennifer used her cell phone to dial dispatch. "I need Mayor Hart's home address." Twenty seconds later, she had it. She disconnected, and called Max.

"Ballard."

"Are you still at the lab?"

"Just finishing up here. Amazing how fast things work when one top dog calls another. The gas chromatograph results from the sampling tubes show traces of red phosphorous. That's what sparked the three separate burns at Fitzgerald's house.''

''Max, is it logical to think a former science teacher might know the red-phosphorous-in-the-balloon trick?''

''Probably. He would for sure know that red phosphorous ignites when it hits oxygen.''

''Make that she. Remember in the Harts' limo how the mayor bragged that since Hannah had spent five years teaching high school, her overseeing social functions was a snap?''

''Christ.'' Max groaned. ''She taught science, right?''

''Right.'' Jennifer unlocked the door on her cruiser, climbed in. ''We've got another problem. After we left the mayor's office, he didn't go to the Chamber of Commerce. He came to his campaign headquarters and got Hannah. They left in a big hurry. I'm going to their house in case they're there.''

''Where do they live?''

Jennifer recited the address dispatch had given her, then said, ''That's not far from where Fitzgerald lived.''

''And died,'' Max added. ''I'll leave the lab now and meet you at the Harts'.''

''See you there,'' Jennifer said, then hooked her cell phone on the belt of her black trench coat.

TEN MINUTES LATER, Jennifer turned in to the addition where huge houses sat on sprawling lawns. Even in the winter, the brick-lined flower beds and grass looked well tended. She spotted the brass numbers that marked the massive stone house where the Harts lived. The circular driveway was bordered in flagstone, and empty of cars.

Jennifer parked at the curb and climbed out. On the sidewalk across the street from the Harts' house stood a silver-haired woman wearing mink earmuffs, a matching ankle-length mink coat and pink leather tennis shoes. She had one gloved hand wrapped around a gold leash attached to the collar worn by a creaky-looking white poodle sporting a red sweater and matching hair bow. Both woman and dog stood motionless, staring at the Harts' house.

With the icy wind capable of snapping bones, Jennifer knew no one would stand around staring at a house without good reason. Flipping open her badge case, she approached the woman.

"Ma'am, I'm Sergeant Weathers. Is something wrong?"

The woman glanced at Jennifer's badge, then pursed her mouth. "Well, I don't know. Less than five minutes ago, Adam stalked out of the front door, climbed into his own car and sped out of the driveway like a bat out of hell. That's not like him. He's always so controlled."

"Was his wife with him, Mrs....?"

"Lang. Clarissa Lang." She stabbed a gloved finger across one of her shoulders. "I live there."

The house had a perfect view of the Harts', Jennifer noted, taking in the stately brick structure. Windows dotted its facade, all with their drapes drawn back. She suspected Mrs. Lang was the neighborhood snoop.

"Only Adam left," the woman answered. "Hannah's in the house—I saw her get out of the limo with Adam two hours ago. They both looked upset. The limo drove off, and Adam started yelling before they'd even gotten to the front door."

"Did you hear what he said?"

"No, I was indoors." The woman glanced down at the poodle, shivering despite its red sweater. "Spice wanted to come outside for a stroll. We were standing here, trying to decide if we should go see if Hannah needs anything.''

Jennifer clenched her fingers, unclenched them. It was possible the Harts had conspired to murder Spencer Fitzgerald. Adam Hart had missed a meeting to go drag his wife out of his own campaign headquarters. Jennifer had worked homicides where more than one suspect had done the deed. Suspects sometimes argued. In a few cases, they killed each other, thinking they could save their own skin.

She looked back at Mrs. Lang. ''Do you know if the Harts' housekeeper is there?''

''No, it's Yolanda's day off.''

''I'll check on Mrs. Hart,'' Jennifer said. ''And I'll let her know you're concerned.''

Jennifer knew she couldn't wait for Max to arrive. Not when the smallest possibility existed that Hart had injured his wife.

Unbuttoning her coat for access to her Glock, Jennifer walked up the Harts' circular drive, then used the side steps leading onto the wide porch lined by windows. She glanced through the first window she reached, noting a dining room filled with dark, rich furniture. Behind another window was a formal living room where a shiny black baby grand piano dominated one corner.

She came abreast of the next window, and froze. In what appeared to be a study, Hannah Hart stood beside an expansive wooden desk. On the section of the desk Jennifer could see sat a bottle of Scotch and a tumbler filled to the brim. Her hands trembling, Hannah opened a gold case and dumped a mound of blue pills into one palm.

Suicide!

Jennifer dashed to the front door. She jabbed at the

doorbell at the same time she tried the knob. When it turned in her hand, she shoved the door open. Her rushing footsteps echoed against the marbled-floored foyer as she raced toward the room's arched entrance.

If Hannah was aware of Jennifer's presence, she gave no sign. She remained beside the desk, standing in profile to the study's entrance while she stared into space. With her deathly pale face tear-streaked and her dark hair disheveled, she barely resembled the sleek, stylish woman Jennifer had met the previous week.

Dropping her gaze, Jennifer saw that the hand Hannah had held the blue pills in now hung limply at her side. Her other hand was crammed into the pocket on the jacket of her turquoise pantsuit. The tumbler of Scotch sitting on the desk was now half empty. Hanna's body shook as if she were standing in an icy gale.

Jennifer took a step into the room. "Mrs. Hart?"

Hannah slowly turned her head. "He called you," she said dully. "I know Adam called you. He'll never forgive me. How could I even ask him to?"

"Mrs. Hart…Hannah, how many pills did you take?"

"Leave me alone."

"What kind of pills are they?" As she spoke, Jennifer took cautious steps into the spacious study lined with floor-to-ceiling bookcases. "Whatever made you take the pills, we'll work it out." Her hand went to the cell phone clipped to her coat's belt. "I'm going to make a call and get you help."

"No!" Hannah jerked her hand from her pocket. "This ends now. It has to end!"

Jennifer's mind went cold, analytical as she stared into the dark barrel of the nickel-plated .22 automatic clenched in Hannah's hand. Moving her right index finger, Jennifer pressed the cell phone's redial button. She waited long enough for Max to answer, then said, ''Hannah, put the gun down.''

''All of them!'' Hannah's arm jabbed forward, aiming the automatic at Jennifer's heart. ''I took all the pills. In case they don't work, I'm going to shoot myself. What I've done is unforgivable. I can't bear it any longer.''

''No matter what you and your husband have done, it's not worth killing yourself.'' Jennifer felt the weight of her Glock holstered at her waist. She could draw her weapon in seconds, but it wouldn't be faster than an aimed .22. All she could hope for was that Max was listening on his cell phone.

''Adam…hates me now.'' Hannah pressed her lips together as tears streamed down her face. ''He hasn't done anything. It was me. All me. He had no idea why I came to him about that vote until this morning when you saw him. No idea I'd been unfaithful. That I'd….''

''You had an affair with Spencer Fitzgerald?'' Jennifer guessed quietly. She was close enough that if she could divert the woman's attention, she could lunge and disarm her.

''Yes.'' Keeping her eyes on Jennifer's, Hannah reached for the half-filled tumbler, drained its contents. The empty glass slid from her hand, shattered against the thick oak floor. ''Adam is a good man. He cares for me, but…his work. That's his life. Politics comes first. Always. I needed….'' She shook her head. ''I met Spence at a museum fund-raiser. He was so witty and attentive. For the first time in years, I felt desirable. Needed.''

Jennifer's gaze darted around the richly furnished study, looking for something—anything—to use to divert the woman's attention. She saw nothing nearby.

''It was more than just an affair,'' Hannah continued.

"To me. I fell in love." She shoved a hand through her dark hair but kept the gun steady. "I thought Spence loved me. He said he loved me. Then he showed me the pictures. He was a photographer, he had cameras hidden in a secret room off his bedroom. He took pictures of us in bed, then edited them so only my face showed. He threatened to send them to Adam unless I influenced him to change the vote. Spence swore if I did that he would give me the pictures, the negatives."

Even as her pulse hammered, Jennifer's mind analyzed the new data. "You went to your husband and talked him into applying pressure to get the vote changed on the land re-zoning. Did he think it odd you had a sudden interest in a land issue?"

"No. I'm on boards. Belong to various groups. People ask me to promote their cause to Adam."

Jennifer now understood why she'd glimpsed the shadowy realization in the mayor's face. He hadn't known until this morning that Fitzgerald had sent Hannah to get the vote changed. With Jennifer bringing up the prospect of blackmail, the mayor had reached the logical conclusion that Fitzgerald had some hold over Hannah. Hart had left his office and confronted his wife.

"I...." Blinking, Hannah shook her head as if to clear it. Her dark eyes were huge now, the pupils pinpricks. The Scotch, along with whatever drug she'd taken, was slowly taking hold. She was breathing fast, yet she kept the gun aimed.

Jennifer swallowed hard. The automatic had been freshly oiled; she could smell it. "I take it Fitzgerald changed his mind about giving you the photos?" *Where was Max? Why hadn't he gotten there? What if the call hadn't gone through?*

"Yes. When he heard Adam intended to run for governor, Spence decided to keep the photos. He said he might need Adam's help again some day.'' Tears slid down her cheeks. The gun made a small arc. ''Spence was so awful, so hideously polite while he told me what he'd do if I didn't cooperate. He betrayed me. I couldn't stand knowing he might go to Adam, tell him what I'd done. Show him.''

''Tell me about the fire, Hannah.''

''Spence called and offered to host the party for Adam's campaign. I knew Spence meant that as proof to me he wouldn't back off. He kept the photos in that damn hidden room. I didn't know where it was, how to get in. I offered to plan the party so I could be at the house after everyone was gone.''

''To start the fire.''

''He left me no choice!'' She pressed a hand over her mouth to hold back a sob. ''I've lost everything. I just…want to die.''

Her gun hand wavered, but not enough for Jennifer to take a chance.

Out of the corner of her eye, she caught movement at the window off the front porch. Grim-faced, Max stood at an angle where only she could see him. He held up his cell phone to signal he'd heard the conversation. He raised his other hand. He had his fingers curled around a red brick from one of the Harts' pristine flower beds.

Her stomach churning, Jennifer squared her shoulders. Max intended to provide the diversion she needed.

Forcing herself to look into Hannah's face, Jennifer felt the automatic's presence without gazing into its barrel's dark eye. Her pulse hammered in her ears.

It happened fast. Glass shattered. The brick smashed onto a table. Hannah whirled, swinging the weapon toward the window.

Jennifer sprang, clamped her hand on Hannah's wrist while using the force of her body to drive her down onto the glass-littered floor. In one twisting motion, Jennifer wrenched the .22 free.

"HANNAH HART DOESN'T LOOK so classy under guard in a hospital room," Max said that night as he lay in Jennifer's bed.

"Getting charged with murder, then having your stomach pumped all in the same day has that effect."

"Good point." He slid his hand down Jennifer's bare back, savoring the sensation.

It felt right having her sprawled half on top of him, her head settled on his shoulder, one shapely leg tossed over his own. Resting on his chest was her bandaged palm from which an ER doctor had removed the inch-long shard that had embedded there when she toppled Hannah to the study's glass-strewn floor.

"I imagine the Harts' attorney has already talked to the D.A. about a temporary insanity plea," Jennifer observed.

"You think that will fly?"

"She's got the best defense team money can buy. I can already hear them claiming that, for Hannah, Fitzgerald's betrayal was a flammable fuel that drove her over the edge."

"You're probably right." Max glanced around the bedroom where candles flickered, their flames casting dancing shadows against the wall. Fire, he thought, had been the thing that had finally brought Jennifer and himself together. Tonight, they had made love while the room shimmered in candlelight.

She snuggled against him, soft and warm. "We were sure off when we thought Adam Hart killed Fitzgerald."

"We got it figured out." Max closed his eyes. *Almost too late.* Even now it jolted him, the image of Jennifer being held at gunpoint. "New Year's, I need to tell you something."

"What?"

Nudging her onto her back, he propped up on one elbow so he could gaze down into her face. Candlelight tinted her skin gold. "When my cell phone rang and I heard you tell Hannah to put down the gun, I was afraid. Scared to death. I thought she would kill you before I could get there."

"I was afraid, too." Using her uninjured hand, Jennifer cupped her palm to his cheek. "Calling you was all I could think to do."

"That was a brilliant idea, Sergeant."

Her mouth curved. "Think so, Inspector?"

"I do."

Her brow furrowed as she looked up at him. "You know how people say they get into a certain situation and they see their life flash by?"

"Yeah, I know." His own life had suddenly passed before his eyes at the thought of losing her.

"I felt that way today, Max. Standing there, knowing Hannah might squeeze the trigger, I saw my life flash by."

He stroked her hair that spread like warm sunshine across the pillow. "Was it a good or bad flash?"

"An eye-opening one. I saw how one-sided my life has been. All I've ever focused on is work. On being a cop. That's all I have. All I ever let myself have."

Her hand moved from his cheek to his chest. "I hadn't realized my mother's walking out had done that to me. You were right this morning, Max. I've never risked my heart. My life, yes, but never my heart. After we kissed

New Year's Eve, I think I avoided you because I knew deep inside you could make me step back from who I always thought Jennifer Weathers was. You could make me go purely with emotion, when just the thought of doing that petrified me.''

"I was pretty unsettled myself that night. For the first time in my life, a kiss grabbed me by the throat and wouldn't let go. I didn't know what to think. All I knew was I wasn't going to let you get away." Sliding his hand beneath the sheet, he settled his palm at the curve of her hip. "So, now that we both know we scared the hell out of each other that night, what do you think we should do about it?"

"I want to see if you're right."

"About what?"

"That we're a fit."

Grinning, he dipped his head, brushed his mouth against hers. "We're a fit all right, New Year's. The perfect fit."

ST. VALENTINE'S DIAMOND

by Jonathan Harrington

For my Valentine

Wren

and in loving memory of
Delores A. Arundell
1945–2001

ONE

"DON'T BUY BLOODY DIAMONDS! Don't buy bloody diamonds!"

As I climb out of the subway at Sixth Avenue and 47th Street, I push my way through a knot of protesters picketing in the street. Their placards read: *Diamonds Fund Wars!* And they chant in unison, "Don't buy bloody diamonds."

It's snowing and the streets and sidewalks are frosted with white. The air is cold and damp. I hunch my shoulders against the swirling flurries and push my way through the crowd of demonstrators. The storm began about two o'clock this afternoon during my last period class and snow has fallen steadily since then. The ground sparkles with crystals of new-fallen flakes. It's February 13. Darkness has settled over Manhattan and the snow is not actually falling—it's rising—swirling upward on drafts of air. I know the thirteenth is supposed to be an unlucky day, but today is also the day before Valentine's Day. A blue banner hanging beneath a streetlight reads: *Welcome to the Diamond District.*

"Want to sell?" a guy asks as he gets in step beside me. He sticks a yellow flyer in my hand: *Loans! High Immediate Cash Against Your Collateralized Diamonds.*

"No thanks."

Groups of Hasidic men stand in the street talking. As

I walk east on 47th Street, the snow crunching underfoot,
I have an odd feeling I'm being followed. I glance back
at two men walking behind me, their long black coats
pulled tightly across their chests against the wind. They
wear black felt hats, ankle-length black overcoats and
cloth belts looped around their waists with frayed ends
dangling. Long salt-and-pepper beards hang over their
chests, and the hair on the sides of their heads is twisted
into *peyas* or sidecurls that dangle down over their ears.
Both of them are talking into cell phones clapped to the
sides of their heads as they stride briskly through the
blowing snow.

47th Street between Fifth and Sixth avenues in Manhattan is the heart of New York's diamond industry.
There are signs in English, Hebrew, Chinese and Ko-
rean. I hear at least as many languages from the
thousands of passersby. Despite the snow, the sidewalks
are shoulder-to-shoulder with shoppers. The storefronts
have put out their best Valentine's Day displays: diamond engagement rings, diamond solitaire necklaces, di-
amond-stud earrings, diamond tennis bracelets, diamonds in every shape and color imaginable. The smell
of hot dogs emanates from a pushcart selling Kosher
franks parked in the street in front of Kaplan Diamond
Center where dozens of shoppers press their noses to the
glass with signs proclaiming: *We Buy Diamonds! Diamond City!*

Some of the shops have already removed their displays from the windows to guard against smash-and-grab
thieves. There's something eerie about the mannequin
necks and fingers stripped of their jewels. But the dealers
inside still do a brisk business. The only shop I pass not
related to diamonds is the Gotham Book Mart.

I'm on my way to see Moishe Finkelstein, an old

friend of my late father's. Before his death in 1995, Dad owned the O'Flaherty Funeral Parlor. I grew up in a two-bedroom apartment over the funeral parlor in the Inwood section of Manhattan. I still live in the same apartment. As much as Dad wanted me to become a mortician, I became a teacher instead. I'm forty-five years old and am not married…yet. For now, I'm your classic Irish bachelor. I'm hoping to change that soon. Maybe by tomorrow—Valentine's Day.

I pass the Plaza Arcade, an alleyway with booths of diamond dealers on both sides. Three Brinks armored trucks idle in the street out front. Two more armored trucks, Dunbar and Ferrari Express, are parked in front of a heavy metal door leading to an alley marked "Freight."

I pause to look into the window of the Diamond Exchange, which has microscopes set out on glass tables inside the store for examining gemstones. I'm going to Moishe Finkelstein's shop to purchase a Valentine's Day gift. Last year, just after St. Patrick's Day, I presented my girlfriend, Fidelma Muldoon, with a diamond engagement ring and asked her to marry me. Not one to rush into a decision like that, Fidelma told me she'd have to sleep on it and give me an answer in the morning. That was almost a year ago and she hasn't given me an answer yet. So I've decided that tomorrow—Valentine's Day—is a good time to present her with something special and pop the question all over again. I've never been good at Valentine's Day. Last year I sent a singing telegram and there was a mix-up taking the order. When Fidelma opened her door she was greeted by a female stripper holding a bouquet of heart-shaped balloons. This year I'm determined to get it right.

I've worked hard all week, sometimes well past

school hours. I'm trying to develop a special section on the Famine for the Irish History curriculum at John F. Kennedy High School in the Bronx where I teach history and social studies. New York State recently passed a law requiring that a section on the Great Famine—*An Gorta Mor*—be taught in public schools. I finally left school about 7 p.m. I'm tired, and wired at the same time. What my mother used to call overtired when I was a kid. I almost feel like bawling.

Although Moishe's shop is not actually a retail outlet, he has been in the business for three generations and gave me a good deal on the engagement ring last year. Moishe is a wholesaler. He buys loose diamonds and sells them to jewelers. In some cases he sells finished jewelry.

Moishe's new office sits between a pawnbroker's on the left—*Immediate Cash Loans!*—and Berger's Deli on the right. A black Lincoln Town Car with diplomatic plates is double-parked in front of the building. There are more protesters picketing at this end of the street. Their placards read: *Don't Buy Bloody Diamonds!*

"Conflict diamonds" have gotten a lot of press lately. Since some revolutionary groups in Africa use diamonds from mines they have captured to buy weapons, these protesters believe that consumers who buy jewelry are helping fund wars. I'm sympathetic, but only a small portion of all stones are in any way tainted by war. Since it is virtually impossible to track the source of gems, it seems misguided to hurt the legitimate dealers by boycotting *all* diamonds. But still, the protesters have a point.

I sign in at the guard's desk, and glance over the list of those who have come in before me. A surveillance camera overhead follows my every move as I push the button for the fourth floor. In the elevator, I brush the snow off my jacket, remove my Donegal tweed cap, slap it against my leg to dislodge the snow, and examine myself in the mirror. There is a bit more salt than pepper in my curly hair than there was last year. Fifteen years of teaching high school in the inner-city has added a few extra wrinkles around my brown eyes.

The elevator stops at the fourth floor. I step out, smile up at the surveillance camera as I enter the hallway. I find the sign that reads: *Moishe Finkelstein* and under that another sign: *Protected by Alarm System*.

When I push the buzzer, the receptionist inside says through the speaker: "May I help you?"

I look up at yet another security camera and know she is watching on closed-circuit TV as she talks to me. "My name is Danny O'Flaherty. I'm here to see Mr. Finkelstein."

She buzzes me in through one set of doors and then another door with a *mezuzah* on it. When I enter the waiting room of the office, I see three other people who signed in ahead of me.

A tall black man in flowing white robes sits on a worn sofa in a corner of the room under a portrait of the late Rabbi Menachem Schneerson. The black gentleman wears a white turban wound around his head and he has a regal bearing. I'm thinking maybe he owns the Town Car out front with the diplomatic plates.

On a chair across the room sits a middle-aged man in snakeskin cowboy boots, a bolo string tie with a jade clasp, a black Stetson and the sunburned face of a man who has spent his life outdoors.

A finely groomed woman paces the floor, glancing impatiently at a diamond-studded watch on her wrist. She is tall, elegant, with an expensive hairdo, fresh make-up and a string of pearls around her creamy-white neck. She stops in front of the cowboy and says, "I can't wait any longer. I have a show tonight."

"Zat right?" asks the cowboy in his down-home accent. "Should I know who you are?"

"Yes, that is right," she enunciates as if giving him elocution lessons. "And yes, you *should* know who I am. I'm Isabel Quick. I cover the role of Trixie in the Broadway production of *Kittens*. Starting tonight I'm on for sixteen straight shows in the main role while the lead—" she rolls her eyes "—Sabrina Von Dam, takes a sick leave."

"What's wrong with Miss Von Dam?" the cowboy asks.

"Well, I've heard Sabrina's so-called sick leave," she says cattily, "includes a face lift at some upscale plastic surgery camp on the West Coast."

"Mr. O'Flaherty," the receptionist greets me in what I guess is a South Asian accent. India, most likely. "How nice to see you again."

"Nice to see you, too." She's an attractive woman. Slender, with long black hair tied in back to show off her full red lips, mocha-colored eyes and fine delicate features. Her fingernails are the color of blood. I remember her from my last visit here, but can't recall her name. "Will I have to wait long?"

"No, he's expecting you. Go right in."

"Thanks… Sorry, I've forgotten your name."

"Priti Patel."

Of course. How could I forget a name like that? "Thanks, Priti." She *is* pretty.

I'm a little surprised that I'm allowed to go in while three others are waiting, but I certainly don't argue, and Priti buzzes me through another door. As I leave the reception area, I hear the actress with the wristwatch say, "I've been waiting half an hour."

The man in robes asks: "I wonder why he is being given preferential treatment?"

"What's so special about him?" asks the guy in the cowboy hat.

As I enter the back room, Moishe Finkelstein is bent over a white Formica-topped table lit by a fluorescent lamp. He has a loupe in his hand and is sorting diamonds. He stands up with a smile on his face and a loose diamond held aloft with a pair of silver tweezers. He is a youthful seventy years old with a neatly trimmed mustache, short graying hair, a dazzlingly white long-sleeved shirt with diamond cufflinks, a diamond stickpin in his blue tie and a *yarmulke* on his head. "Danny, where have you been hiding? You're as bad as my kids. You never come to see me anymore. Nice to see you."

"It's good to see you, too, Mr. Finkelstein."

Moishe puts down the diamond, takes a folded sheet of cellophane from his coat pocket, opens it and takes another stone out with the tweezers. "Look at this," he says offering me the diamond along with a loupe. I hold the gem in one hand and the loupe in the other. I'm not sure what I'm looking at, but the diamond sparkles like a million stars.

"Five carats," says Moishe. "Beautiful piece of work. Excellent quality, well cut, no inclusions. You don't find a diamond like this every day."

"What's an inclusion?" I ask. Moishe loves talking about the diamond business. I've often wanted to ask him to talk to one of my classes.

"What's an inclusion he wants to know. An inclusion is a flaw inside the stone. Sometimes it's a carbon spot or a seed garnet."

"How much is this diamond worth?"

"About thirty thousand dollars."

"A bit outside the budget of a high school teacher," I say, handing it back.

Moishe smiles, puts the diamond back in the cellophane and tosses the package onto a table behind him.

One of the surprising things about diamond dealers is the nonchalant way they handle these very expensive stones.

"What do you think of these protesters outside?" I ask him.

"Protesters? Oh, those. Yes. I'm as concerned as they are," Moishe answers as he takes a handkerchief out of his shirt pocket and polishes his loupe. "In fact, the whole diamond industry is doing everything we can to solve the problem. But only four percent of the world's diamond production is in any way involved with conflict diamonds. Shouting in the street is a solution? I don't think so. Industry regulation is the solution."

Moishe is a member of the elite Diamond Dealers Club on 47th Street and, of course, it doesn't surprise me that he rushes to the defense of the industry. The DDC was formed in 1931 as a central, secure place for trading diamonds. Because of security, few outsiders are allowed in.

"What *is* the industry doing?"

"What's the industry doing, he asks? Certification, that's what the industry is doing. Laser branding. The problem is being able to certify the source of any given diamond. No easy thing. Needle in a haystack. But some companies are already tackling the problem. They imprint a tiny brand, invisible to the naked eye, on all stones coming from their mines."

"I see. So, a dealer can be sure that the diamond is not associated with conflict diamonds."

"Yes and no. Even that's not foolproof. Brands can be forged. I agree with the protesters, but it's an industry problem. Let me tell you something, Danny. I don't know if I ever showed you this." Moishe removes a cufflink and pushes the sleeve up on his right arm. A number is tattooed above the wrist. "I was at Treblinka."

"Yes, the concentration camp. I know. Dad told me."

"I'm afraid so, Danny. My father and mother died there. Believe me, I know what these poor people in Africa are going through. I would never sell a single diamond if I knew it was acquired at the expense of an innocent person's life. Now," he says a bit impatiently, pulling down his sleeve and fastening the cufflink again, "I know you didn't come here to talk about dirty diamonds. What's on your mind, Danny Boy?"

"I'm here to buy a Valentine's Day gift for my girl-friend."

"Oh, yes. How did she like the engagement ring?" he asks. "That was a nice one, and you got a good price on it. Good price. Truth is, you stole it from me."

"She seemed to like it."

"When's the date for the wedding?"

"Well, uh, we're not sure yet...exactly."

"Oh." Moishe seems surprised. He looks at me curiously. "Why not...exactly?"

"She didn't actually say she'd marry me yet." I push my glasses up off my nose. "Said she needed time to decide."

Moishe sits down wearily behind the Formica table and sighs. "What's that about? Time to decide? What's taking her so long? She should be throwing herself into your arms.''

"She needed to think.''

"Think *schmink*. Should I do this…should I do that?'' Moishe clucks. "Danny, Danny, Danny. What's the matter with you? Does she love you?''

He doesn't give me time to answer.

"Do you love her? What's so hard to understand? Two people who love each other get married. That's the way the world works. It takes an Einstein to figure this out?''

"So I thought I'd give her something special for Valentine's Day. See if that might prod her toward a decision.''

"Now you're talking. You said she loves you. Let me tell you, she's not thinking. She's making you *think* she's thinking. She wants to see what you're going to put on the table.''

"Well, I don't believe Fidelma is really like that.''

"Get out of here…he doesn't believe Fiona is like that, he tells me.''

"It's Fidelma.''

"Fidelma, Fiona, Falulu…forget about it. She wants to know you care. Let me tell you, kid, there's only one thing you need to know about making a woman pay attention to you. Are you listening?''

"I'm listening.''

"I'm only going to say it once.'' Moishe pauses dramatically.

"I'm listening, I'm listening.''

"You have to make her know you really care.'' Moishe shrugs. "And diamonds are a nice way to show her.''

Moishe truly loves the diamond business and like my

own dad, was disappointed when his son, Abe, didn't follow in his father's footsteps. Like me, Abe became a high school teacher.

Moishe invites me to sit down at the white table. "Now," he says. "You want this girl to set the date by tomorrow? No problem. And naturally you want to keep your costs down. Let me show you something."

He stands up, disappears for a moment, then returns with a cloth case that he sets on the table. He snaps off the Velcro flap and opens the four overlapping sides. Inside are four pockets, each containing a chain with a single diamond.

He lets the loupe he is gripping between his eyelids fall to the cloth case and examines me for a moment. "Give her one of these for Valentine's Day and she'll be saying 'I do' before you ever get to the altar."

I pick up one of the necklaces and examine it with the loupe. It's a diamond solitaire. A single diamond on a gold chain. "How much for this one?"

"Retail, about a thousand."

"Ouch." I drop it like a hot frying pan.

"But that's negotiable," he adds hastily, putting it back in my hand. "Besides, what's money at a time like this? Danny, I'm surprised at you."

"Have you seen what they're paying schoolteachers in this city?"

"Have I seen? Have I seen, he asks me. You bet I've seen. That's why I tell my son Abe I can set him up in business and he can make twenty times what he's making baby-sitting a bunch of delinquents. But does he listen to his father? Oh, no, not Abe. He's out to save the world. Well, let me tell you how you save the world. You save the world by starting with your own family.

Save them first, and you can get to the rest of the world later in the day.''

We banter back and forth over the price of the necklace for a good fifteen minutes. I can tell that the money means nothing to Moishe. He simply enjoys bargaining. Finally, he agrees to sell it to me for four hundred dollars.

"I don't know how you can do this to me, Danny. Your father and I were good friends and you come in and practically shoplift this diamond you're getting it so cheap.''

"Well, I appreciate…''

"Appreciate nothing. I'm taking a bath on this one,'' he says. "I don't know how I'm supposed to pay the rent on this place if I keep giving away jewelry to every guy off the street who can't get his girl to say 'yes.'''

"Thanks a lot, Mr. Finkelstein.''

"Take your diamond and get out of here.''

I pay him in cash and we shake hands.

"Mazal U'Bracha," he says, the traditional way of sealing deals in the diamond industry. He's smiling and there's a twinkle in his eyes. "With luck and blessings.''

Back in the waiting room, the receptionist, Priti, brings out a plate of heart-shaped cookies with red frosting and plastic glasses of red punch that she passes among the waiting clients.

"Valentine's Day cookie, Mr. O'Flaherty?'' she offers.

"No, thanks.'' I'm thinking Valentine's Day is no Jewish holiday.

"Oh, come on,'' she insists and pushes one of the cookies toward me with a red fingernail. "Macadamia nut.''

I take the cookie, put it in my mouth and bite into a

nut that nearly cracks my tooth. But I smile pleasantly and wash it down with a cup of punch.

Back on the street, the snow is still falling. I make my way to the subway station on 50th Street. Just at the entrance to the 1-Train, I turn around and realize a tough-looking kid in a hooded sweater has been following me. I'm paranoid about carrying a thousand-dollar diamond necklace in my coat pocket, so I pick up the pace and hurry toward the station. Still, with all the diamonds here, I can't imagine why *I'm* being followed. As I scramble down the stairs of the subway station I see the tough kid coming down the opposite set of stairs. I fumble in my coat pocket for my Metro card, and sweep it through the turnstile just as the train enters the station.

As I get aboard, I see the young tough vault over the turnstile, but the door of the train closes before he gets on.

To my surprise, when I get out at 207th Street, the kid follows me as I walk toward my apartment. I thought he had missed the train, but apparently not. My hand is sweaty as I clutch the necklace in my jacket pocket and hustle toward my building. He closes in as I approach the door.

"Hey, you!" he shouts as I get the key into the front door with shaky hands. "Hey, you!" he shouts again, bounding up the outside stairs of the building just as I slip into the lobby and slam the door behind me, my heart racing. I just have time to grab my mail.

TWO

UPSTAIRS, AS I OPEN the third lock on the door to my apartment, I hear someone talking inside. "What the hell?" I mutter, throwing open the door.

"...so, I'll see you tonight."

The message machine. I lunge for the phone...

"I'm waiting!"

...just as Fidelma hangs up.

"Hello," I shout into the phone, too late.

I throw the mail I picked up downstairs in the lobby on the kitchen table, and push the rewind on the message machine and play back my messages.

My cat, Barnabus, arches his back and rubs his rib-cage against my shins, glad to see me, then skitters away, nervous about something. I see that Fidelma has fed Barnabus because his bowl is half-filled and the bag of cat food was left out. Fidelma was coming over today to give Barny his medicine. My cat has been taking pills three times a day in his food all week. I've given it to him in the morning and at night and Fidelma has come over every day this week to give it to him in the afternoon while I'm at school. She lives across from Van Cortland Park where she shares a two-bedroom apartment with a guy she swears is gay. Although I've never actually met Morris Greg, I have my doubts about his true sexual orientation. Yes, I'm jealous, and Fidelma knows it.

In the living room the light is on. I also notice one of the dining room chairs is tipped over and I pick it up. I don't remember leaving the light on this morning—maybe Fidelma did.

I live on 207th in Manhattan—Inwood, which used to be the heart of Irish New York. Today, it is a mixed area of Irish and Dominicans. I open the blinds. Outside, the darkened streets still buzz with pedestrians despite the snowstorm, but I don't see the tough kid who followed me home. Most of the Irish moved to Bainbridge Avenue, or Yonkers, or Woodside, Queens, years ago. The handful of Irish left in my neighborhood are mostly elderly or, like me, younger Irish-Americans who moved into their immigrant parents' rent-controlled apartments.

"This is a message for Danny O'Flaherty…" Another salesperson trying to sign me up for a new kind of telephone service. I push the button and skip his call.

"Danny, this is Aunt Bertie. You must be working. Give me a call and we'll do lunch."

Do lunch? Is Aunt Bertie talking like that now?

It's almost 9 p.m. and I haven't called Fidelma. We made no definite plans for tonight, but I said I'd get in touch as soon as I got home and we'd go out. Buying the necklace took longer than I thought it would and the train was delayed getting back uptown.

"Hi, Danny. It's me." Another message from Fidelma. "Are you still not home? I guess you're working late again, as usual. Anyway, I've got some good news. I've gotten tickets for *Kittens* tonight. They'll hold yours at the box office. See you at the show."

I glance at my watch. *Kittens?* Didn't the actress in Mr. Finkelstein's shop say she was in that show? It is now after nine o'clock. Fidelma's going to be furious. I can't tell her I'm late getting home because I was out buying her a diamond necklace. It's supposed to be a surprise.

I sort through the mail: Con Ed, NYNEX, Verizon. As the message machine continues playing its litany of sales calls, a peculiar smell draws me to the refrigerator, afraid of the science projects I am likely to find. It looks like a typical bachelor's fridge. There isn't much: a couple of pieces of dried-up pita bread and an empty bottle of *salsa picante* that I pitch into the garbage. In short, not a thing to eat. One lousy bottle of Harp that I open and pour into a glass. I kick off my shoes and fumble with the cords of my laptop, boot it up and set it on the kitchen table. I take out a stack of folders containing my research on the Irish Famine and start plucking out facts to craft into a multiple choice exam:

The Irish Famine was caused by:
a) excessive rain
b) failure of the wheat crop
c) a fungus that infected the potato crop
d) the English

The correct answer is c). The collapse of the potato crop in Ireland as a result of a fungus during the summer of 1845 led to the deaths of over one million people between 1845 and 1854. At least another two million emigrated. Some fifteen percent of those died en route. Many of the Irish Catholics in America are descendants of famine survivors. But not my grandparents. They were much more recent immigrants from County Clare and County Mayo.

I might give partial credit for d) the English. In fact,

the English had a surplus of wheat in storage throughout Ireland and could have prevented the starvation of millions. But they held back the surplus food in order to keep the price of wheat from collapsing. Nice folks.

The funny smell makes my nose twitch again, and I wonder if maybe I left something in the oven before I went to school this morning. I get up and look, but don't find anything except a layer of gunk I need to scrub out.

I check my e-mail messages, then go offline to free up the phone line and almost immediately the telephone rings.

"Hello?"

"So you finally made it back."

It's Fidelma. "Yeah, I'm beat."

"And you didn't call me?"

"I just walked in."

"Well, your phone's been busy."

"I was checking e-mail."

Fidelma doesn't answer and I guess she is pissed. Finally, she says, "I'm calling from the lobby of the theater. It's already intermission. You missed the show."

"I know. I'm sorry."

I cradle the cordless phone between my shoulder and chin, pick up the stack of folders containing my research, place them beside my laptop and boot up Windows 2000. I also take the necklace from my pocket and lay it on the table in front of me. "Fidelma, I have something very important to talk to you about tomorrow."

"Why tomorrow?" she asks. "Where were you tonight?"

"I had an important errand to run after school."

"Oh, did you? How important was it? You know, Danny, you never seem to be around for the *important* moments in my life. Where were you, anyway?"

"I can't tell you."

"Why not?"

"I just can't."

"My roommate says…"

"What are you talking about? And can we put a lid on the roommate stuff?" Although I've never actually met this Morris Greg, everything about him rubs me the wrong way—primarily because *Fidelma* has nothing but good things to say about him. "What does that jerk know about me, anyway?"

"Apparently, much more than you know about yourself."

I fiddle with the mouse on my computer and open up the file I started on study questions for the Irish Famine test.

"Are you sitting there playing with your computer," Fidelma asks furiously, "while our relationship falls apart?"

"Playing with my computer?" I start the SpellCheck on my study questions. The preponderance of Irish and Gaelic place names makes the SpellCheck go crazy. "Fidelma, do you really think I'm that insensitive? I mean, really!" I try to sound offended as I click through the SpellCheck. "Can we meet tomorrow for Valentine's Day?"

"I think," Fidelma cuts me off, "and my roommate agrees, we should take a little time off."

"Time off? What are you talking about? And what does that dipshit have to do with us? If I ever see that guy I'll kick his…"

"Don't be vulgar, Danny."

After five years of our on-again off-again love affair, we're no closer to seeing eye-to-eye than the day we met in a cemetery in County Clare. But I love Fidelma and I know she loves me.

I take a deep breath. "I don't think I understand."

"I think we should stop seeing each other for a while."

"Fidelma!"

"I'm sorry. We'll talk later. And turn that damn computer off. You care more about your students than you do about me."

"That's not true!" I stare at the screen on my laptop, and she hangs up.

I get up from my seat, with the necklace in my hand, stunned. Just ten minutes in my apartment and we've already had an argument. Fidelma and I have a relationship that is combative in a healthy way, but this time I wonder. I look at the necklace for a long time, then put it back in my pocket.

Suddenly, I feel overwhelmingly fatigued and just want to lie down and sleep for a week. As I drag myself toward the bedroom, the smell that has been bothering me since I entered the apartment seems stronger. When I open the door to the bedroom I almost pass out from shock.

Blood is everywhere: on the floor, on the walls, on the furniture and books. The carpet is so saturated it squishes under my feet. A blood splatter high up on the wall looks like a Rorschach test. A young man, naked from the waist up, lies across the bed, face up, his eyes staring at the ceiling, his mouth agape. The sheets and blankets are soaked in blood. He has been cut open from the chestbone to his genitals.

I back out of the room, into the bathroom, and vomit into the toilet. There are even swirls of blood in the tub and someone's bloody handprints are all over my towels.

When I have my racing heart under control, I go back to the kitchen and dial 911.

A patrol unit arrives within minutes, double parks in the street out front with its lights flashing and two patrol officers come upstairs. One is a Latina—her nameplate identifies her as Jessica Rivera—and the other an Irishman with a face the color of raw meat.

I show them the way to the bedroom and try to avoid looking at the corpse splayed across my blood-soaked sheets. My heart is still hammering and I'm dizzy and nauseated. But I can't tear my eyes away from the corpse. The body lies face up across the mattress. His feet dangle over the side of the bed—one shoe off and one still on. His hands are tied behind him with a leather belt. His eyes are half-closed, his mouth open, and a lock of his reddish hair has fallen across his forehead. I almost feel like brushing it away.

After a quick look at the body, Officer Rivera plucks a cell phone from the pocket of her uniform and flips it open. "Could I get a glass of water?" she says to me.

I walk into the kitchen on shaky legs and pour a glass of water from the pitcher in the refrigerator. I have to support myself for a moment on the door of the refrigerator to keep from fainting. Then I bring the water back to where Rivera confers with Patrolman Tom Murphy who surveys the room carefully, making sure not to touch or step on anything.

"Thanks," she says, taking the glass and punching in the numbers on her cell phone. "This is Officer Rivera. Can you send Detective Washington. We've got a DB down here."

Dead body.

When she gets off I ask, "Did you say Washington?"

"Yeah. You know him?"

My voice is quavering and I feel as if I might vomit again. "I do. I helped him find the killer of the Grand Marshall of the St. Patrick's Day parade last year."

"Oh, you're the high school teacher? Thanks for the water. Well, after that high-profile arrest he got booted upstairs. He's a senior supervisor of detectives at the Thirty-fourth Precinct now."

"Really?" It seems odd having this conversation while there's a dead body on my bed. "How is he?" It's as if the reality hasn't hit me yet.

Officer Rivera laughs. "Okay, I guess. I'll bet he'll be thrilled to see you again," she adds sarcastically.

How can Officer Rivera take this all in stride? Just another day on the job?

Detective Washington appears on the scene more quickly than I imagine humanly possible. He barely acknowledges my presence as he limps into the room wearing blue dress pants held up by matching suspenders, a white shirt, blue tie and his .9mm Glock clipped to his waist. Detective First Grade George Washington is a tall black man with sharp, handsome features. His mustache and hair have gone gray but his muscular arms and chest still exude a powerful, athletic air.

"Jesus," he mutters with disgust as he looks at the body in the bedroom. "What a mess."

He almost seems angry about my soiled sheets. "Who's the first officer on the scene here?"

"I am," says Rivera.

"Are you keeping a log of everyone who enters and exits the crime scene?"

"Yes, sir."

"Alright, rope it off downstairs and secure the scene," he says to Murphy. "No one leaves or enters the building until I talk to them. If they have to go out, take names and phone numbers.'' He removes a packet of business cards from his shirt pocket and hands them to Murphy. "Give 'em one of these and tell them I'll be in touch.''

Detective Washington says to Officer Rivera: "Get a photographer down at once. Then start taking statements from all the neighbors. Have you found the murder weapon yet?''

"Not yet, sir.''

"Get on it.''

"Yes, sir.''

I have three neighbors on this floor. Mrs. Zarzinski in 10-A; the Lopez family in 10-B; Mr. and Mrs. Bergman in 10-C. I live in 10-D.

He turns to me for the first time as if just realizing who I am. "So we meet again, O'Flaherty.''

"I can't believe it.'' I still feel dizzy and nauseated and I support myself on a chair back.

"Why don't we go down to my car and have a little chat,'' he says, scraping his thumbnail against the stubble on his chin.

"Okay.''

When I get into the back seat of the squad car, I see the super of my building, Jose, watching. It is almost 10:30 p.m. and I can hardly believe what is happening.

"What time did you get home?''

"About nine o'clock.''

"So, you say you don't know this guy?'' Washington asks.

"Never saw him before in my life.''

"He just walks into your apartment, lays down on the bed and gets zipped open from head to foot?''

Just like the first time I met him, Washington is all business. "How did he get into your apartment?''

"I have no idea."

"Mind if I smoke?" Washington lights a thin foul-smelling cigar before I can object. He blows a cloud of blue smoke into the back seat. "There's no sign of forced entry. Did you leave the door unlocked?"

"Of course not."

"Were the lights on when you got home?"

"No." I stop and think a moment. "Actually, yes. The light in the living room was on."

"You didn't leave it on?"

"I don't remember leaving it on."

"Who's got keys to your apartment?" Washington asks.

"The woman across the hall, Mrs. Zarzinski."

"That's it?"

"Yeah, well, let's see, Fidelma has a key."

"That's your girlfriend, right?" asks Washington. "The Irish girl?"

"Woman," I say. "And she's not exactly my girlfriend anymore."

"Too bad."

"My God." It has just occurred to me that Fidelma might have been in danger this afternoon.

"What's wrong?" asks Washington.

"Fidelma came over sometime this afternoon to give my cat his medicine."

"What time?"

"I'm not sure, but when I came in I saw that she had left the cat food out." Now I'm shaking even harder just thinking about what might have happened to Fidelma if she had been there at the same time as the murderer.

"You see anything else unusual before you found the body?"

"Yeah. A chair in the dining room was tipped over."

Officer Rivera comes out of the building and Washington gets out of the car. They talk for a long time, Washington looks at me and nods several times. When he gets back into the car he looks tired. "They found the murder weapon wrapped in some towels in the bathroom. Steak knife that matches the set in your kitchen."

"I can't believe this."

"Where were you this afternoon before you got home?" he asks.

"I went down to the diamond district to buy a Valentine's Day gift for my girlfriend."

"Fidelma?"

"That's right."

"I thought you said she *wasn't* your girlfriend," says Washington.

"Well, I thought she was then."

"This afternoon she's your girlfriend." Washington closes one eye and peers at me through the other. "Now you don't think so."

What's he getting at, I wonder? "We had an argument over the phone."

"I see." Washington pauses for a long time. "You argue with your girlfriend. Then some guy you don't know walks into your apartment and gets murdered in your bed."

"You make it sound like—"

Washington turns over his hand and looks into his palm as if reading his own fortune. "What *is* it like, O'Flaherty?"

"I don't know what he was doing in my apartment. I've never met this guy before in my life. I come home after shopping for a gift for Fidelma. This guy follows me home—"

"What guy?"

"Some punk followed me from the place where I bought the necklace. He must have known I was carrying diamonds and wanted to rob me. I thought I lost him in Midtown but he got out of the subway with me at 207th Street and tried to stop me before I got to my apartment."

"Was he alone?"

Everyone who walks by the police car looks in at me like I'm some kind of criminal. "Yes."

"Ever see this kid before?" asks Washington. "In the neighborhood, maybe?"

"No."

"Did you hear anything before you got into the apartment?"

"At first I thought someone was talking inside. But it was just the answering machine playing."

"Who was it?"

"Fidelma."

"Then what, O'Flaherty?" he says as he leans into my face. "This kid gets into the apartment without forcing the door seconds before you do, murders a total stranger in your bed and runs out of there?"

"Look, Detective. I don't know who this guy is, how he got into my apartment or who might have killed him."

Officer Rivera comes back. Washington gets out of the car and they have another, much longer, chat.

When Washington gets back in the car he says: "You still telling me you don't know this guy?"

"I swear I have no idea who he is," I say.

"Never saw him before in your life?"

"No!"

Washington's eyes probe my face. "You're sticking with that story?"

"It's not a *story!*"

Washington heaves a deep sigh and starts the engine. "You got a real problem, O'Flaherty."

"What do you mean?'

Washington swings the car onto 207th Street.

"Where are we going?" I ask.

"We're gonna have to go to the precinct and talk about this some more."

"What's wrong?"

"The dead guy upstairs...We got his ID out of his wallet. Called his house."

"Yes?"

"Guess who answered?" asks Washington.

"How would I know?"

"Your girlfriend, Fidelma, answered the phone, that's who."

"What?" I'm shaking my head in disbelief. "That's not possible."

His eyes slide over to my side of the car and then back to the street. "The name of the dead guy upstairs is Morris Greg."

"What? No! It can't be!"

"You've got a lot of explaining to do, O'Flaherty." He glances in the rearview mirror and pulls into traffic. "Up until the time he got murdered in your apartment, Morris Greg lived with your ex-girlfriend, Fidelma Muldoon. Sounds like he was poking his nose into your relationship."

"What's that supposed to mean?"

"Your girlfriend said you didn't like him. She said you were jealous because she had a male roommate. Is that right, O'Flaherty? Were you jealous?"

"Maybe."

"So you killed him?"

"No!"

"You threatened to assault him?"

"What? No!"

"Said you'd kick his butt if you ever saw him?"

"That's just a figure of speech. I didn't mean it literally."

"Called him a dipshit," Washington adds.

"Okay. Okay. I called him a dipshit, but that doesn't mean I murdered him. Besides, I wouldn't know him if I passed him on the street. I've never met the guy in my life. I don't know what he was doing in my apartment."

Washington shakes his head and says almost sadly, "You're in a lot of trouble, O'Flaherty."

THREE

IT TAKES THREE HOURS at the 34th Precinct to convince Washington, and two other detectives, that I didn't recognize Morris Greg because I've never seen him before in my life. Besides, it would take some presence of mind for a man to do something like that in his own apartment and then call the police himself. He'd have to shower and clean himself up before the police came.

"Looks like someone *did* use your tub to clean up," Washington says.

"Well, it wasn't me!"

Finally, Detective Washington admits that even if I didn't kill Morris Greg, he is not convinced that this is all just a coincidence. He believes I'm withholding information that could solve the case. He sends an officer to take a statement from Fidelma and she helps solve part of the mystery. She couldn't get over to give the cat his medicine because she had to pick up tickets to *Kittens*. So her roommate agreed to go to my apartment, feed Barnabus and give him his medicine. She gave Morris Greg the key to my apartment and sometime between 8 p.m. and when I got home around 9 p.m. someone must have followed him into the apartment and murdered him. But why?

"She still keeps saying," Washington adds, "that you didn't like Morris Greg. That you were jealous."

"She said that?"

"Were you?" asks Washington.

"Why should I be jealous? He was gay."

"She said you didn't believe that."

What the hell was Fidelma trying to do, get me arrested? "I don't know what the guy's sexual orientation is."

"*Was.*"

"Whatever."

"You don't sound too upset about his death," Washington says.

"I told you, I didn't even know the guy!"

"Then why did you call him a dipshit?" Washington asks.

"He told Fidelma…" I hesitate, not sure if I want to go into all this.

"He told Fidelma what?" Washington asks.

"He told Fidelma that he thought she and I should stop seeing each other."

"He tried to break up your relationship."

I don't say anything.

"Well?" Washington prompts.

"He was interfering."

"This won't look good for you, O'Flaherty."

"When did you last see your girlfriend?" the detective asks.

"Yesterday, after school we had dinner. We were supposed to see a show tonight."

"You stood her up?"

"I was out buying her a Valentine's Day gift!" I say, raising my voice.

"Do you know, or did your girlfriend ever mention, anyone who might have had a grudge against this Morris Greg?"

"No."

"Okay. So Fidelma gave Morris Greg a key to your apartment to give your cat medicine. That still doesn't explain how the murderer got into your building, then your apartment, all without forcing the door."

After almost three hours of grilling at the 34th Precinct, I start to go home but realize I can't. A man has just been butchered in my bedroom. The carpet will have to be ripped out and tossed away, the mattress and box spring are ruined. Murder is a messy business. But I never actually thought about who cleans up after the police leave. Is there some kind of cleaning service that specializes in crime scenes? I shudder just thinking about it.

The coroner's office would have removed the body by now, but I still don't feel good about going home. The whole place has been violated, infected. I feel creepy about my own apartment. How will I ever be able to live there again? But the worst thing is that I have to face Fidelma and somehow explain why her roommate was murdered in my bedroom. She couldn't possibly think I had anything to do with it.

I'm standing on the corner of Broadway and 182nd trying to hail a cab. It's almost 2 a.m. and the snow-covered streets are as quiet as it gets in Manhattan. Six inches of snow have accumulated since yesterday afternoon. A hush has fallen over the noisy city and I can hear the traffic lights click as they change in the gently falling snow. When I look up at the streetlights, I see flurries swirling around the light. I'm so tired I'm about to pass out. There's not a taxi in sight, but soon a car-service car emerges from a side street coming toward me. Gypsy cabs look like any other car, but it's easy to spot one once you know what to look for. They are usually Lincoln Town Cars with a small rectangular sign on the passenger side front window identifying them as cabs. I stick out my hand and the car pulls over. As I open the back door, I notice there is someone already in the back seat.

"Oh, sorry," I say to the driver. "I thought you were free."

"Get in."

"No, sorry."

"Get in," says the passenger in back. That's when I recognize him as the tall black man in flowing white robes and white turban who was sitting in Moishe Finkelstein's waiting room this afternoon when I bought the necklace.

As I back out of the door, the driver leaps out of the car, gets behind me and pushes me into the back seat and slams the door. Then he gets behind the wheel and turns downtown. I reach for the door handle but the locks snap shut.

My heart is pounding as I look around the darkened interior of the car. The man in the white turban speaks in a deep gravelly voice. "Mr. O'Flaherty?"

"That's my name."

"May I call you Danny?"

"What is this?"

The car speeds south, sailing through red lights; the driver reaches over and tears the phony car-service sign from the inside windshield of the passenger side.

"Mr. Danny," the turbaned man with the voice like Nat King Cole says, "I'll get right to the point. I want the diamond."

I've almost forgotten about the damned necklace, and I reach into my jacket pocket to make sure it's still there. I can't believe this is happening just because I wanted to buy a Valentine's Day gift for my girlfriend. Someone has been murdered in my apartment and now this?

The man in the turban looks at me with piercing black eyes and says again. "The diamond. Where is it?"

These guys look dangerous. I don't feel like getting myself killed for four hundred dollars. I'll buy Fidelma another necklace…that is, if she ever talks to me again. Before I even have a chance to take it out of my pocket, the driver reaches back and grabs me by the shirt collar. He still has one hand on the steering wheel, but he manages to pull my face up against the front seat and hiss, "Give it to us."

"Please, please," says the man in the turban. "That is not necessary."

The driver lets me go and I take the necklace out of my jacket pocket and hand it to the man in back. "Here. Take it."

The man looks at the necklace dangling from my hand as if it's a dirty sock. There is tense silence inside the car for several seconds and then the man breaks into laughter.

I look at him, bewildered. When he has his laughter under control, he takes a handkerchief from inside his robe and wipes tears from his eyes. "That's really very funny, Mr. Danny."

"Take it!" I say.

The man shakes his head slowly, and he is not laughing anymore. "This is serious, Mr. Danny. Now give me the diamond."

"Here." I thrust it in his face. "Take it and let me out of here."

"You know what diamond I'm talking about," he says.

"What?"

"St. Valentine's Diamond."

"I don't understand."

The man shakes his head again. "Please, don't play dumb, Mr. Danny. We know you have it."

"I don't know what you're talking about. I went to Moishe Finkelstein's shop to buy a gift for my girlfriend. What the hell is a St. Valentine's Diamond?" I glance into the rearview mirror, and a car seems to be following close behind. I'm wondering if I might be able to attract attention and perhaps get help. But this is New York, after all.

"Don't play games, Mr. Danny. We know you are the courier. We know Finkelstein gave you the diamond. We've been watching his office."

"You've made some kind of mistake."

The driver reaches into the back seat again and grabs me by the shirt collar. This time the man in the white robes doesn't interfere.

"I don't want to do it this way, Mr. Danny," says the man in back, "but if you don't hand over the diamond we'll have to do it this way."

The driver twists my shirt collar, cutting off my air. I've been watching to see who controls the door locks and I see the console on the driver's side with all the switches for the doors. We've been heading downtown on Broadway. The streets are nearly deserted. I'm gasping for air and I check out the rearview and see the car is still behind us. Out the window, I notice Cannon's Pub on 108th Street and Broadway is still open. Good old Cannon's doesn't close until 4 a.m.

"I don't have any diamond. Just this necklace."

The driver twists my collar tighter. "Give it to us!"

"Watch out!" I croak, my windpipe almost closed.

The driver lets go of my collar, yanks the steering

wheel to the left and slams on brakes. I slam him against the steering wheel as I reach over the seat and push as many buttons as I can on the door lock console. Then I rip open my door, tumble out onto the sidewalk in front of Kim's Cleaner, get up with difficulty, leap into the tree-lined medium on Broadway, race across the other side of the street, nearly get hit by a cab and stagger toward the door of Cannon's Pub as the Lincoln Town Car speeds away. As I enter the bar, I see the car that has been following us screech to a halt out front.

Inside I brush myself off, order a Harp and a shot, then ease my aching body into a booth. My hands are bleeding from where I hit the pavement and my pants are ripped at both knees. I down my shot of Bushmills in a single gulp and the burning in my throat takes my mind off my throbbing hands and knees for a second. I'm taking a deep gulp from my pint when a man comes through the door of the pub, looks around, makes straight for my booth and slides in across from me.

"We've got to talk," he says, his eyes darting around the bar.

It's 3 a.m. and I haven't slept for nearly twenty hours. Eight hours ago I set out to buy a Valentine's present for Fidelma. Since then I've been followed by a thug, dumped by my girlfriend, a man has been butchered in my apartment and I've been implicated in the crime. Then a couple of African nut cases pick me up and start asking me about St. Valentine's Diamond, and now I'm looking at a man I've never seen in my life who says we've got to talk. All I want to do is go home and fall into bed. Except that my bed is saturated with the insides of Morris Greg. Even for New York it's been a tough day.

"My name is Vincent de Leon," the guy says. He

looks like he's just come back from the Caribbean. His face and arms are tanned, his hair and mustache freshly trimmed, and he has the rugged good looks of an outdoorsman.

He reaches into his back pocket and pulls out his driver's license and a membership card in the American Association of Travel Writers. "I'm a freelance travel writer."

"Great." I take a sip of my Harp. "Have you done the Statue of Liberty yet?"

He just looks at me.

"Ellis Island?" I pick up a napkin and dab at my bleeding hands.

"Let me get right to the point," he says.

"That's what the last guy who nearly killed me said." I'm feeling dizzy and I still can't believe all this is happening.

"I don't want to kill you. I just want to know about St. Valentine's Diamond."

Oh, boy.

"Of course, you know about it," he says without waiting for my response. "I first heard about the rock myself last summer when I was staying at the Iturbe Lodge in South Africa. I work for a publisher, *Travel World,* updating guidebooks. They sent me to South Africa to update the information on this lodge. I did that, but in the meantime I stumbled onto a big story."

I'm almost nodding off from lack of sleep and all the crazy events of the day and I'm struggling to stay focused.

"I met a reporter named Rob Bates who was on assignment for a jewelry trade magazine. He told me that a ten-carat diamond had been smuggled out of a mine in Lesotho, South Africa, by a worker."

"This worker just finds a diamond lying around?"

de Leon motions to the waitress. "It's not that simple. Raw diamonds are embedded in kimberlite. So the workers are down there breaking pieces of kimberlite from the walls of the mine. It's then put on a conveyer belt where it goes to a separation plant. At the separation plant, two giant wheels crush the kimberlite into tiny particles that are screened by sieves. Then these tiny particles are put on another set of conveyor belts and passed through cyclone baths. This separates the diamonds which are of heavier density from the other materials. Lighter materials rise and are skimmed off. About ninety-nine percent of the ore is removed in this way."

"I had no idea it was that complicated." And I'm wondering why I should care.

The waitress finally comes over and de Leon orders a bottle of Corona with a slice of lime.

"That's not all. Then this material is passed through what they call a 'sortex.' It's an X ray. Diamonds gleam under these x-rays. Then a photoelectric eye recognizes the glimmer of the diamond," de Leon continues, "and triggers a jet of air that blows the diamond off the conveyer belt and down a chute to a sorting room."

The waitress brings de Leon his Corona.

"Then where did this mine worker find the diamond?" I ask.

"It is very rare, but sometimes it happens that a miner spots a diamond right at the beginning of the process in the kimberlite itself. Apparently, that's what happened in this case."

"How do you know all this?" I ask.

"It came out in the worker's trial." de Leon pushes

the slice of lime in the neck of the bottle down into the beer and watches it fizz.

"So they caught him?"

"Yeah, but not before he had already sold the diamond to two South Africans."

The facts he's laying before me skitter away from my exhausted mind. "But how did he get it out of the mine? They must guard those places like Fort Knox."

"You're not going to believe this," he says.

"Try me."

de Leon turns the beer bottle in his hand. "A pigeon."

"Excuse me?"

"The worker used a homing pigeon to smuggle the diamond out of the mine," he says, finally taking a hit of his beer. It's half gone in one swallow. "When he found the diamond he hid it in the mine. Then he brought a live homing pigeon into the mine with him in his lunch box the next day. He attached the diamond to the pigeon's leg. It flew out of the mine right back to the worker's home."

"You're kidding me."

"Nope. In fact, the mining company hires men to shoot any homing pigeons within the immediate area of the mine. It's illegal to keep them. Somehow, this guy had one."

"Amazing!" I say, and it suddenly occurs to me that the day has been so surreal, it's almost like a dream.

"Anyway, this was a pink diamond...very rare...very valuable. Supposedly the worker sold the diamond to two South Africans." de Leon takes another sip of his Corona and shakes his head. "One of the South Africans he was supposed to have sold the diamond to was later found dead in a Johannesburg hotel room, apparently double-crossed by his partner."

I'm trying to decide if I trust this guy or not. "How do you know all this?"

"Like I said, this guy Rob Bates told me. He was following the story himself. Anyway, the partner fled with the rough stone to Antwerp and he was later found dead. A safe deposit box in his name was found to contain half a million dollars in cash, but no diamond. The authorities believe the diamond had been sold and cut in Antwerp into a heart shape."

"Are you telling me that—"

"The Belgium police received a tip from a suspicious diamond dealer who had been offered a giant pink heart-shaped diamond that the seller called St. Valentine's Diamond. The seller claimed it was owned by the Saudi Royal family and he was selling it on their behalf. But the diamond dealer was suspicious. Made some phone calls. Found out that the Saudi family owned no such diamond. In the meantime, the man who had offered to sell it disappeared and is believed to be in New York attempting to unload St. Valentine's Diamond."

"Who is this man?"

"That's what I'd like to know." de Leon reaches into his shirt pocket and takes out a business card. "That's what I'm hoping you can tell me," he says, handing me his card.

"I don't know anything about any of this. How much is this rock worth, anyway?" I ask.

His gaze is locked on mine. "Over a million dollars."

"Wow." Interesting story, but I still can't figure out how I'm involved.

"Guess how much the worker who smuggled it out of the mine got?" His eyes meet mine as he takes another swig of his beer.

"Tell me."

"About two thousand dollars." de Leon wipes his mouth with the back of his hand. "And he was sentenced to ten years in prison."

"How big is it?"

"Not that big." He holds up his thumb and measures off a portion with his index finger. "About the size of a pea. It's the fact that it's a pink that makes it so valuable. And supposedly whoever cut it is one of the best in the industry. It's completely flawless and a perfect pink color. A regular work of art."

"Who cut it?" I ask.

"I'm still trying to find that out," says de Leon. "Now, make sure you talk to me first. Don't talk to any other reporters. If you hear anything, make sure you call me. I'll keep you informed, you keep me informed."

I study him, trying to figure his angle. Is he planning to save this story for the *New York Times?* "Why are you interested in all of this?"

"Well, at first I wanted to track down the diamond myself to write a story about it. But then I found out that a hundred thousand dollar reward is offered by Kruger and Kruger, Ltd., for anyone giving information leading to the recovery of St. Valentine's Diamond."

My head is spinning from all of this information. "You were following the car I just jumped out of."

"That's right. Now, like I said. You call me if you find out anything. If this guy Rob Bates calls, don't talk to him. I don't trust him completely. And as far as this reward…you give me the information I need and maybe we can work something out, a compromise of some kind."

"But I don't know anything."

"I'm not so sure about that." de Leon kills what's

left of his Corona and sets the bottle on the table with a clunk. "I think you do."

"Do you know those guys...the Africans?"

"Know of them," says de Leon, shrugging. "The guy in the robes is a delegate to the United Nations from Zimbibia. His name is Abdul Momodu."

"I've never heard of Zimbibia."

"It's a newly independent nation wedged between Namibia, Zimbabwe and Zambia. I was there last year. Did an article on a game preserve they have there."

"Why does he want the diamond?" I ask. "He must be a crook."

"On the contrary. He's one of the few honest people in the Zimbibian government. He's trying to locate that diamond in order to prevent the overthrow of the government of Zimbibia."

"You've lost me."

"It's believed that the dealer trying to sell the diamond is actually working on behalf of a key figure in the ZLF—the Zimbianese Liberation Front, a group seeking to overthrow the government of Zimbibia. A courier is supposed to bring that diamond to a weapons dealer here in New York. Momodu believes that it is going to be used as currency to purchase a shipment of Kalashnikovs. These arms will be used to overthrow the Zimbibian government. If Momodu can find the diamond, then he can stop the coup."

I take a sip of my Harp and let all of this information sink in. But I'm not prepared for what de Leon says next.

"Some people think that *you* are the courier who is delivering the diamond."

I choke on my beer, spraying a mouthful on the table. "What?"

"Look, O'Flaherty. I don't care what your role is. I'm

looking for the diamond. I'm not a cop, I'm a reporter. You help me and I can help you.''

"But why do you think I know anything about this diamond?''

"My sources tell me that Finkelstein has the diamond. I'm thinking he brokered a deal between the ZLF and an arms dealer from Oklahoma named Hector Westman.''

Now he's making me angry. I slam my pint glass on the table. "Moishe Finkelstein is a completely honest businessman!'' I inform him. "And I know for a fact he would never be involved with conflict diamonds. Never!''

He shrugs. "Maybe. Anyway, Finkelstein is not going to just hand over the diamond. He needs someone to deliver it to the arms dealer. I was tipped off that someone was going to show up at Finkelstein's office around seven o'clock on the thirteenth to pick up the diamond. There are people who believe that someone is you.''

"That's absurd. I was there to buy a Valentine's Day gift for my girlfriend.''

de Leon stands up. "Here's another one of my cards. Put it in your Rolodex. You're in this deep, O'Flaherty, deep. If you want to cut your losses while you have a chance, talk to me. We can maybe work out a percentage of the reward and save a lot of innocent lives in Africa in the bargain.''

"I told you, I don't know anything!''

"Call me," he says as he goes out the door.

I walk out of Cannons's Pub ready to flag a cab. There's a public phone right outside the front door of the bar and I call home to see if I have any messages. There's a message from Fidelma. "Danny,'' she says, crying, 'just give yourself up. I don't know why you hated Morris. There was nothing between us. Nothing. Just give yourself up, please.''

What? She couldn't possibly believe I did this?

The next message is from Washington. "Are you there, O'Flaherty? Pick up the phone. O'Flaherty! It's Detective Washington. Pick up the phone! You better not have skipped town. We need to talk.'' He sounds annoyed. Then, in the next message an edge of hysteria has crept into his voice. "Where are you, O'Flaherty? I told you to go straight home and not leave town. Call me! Now!''

I call the 34th Precinct and the receptionist puts me through to Washington. "It's 3:30 a.m.," I say, "and you're still at work?''

"Never mind where I am, O'Flaherty. Where are *you?* I want you to get down here now before I put out an all-points bulletin!''

"I've had an unusual evening.''

There is silence at the other end of the phone, then I hear Washington munching on something like a stalk of celery. Neither one of us says anything for a long time, then Washington says, "Tell me something, O'Flaherty. Are you right-handed or left-handed?''

"Left-handed. Why?''

"The medical examiner seems to think that the knife wounds on Morris Greg were made by a lefty.''

I'm too stunned to say anything.

"And your prints were all over the murder weapon.''

"I live there, for God's sake. I eat with those knives.''

"Your girlfriend seems pretty convinced you had something to do with his death. You're holding out on me, O'Flaherty.''

"No, I'm not,'' I lie.

"The crime lab did some tests at the scene of the

crime. Found the usual stuff on the body: defense wounds where he tried to fight off his assailant, blood and skin under his fingernails where he scratched his murderer. We're running DNA on that. But then they found something else very interesting.''

''What?''

''Diamond dust.''

''Did you say diamond dust?'' I ask.

''That's right. When they were lifting fingerprints they found an unusual substance on the prints themselves. Did some tests. Found out it was diamond dust.''

I'm not sure exactly what diamond dust is. ''What does this mean?''

''When a diamond is cut or drilled or whatever, it gives off a fine dust. The only person in the world likely to be walking around with diamond dust on his fingers is someone who cuts diamonds for a living.''

''I see.''

''By the way,'' Washington adds, ''we picked up your buddy this evening.''

''What buddy? Who are you talking about?''

''Moishe Finkelstein.''

''What? Moishe Finkelstein is a completely innocent, honest businessman.''

''Keep telling yourself that, O'Flaherty,'' says Washington, ''and you might end up believing it.''

''What are the charges?''

''We just brought him in for questioning.''

''On what grounds?''

''Are you an attorney now?'' Washington asks sarcastically. ''As well as a private detective?''

''He's a completely honest diamond dealer.''

''Yeah, right. When we took his prints they were covered with diamond dust.''

"What's that supposed to prove? He handles diamonds every day."

"Oh, yeah? In the meantime, I want you to get down here as soon as possible. There are a couple of holes in your story that my supervisor wants to go over with you. If you don't get here within half an hour I'll send a patrol unit to pick you up. You got that?"

"I understand. I'll be right there."

Just as I'm about to hang up on Washington I feel something in my back. I whip around and the cowboy from Moishe Finkelstein's shop is pushing the barrel of a snub-nosed handgun between my shoulder blades.

FOUR

"LET'S TAKE A RIDE," Cowboy whispers, taking the phone from my hands.

"O'Flaherty!" I hear Washington yell over the phone. "O'Flaherty, where are you?"

The cowboy hangs up the phone and pushes me into a car parked beside the phone booth. There's a pimply faced Hispanic kid with a thin mustache in his early twenties behind the wheel. He's wearing a red and green bandana knotted sideways on his head. Cowboy puts the cold barrel of the gun into my right ear. As we pull onto Broadway, beads of sweat pop out on my forehead.

"What do you want?" I whisper, barely able to recognize my own squeaky voice. I'm staring at the gun out of the corner of my eye. "Who are you?"

"Never mind who I am," he snarls, screwing the gun deeper into my ear. "Don't ask any more questions or my driver here will be wiping your brains off the back seat. *Comprende?*"

His Spanish pronunciation is horrible but I'm not about to tell him that. I nod my head and my whole body is shaking. I'm sweating so much inside my clothes I can smell it. There's something familiar about the cowboy's driver. The driver glances in the rearview and I see a light-skinned Dominican with a thin mustache and acne scars on his cheeks.

"Now, we're going to take a little drive. See some of the sights of New Jersey. You like New Jersey?"

"My favorite state," I manage to squeak.

"Good. 'Cause we're going to tour some of the marsh areas. You an environmentalist?"

"Absolutely."

"That's good, too." He pushes the barrel of the gun so far into my ear I'm getting a headache. "Because if you don't tell us where St. Valentine's Diamond is, I'll blow your brains out all over the marshlands and let the little birdies nibble on pieces of your skull."

This guy is getting himself worked up. It seems useless to tell him I don't know where the diamond is—or why everyone thinks I do. We turn onto the West Side Highway and speed uptown. Traffic is light at this hour as we race north, the Hudson River on our left, the lights of New Jersey twinkling on the opposite shore.

We're almost at the exit for the George Washington Bridge. When the driver glances in the rearview for a second, I still have the feeling I've seen him somewhere before.

"I'll show you where the diamond is," I say, surprising myself by my own voice. I'm not even sure why I've said this but I have a bad feeling that if we go over the George Washington Bridge it's going to be a one-way trip for me.

"He's going to tell us where the diamond is. You hear that, Pancho?"

"My name ain't Pancho," says the driver.

"Pancho, Paco, Pablo, Pogo, whatever."

Something tells me these guys don't know each other that well. "I'll take you to the diamond," I say.

"Now, that's what I like to hear," the cowboy enthuses.

"It's near my apartment."

"I knew you didn't want your brains fed to the pigeons."

I glance at the guy. I wonder why he mentions pigeons?

When the driver passes the exit for the GWB and continues uptown, I heave a sigh of relief. When he keeps driving without asking where we're going as if he knows exactly how to get to my apartment, something clicks for me. He glances again in the rearview and confirms my suspicion. The driver is the kid who followed me home from Moishe Finkelstein's shop.

Just before the Dyckman Street exit, there is an exit for the Cloisters, a complex of five different cloisters from medieval monasteries that sits high on a hill in Fort Tryon Park overlooking northern Manhattan. "Up there," I say, pointing to the Cloisters.

"What for?"

"I'm going to show you where the diamond is."

Cowboy pushes my head with the gun barrel. "No funny stuff, Teach."

He seems to know a lot about me.

"Do what he says," the cowboy tells the driver just in time to squeal off the exit into Fort Tryon Park.

Up at the Cloisters the driver pulls into a secluded parking area near the herb garden. The sun is just coming up and the deserted park surrounding the castle-like Cloisters looks gloomy in the dawn. Deep snow blankets the grounds surrounding the castle. The shrubbery is heavy with snow, and the withered fingers of the trees are glittering with ice. A shiver runs up my spine as I see a lone light go out in the tower looming over the Cloisters as if a monk has blown out his candle and turned in for the night. I'm hoping it's not a metaphor.

"Show and tell time, Teach," says Cowboy.

I take a deep breath and count to five, trying to calm my racing heart. A half moon hangs over the Cloisters. "I think you better tell him," I say to the driver.

There is a long silence. Then the kid behind the wheel swings his head around with an incredulous look on his face. "What?"

"The jig is up," I say, trying to remember gangster talk from the movies.

"What's going on?" Cowboy asks, lost.

"Tell him," I say to the kid.

"What you talking about, man?" the kid asks, a nervous tick in his voice.

"No use getting us both killed," I add.

Cowboy eases the gun out of my ear and looks at the driver. "What's he talking about?"

"Guy's crazy. I don't know what the hell he's talking about."

I turn to Cowboy. "He followed me from Finkelstein's shop."

"Yeah. So what? We've been watching you."

"Tell him," I say to the driver.

The kid's voice rises in pitch. "Man, I don't know what you're talking about."

Cowboy waves the gun back and forth now between me and his partner.

"Somebody's holding out on you, Tex," I say to Cowboy.

"What?"

"Your buddy here followed me from Finkelstein's shop in order to get the diamond."

"He never got into your apartment," Cowboy says. "I watched him from the car."

"Oh, yeah? Is that right?" I'm stalling, trying to figure out where to take this. "Is that what he told you, Tex?"

"Don't call me Tex!" he shouts. "I'm from Oklahoma."

I've rattled him and I think I've touched a raw nerve. The gun is shaking in his hand and he doesn't seem to know whether to point it at me or his partner.

"He's got the diamond," I say.

"You're bluffing." A note of uncertainty has entered his voice.

"Don't listen to him," says the driver.

"Shut up!" Cowboy swings the gun around and points it at his partner. There is a tense moment while I glance outside the car. We're parked in the lot on the west side of the park between the Cloisters and the Hudson River.

"He double-crossed you," I say, waiting a beat before I add, *"Tex!"*

Cowboy snaps, shoving the gun behind the driver's head and screaming, "You greaseball, where's my diamond?!"

"He's lying, man! He's freaking lying."

I decide to leave the quarreling couple to themselves. While Cowboy has the gun pointed at his partner, I lunge for the lock of my door and bail out.

"Hey!" Cowboy swings around and fires a shot that rips a hole in the shoulder of my jacket. I get up running, leap the retaining wall separating the sidewalk leading to the museum from the snow-covered hill that plunges down to the Henry Hudson Parkway.

"He's getting away!"

I slip down about twenty feet of ice and snow-covered slope until I come to a stop on an outcropping above the highway. The sun has risen and I can see Cowboy and his partner scrambling down the rocky slope after me.

"There he is!" Cowboy fires another shot that shatters a rock next to my foot. Another bullet whizzes by my ear as I leap for a tree about ten feet in front of me. My legs burn as I slide down the tree, hit the ground, and roll onto the northbound lane of the Henry Hudson. A car swerves into the southbound lane to avoid me, its horn blaring.

"You idiot!" the driver screams out the window.

I scramble across the highway, desperately trying to flag a southbound car. As another bullet whizzes by me I realize that nobody in his right mind is going to stop for somebody standing in the highway at sunrise waving his arms like a madman, dodging bullets.

Just as I see Cowboy and his sidekick slide down onto the highway, a miracle occurs.

A yellow cab pulls over.

I jerk open the door, dive into the cab, and scream, "Get out of here!"

The driver is in no hurry and I see Cowboy and his sidekick run across the highway toward us as we pull slowly back onto the road. "Get going for God's sake!"

"You are agitated again, sir."

I watch my two attackers recede in the rearview mirror, shouting and waving their fists as we pull into the right lane. Then I lock eyes on the driver in the mirror. My God! It's the Indian cab driver I met a year ago. I glance at his ID taped to the Plexiglas partition between us: Ravi Ajmera. He's wearing the same purple turban and his face has the same look of utter serenity. "You just saved my life," I say, my chest heaving.

"I am not capable of saving your life," he says,

switching lanes. "Life and death are beyond the control of man."

"Do you remember me? We met last year."

"Of course I do, sir."

He acts as if meeting again like this in a city of eight million people is not in the least remarkable. I can hardly believe it. "If you hadn't shown up just then, I'd be dead. How can I thank you enough?"

"I was at that particular place in the world at that particular time because it was my destiny to be there. As it was *your* destiny. You cannot possibly thank me for an action over which I have no control."

"But I might have died. Those two guys were trying to kill me!"

"Might, sir?" he asks. "There is nothing conditional about death. Death is an absolute certainty. When it is your time and place to die…you shall. And neither you nor I nor those two men back there can do anything about it."

This whole day has been so bizarre that I chalk this chance meeting up as just another crazy event. I think that in the nine plus hours since leaving Moishe Finkelstein's office, the only person from the office I have *not* seen is the Broadway actress, Isabel Quick, who was sitting in the waiting room when I got there. It's just 6 a.m. I need to get to the 34th Precinct to talk to Washington. But before I do, even though I'm about to pass out from exhaustion, I decide to go ahead and see if I can find Isabel Quick and maybe figure out how she fits into this whole mess…if at all.

It's calming talking to Ravi Ajmera and by the time we get to midtown my shattered nerves are starting to recover. He drops me at Columbus Circle.

"I still can't believe we met like this again."

Ajmera smiles. "Nothing in life is coincidental. Nothing happens by chance. It is all predetermined. It was a pleasure to see you again, sir. Until we meet again, then…if that is our destiny." The cab disappears into the city.

I CALL INFORMATION, find that Isabel Quick has a listed number, and get the address from the operator. She lives on West 51st Street between 10th and 11th avenues—Hell's Kitchen.

Hell's Kitchen, now sometimes called Clinton, depending on who you talk to, was once a home to breweries, factories and Irish immigrants. In recent years actors, directors and others from the nearby theaters have moved in followed by the usual galleries and upscale restaurants.

I ring the buzzer at the front of her building, wait a long time, then ring again. After two or three minutes, I ring again and a tired, angry voice comes over the speaker.

"Who is it?"

"My name is Danny O'Flaherty."

"Who?" Pause. "It's six o'clock in the damn morning. What do you want?"

"I'm here about a diamond. St. Valentine's Diamond."

I don't hear anything for a long time and then finally she buzzes me in.

It's a four-floor walkup and Isabel's apartment is on the top floor. I climb the rickety stairs, thinking it's not exactly the kind of place where I would expect a Broadway star to live. When I get to the fourth floor she is standing in the door of her apartment. She still has the chain attached and watches me through the crack of the partially opened door. She looks sleepy and twenty years older without her makeup.

"What do you want?" she demands as soon as I approach her door.

I'm so tired I can hardly stand up and the four flights of stairs haven't helped any. My hands are throbbing from where I hit the pavement in front of Cannon's Pub and I've skinned the inside of my legs from sliding down the tree near the Cloisters. Both knees of my pants are ripped and I have a bullet hole in the shoulder of my jacket. "I'm not sure, exactly."

"Great," she says, rubbing her temples with the tips of her fingers. "You wake me up at six in the morning and you don't know what you want. I had a show last night. I didn't get home until midnight, and I didn't get to bed until 2 a.m., I have a matinee today and an evening performance, and to tell you the truth I've got a bitch of a hangover. Who the hell *are* you?"

"Sorry to bother you. At least you got some sleep. I didn't get to bed at all last night."

"That's not my problem!"

True enough. "May I come in?"

She looks at me oddly, then snaps her finger. "Now I remember you. You were at the diamond dealer's office yesterday."

Was that yesterday? It seems like a million years ago. "I'm trying to find out what you might know about a missing diamond," I say.

"Oh?" She unhooks the chain and reluctantly opens the door. "You better come in. You look like you're about to pass out. What happened to you, anyway?"

"It's been a long night."

Despite the shabby exterior of the building, the inside of the apartment looks like something out of *Metropol-*

itan Home. The walls are painted a creamy eggshell with dark wooden crown mouldings, baseboards and door-frames.

"You want coffee?" she asks.

I think I'm actually beginning to hallucinate from sleep deprivation. "I've never wanted a cup of coffee so much in my life."

While Isabel bangs around in the kitchen, I check out the living room. A grand piano takes up nearly half the space. Modern paintings hang throughout the room. One by Paul Klee looks like it might be an original. Matching table lamps sit on both sides of a plush white sofa and the rest of the room is furnished with a blend of antique and modern furniture. She has her own framed headshot from at least twenty years ago on one wall. A vintage movie poster of Fred Astaire and Ginger Rogers—*Singing in the Rain*—hangs on another wall. Musical scores lie scattered around and crammed onto bookshelves. I look down a hall into her bedroom. To my surprise I see a young guy, naked, with a body like a weight lifter and a face like Leonardo DiCaprio sleeping in Isabel Quick's bed. He's young enough to be her grandson.

In the living room something else catches my eye. Looking out of place on a bookshelf among dozens of musical scores is a large, hardbound volume, *The Fine Art of Diamond Cutting* by Sammy Lipschitz. Just as I reach for the book, Isabel pads back into the room in French poodle bedroom slippers, her bright red toenails peeking out through the dogs' mouths. She carries two cups of coffee on a silver tray with cream and sugar.

She glances at the book as she enters the room, then walks over and sets the tray down on an end table beside a bottle of Kahlua. She opens the Kahlua and pours a generous shot into her coffee, settles herself on the white sofa and crosses her legs. She raises her coffee cup to me in a toast. "Hair of the dog."

"I see."

"In case you're wondering, my ex-husband was a diamond cutter," she says, acknowledging the book with a nod of her head.

I limp over to a lounge chair and ease into it. I feel like I've aged ninety years since yesterday. "Interesting. Did you say *was?*"

"That's right. He wrote the definitive text on diamond cutting." She's twitching her crossed leg so that the French poodle on her foot almost looks alive. "You see, the cutter uses a saw coated with oil and diamond dust."

"Diamond dust?"

"That's right. Only diamonds are hard enough to cut diamonds. Once the cuts are made, the stone is passed on to a 'girdler.' He rounds out the edges of the newly cut stone with another diamond. Then a polisher uses a spinning wheel coated with oil and diamond dust to grind off the rough outer surface of the gem which creates the facets, the flat surfaces that make a diamond sparkle."

I'm thinking about what Washington told me—that diamond dust was found on Morris Greg's body. "Where do cutters get their stones?"

"Most cutters work on a contract basis. They don't actually own the stones. But my ex-husband bought his own diamonds from a sight-holder. The diamond trade is a complicated and tradition-bound business. But in simple terms it works like this. Ten times a year, one hundred and twenty-five sight-holders are invited to London by De Beers where they are offered a box of diamonds—called a sight—for a fixed price. The box contains a mixed grade of uncut diamonds and the sight-holder has to pay the set price no matter what's in the box. In other words, he takes the good stones with the bad. Later, the diamond dealer takes them to a cutter to cut and polish to his specifications and sells them to retailers to mount in settings. Now, Sammy bought stones himself and cut them in his own one-man shop.''

"I thought they used lasers to cut diamonds now.''

"Sometimes they do for certain kinds of cuts. But my ex-husband did it the old-fashioned way.'' She gets up, walks over to the sidetable and refills her coffee cup with Kahlua, skipping the coffee this time. "Even though he still called himself a cutter, in the last couple of years he was strictly a marker.''

"What's a marker?''

She takes a gulp of her drink. "He's like an architect of diamond cutting. He studies the rough stone to determine where each internal flaw is located. He decides where to make each cut so that the greatest number of these flaws can be eliminated by the cutter and the polisher. He decides how to get the most value out of any given diamond.'' She sets her cup on the end table beside her and brushes a stray hair from her face. "Once he maps out how the diamond is to be cut, he gives the rough stone to the cutters and polishers who work the stone into a finished diamond.''

"You know a lot about diamonds," I say.

"Yeah, well, I should. My ex never stopped talking about his work. Never asked a thing about *my* career, but he could go on for days about diamond cutting.'' She points her chin toward her room. "At least the pretty boy you saw in my bedroom keeps his mouth shut. It's better that way.''

"Where is your ex-husband now?''

She looks at the movie poster on the opposite wall for a moment and says in a flat voice, "He's dead."

"I'm so sorry."

She doesn't reply so it's hard to tell if she's sorry or not.

"Was he ill?" I ask.

She re-crosses her legs and clasps her hands over her knee. "Murdered."

"My God!" She seems rather calm about it, even if it was an ex-husband. Actually, she seems almost chipper. "When?"

"A week ago."

"What happened?"

"You know, a diamond is just a rock. And not a very pretty rock, really." She picks up her coffee cup again, takes a sip, and points toward the tray. "Cream?"

"Black's fine." I grab my own coffee and drain half the cup.

"It takes a master craftsman to release a diamond's beauty and sparkle," she goes on. "When a stone is cut in the right way, light is reflected from one facet to another so that it disperses up through the table." She points to the top of her coffee cup, using it for a visual aid as if it were a gigantic gem. "Cut it too deep and the light spills out the girdle of the stone or down through the lower facets. You can take an extremely valuable diamond, cut it the wrong way, and you can cut its value in half in the process."

I'm wondering what any of this has to do with her husband's murder, but I don't ask.

"Sammy was approached by a man who wanted a diamond cut to make two stones out of one."

"Is that unusual?"

"Not necessarily. Sometimes clients would come to

him with gems that had old-fashioned cuts. They wanted the stones modernized. Just as you can reduce the value of a diamond with a bad cut, by the same token you can increase its value with an improved cut."

"I see."

"But what this man wanted to do was to change the diamond from a heart-shape to two pear-shaped stones."

"Why would anyone do that?" I ask.

"No one in his right mind would have wanted to cut that beautiful heart-shaped diamond into two different stones. My ex-husband told me he recognized the work of the original cutter—a colleague of his in Antwerp. It was a beautiful job. Sammy suspected the only reason anyone would cut the stone into two was that the diamond was stolen and whoever had it wanted to change it so that it couldn't be traced."

"Interesting."

"Sammy wasn't much of a husband, but he was an artist when it came to his work, a craftsman. He wasn't about to ruin that beautiful jewel. He refused."

"How do you know all this?"

"We divorced three years ago. Haven't lived together for five years. But we remained friends. In a way, the divorce was the best thing that ever happened to our relationship. At least I thought so. Sammy didn't agree. He was always anxious for us to get back together. He sent me flowers, gave me jewels, always trying to get us to move in together again. I told him he should see other people."

"Did he?"

"Yeah. He did start dating an Indian woman. But even then, I had the feeling he was doing it to try to make me jealous. But I knew it was best that we stayed apart. Anyway, my ex-husband told me about this man coming to see him with the heart-shaped gem on a Monday. He told me that he refused to cut the diamond. He also said he was going to contact the Diamond Dealers Club to warn them that this stone was circulating in New York. The next day, Sammy was shot outside of his office. Police called it a random drive-by shooting with no apparent motive. I don't believe it.''

"What do you think happened?"

"Whoever wanted that diamond cut realized my husband knew what they were up to. So they wanted to silence him.''

"Who's they?"

"I don't know. Sammy didn't recognize the man who showed him the stone. I told the police everything I know, but they've come up with nothing.''

"This heart-shaped stone...could it have been St. Valentine's Diamond?''

"I'd never heard of St. Valentine's Diamond until you mentioned it. What is it?''

I tell her everything I've found out so far, including the fact that I almost got killed by two men who were after the gem.

"I'm sure it's the same stone," she says after hearing my story. "Which means that whoever killed my ex-husband probably killed Morris Greg as well.''

"Do you think it's the guy with the cowboy hat?" I ask.

"Maybe. But when I talked to him in Mr. Finkelstein's office he said he was an oilman from out West who was there to buy a diamond for his wife.''

"This guy is no oilman." Then I finally ask her what I've been wondering all along. "Why were *you* at Moishe Finkelstein's office?''

"I went to Finkelstein's office because I found out

that he had a ten-carat diamond out on memo to my ex-husband.''

"What do you mean 'out on memo'?" I ask.

"You see, the diamond trade still operates on an old-fashioned system of trust. When a dealer puts a diamond out on memo, that means he's loaning a diamond to another dealer. If the borrower sells the stone, then he gives the person who loaned it to him the agreed upon price. If he can't sell it, he returns it to the dealer. Usually this is a very informal arrangement. Sometimes there's no receipt at all. Most transactions are in cash, and million-dollar deals are closed with a handshake and a spoken promise of payment.''

"I see."

"However," she goes on, "in other cases the dealer might scribble his signature on the back of a business card with a memo regarding the size and price of the diamond. I found one of Moishe Finkelstein's business cards among my husband's diamond-cutting tools in his shop. There was a note on the back of the card stating that Moishe had loaned my husband a ten-carat diamond before he was murdered.''

"Is that so?"

"Naturally, I wanted to return the stone to Mr. Finkelstein. So I brought the memo to his office. I wanted to explain to him that it might take me some time to find the diamond since I wasn't sure where all of Sammy's things were.''

"What did Moishe say?"

"Well, I was in for quite a surprise. He said Sammy didn't owe him anything.''

"Why not?"

"Because he never gave him any diamond. He had no idea what I was talking about.''

"Did you show him the memo?"

"Yes. He said it looked like his handwriting, but it wasn't." She turns a gold ring nervously on her finger. "He never loaned a diamond to my ex-husband."

Something has been nagging me ever since this whole business began. Finally, I ask Isabel. "Do you think Moishe Finkelstein is involved in anything illegal?"

The actress doesn't hesitate a moment. "Absolutely not."

I feel a huge sense of relief. "What makes you so sure?"

Isabel crosses her legs again but the poodle on her foot has stopped fidgeting. "Well, look at it this way. The memo I took to Mr. Finkelstein's shop was for five hundred thousand dollars. If he was dishonest he could have demanded payment. My husband wasn't alive to say whether or not he really owed Mr. Finkelstein money. And if I couldn't find the diamond I would have to give Finkelstein the money. But he didn't want any money." She hesitates a moment, then asks, "Does that sound like a dishonest businessman to you?"

No, it doesn't. But this whole mess has gotten so crazy I don't know what to think anymore. There is another way to look at this, too. Maybe Moishe really is mixed up with St. Valentine's Diamond and put the stone out on memo to Sammy Lipschitz. Suppose someone came along, murdered Lipschitz and ripped off the diamond. When Isabel Quick brings the memo to Moishe's shop, he can't very well say, "oh, yeah, you owe me five hundred thousand dollars for the stolen diamond your husband was trying to sell for me before he got killed." In fact, he's got to do just the opposite and deny that he knows anything about St. Valentine's Diamond even if it costs him half a million dollars. Otherwise the stone could be traced back to him. But I have a hard time believing this scenario. The idea that Moishe Finkelstein is dealing in illegal jewels is as preposterous as if someone told me he was selling crack cocaine.

"Isabel, let me ask you something. Who was the diamond cutter in Antwerp whom your ex-husband believed cut the heart-shaped stone?"

"He didn't say what his name was."

"What *did* he say?"

"That it was the work of a master craftsman."

"Like your ex-husband?"

She looks across the room at the Paul Klee. Frown lines wrinkle her brow. "Yes, Sammy *was* a master. Why?"

"How did he know this cutter in Antwerp?"

"Sammy ran a small cutting facility in Antwerp, as well as New York."

"I see. May I use your phone?"

"Of course."

It has been nearly nine hours since I discovered the body of Morris Greg in my apartment and I still haven't called Fidelma. I dread doing it, but before I leave to go uptown, I decide to call her from Isabel's house.

When Fidelma picks up the phone her voice is sleepy and scared. "Hello?"

"Fidelma?"

There is a long silence.

"Fidelma?"

"Danny, don't call me anymore."

"Fidelma, please. You don't understand!"

"Just turn yourself in, Danny."

"I didn't do anything!"

"You need help."

"I need *your* help, Fidelma. I'm in trouble."

"Danny, maybe there's some explanation. Did you find Morris in your apartment and think he was a burglar or something?"

"Fidelma, this is crazy. I didn't do anything."

"I've talked to Detective Washington," says Fidelma. "Maybe you can get a reduced sentence if you cooperate. How did you get mixed up in this diamond business?"

"I'm not mixed...I can't tell you. I'll explain later. Just do me a favor for God's sake and I can prove I'm innocent."

"What favor?" Fidelma's voice is shaking.

"I want you to go to my apartment..."

I hear Fidelma suck in her breath. "Oh, God, Danny. You think I can go in there? After what you've done? Why, Danny? Why? He meant nothing to me. We were just friends!"

"Fidelma, this is ridiculous. Please, I didn't do anything. I found Morris in my apartment, dead. Now help me, please. It's important."

Just then, Isabel Quick's boy toy comes out of the bathroom and she calls across the room to him: "Hey, lover boy, thanks for a good time last night."

"Who is that?" Fidelma asks, suspicious. "Who are you with?"

"Fidelma, I'll explain later."

"I heard a woman's voice. What did she say about last night? It's just six-thirty in the morning. Where are you?"

"I'll explain later. I want you to go to my apartment. It won't take a minute. Just push redial on the phone and find out who the last outgoing call on my phone was made to."

"Danny, you're sick. You need help. You killed my

roommate last night and now you're already sleeping with someone else. Get help!'' she screams and bangs down the phone.

I immediately put in a call to Detective Washington.

"O'Flaherty, you're in a lot of trouble," the detective says before I even have a chance to say hello. "I told you to get up here right away. I've got patrolmen combing the city looking for you now. Where the hell are you? Your prints are all over the murder scene."

"Of course they are…I live there, remember?" Is he joking? "Besides, how did you know they were my prints?"

"Because Officer Rivera took your print from the glass of water you brought her."

"Oh, yeah," I say. "So that's what that was all about."

"Where have you been?"

"I got picked up by two gentleman who almost killed me."

"Who?"

I describe the Cowboy and his sidekick as well as the car they were driving.

"Where are you now?"

"I'm in Hell's Kitchen." I give him Isabel Quick's address. "And what have you been telling Fidelma? That I murdered her roommate?"

"You get your butt up here now!" Washington shouts. I've never actually heard him lose his cool before. "I'm putting you under arrest when you do get here."

"Under arrest?" I can't believe this. "What for?"

"Murder one, trafficking in stolen diamonds, obstruction of justice, withholding evidence."

This is ludicrous. "What evidence?"

"We know all about St. Valentine's Diamond, O'Flaherty. We've already booked Moishe Finkelstein."

"No!"

"I'm afraid so."

"What's the charge?"

"Never mind. Just get up here before one of my men drags you up here. I'm not sure yet how you're mixed up in all this. But give yourself up and it will look better for you in court."

Court? Give myself up? I can't believe this is happening.

FIVE

AS I LEAVE Isabel Quick's building and step into the street, I spot a coffee pushcart just setting up and realize I haven't eaten since yesterday morning. I buy a bagel and a cup of black coffee from the Middle-Eastern guy running the cart. As I'm eating my bagel, I spot two uniformed cops sitting in an unmarked car across the street and my heart starts racing. I've never felt like this before in my life, but all of a sudden I feel paranoid about cops. I want to go directly to Washington rather than be hauled in by a couple of patrolmen.

As I finish my bagel, the cop behind the wheel steps out of his car, puts his night stick through the loop in his belt and strolls toward me. He's an enormous man, at least six feet six and weighing close to three hundred pounds and his uniform is too small for him. My heart is practically banging a hole in my chest. I polish off my coffee, drop the cup in a garbage can and walk briskly away.

"Hey, you!" the cop calls.

Then—don't ask me why—I start running.

I look back and the second cop has gotten out of the car and is racing after me. He's a short guy, under five-five and runs like a sprinter. The big cop is back behind the wheel. The cop chasing me is in a lot better shape than I am and gaining on me quickly. I can hear his heaving breath behind me and the thump of his shoes on the sidewalk. I'm not sure why I'm running, but now it's too late to stop. If Moishe Finkelstein can be arrested, then anyone can. How can I help Moishe if I'm in jail, too?

"Stop!" The patrolman yells as he gains on me. "Police!"

My legs are burning and my right side feels like someone has driven a sword into it. In the meantime, the big cop behind the wheel swings the unmarked car into the street and races after me.

I dash across Eleventh Avenue and nearly get creamed by a delivery truck whose driver screams at me as he swerves to miss an oncoming car. In the confusion, I've lost the cop who was chasing me on foot and duck into an alley to catch my breath. My chest is heaving, my gut burning, and I look around for some way to escape. At the back of the alley, dozens of garbage cans are stacked, their contents spilling out. I kick aside a tier of cans and leap through a hole in a chain link fence into the back court of the adjoining building.

When I emerge on 52nd Street, the cop I thought I'd ditched blindsides me. "Alright, buddy," he says, pushing me against the wall. He rakes my face against the brick as he slings me to the ground and jerks my arms behind my back while he reaches for his handcuffs. "You're under arrest." He jams his knee into the small of my back and clamps the handcuffs on my wrists so tightly it cuts off the circulation. Then he hauls me to my feet, spins me around, and knees me in the groin. I double over in pain as he slams his knee back up again under my chin, snapping my head back and knocking me on my butt.

"Get up!"

I'm dazed, and I push my tongue against a loose tooth

at the back of my mouth and spit a mouthful of blood on the ground.

"I said get up!" he shouts.

I stand up and he pushes me ahead of him all the way around the block and back to 51st Street. As we step off the sidewalk, his partner in the unmarked car pulls up, runs around, opens the rear door and throws me in the back seat. The two cops get in front and slap their open palms together in a high five.

A small crowd has gathered. As we pull away from the curb, the little cop on the passenger side puts his head out the window and says: "Everything's okay now, folks. You can go home. We've just taken another piece of scum off the streets of Manhattan."

"That's enough now," says the cop behind the wheel.

We race toward the West Side Highway. The cop behind the wheel takes his patrolman's cap off and starts unbuttoning his shirt.

The cop on the passenger side turns around and says to me: "You have the right to remain silent, anything you say..."

"Cut the rights crap," his partner says as he slips one arm out of his shirt, his right hand still on the wheel.

"Oh, come on, I always wanted to read someone his rights."

"Shut up!" says the driver.

"Come on, man. It's fun to be the one saying it to someone *else* for a change."

What are they talking about?

"You really hammed it up with that cop stuff. Now shut up and get out of that uniform," his partner orders.

Get out of the uniform?

"Alright, alright," says the little cop as he starts undressing, too. "Is that all you ever say?" he adds, whining. "Shut up?"

"Shut up!" The cop behind the wheel says again, "We'll toss these uniforms when we get downtown."

Toss their uniforms?

"Ah, come on, man," his partner whines. "I want to keep mine."

"Shut up, butt-wipe! You want to do time in Sing Sing for impersonating a police officer? We got to ditch these things."

Now I know I'm really in trouble. It was bad enough when I thought these guys were actually cops. "Where are we going?" I ask, nervously.

The two roll eyes at each other. "Should we tell him?" asks the driver.

The little guy giggles like a schoolgirl. "Sure, why not?"

"Well, we're going to a very *rare* part of the city," says the driver and they both break into hysterical laughter.

"Yeah," the little one adds in a fake British accent. "It's a *bloody* nice place."

These two idiots are laughing so much that we almost smash into a school bus as we turn onto the West Side Highway and speed south.

"Where the hell are you taking me?" I scream.

"Hey," says the driver, suddenly serious, holding up an index finger the size of a polish sausage. "There's no need to yell. Just relax. We're taking you to the…" He breaks into laughter again and can't finish the sentence.

"The Meat Packing District," his partner finishes for him in a high-pitched squeal. He is laughing so hard tears are running down his cheeks.

The Meat Packing District is south of Chelsea on the west side near Ninth Avenue…roughly from 17th Street to West 12th Street. Its grungy, desolate streets are home to butchers, slaughterhouses, coolers for storing animal carcasses, meat-packing houses. To add to the strangeness of this grisly network of streets, it has become the new hip place in Manhattan among the sexual cutting edge, so there are S&M clubs, fetish clubs and hip bars sandwiched between packing houses and wholesale meat shops.

"Now, don't have a *cow*," the big guy behind the wheel says, and the two of them break into maniacal cackles.

Once the guy in the passenger seat has his laughter under control, he says to me, "Hey, what's your *beef?*" Then both of them break into the same scary, twisted laughter.

Within minutes we turn off the West Side Highway onto Twenty-Third Street, then turn south on Ninth Avenue. We pass the Old Homestead with its life-size plastic cow over the entrance—*We're the King of Beef*—and turn right on Fourteenth Street. We pass the Plymouth Beef Company, M&W Packing, Inc., then turn left onto Washington Street.

Men in white ankle-length coats are unloading a semi truck. An enormous metal arm swings from the building to the back of the truck. The arm has meat hooks hanging from it and the men slip the trussed back legs of whole butchered cattle onto the hooks. We pass a bar on the left—Hogs & Heifers. *No Club Colors,* says the sign out front. The place looks like a dump, but it's a hangout for people like Paul McCartney and Mick Jagger. We turn left on Little West 12th Street and about halfway up the block, we pull in front of a metal garage door between two loading docks. Above each loading dock is a metal framework with meat hooks hanging from it. The big guy behind the wheel noses the car to the door of the garage. A sign over the garage door says: *Suckling pigs, lamb, sides of beef, pig's feet.*

The driver takes a garage door opener from the dashboard, points it at the door and pushes the button. The garage door opens and as we pull inside, the little guy says in an exaggerated falsetto, "Honey, we're home!"

The garage door closes behind us and I can smell death.

The guy in the passenger seat gets out and pulls me roughly out of the back seat. The floor of the narrow garage is sticky with blood and the air smells of fresh meat. Along the sides of the walls are clear plastic bags of discarded chicken parts. The guy shoves me forward to a metal door that he pulls open. We are hit with a blast of freezing air as we step inside. The driver turns off the car and follows, closing the door to the freezer behind us. Sides of beef dangle from the ceiling on meat hooks. At the back of the freezer the little guy opens another door and all three of us step into a room used for cutting meat. There are long wooden tables and blood-stained white aprons hanging on hooks along the walls. Rows of boning knives, meat cleavers and tenderizing tools hang on metal racks suspended from the ceiling.

"You know what I like about this job?" asks his partner.

"No. What do you like about this job?"

"Well, you might not believe this, but when I was a little boy I wanted to be a cop."

"You? A cop?"

"Don't laugh. And then a few minutes ago, I *got* to be a cop. I mean that was real, man. We busted this guy just like we were on *NYPD Blue.*"

"You're a moron."

I'm hyperventilating, sweating profusely, knowing

these two are capable of anything. I feel like I'm going to pass out.

"Relax, man," the big guy says to me. "Just relax."

They grab me and lay me face up on a long wooden butcher block set up on legs, my hands still in cuffs. I'm having visions of Morris Greg laid out on my bed. They strap me down to the butcher block with straps around my legs and across my chest.

"Yeah, relax," says his partner when they are finished strapping me down. He takes down a long butcher knife from the overhead rack. "This won't hurt a bit."

"My God!"

"Now," the little guy says to his buddy. "I'll tell you something else."

"Okay. You tell me something else."

"When I was in high school I wanted to be a doctor."

"Oh, really? Don't you have to know your numbers and colors to do that?"

"Go ahead and laugh. Actually, I wanted to be a surgeon. And now…" He held the gleaming butcher knife above my chest with his left hand. "My second operation."

"No!" I gasp.

"Wait, let me guess," says the other guy. *"Dr. Kildare?"*

"Man, you're so out of it. *ER,* man, *ER!"*

Bullets of sweat have popped out on my forehead and my heart is racing. "What are you doing?" I gasp.

"In medical terminology," the little guy says, playing doctor, "it's called a diamondectomy."

Suddenly, as if in a flash, it has all become clear to me.

"You see," the short guy goes on, still playing doctor, "at this point the diamond is lodged most likely in…"

he points the tip of the knife blade just below my navel "...the small intestine."

"Please, think about what you're doing..."

"Oh, I've considered it for some time now. Every operation is carefully thought out and planned. We'll have to make an incision here..."

"Please, you guys don't want to do this."

"Not without anesthesia, no. You are quite correct. But our anesthesiologist took the day off. She had to get a pedicure."

I try to wiggle loose, but the straps hold tight.

"Relax. It will all be over soon."

"Get on with it," says the driver. "I want to get out of this creepy place."

"You need to work on your bedside manner," the little guy says to his partner. Then he puts the tip of the blade back under my navel and starts to apply pressure.

"Shut up and get the diamond."

Sweat drips down my forehead and my hands are icy with fear. I don't yet know why all this is happening, but I do know why I have a diamond in my gut...and I know who is responsible for putting it there. "You two guys cut open Morris Greg because you thought he had the diamond."

"Not exactly. We cut up the guy because we thought he was you!"

The little guy pushes harder on the knife and a bead of blood pops out on my stomach. Just as I feel myself losing consciousness I hear a banging back in the freezer.

"What was that?"

"Get him open and let's get the diamond."

"I heard something," says the little guy.

"It's nothing, let's go."

I hear the banging again as if someone is lifting the garage door.

"What was that?"

"Just get on with it."

He lunges down with the knife just as the freezer door swings open and I hear shots fired. The knife drops from his hand and he collapses on the floor.

"Get your hands up!" Washington shouts, his Glock held firmly in both hands. "Get them up!"

A swarm of blue-suited officers descends on the place. The big guy whirls and fires. One of the policemen tackles him. Two more patrolmen wrestle the gun away from him, slap on handcuffs, and put him under arrest.

"You've got a lot of explaining to do, O'Flaherty," Washington says angrily as he takes off the straps.

The little guy on the floor is whimpering. He seems to have taken a bullet to the shoulder. Washington barks at one of his officers to get an ambulance.

"How did you find me?" I ask.

"Lucky for you," Washington says, "Isabel Quick was watching from her window when you got 'arrested.' She thought there was something not quite right about it."

"But how did she know to call you?"

"She just pushed redial on her phone and got right through to me. I radioed ahead and had these two bozos tailed from the minute they left midtown. So these are the two who killed Morris Greg?"

"Yes. Thank God you got here in time or they would have killed me, too."

"Thank the NYPD, O'Flaherty. But before you start thanking anybody," he says as he leads me out to his car, "you still have a lot of explaining to do."

"There's someone who can explain everything. I'll take you to her."

"Where?"

"The Diamond District."

"I've got someone who's anxious to see you first."

Just then, I see Fidelma sitting in back of the police car. She opens the door and flies into my arms. "Danny, I'm so sorry. Are you all right, love? Will you ever forgive me?"

"Fidelma, I'm sorry about Morris. I know I said some awful things about him."

"Danny, I said some awful things, too. I don't know how I could have ever suspected you of doing something like that. I must have been out of my mind. I've been worried sick about you."

"You have?"

"Of course I have. Are you alright?" she asks.

"Yes and no. It's been a pretty crazy night. And it's been the craziest Valentine's Day of my life," I say, kissing her. I have one arm around Fidelma's waist and my hand on the diamond necklace, still in my jacket pocket. "Did you find out the number of the last outgoing call from my apartment?"

"Yes." Fidelma reaches into her coat pocket and hands me a slip of paper. I look at it and nod.

"What is it, O'Flaherty?" asks Washington as he gets behind the wheel of the car.

"The phone number of the person responsible for Morris Greg's death, Sammy Lipschitz's death...and an attempted murder on me."

"Who's Sammy Lipschitz?"

"I'll explain on the way to the Diamond District."

I TELL WASHINGTON everything I've learned, as well as my own theory of the crime, on the way to 47th Street. When we pull into a parking spot in front of Moishe Finkelstein's office, Washington takes out his cell phone and says, "Give me the number." He punches it in as we sign the log at the security desk and ride the elevator upstairs.

"Hello," he says into the phone. "This is Detective Washington of the NYPD." Washington looks at me. "She hung up."

The elevator door opens. Just as we get off, Priti Patel flies out the door of the office heading for the stairs, and smashes into Washington. "Going somewhere, miss?" says the detective, taking her gently by the elbow.

Priti looks frantically from me to Washington. Her face is flushed; a strand of her black hair has fallen across her forehead.

"Hope you're not in a hurry," says Washington, guiding her back into the office. "Well, it doesn't matter if you are. I've got a few questions for you."

"I want to talk to my lawyer," Priti snaps belligerently, her chest heaving.

"Fine." Washington offers his cell phone. "Call's on me."

She just looks at him.

"Let's go back inside," says Washington.

We step into the reception area of Moishe Finkelstein's office. Priti seats herself back behind her desk and fidgets with a mound of paperclips. I sit down on the sofa across the room. Washington perches on a corner of Priti's desk. "What I want to know is *how* Danny ended up with a diamond in his gut?"

"Ask him."

"I'm asking you," says Washington.

She glances at me then back at Washington. "You've already arrested Mr. Finkelstein. What do you want with me?"

Washington reaches over and picks up the phone on her desk and hands it to her. "Call your lawyer. I'm taking you in. Your counsel should probably be present when we question you at the station.''

"Please,'' she says. "I know who's behind all this.''

"Who?''

"A man named Jake Rinzler. He's a greedy diamond smuggler who double-crossed his partner in Africa. They bought St. Valentine's Diamond from a miner for two thousand dollars. But Rinzler murdered his partner in Johannesburg, took the pink diamond for himself and fled to Antwerp. He took it to a diamond cutter there.''

I interrupt for the first time. "Sammy Lipschitz?''

"That's right. Rinzler approached Sammy in Antwerp. Sammy agreed to cut the raw stone into a heart shape. He maintained a diamond-cutting facility in Antwerp and New York. But once Sammy saw that diamond, he knew he had to have it. Sammy tricked Jake Rinzler. He took a Moissanite, or some kind of synthetic stone, cut it in a heart shape and had it artificially treated to color it pink.''

"What's Moissanite?'' asks Washington.

"It's an artificial diamond that not even experienced diamond dealers can always distinguish from the genuine article,'' Priti explains. Then she continues. "Sammy later cut the *real* diamond and smuggled it into New York among a shipment of legitimate stones to Mr. Finkelstein. I removed St. Valentine's Diamond when I received the shipment.''

"I see.'' Washington strokes his chin with his hand.

"Jake Rinzler in the meantime sold the fake diamond, the Moissanite stone, to a known arms dealer named Hector Westman for five hundred thousand dollars. Later, when Westman realized it was a fake, he killed Rinzler.''

"Yeah,'' I add. "That's why the Belgian police found

five hundred thousand dollars in a safe deposit box in Antwerp registered to Jake Rinzler, but no diamond.''

''That's right.''

''Finkelstein didn't know what was going on?'' Washington asks. ''That his office had been used to smuggle an illicit stone?''

''Nobody knew.''

''So how did you get involved?''

The skin around Priti's eyes and mouth tightens. ''How do women usually get involved with jerks?''

''You tell me.''

''Love's got a lot to do with it,'' she says. ''I loved him. But he just used me to smuggle St. Valentine's Diamond into the country.''

''Who?''

''Sammy Lipschitz,'' she says. ''I helped him smuggle the diamond into New York, but I didn't kill anyone.''

Washington says, ''Tell me more.''

''Hector Westman started trying to find who had the real diamond. He suspected that whoever had originally cut the diamond had switched it on Jake Rinzler. He started asking around Antwerp. Found out Sammy Lipschitz had cut the diamond for Rinzler. So Westman came to Sammy's shop here in New York. Hector Westman showed Sammy the Moissanite stone, pretending that he wanted to have it cut into two pear-shaped stones. He just wanted to see how Sammy would react. Sammy was visibly shaken, confirming Westman's suspicion that he had switched stones on Jake Rinzler.''

''Lipschitz told you all this?''

''Sammy told me everything he thought I needed to know.''

''Then what?'' asks Washington.

''Hector Westman went back to Sammy Lipschitz's

shop. Demanded to know where the *real* St. Valentine's Diamond was. Threatened him. Sammy told Westman that Mr. Finkelstein had the diamond. Westman murdered Sammy, anyway."

"How do you know all this?"

"Sammy was a very handsome man," Priti says absently, as if lost in her own thoughts. "A very charming man...or at least he knew how to put on the charm. We met at the Russian Tea Room. He made it seem like a chance meeting. But he had planned it all in advance. I thought he was attracted to me. I fell for him. He wined and dined me...gave me jewelry...champagne, flowers. He treated me like a queen. He said he wanted to marry me. But he just used me."

"First to get St. Valentine's Diamond into the country through Moishe Finkelstein's office," I say. "Then to get it out of the office."

Priti Patel nods. "You're starting to get the picture. He was willing to do anything, pay any price to own it. But it wasn't for the money."

"Oh, no?" Washington raises his eyebrows.

"Even for Sammy, not everything had to do with money. Love had a lot to do with it again. But it didn't have anything to do with me." There is a catch in her voice. "All along he was still in love with Isabel Quick. He wanted to win her back with the diamond. I didn't know it at the time, but I found out he wanted to give the real diamond to Isabel Quick for Valentine's Day."

"How touching," says Washington sarcastically.

"He still had to get it out of Moishe's office," I add.

"I loved Sammy," says Priti. "I would have done anything for him."

"Kill someone?" I ask.

Priti moves uncomfortably in her chair, then plunges back into her story. "When...when Sammy was found shot outside of his shop, I knew Hector Westman had found him out. I knew Westman would be coming to the shop eventually to get the diamond. It was my idea to swallow the stone and walk out with it. I prepared a batch of cookies here in the office, in the microwave, with the diamond in one. Then, yesterday, Hector Westman showed up at the shop, claiming he was an oilman who wanted to buy jewelry for his wife. But I knew it was Westman. I just knew. And I knew I had to get the diamond out of the office right away. But I had no idea it would turn out like this.''

''Those goons almost cut me wide open.'' I'm so angry my voice is shaking. ''I'm sure you knew about all those other cases where thieves swallowed diamonds. So you figured you'd make me your human jewelry box.''

''That's enough,'' says Washington.

''So I fed the diamond to Danny in a Valentine's Day cookie when he came to the office.''

''I should have known that was no macadamia nut I bit into.''

''But why use Danny?'' asks Washington. ''Why not swallow the diamond yourself, or just walk out of here with it?''

''Sammy had been very careful all along. Before he was killed he knew the shop was being watched. The embassy of Zimbibia had been snooping around. The customs department sent a man over to talk to Moishe. Sammy had reason to believe that federal authorities were involved. Word had somehow gotten out that the diamond was going to be sold through this office. I'd been followed from Mr. Finkelstein's office almost every night since I met Sammy. He was afraid I'd get caught with the diamond on me.''

''So, once Sammy was dead,'' Washington adds, ''you had the diamond all to yourself?''

Priti looks up and says quietly, "Yes. All to myself."

"But you knew Hector Westman would be gunning for you."

"It was one of the most beautiful stones I'd ever seen in my life. But I didn't expect Hector Westman to find out where it was so fast. So, when he showed up at the office, I panicked and fed the diamond to Danny."

I feel a pain in my gut.

"But Westman must have figured out what I'd done." She glares at me, then says, "Soon after Danny left, Westman left, too. He and his partner must have followed Danny uptown. Got into his apartment and killed…"

"You're lying," I shout, standing up from the couch and moving toward her. Both Washington and Priti look at me, startled. "Neither Westman nor his partner ever got into my apartment. You're lying about Sammy Lipschitz, too."

"No," she says. "Hector Westman killed him."

"You're the one who killed Sammy Lipschitz."

"No! I loved Sammy."

"You did kill him. Hector Westman may be a thief and a gun-runner. And he may have killed Jake Rinzler in Antwerp. But you ordered a hit on Sammy Lipschitz. When you found out he didn't love you, that he still loved Isabel Quick, you hired those two goons who almost killed me to kill Sammy."

"That's not true!"

"Yes, it is. Whoever killed Morris Greg made a phone call from my apartment to this phone." I point at the phone on Priti's desk. "Are you trying to tell me that Hector Westman called you to say there was no diamond inside Morris Greg when he cut him open? I don't think so. It was somebody else who called to tell you there was no diamond inside Morris Greg. Sure, Westman and

his sidekick followed me uptown. But it was the same
two bumbling hitmen that *you* hired to kill Sammy Lipschitz who killed Morris Greg. Westman knew what I
looked like. Those two idiots killed the wrong man.''

Priti Patel's eyes fill with tears.

"But tell me this," I continue. "Are they the ones
who planted that phony memo on Sammy Lipschitz?"

"What memo?" asks Washington.

"You forged that memo to incriminate Moishe Finkelstein, didn't you?" I ask Priti. "You wanted to make
it look like Moishe had put a diamond out on memo to
Sammy Lipschitz worth five hundred thousand dollars.
You figured if anybody found out that someone had ordered the hit on Sammy, the cops would find the memo.
Maybe they'd figure Moishe had Sammy killed because
Lipschitz owed him five hundred thousand dollars and
wouldn't pay him."

Priti Patel looks at her hands folded in front of her on
the desk.

Now, I'm shaking with anger. "I'll bet you didn't
know that those two stupid hitmen left diamond dust all
over Morris Greg's body, did you? They had diamond
dust on their fingers because they picked it up when they
planted that phony memo in Sammy Lipschitz's shop
before they killed him."

Priti Patel turns away from me and faces Washington.
"Yes, I called those two awful men again as soon as
Danny left the office. Told them that Danny O'Flaherty
had swallowed the diamond and I told them his address."

"So those two guys were waiting at my apartment,"
I add. "But instead, Morris Greg showed up to give my
cat his medicine. They assumed *he* was Danny
O'Flaherty. Those two goons murdered Morris Greg and
cut him open in an attempt to recover the million-dollar

diamond. But surprise! No diamond. So, like the idiots they are, they actually use my phone to call you and tell you they can't find the diamond."

"Yes," says Priti. "Like idiots! And now I knew you were walking around the city with *my* diamond. My beautiful St. Valentine's Diamond. I told those jerks I wanted that diamond, no matter what it took to get it."

I can hardly believe it. My stomach is churning just thinking about all of this, not to mention the fact that I've got a million dollars in my gut. "Where did you find those two losers, anyway? The Internet? *Hitmen-R-Us?*"

"That's enough, O'Flaherty," says Washington.

"I hope you got a discount on those hitmen, because if brains were gasoline those two clowns wouldn't have enough to start a flea's motorcycle and drive halfway around a marble."

"I said that's enough," Washington shouts.

Priti reaches for a box of tissue on her desk, takes one, and blows her nose. "Sammy lied to me. He never loved me. He wanted the diamond for his *true* love. I had him killed for that. Now he'll never have her. And she'll never have St. Valentine's Diamond."

After Detective Washington reads Priti Patel her rights and arrests her, he takes her downstairs and puts her in the back of the squad car. A call comes in on his cell phone and Washington talks for five minutes. Then he snaps the cell phone shut and turns to me. "The FBI just found Hector Westman and his sidekick."

"Excellent. Are they under arrest?

"Dead," says Washington. "The Feds have been following them for some time now. The reason Westman and his partner were so desperate to get the real St. Valentine's Diamond back is that they had already traded the fake one for a shipment of Kalashnikovs that they

were negotiating to sell to the Zimbianese Liberation
Front. The gun dealers they bought the weapons from
also discovered it was a fake diamond. They gave Westman twenty-four hours to come up with the real stone.
I'm afraid the clock ran out on him.''

"My God. Where did they find them?''

"In a marsh outside of Jersey City. The Feds said that
by the time they found them, birds from a nearby landfill
were picking their brains.''

Fidelma gets out of one of the other police cars, runs
over and puts her arms around my neck. "Oh, Danny.
Thank God you're safe.''

Washington winks at me as he gets behind the wheel
of the squad car.

A small crowd has gathered around the cop cars
parked in the street. I'm so tired my knees are about to
buckle under me. All I want to do is go home and get
some rest. Tonight I'll take Fidelma out for a nice dinner
and give her the necklace. Right now I'm dirty, the knees
of my pants are ripped, and I have a bullet hole in the
shoulder of my jacket.

"Fidelma,'' I say. "Let's celebrate Valentine's Day
tonight over dinner. I have a surprise for you. But right
now I have to get some sleep.''

"I understand, Danny. You go ahead.''

Washington interrupts. "You're not going anywhere,
O'Flaherty.''

"What?''

"You still have a lot of questions to answer. Besides,
I want that diamond on my desk. We'll need it for evidence. We'll keep you in a holding cell until we get the
diamond back.''

"No!''

"I'm afraid so. There's no way you can walk out of

here now. Not when you're toting a million bucks and evidence in a murder one case in your belly.''

I almost pass out from exhaustion in Fidelma's arms.

"Go, ahead, Danny. I'll make dinner for us tonight.''

"But Fidelma, I have something for you.'' It's not clear when I'll get home from the precinct. I take the diamond necklace from my coat pocket. "Happy Valentine's Day, darling,'' I say, handing it to her.

"Oh, Danny! It's lovely. When did you get it?''

"That's why I couldn't tell you how I'd gotten mixed up in this diamond business. I was out shopping for a necklace for you.''

"Oh, Danny!'' Tears spring into Fidelma's eyes and she throws her arms around me. "I'm so sorry.''

I go around behind her. "Let me put it on.'' When I've finished fastening the tiny clasp on the gold chain, I take a deep breath and place my hands on Fidelma's shoulders. "Honey, before they take me uptown, I have an important question to ask you.''

I feel Fidelma's shoulders rise under my hands. "Yes?''

"Will you...will you make me the happiest man in the world?''

Fidelma turns around and looks up at me. Her blazing red hair cascades down her back and the necklace dangles between the soft V of her breasts. Her lips part in a joyous smile and her dazzling green eyes sparkle like a million dollars in diamonds.

THE LOVEBIRDS
by B.J. Daniels

Acknowledgments

With special thanks to former Gallatin County Coroner Rob Myers for his expertise when it comes to corpses; to fellow writers Carmen Lassiter and Judy Kinnaman for their input and encouragement; and as always, to my loving husband, Parker.

ONE

PEGGY KANE GLARED at the string of naked pink cupids fluttering over the floral shop counter. "Lovebirds?" she demanded into the cell phone as she turned her back to the cupids—and the clerk.

"Yes." Oliver Sanders sounded distracted. She could imagine him behind his big mahogany desk loosening his tie, his suit jacket already off and hanging neatly over the back of his chair, the scent of his expensive cologne mingling with the rich smell of leather and wood.

"I should have thought of them before," he said. She could hear the scrape of a pen on paper. He must be signing the letters she'd typed for him before he sent her to buy Valentine's Day presents for his wife. "You got the good chocolate right, the stuff from Bulgaria or whatever?"

"Belgium. Yes." Only the best for Mitzy Baxter Sanders. "I went to the little shop you told me to go to."

"And the flowers?" Peggy could tell by his tone that he'd stopped what he was doing and was finally giving her his undivided attention. "You didn't forget flowers?"

He didn't call her Miss Efficiency for nothing. "Roses. Red Beauties. Two dozen. They are the largest, reddest and sweetest ones you can buy."

She could hear the smile of approval in his voice. "I

knew I could count on you. And you've got the key I gave you for the elevator to the penthouse. You're going to have to hurry to get everything there before she gets home. It has to be perfect. You know how important tonight is.''

She knew. ''It will be,'' she said glancing at her watch. How was she expected to get everything to the hotel before Mitzy got home, she wanted to know, but didn't ask, reminding herself how lucky she was. The day she'd become Oliver Sanders' secretary, her dreams had finally begun to come true.

She hung up and asked the florist behind the counter where she could find lovebirds in a resort town like River's Edge, Montana.

''There's a new pet shop in that mall on the way to the ski hill,'' the starry-eyed young woman told her. ''Roses and lovebirds?''

Peggy nodded as she gathered up all of her purchases.

''Oh, how sweet and so-o-o-o romantic!'' the clerk cooed.

Yeah. Peggy batted away one of the cupids hanging over the door as she left, sick to death of hearts and flowers. She'd spent years of watching other women get boxes filled with chocolate and big, bright bouquets in pretty vases.

''Oh, look, I got flowers! Here, smell them!''

Smell them?

Peggy swore under her breath. What sadist, she wanted to know, had come up with a holiday that so flaunted the fact you didn't have anyone? Wasn't it bad enough that all year long someone was trying to fix you up with blind dates? That your mother probably thought you were a lesbian since you were thirty-two and man-less? That the man of your dreams was married to someone else and buying *her* all the wonderful Valentine's Day presents you'd ever dreamed of? And some presents you hadn't even thought of? Like lovebirds?

Lovebirds! She bought a peach-colored pair, trying not to gag at the sight of them cuddled together before she covered them. Then with her car full, she headed for The Riverside.

The Riverside was once a stagecoach stop in the middle of nowhere until the ski hill went in and River's Edge was born as a winter ski and summer fishing resort. Oliver Sanders's father, Otto, bought the massive stone building and turned it into an elegant old-style hotel complete with a penthouse that overlooked the town, the ski hill and the river.

Peggy slipped past the desk clerk, a fastidious man in a blue and gold uniform who was busy on the phone but motioned frantically for her to wait for a bellhop to help her. Luckily for her, both the clerk and bellhop were busy with a busload of Minnesota skiers.

She was dying to see the penthouse where Oliver lived and she didn't want some bellhop watching her every move. She hurried into the private elevator. The door closed before the bellhop could get a cart for her purchases, let alone catch her. She used the key for access to the penthouse.

In the quiet of the elevator, she leaned against the wall, tired, hungry and irritable. The coo of the lovebirds irritated the hell out of her and she felt antsy.

Only one thing made her feel better. Thinking about Oliver. That alone had sustained her all these years. It hadn't been easy, feeling the way she did about him. She had to leave town when he married Mitzy right after high school, unable to stand it.

Mitzy. Her momentary good mood evaporated at just

the thought of Mitzy as the elevator slowed to a stop. Mitzy was two years younger and had captured Oliver's attention from the time they were all kids. Mitzy in her twin blond ponytails bobbing under pretty pink bows. Mitzy in high school in the same color pink, but only a cashmere sweater that stretched over her twin perky breasts that bobbed as she walked. The same pink as cupids.

The elevator door opened directly into the penthouse foyer. Gathering up the presents, Peggy stepped onto the shining white marble and braced herself for the wave of jealousy she knew was about to hit her.

It was worse than she'd thought. She put down the lovebirds, the roses, the massive box of chocolates, the champagne, the velvet box with the diamond tennis bracelet nestled in it and the tiny vial of one-of-a-kind perfume. She carefully put the last beside all the rest on the antique table next to the door, arranging them, just as Oliver had instructed.

Then she moved slowly into the apartment, trying not to drool. *This* was exactly what she'd always dreamed of. A life like this. With Oliver. It would silence all the years of being called Piggy and pudgy and plain old fat. She hadn't been fat for several years but she still *felt* fat inside. Probably because she knew Piggy Kane was only a Sara Lee cheesecake away.

She didn't have much time. Mitzy would be home soon. Mitzy, who'd taken one look at her after returning to town and said, ''My God, you've lost a ton of weight. I barely recognized you!''

Mitzy, who'd suggested lining her up with Oliver's aging mechanic. The same Mitzy who would never know that her husband had sent his secretary out to do his Valentine's Day shopping at the very last minute.

That is, she'd never know as long as Peggy got out of the penthouse and soon.

Peggy walked through the apartment, touching the lush furnishings, wanting to lick her fingers everything felt so good. In the bedroom, she opened the door to the huge walk-in closet and stepped in to feel the fine fabric of Oliver's suits. When she pressed a sleeve to her face, she could smell his cologne and almost imagine him here in this room with her.

She turned and saw Mitzy's side of the closet filled with more clothes than Peggy had even dreamed of ever owning in a lifetime. Fancy gowns, nice suits, beautiful dresses, lush furs. All in size six. Little, cute Mitzy.

Peggy frowned, the old bitter taste in her mouth reminding her that she would never be a size six, would never be prom queen, would never be Mitzy—even if *she* were married to Oliver. And because of that she would never forgive Mitzy.

But then, like poking a stick in an open wound, she reminded herself that it hadn't just been Mitzy who'd made fun of her when she was overweight. Oliver had laughed, then pretended he didn't think it was funny, when Mitzy nicknamed her Piggy, a nickname that had stuck like fat.

Peggy shoved the thought away. It had been her own fault, sitting off by herself at lunchtime, stuffing her face with food, watching Mitzy and Oliver with such envy, wishing— She'd spent years wishing. Then finally done something about it. She'd come back here and gotten the job as Oliver's secretary. Not that she hadn't tortured herself at first with the thought that he'd only hired her out of guilt or pity or both.

As she closed the closet, she turned to stare at the

king-size bed, seeing herself between the satin sheets with Oliver.

A sound from the foyer startled her. She froze, listening. The elevator. She heard it open and close again. Hurriedly, she glanced at her watch. Had Mitzy come home early?

Her heart began to race and she felt sick to her stomach. If she got caught in Mitzy's bedroom— She couldn't hide in the closet. Or under the bed. She'd be trapped and eventually discovered. Her humiliations in high school would pale next to this. Everything would be ruined and Oliver would be furious!

Her stomach growled loudly. Right now, she would have killed for a Big Mac and fries. She closed her eyes, listening with every cell of her body. She should have just dropped off the presents and left. She'd known this place was going to upset her and now all she wanted to do was get out of here and go some place and eat. Eat something rich and fattening that would make her feel better. Something forbidden.

She thought she heard the elevator open again. And close. Was it possible the bellhop had come up looking for her, seen the presents and just assumed she'd left already?

She glanced at her watch again. She still had time to get out of here without being caught by Mitzy. Without upsetting Oliver. If she left right now.

She crept soundlessly over the thick, plush carpet, peering in doorways as she went, trying to convince herself she really was alone in the apartment. She could smell Mitzy's perfume. And Oliver's cologne. The mingling of the two made her sick to her stomach.

The presents were where she'd left them on the table,

the lovebirds cuddling and cooing. Everything looked just as she'd left it, except....

The bow on the candy box had fallen to the floor.

She stepped closer, counting off the gifts, almost afraid she'd find one missing. Birds, flowers, perfume, champagne, jewelry, candy— That was odd. The lid on the heart-shaped box of chocolates!

Someone had opened the box and left the lid half off, probably in a hurry to get out of the penthouse.

Her heart lurched at a sudden thought. Surely the bell-hop wouldn't have taken a piece of the chocolate. No! Panic filled her, making her grab the edge of the table for support. Oliver had been very specific about how everything had to be. It had to be *perfect.*

He'd think *she* took the candy! That she hadn't over-come her "problem" with food. That it was just a matter of time before she became Piggy Kane again. He would never believe the bellhop had taken the candy even if Peggy got the chance to explain. Not that she could ad-mit she'd been in the bedroom snooping around and heard the bellhop come in.

She felt sicker. How much had he taken? Maybe none. Maybe he'd just looked into the box. Her fingers trem-bled as she slowly lifted the lid all the way off, praying all of the chocolate would be nestled in their little red foil cups.

One was missing!

Peggy had watched the woman at the candy shop place the chocolate in an intricate heart pattern. The air thick with the smell of chocolate, she'd watched each specially made morsel go in, right up until the last piece—a perfect heart of milk chocolate drizzled with semi-sweet chocolate.

And now it was gone, leaving only an empty bright

red foil hole gaping at the center of the design and all
of the pieces askew and no longer resembling a heart at
all as if the box had been dropped!

In horror, Peggy realized Mitzy would notice immediately and call it to her husband's attention. Oliver
would have to confess that Peggy had picked up the
presents. Had to have been Peggy who'd taken the piece
of candy.

Mitzy would make a big deal out of it. Peggy could
just hear her, "Poor Piggy Kane, had to steal Valentine's
Day chocolate because it wasn't like anyone was going
to give *her* chocolate. That would be like giving tequila
to an alcoholic."

But that wasn't the worst part. Mitzy wouldn't want
the chocolates, not after Piggy Kane had been in them.
Oliver would be furious. Didn't Peggy know how important it was for tonight to be perfect?

She stared down at the box of candy. Smooth pale
milk chocolates. Dark rich bittersweet chocolates. All
filled with heavenly cremes, mouth-melting caramels
and buttery nuts.

She watched her hand as if seeing it from a great
distance away. Watched her finger and thumb gently lift
one of the milk chocolate cremes from its foil nest as if
lifting out a priceless jewel. Watched the chocolate approach her mouth, the sight of it making her dizzy, the
intoxicating scent of it making her weak with anticipa-
tion.

The forbidden chocolate brushed her lips as lightly as
a kiss and then it was on her tongue. She closed her
warm mouth around it, sucking it in, lips parting slightly
as she released a cocoa-scented sigh. Her breath caught
in her throat as the chocolate slowly, achingly began to
melt.

She had never tasted anything so smooth, so rich. She deserved this. She deserved so…much…more. Then the warm chocolate seemed to burst and the sweet, incredible creme oozed out, filling her mouth. She groaned from the pleasure of it, licking her lips as she closed her eyes, willing herself to fight the urge and hold it in her mouth as long as she could, knowing how quickly the sensation would be gone once she swallowed.

This was heaven. Unfortunately, she knew from experience, it never lasted long enough.

Her hand was already reaching for another chocolate, her mind already crumpling the empty incriminating red foil into her coat pocket and rearranging the chocolates, already convincing herself that no one would ever have to know, especially Oliver. That was when the poison hit.

She had only enough time to pull the Valentine from her pocket before she hit the floor.

TWO

"WHO FOUND THE BODY?" Sheriff Jack McAllister asked the deputy as he rode up the elevator to The Riverside penthouse. He couldn't believe it. He'd been sheriff for less than twenty-four hours and he already had a dead body on his hands. Just his luck, since he'd come home to River's Edge to get away from this very thing.

"*Mrs.* Sanders found her."

He shot a look at the deputy and realized the only Mrs. Sanders he knew would be hugging eighty by now—if she was still alive. He hadn't thought about which Sanders lived in the hotel penthouse. "Ellie Sanders, old man Sanders's wife?"

Deputy Reed, whom Jack had just met that morning, shook his head, his expression suspiciously closed. "Mrs. *Oliver* Sanders. Old man—Mr. Otto Sanders is deceased. His wife, Ellie, resides in Hawaii now."

Good for Ellie. Jack hoped she was having a great time, spending the old man's money.

"Who'd Oliver marry?" he had to ask. Keeping track of the comings and goings in River's Edge had been the last thing on his mind. He'd left pretty soon after high school, taking the best of River's Edge with him, and had never looked back, never planned to come back. As he rode up the elevator, he was starting to remember why.

"Oliver married Mitzy Baxter," Reed said and had to clear his throat.

Jack let out a low whistle. Mitzy Baxter Sanders. Mitzy. Oh, boy.

The elevator door opened onto a slab of white marble floor complete with a dead body and a hysterical woman. He recognized the loud high-pitched complaining voice in the background as Mitzy's. Some things did not change.

A second deputy stood next to the elevator door, protecting the possible crime scene just as Jack had asked. But the poor man looked as if he'd rather be anywhere than here. Jack understood perfectly.

"Mrs. Sanders is a little upset," Deputy Dodson said. "As would be expected," he added quickly.

Jack had to smile. "Yes, as would be expected." He looked from the deputy to the foyer table covered in gifts and the body of a woman lying on the floor beside it. A box of spilled chocolates dotted the marble floor around the body like thrown dirt clods.

Under the table was a woman's large black leather purse with a shopping bag next to it. Against the opposite foyer wall were two more shopping bags and another purse, this one pink and dainty.

Jack bent down, and without touching anything, took a look at the murder victim.

"She's Mr. Sanders's secretary," Dodson informed him. "Her name is Peggy Kane."

That news startled him. Both seemed implausible. He'd gone to school with Peggy Kane. Knew her relationship with not only Oliver, but Mitzy. At least he thought he did. It seemed a number of things *had* changed since he'd been gone—and Peggy Kane had changed the most.

This woman looked nothing like the one he remembered even if her face hadn't been blue. Peggy Kane had lost a lot of weight, but it was more than that, he realized. It was the way she was dressed, the expensive jewelry, the hair, the whole look. It made him wonder what Oliver paid her.

In River's Edge, there were two classes of families. The ones with money who owned the condos, huge seasonal homes and the businesses that thrived because of them. And the ones who worked for the businesses. The Kane family fell into the latter group, just as the McAllisters had.

Peggy had a piece of chocolate gripped in her right hand. It had melted down to just the nut. On closer inspection, in her other hand was what appeared to be a crumpled piece of white paper. He didn't touch it and wondered if anyone else had noticed it.

"I took down everyone's statement, just as you instructed," Dobson said. "I'm also the crime photographer. I shot the elevator, all of the rooms in the penthouse and the possible crime scene." Standard procedure in a sudden death of this nature. "I've sent the photos to the lab. You should have them within the hour."

"Good work," Jack said, pushing himself to his feet again. He asked both deputies to remain at the elevator door and protect the scene until the coroner arrived to tell them whether or not a crime had actually been committed. Then bracing himself, he followed the irritating sound of Mitzy's voice into the living room.

Mitzy actually stopped talking when she saw him. Her mouth remained open, but thankfully nothing came out. Her husband, Oliver Sanders, was at the bar making drinks, his back to Jack. Jack caught his own reflection in the mirror over the bar, seeing himself the way Mitzy must. Older. His dark blond hair still thick although graying at the temples. His blue eyes faded like old denim and lined from the sun. Just seeing how life had weathered and aged him, he remembered with a jolt his real reason for coming back here.

Oliver turned at the sudden quiet, his eyes narrowing at the sight of the new sheriff.

"Well, I'll be damned," was all Oliver said, but he seemed to tense as if expecting a blow.

Jack knew that one of the town councilmen had voted against hiring him as sheriff and figured it had been Oliver Sanders. He told himself that Oliver's obvious anxiety at seeing him could be nothing more than having a dead woman in his foyer. Or it could be the past. Considering his and Jack's past, it could easily have been that alone.

"Jack?" Mitzy cried, finding her voice too soon. "Jack McAllister?"

She'd remembered his name. But he'd have hoped as much considering how…intimate they'd been for a short period of time during his junior year in high school—a time he would have just as soon forgotten.

He reminded himself that she probably felt the same way, in fact, might *have* forgotten him and only remembered when she saw his photo in today's paper. Then again, the story about the new sheriff moving into his office hadn't gotten a lot of play in the resort town's only newspaper—not like Oliver Sanders's new expensive condo development.

Mitzy pushed herself up from a plump velvet couch, but appeared uncertain what to do next. Running into his arms seemed somehow inappropriate, he thought. So did shaking hands, but he held his hand out to her.

"Mrs. Sanders," he said in his cop voice, amazed how much she looked like she had in high school. He'd almost forgotten how partial she was to pink. She wore a pale pink suit with matching high heels and a white silk blouse, all expensive and carefully chosen for effect rather than comfort, just like the decor of this place.

Her sculpted blond hair curled at her suit jacket collar and framed her doll-adorable face, accenting her big baby blues in a way that told him it hadn't been unwittingly. Her still very nicely rounded body had fitness center written all over it.

She took his hand almost coyly, something Jack was sure Oliver hadn't missed. Some things just didn't change.

"Oh, Jack," Mitzy said in that breathy voice of hers. "Sheriff? In River's Edge?" She seemed to find humor in that. Or pity. With Mitzy it was hard to tell.

Jack's gaze moved past Mitzy to the third person in the room.

A slim woman stood silhouetted against the bank of windows looking out over the town and the mountains. It wasn't until she turned that he realized he knew her. That is, had known her. He fought to hide his surprise as she moved toward him, hand outstretched, amusement in her dark eyes.

"Tempest Bailey," she said, as if he wouldn't remember her.

Not a chance. "Tempest," he said, wondering what she was doing here

She nodded as if seeing him wondering. She didn't miss much. "I'm The Riverside's version of a house detective—at least temporarily," she said, making him remember her voice. Soft and deep with a hint of humor. It was one of the sexy things about her, although she hid the rest well. She wore khakis, a white blouse under a navy-blue sweater and cross-trainers. Her hair was long and dark, pulled back into a braid that hung to the center of her back. She wore no makeup, her face lightly freckled. There was something about the privileged. No matter how much they dressed down, they couldn't hide the fact that they'd come from money.

He realized he was staring at her. "Temporarily?" he asked when her words finally registered.

"I've been offered the undersheriff job," she said, tilting her head a little, her eyes glinting.

T. J. Bailey. My God, he'd never dreamed the T. J. Bailey, the applicant the town council had offered the undersheriff position to, was Tempest. He tried to think of something to say to cover his shock and discomfort, but it was impossible with his foot stuck in his mouth.

"Congratulations," he finally managed.

She cocked her head. "It's a little premature for that. I haven't accepted." She met his gaze, her eyes as dark as an abyss.

"Jack!" Mitzy cried, reminding him she had to be the center of attention. "I have a dead woman in my foyer!"

"Yes." It didn't surprise him that she wouldn't refer to Peggy Kane by name. "That's why I'm here. I'll need to get statements from all of you."

"Statements?" Mitzy looked horrified. "She choked to death on one of *my* chocolates. What more is there to say?"

"We won't know what killed her until the coroner—"

"Of course, she choked," Mitzy interrupted. "What else could it have been? Unless it was a heart attack. She did carry a lot of weight for a lot of years." She must have seen his expression. "I'm not speaking ill of the dead. *You* all know it's the truth. She was *huge.*"

Jack pulled the tape recorder from his pocket as Oliver pushed a large martini into his wife's hand.

"I'd offer you a drink, Jack," Oliver said, motioning to his own glass, "but you're on duty, right? Just like Tempest here."

"Why don't we all sit," Jack suggested as he took Mitzy's drink from her hand and put it down on the glass coffee table out of her reach. "If you don't mind."

"I think he'd like to get your statement while you're still halfway sober, my dear," Oliver said to his wife. "Jack obviously knows you."

The tension in the room jumped up a notch as Mitzy shot her husband a .357 point-blank, drop-dead look, but it didn't even seem to wound him, making Jack wonder about their relationship.

"You might want to slow down a little yourself," Jack suggested to Oliver. "Just until I get your statement."

Mitzy smiled at that, then sat on the couch, smoothing the pink fabric over her thighs with both hands. "To think she choked to death on *my* chocolates."

Jack didn't correct her. For all he knew, she might be right. He met Tempest's gaze across the expanse of glass coffee table as she took a chair opposite the couch. He got the distinct impression she didn't think Peggy Kane had choked to death. At least not without help.

He sat in the chair at the end of the coffee table between Mitzy and Tempest. Oliver continued to stand behind the couch, sipping his drink. It was just like him to refuse to sit. After all, he was a Sanders and they didn't take orders from anyone in River's Edge. Especially from some ex-high-school-jock from the wrong side of the tracks named Jack McAllister, even if he was the new sheriff.

"Mitzy, why don't you tell me exactly what you re-member," Jack said as he set the tape recorder on the table. "I'd appreciate it if no one interrupted her." He glanced pointedly at Oliver, who bristled visibly.

"I already told everything to that other cop," Mitzy said irritably. "I don't see why I have to go over it again. It's just all so…ghastly."

"I need to hear it for the record," Jack said as he pushed the record button.

Mitzy stared at the tape recorder, then at her drink for a moment, before she wet her lips and began speaking. "I came home at my usual time. I'm a Realtor, a very good one, in case you haven't heard." She directed the comment and a broad smile at Jack.

"You came home at your usual time," he prompted.

"Yes, I was anxious to get home. It's Valentine's Day," she said and looked from Jack to Tempest as if she doubted either was aware of that fact. "Anyway," she sighed, "I got into the private elevator, started to insert my key for the penthouse when I noticed there was already a key in it." She rolled her eyes. "I thought, damn Oliver! How many times have I told him not to leave his key in the elevator where anyone off the street can just walk right into our penthouse."

"Oliver's left his key in before?" Jack asked.

"Only once or twice," he said with obvious irritation. "The bellhop usually sees it and either brings it up or calls to let me know it's at the desk. It really isn't a big deal. I find the whole key thing to be a real nuisance."

"Anyway," Mitzy continued. "There was the key, so I just assumed Oliver had beat me home. I came up, excited to give him his gift. I bought him a new Rolex. Oh, sorry, dear," she added quickly, glancing at her hus-band. "I guess it won't be much of a surprise now."

Her gaze swung back to Jack. "But then *my* Valentine's Day was ruined the moment I saw Peggy sprawled dead in the middle of my chocolates, wasn't it?" She was completely ignoring Tempest. Nothing new here.

"You were saying what happened when the elevator door opened," Jack reminded her.

She looked at him aghast. "What do you think happened? I saw Peggy and screamed."

"Did you check for a pulse or see if you could help her?" Jack asked.

Mitzy blinked. "I could see that she was dead. I wasn't about to…touch her."

Jack looked to Tempest. "So that's when you came on the scene?"

She nodded. "I was on the floor below. I came right up."

"By elevator?" he asked.

"No, Mrs. Sanders had the elevator door blocked open with her bags. I took the emergency stairs off the fire escape and entered through the fire exit door." Tempest seemed to read his mind. "I insisted Mrs. Sanders leave everything just as she'd found it—including the bags she'd used to block the elevator."

The two shopping bags he'd noticed against the opposite wall from the body.

He turned his attention back to Mitzy, trying not to think about the possibility of working with Tempest Bailey. With luck, she wouldn't take the job. "Did you touch anything?" he asked Mitzy.

"I just screamed and the next thing I knew—" she swung her gaze at Tempest "—she came through my house. It appears Oliver didn't use the dead bolt on the fire escape exit." Mitzy shook her head in disgust.

"Then she called your office and ordered me to go back down to the lobby."

Jack knew the answer to this one. "But you didn't."

"Of course not," Mitzy said. "I couldn't have a bunch of strangers up here unsupervised." Tempest Bailey was far from a stranger to Mitzy even if Tempest hadn't been the hotel detective. "There wasn't any reason I couldn't wait in the living room and just step around the body if I had to."

He glanced at Tempest. She said nothing, but her expression told him everything he needed to know about her confrontation with Mitzy. "You called the sheriff's department from your own cell phone?"

Tempest nodded. "I touched nothing nor did I let anyone else touch anything around the victim or the penthouse until I turned it over to the two deputies and it could be photographed and fingerprints taken. I have been here with both…witnesses the entire time."

"Good work."

"I was just doing my job."

Mitzy looked as if she wanted to argue that.

"How many keys are there to the penthouse?" he asked Tempest.

"Four," she answered without hesitation. "Mrs. Sanders and I each have one. Mr. Sanders has two."

Jack shot Oliver a look.

"I have a tendency to misplace mine," he said.

So it seemed. "May I see everyone's key?" Jack asked.

Tempest produced hers. Mitzy had to have her little pink bag brought in from the foyer. She dug around for a moment, then finally came up with it. Out of the corner of his eye, Jack saw Oliver reach into the pocket of his suit pants, frown, then move to the bar where he began to mix himself another drink.

"Don't you have your keys?" Jack asked.

"No, I guess I left mine at my office," Oliver said after a moment, his back to everyone.

"So whose key did Peggy have?" Jack asked as if he didn't know the answer.

Oliver turned slowly from the bar, another full drink in his hand. He stared down into the frothy liquid for a moment, then glanced at his wife, who'd swung around on the couch to look at him. He let out a long sigh. "I asked Peggy to drop off the presents I'd purchased for Mitzy. She offered and since she didn't have any plans and I wanted everything here before Mitzy got home and I wasn't sure what time I could get off work, I thought, why not?"

Oliver had rattled that off a little too quickly. Jack looked at him, wondering why the man would lie about something as innocuous as having Peggy drop off the gifts. Except for the fact that the woman was now dead in his foyer.

"So you had already bought all the presents?" Jack asked, trying to pin down the lie. "When was that?"

"What does it matter?" Oliver snapped. Mitzy hadn't said a word but she was still looking at her husband, a hard brittleness in her gaze.

"It matters to me," Jack said. And it appeared to matter to Mitzy as well. "When did you purchase the gifts? I'm sure you have the receipts or the clerks at the stores can substantiate your story."

Oliver glared at him. "I had Peggy buy everything this afternoon."

Mitzy turned back around, picked up her martini and drained half of it.

"Where did Ms. Kane buy the chocolates?" Jack asked.

Oliver seemed to hesitate as if he might be considering lying. "Sweet Things."

"Her choice? Or yours?" Jack asked.

"Mine. I'd called ahead so I got exactly what I wanted," he said, glancing at his wife's back, as if he thought that fact was going to save him. But Mitzy seemed more interested in her drink than her husband now. Jack could understand that.

"Cash? Or charge?" Jack asked.

Again Oliver seemed to hesitate, then said, "Charge. I would imagine Peggy still has my credit card." The realization definitely didn't make him happy. "I should have known Peggy couldn't handle this." He didn't seem torn up over his secretary's death and that bothered Jack. But Oliver was upset over something and it had to be more than getting caught sending his secretary out to do his Valentine's Day shopping.

It also made Jack wonder how Peggy had gotten the job and why. "How long has Peggy been your secretary?"

"Too long," Mitzy commented under her breath, then turned her baby blues on Jack. "Obviously, Oliver only hired her because he felt sorry for her and look where it's gotten him."

Where had it gotten him? Jack wondered.

"Just a little over a year," Oliver said as if Mitzy hadn't spoken.

"Are you saying she wasn't a good secretary?"

"Adequate," Oliver said and finished his drink.

"But you kept her on," Jack persisted.

"Finding anyone who wants to *work* in River's Edge is next to impossible," Oliver said.

Mitzy emptied her glass.

"When did you arrive at the penthouse?" Jack asked Oliver.

"Right after Mitzy." Oliver glanced at Tempest as if he expected her to either corroborate his story—or contradict it. "I came up the back stairs."

Jack lifted a brow.

"The elevator was blocked, remember?" Oliver said. "I wasn't even aware I didn't have my key."

THREE

THE MISSING EXTRA KEY bothered Jack. But what bothered him more was the way Oliver had looked to Tempest.

Jack glanced at her now. She said nothing, but from the set of her jaw, Jack guessed she wasn't happy about something.

"Excuse me, Sheriff," Deputy Reed said from the living room doorway. "The coroner is in the lobby."

"Bring him up," Jack said, reaching over to turn off the tape recorder.

Mitzy shoved herself up off the couch and headed for the bar, breezing past Oliver without looking at him.

Jack rose, tucking the recorder into his jacket pocket again. "I assume neither of you is planning to leave town?"

He caught a look pass between Mitzy and Oliver.

"We're not going anywhere, Sheriff," Oliver said impatiently.

Jack turned his attention to Tempest, anxious to talk to her alone. She was already on her feet, no doubt eager as anyone to get away from this pair. "If you have a few minutes...." He motioned toward the foyer.

She nodded and followed him out to where the coroner was just getting off the elevator.

"Damn," Lou Ramsey said, scowling down at the body, then at Jack. "You bring this kind of stuff with you from the big city?"

It did feel as if he'd brought something back with him, more old baggage than even he'd realized. "I can't believe you're still alive—let alone still the coroner," Jack said to the cantankerous old veterinarian/councilman/coroner.

White-headed, stooped-shouldered and more temperamental than a de-hibernated grizzly in spring, Ramsey guffawed, then put down his bag. "I'm really looking forward to working with you," he said. "Yeah, right."

Ramsey asked Dobson if he'd shot the scene as he snapped on a pair of latex gloves from his bag. Dobson nodded. Jack sent Deputy Reed to keep the Sanderses company and make sure they remained in the living room until they could have their foyer back.

With a series of creaks and groans, Ramsey lowered himself to the floor, obviously being careful not to touch any of the candy around the body. Jack watched him check Peggy's throat.

"Want the gist of it? Nothing stuck in the throat to choke on, too young in my opinion to have had a stroke. Unless she has a medical history to explain this, I'd say you got yourself a murder, McAllister," the coroner said quietly after a moment. Then without turning, Ramsey pulled his bag closer and told Dobson to bag the chocolates as evidence, handing the young deputy latex gloves and evidence bags. "You're sure?" Jack foolishly asked.

Ramsey shot him a look over the shoulder. "Don't tell me you didn't already suspect as much based on her blue skin color. She bit her tongue more than once, indicating convulsions. I'd guess she was poisoned but we won't know for sure until we check her stomach contents.'' A Ramsey ''guess'' was a good bet any day, Jack thought as he watched the coroner take out tweezers and remove the nut from Peggy's clenched fist, then scrape off the chocolate from her palm into one of the evidence bags.

Jack watched as the old coroner carefully opened her other hand. ''Well, what do we have here!'' Ramsey said.

''A valentine.'' Tempest had been watching as Ramsey opened it with the tweezers. ''The kind we used to give each other as kids.'' Her gaze lifted for an instant to meet Jack's, then dropped again to the coroner's gnarled hands.

Tempest was right. It was a kid's valentine, bright colored with a clown on the front, folded in half so it fit into the flimsy paper envelope. It read: ''You're one smart cookie, but I'm smarter because I have you.'' It was signed: ''You Know Who.''

''Do you recognize the handwriting?'' Jack asked.

She didn't answer. He watched her frown as she stared down at the valentine. She seemed to be miles away. He remembered the valentine boxes they made in grade school. By the end of the day, some boxes would be stuffed with valentines. There was always at least one kid who wouldn't get any, like Peggy Kane. Kids could be so incredibly cruel.

But now Jack wondered how many Tempest had gotten.

Ramsey bagged the valentine, then took a peek in the

shopping bag near the edge of the foyer table next to what Jack assumed was Peggy's purse. "Hmm, interesting," the coroner said and shot Jack a look. "There's another box of chocolates in here. Looks identical to the one on the table."

"Maybe she bought herself a box at Sweet Things when she got this one for Mitzi," Jack suggested. And charged it to her boss.

"I don't think she'd do that," Tempest said.

He raised a brow.

"Buying yourself a huge satin-quilted, heart-shaped box of expensive chocolates on Valentine's Day—" She waved a hand through the air. "What woman would purposely make herself feel that badly?"

"Maybe Oliver told her to buy herself one," Jack suggested.

"Yeah, right," Tempest said, echoing Ramsey's earlier words. She shrugged. "I suppose she could have bought the box of chocolates as cover. Pretend to the clerk that the chocolates were for someone else. Still, I don't think Peggy would do that."

Jack had never understood the workings of a woman's mind, but he did wonder why Tempest felt so strongly about this. He had a feeling, though, that it had nothing to do with logic or evidence or even her training.

He pulled out his cell phone, dialed information and called Sweet Things. He could feel Tempest's gaze on him as he questioned the clerk at the store. As he hung up, he gave Tempest a nod. She'd been right. The clerk remembered Peggy Kane. She had purchased only one box of chocolates. The reason the clerk remembered was because Peggy had paid for the box of chocolates with

Oliver Sanders's credit card and everyone knew the Sanderses.

"Did the Sanderses buy any other boxes of chocolates before or after that?" he'd asked.

"Not that I know of," the clerk said. "But I wasn't the only one working on the Valentine's Day boxes." Jack asked her to check with the other clerks and get back to him. "You're sure that second box came from Sweet Things?" he asked Ramsey.

The old man held it up in his gloved hands, turning it so Jack could see the Sweet Things logo engraved in the bottom. The box was obviously new and hadn't been opened. Jack could hear the rustle of candy inside.

Then Ramsey went through Peggy's pockets, pulling out receipts, which he showed to Jack, then bagged. "What's this?" He held up a key in his latex-gloved weathered fingers, a brow raised in question.

"The elevator key," Tempest said and shot Jack a look.

Peggy hadn't left hers in the elevator. That meant that Oliver had lied. The key now in the elevator had to be his. So how did it get there? The answer seemed obvious.

"Bag the key that's in the elevator and check it for prints," Jack told Dobson. "Tempest, would you mind if we used your key?"

She produced it without hesitation.

With no small amount of effort, Ramsey pushed himself to his feet. "Ready to take the body," he announced.

Jack nodded and walked back into the Sanderses living room. Mitzy stood at the window, her back to the room—and Oliver. Oliver was still at the bar, looking glum and guilty. But of what, Jack wondered.

Deputy Reed stood at the edge of the room, appearing extremely uncomfortable. Neither Mitzy nor Oliver seemed to hear Jack as he entered the room.

"I'm going to need statements from both of you, separately," he said without preamble.

Both turned then, both obviously ready to argue.

"It appears Peggy Kane might have been poisoned," Jack said. "We're considering this a murder investigation." He read them their rights. Mitzy seemed at a loss for words. Oliver hurriedly called his lawyer.

"Deputy Reed will be happy to take you down to the Sheriff's Department or follow you, but I know that you'll both want to cooperate fully on this." Jack nodded to Reed, then went back out to find the black-bagged body loaded onto a stretcher.

"Won't know much more until I open her up and check the stomach contents," Ramsey was saying. "I'll call the crime lab in Missoula. They'll want their own pathologist to do it, but I'll assist. Should be able to tell you something by this afternoon."

Jack nodded. "Take all the gifts as evidence for now," he ordered Dobson. "Ask Reed to get handwriting from both Mr. and Mrs. Sanders."

He had Dobson fish Peggy's keys out of her purse since he was still gloved, then bag the purse and its contents once he knew what she drove and where she lived.

Deputy Reed brought the Sanderses out and took them down the elevator. Jack hung back, wanting to talk to Tempest alone.

As the elevator closed behind the Sanderses and Deputy Reed, Jack glanced into the two shopping bags Mitzy had brought up. Both bags contained new clothing. But they could have once held the second box of chocolates.

He stared at Peggy's shopping bags for a moment, trying to figure out what was bothering him.

"He didn't buy her any lingerie," Jack said finally, turning to Tempest. "Isn't that odd?"

She seemed amused that he would ask her.

"I mean, look at that pile of presents he had Peggy buy. Even those damned cooing birds. But no lingerie." He wished he hadn't said anything, because it probably didn't mean anything and he was starting to feel foolish.

"You think he was trying too hard," Tempest said, bailing him out.

Jack nodded, surprised how easily she'd put her finger on what had been nagging at him.

She smiled and shook her head at him. "Sorry, but not even Oliver would ask his secretary to buy lingerie for his wife."

"Oh." He hadn't thought of that. "I guess not. Too gauche?"

She nodded. "Especially considering the crush Peggy's had on Oliver for years."

He frowned. "Really?"

She mugged a face at him. "Don't tell me you never noticed."

He hadn't. But then he'd had his own problems.

"The gifts are pretty clichéd," Tempest said. "Lingerie does seem like an omission." She shrugged. "He definitely was trying to impress her. He wanted something." She seemed to consider that. "But it wasn't to get her into bed. He had another motive for all the gifts."

Jack found himself studying her, not surprised by how smart she was and not sure what he was looking for in her face. Not sure what he needed from her. Something. Absolution, no doubt. He'd treated her badly in the past and they both knew it.

"I need to get statements from the Sanderses first," he told her. "Then I'd like to talk to you, if you're going to be around later?"

She laughed. Her laugh had aged nicely, just like she had. "I'm not planning to leave town, if that's what you're worried about."

"I thought you might have a date," he said, feeling strangely shy and uncomfortable around her.

She flushed and looked away. "No."

He cursed himself for his lack of tact. "Then I'll give you a call later." She gave him her number.

Once down at the department, he had to wait until Oliver's attorney arrived. When Mitzy finally arrived in her own car, she waived her rights to an attorney.

By then Ramsey had called. He'd had the lab run the chocolates. The cremes were full of poison—strychnine to be exact. Definitely murder.

Jack took Mitzy into the interrogation room, just a small room off the back with a couple of chairs and a table. River's Edge was lucky to have a sheriff's office at all. But since it was the richest part of the county, it got not only an office but a five-person staff.

Mitzy stuck to her story of arriving to find the key in the elevator and Peggy already dead on the floor.

He asked her about the chocolates, whether she'd purchased the second heart-shaped box. Rather than shock or indignation, she'd seemed amused that he thought she'd murdered Peggy.

"What is my motive?" she asked.

"I don't know. Maybe you didn't like her working for your husband," he said.

She smiled, different now that they were alone. Not so coy. Nor as brittle or obnoxious, either. "You know Oliver. He liked having someone who idolized him work for him."

"Did Peggy idolize him?" Jack asked, remembering what Tempest had told him.

She laughed. "Come on, Jack. You know how she used to stare at him all the time in school. She had a major crush on him."

"That was high school," he pointed out.

She raised a brow. "Are we so different now than we were back then?"

He hoped to hell he at least was. "Is there anyone who might want to cause you harm?"

"You mean poison *me?* Of course not."

Right. "Someone who might have been…jealous, maybe. Or had some grudge against you?" Had they still been in high school he could have come up with half a dozen off the top of his head. Except for a selected few friends, Mitzy had been a real bitch to everyone else.

"Jealous?" She laughed. "Why would anyone be jealous of me?" She almost sounded sincere.

"Because you're successful, you live in the only penthouse in River's Edge, you're a well-known town figure and your last name is Sanders."

She laughed. "You have no idea how hard it is being Mitzy Sanders."

Yeah. But it did surprise him that she was trying to play down her success. Earlier at the penthouse she'd been flaunting it. What had changed? Oliver wasn't there, he thought. Or Tempest.

Also she was acting as if being married to Oliver wasn't all it was cracked up to be. He suspected she liked being Mrs. Oliver Sanders more than she liked being married to Oliver, but Mitzy was the kind of woman who liked to keep up appearances.

"Was Peggy jealous of you?" he asked. If he knew Mitzy—which he thought he did—she'd rubbed her affluence, her success and her husband in Peggy's face.

Mitzy stared at him, half smiling. "You don't really think that Peggy tried to…poison me?" She seemed to find even more humor in that. "Peggy didn't have what it takes to kill anyone."

Mitzy made it sound as if she saw the inability to kill as a character flaw. "You seem so sure of that."

"Peggy was a dreamer," Mitzy said. "In that way, she was a lot like Oliver."

He raised a brow.

She pursed her lips as if she wished she hadn't added that last. "Oliver would be nothing without a good woman behind him. But then I suppose that could be said of most men." She smiled, but he couldn't miss the bitterness in her tone. It didn't surprise him that Oliver might be a disappointment.

"Anyway," she continued, "how stupid would that be? Peggy plotting to poison me, then forgetting and eating the chocolates?" She laughed and shook her head.

"Not even Peggy was that dumb, although you know how she was about chocolate."

No, he didn't. "She had a weakness for it? But she'd lost so much weight...."

Mitzy lifted a finely honed brow. "Just because she was slim, don't kid yourself, Peggy was only masquerading in that body. She knew she'd never be able to keep it. She was like a person who buys a car she can't afford. Eventually the bank is going to come pick it up. With Peggy it was just a matter of time before she started eating again and she knew it."

"That's pretty cold," he said. Even for Mitzy.

She opened her purse to take out a mint, unwrap it and pop it into her mouth. "It's just the truth," she said, sounding almost sad. "It was cruel of Oliver to make Peggy buy me chocolates knowing chocolate is the woman's weakness."

Jack couldn't agree more, especially under the circumstances. So why had Oliver? "Does he usually get you chocolate for Valentine's Day?"

"Valentine's and every other occasion he can think of," Mitzy said. "I swear he buys it for himself. Or maybe just to bug me. He knows I don't eat the stuff."

"Not even one piece?" Jack asked in surprise.

She shrugged. "I usually eat a piece just to appease him and he finishes the box. He's a chocoholic and damned lucky he has the metabolism he does otherwise he'd be fatter than Peggy used to be."

So Mitzy would have eaten one piece to appease Oliver. And it seemed one piece would have been enough to kill her.

"What about Oliver? Did he have any reason to want to harm you?" Jack had to ask.

The question didn't seem to surprise her. "Oliver has no more killer instinct than Peggy did. I assure you, Oliver wouldn't know what to do without me." She looked bored. "Anything else you want to know?"

"Only who might have poisoned Peggy and why," he said and thanked her for coming down.

Oliver and his expensively dressed lawyer were waiting when Jack came out of the interrogation room with Mitzy. The lawyer, a man who introduced himself as Randall Garrison, had that same I've-got-money-and-connections look as Oliver. They could have been twins. They even wore the same cologne. Either that or Oliver had drowned himself in his to mask the smell of alcohol.

Oliver seemed tense. Randall Garrison just seemed anxious to get to dinner.

Oliver told the same story he'd told at the penthouse. He swore he had no idea how both of his keys ended up at the penthouse without him. He said he gave his to Peggy. He thought his other key was at his office, but maybe he'd left it home. Or maybe he gave Peggy both keys. He'd had so much on his mind, he hadn't been paying a lot of attention. No, he hadn't thought to tell Peggy to leave the elevator key at the main desk, that's why he hadn't bothered to even stop at the desk, just went straight up the fire exit when he realized the private elevator wasn't going to be coming down.

"How should I know who put poison in the chocolates?" Oliver demanded. "I was at my office all afternoon while Peggy picked up the presents."

"Did anyone see you there?"

"No, because my secretary and I are the only employees and, as you know, my secretary, was out," Oliver said impatiently.

Out permanently. "You didn't buy another box of chocolates exactly like the one you had Peggy pick up?"

Oliver regarded him for a moment, making Jack too aware of the past and the animosity there'd been between them. It seemed stupid now. After all, it had been high school and wasn't high school hell for a lot of people? But the heart of the problem between them still seemed to run deep. Some odd male competition thing.

"Why would I bother to buy a second box if I couldn't get away from my office to buy the first?" Oliver asked.

"To poison the second box and switch it with the first," Jack suggested. "Or maybe you'd already bought the first box and doctored it."

Oliver's gaze went cold. "Are you calling me a murderer?"

"I'm not calling you anything," Jack said calmly.

The attorney placed a warning hand on Oliver's arm. "Why would I want to kill my secretary?"

"How is your marriage?" Jack was rewarded with another flicker of anger. Much better than that dumbassed stare he'd *been* getting.

"My marriage is just fine," Oliver said between gritted teeth.

So why did Jack doubt that? Because Mitzy hadn't been turning cartwheels. Because Oliver didn't care that Mitzy didn't like chocolate; he bought her a huge box anyway. But both of them seemed to be trying to keep up the pretense, Jack noted.

"Mitzy said she doesn't really like chocolates so why buy her such a big box?" Jack asked.

"Mitzy *loves* chocolate, *Sheriff*." Oliver shook his head in disgust. "Is that really what she told you? She frigging *loves* chocolate. No doubt she wanted you to believe that she's above such mortal desires and temptations as simple as chocolate."

"You're saying she lied to me?" Jack asked.

Oliver glared at him in answer.

"What about you? Would you have eaten some of the chocolates?" Jack asked, wondering why Mitzy lied, if she was the one lying.

"Of course. Who doesn't eat chocolate?" Oliver said. "I would have also drank some of the champagne. That's why I had Peggy get the good stuff. So what's your point? Doesn't that prove I didn't put poison in the chocolates?"

Jack considered this, telling himself, of course, the killer would say he'd have eaten the chocolates. But what did it really matter? Neither Mitzy nor Oliver had eaten the chocolates. Only Peggy.

"But believe me, I won't ever eat chocolates again," Oliver said.

"Does it seem odd to you that Peggy would have opened Mitzy's box of candy and eaten some?" Jack asked.

"I don't know," Oliver said, adding a long-suffering sigh. "She was a woman. Who the hell knows what a woman's going to do?"

Interesting observation, Jack thought. If Peggy had been the intended victim, then it seemed the killer had to have known she would eat some.

"Mitzy said you have a weakness for chocolate," Jack pushed.

The word *weakness* seemed to stick in Oliver's craw. He leaned forward, his voice low. "I know what you're doing. I know why you're back here, why you wanted the sheriff's job. I know."

"Why is that, Oliver?"

"Because of Frannie."

Jack felt himself go deadly still. He'd known it was just a matter of time before someone mentioned Frannie. He just wished it hadn't been Oliver. "I don't want to talk about my wife with you."

"Don't you mean your *late* wife?" Oliver asked.

Jack moved so quickly, he even surprised himself. He shot around the table to grab Oliver's collar, jerk him up and slam him against the wall, stopping just short of burying his fist in Oliver's face.

He could hear the lawyer Randall Garrison protesting behind him, but right at that moment, Jack didn't give a damn. He didn't like Oliver Sanders. And it had nothing to do with all the shitty things Oliver had done to him in high school.

"Go ahead," Oliver goaded, although he looked considerably more pale than he had just moments before. "You've been wanting to hit me for years. Don't you think I know you're planning to frame me for this murder? I know you are. To get even with me over Frannie."

Jack felt a chill of truth in Oliver's words. He released him and stepped back. Only one man had wanted Frannie more than Jack. Oliver Sanders. And Oliver had done his damnedest to take Frannie away from him.

"This murder investigation has nothing to do with her," Jack said. That much at least was true.

Oliver let out a snort. "Like hell. You don't think I know she's the reason you're back here?"

Jack snapped off the tape recorder as he jerked it off the table and headed for the door. "Interview over," he said over his shoulder.

"I heard she left a suicide note."

Jack stopped walking, but he didn't turn around. "What do you want to know, Oliver? If she mentioned you?" He could hear the silence behind him like a toxic hole in the atmosphere.

"Did she?" Oliver asked, his voice barely a whisper.

Jack didn't bother to answer. He strode out, slamming the door behind him, sick inside.

Back in his office, he called Tempest and on impulse asked her to meet him at the nearby café. He wasn't hungry, but he knew he needed to eat and he'd had enough of his office for one day.

She sounded surprised.

"I haven't had dinner," he heard himself overexplain. "I thought maybe if you hadn't either...." He wished he'd given the invitation more thought now.

"No, I haven't eaten yet," she said.

"Great. I'll meet you there. Say half an hour?"

FOUR

SHE SHOWED UP exactly thirty minutes later, wearing slacks and a sweater, her hair freshly washed and scooped up at the nape of her neck, making him want to free it. They took a booth in a corner. It was late enough that the Valentine's Day crowd had already done the date thing, but still it felt awkward being with Tempest.

"I can't believe you're in River's Edge," Jack said after they were seated. She only smiled. "How did you come to be working for the Sanderses?"

She nodded as if she'd been expecting the question, maybe realized that curiosity more than anything had made him suggest dinner tonight. "Ellie Sanders called me and offered me the job." Jack figured Tempest's mother and Ellie Sanders probably still stayed in touch. "Ellie owns the hotel."

That surprised Jack. Obviously Ellie hadn't trusted her son. Jack liked smart women and while he'd detested Otto Sanders and spent half his life battling with Oliver, Jack had always liked Ellie.

But Tempest hadn't told him what he really wanted to know: why she'd come back to River's Edge. "I would think working for Ellie would be all right. So what made you apply for undersheriff?"

Her gaze met his, dark and a little disturbing. "I applied for *sheriff.*"

Ouch. "Sorry, I didn't know."

She shrugged. "I like Ellie, but she promised Oliver she'd turn everything over to him on his thirty-fifth birthday, which is February twenty-first, just a few days away."

The timing was definitely interesting, Jack thought.

He watched Tempest pick up her menu. Once Oliver and Mitzy took over The Riverside, Tempest would be out like a stray cat and she had to know that.

"I still can't get over the fact that you moved back here at all after everything...." Subtle, he wasn't. "I mean, it's funny the two of us coming back here, you just a few weeks before me." The timing definitely seemed coincidental. The sort of timing that bothered him. Just like Peggy's death and Oliver's upcoming birthday.

Tempest didn't look up from the uninteresting café menu. He wondered why she was avoiding telling him what had brought her back. Or if he just wanted to believe she had some ulterior motive. Hell, she could have just missed the place, although he had a really hard time believing that. He cursed his suspicious nature.

"Why do any of us come back?" she said finally without looking up from the menu. "I would imagine Peggy came back a year ago because of Oliver. And you because of Frannie."

He started to tell her he didn't want to talk about Frannie. Couldn't.

"You're looking for answers," Tempest said, lowering the menu to face him. She must have seen his closed expression. "Or did you come back to make amends for standing me up the night of the junior prom?'' She softened her words with a smile.

But still he felt like hell, relieved she wasn't going to talk about Frannie, but embarrassed for what a jerk he'd been. "I can't apologize enough for that." He'd stood her up because of Mitzy. Later he realized that Mitzy had just been using him to make Oliver mad. Which was fine with Jack. But he'd blown off his date with Tempest, a date he'd only agreed to because Frannie had asked him to. He'd liked Frannie even then, even when they were only friends.

Tempest waved it off. "It all turned out the way I guess it was supposed to."

Had it, he wondered. He'd eventually ended up with Frannie, something that seemed to have led to her death. Had he come back looking for answers? Or someone to blame?

The waitress, a bubbly little thing dressed in a red and white heart-print dress, bopped up to take their orders, but her interest quickly shifted to the plant growing by their table.

"On Valentine's Day it's said that you can see the initials of your intended in a heart-shaped ivy leaf," the waitress said dreamily as she fingered a leaf, squinting hard at it. "Ivy is a traditional symbol of fidelity." She brightened and released the leaf. "What can I bring you?"

The moment the waitress left to get their drinks, Jack asked, "When do you start as undersheriff?" trying to steer the conversation away from the past.

"I haven't accepted the job yet," Tempest said.

"What's holding up your decision?" he had to ask, afraid he already knew.

Her dark gaze met his in answer just before the waitress returned with their drinks and put them down on red, heart-shaped napkins. "Did you know..." The girl moved her gum out of the way of her tongue, "...that lovebirds choose their mates on Valentine's Day? Really!"

"I didn't know that," Tempest said.

"Oh, yeah, and on Valentine's Day if you put the guy you like's initials in a piece of bread—I guess you'd have to like carve them in—and put the bread under your pillow, in the morning, if the initials are still there, then he's the one. Cool, huh?"

"Very cool," Tempest said, and took a drink of her iced tea, her amused gaze meeting Jack's over the rim of her glass.

The waitress nodded and bobbed off, humming to herself.

Jack smiled across the table at Tempest, noticing she, too, was trying hard not to laugh. "I'm willing to bet you're as wild about Valentine's Day as I am."

"It's too pink for me," she said.

The waitress came back with two salads, but no more Valentine's Day folklore fortunately. They ate, avoiding talking about the past—or the case—or her job offer. He learned that she'd gone to college back east, mastered in criminology and taught for a while before coming back here to apply for the sheriff's job, most of which he would have seen on her application had he looked.

"I thought you'd be a scientist," he said, putting down his fork to study her. "You were so...smart."

"Nerdy, I believe is the word you were searching for."

"No. I remember being so envious of you in algebra class. You always knew the answers."

His praise seemed to embarrass her. "I never knew

the answers to anything that mattered," she said looking down as she picked at her salad. "I would have given anything to be part of Mitzy's crowd, just to know what to say, how to dress, how to act."

"Our values are so screwed-up at that age," he said and wanted to say more but the waitress appeared with their dinners. They ate in silence for a few moments.

The waitress came back by to see if they needed anything else. "Let me know if you need any…bread," she said to Tempest with a wink.

"I'll do that."

Jack watched Tempest pick at her meal, trying to imagine her putting bread under her pillow. Why had she come back? Like him, she had no kin here anymore, nothing that he could see to drag her back. But he and Tempest weren't the only ones who'd returned recently. Peggy had. "You and Peggy were pretty good friends for a while."

She looked up, surprised either by his abrupt change of subject or that he'd remembered. He'd been a junior. Tempest and Peggy were sophomores, Oliver a senior and Mitzy and Frannie freshmen. It had been such a small high school it seemed impossible they could form cliques. But even on the basketball court or football field, it proved hard to play as a team because of their obvious social differences.

"Outcasts often band together," Tempest said after a moment. "At least for a while." Her chuckle was hard edged. "Peggy realized I was more hopeless than she was. Even nerds have their standards." What she didn't say, he knew, was that even money couldn't overcome that.

While Tempest was one of the privileged, when she was a freshman, her father, a congressman, was charged with corruption. He took off with a female aide he'd been having an affair with, leaving his wife of twenty years and Tempest. The distasteful incident made Tempest and her mother outcasts among their own, except for Ellie Sanders who remained a friend.

Jack wished he hadn't been such a jerk, standing Tempest up, especially since she'd been Frannie's friend. But he'd felt intimidated by Tempest's brain—and her money—and had been running on teenage testosterone. And then there'd been temptation in the form of Mitzy.

He and Tempest finished their meals, the restaurant nearly empty by the time the waitress cleared away their plates.

"I need to get your statement. Do you mind if we do it here rather than back at the office?" he asked as he pulled out the tape recorder. She seemed a little surprised. "You don't mind, do you?"

"It wasn't like I thought this was a date," she said, then reddened.

"Look, I'm sorry if you thought—"

"Let's just not go there." She hit the record button and met his gaze. "What is it you'd like to know?"

Why had she thought he'd asked her to dinner? He felt like a jerk, again. What was it about Tempest that made him so...awkward around her? Frannie. She had known Frannie probably better than he had. Maybe that's why he and Tempest had never gotten along. That and the fact that Tempest had been against the marriage. Jack figured she didn't think he was good enough for Frannie. Which was true.

Tempest was waiting, the tape recorder rolling.

"What do you know about Mitzy and Oliver's relationship?" he asked.

"The word around the community is they're perfect

for each other, but there is all kinds of ways to take that.'' She shrugged. ''To all appearances they seem to be…lovebirds,'' reminding him of the two birds Peggy had brought to the penthouse, birds that, if their waitress could be believed, had mated for life just today.

''Okay, tell me what happened from the time you heard Mitzy scream,'' he said.

Tempest's story matched what Mitzy had told him and yet even as he listened he had the feeling Tempest wasn't telling him everything.

''You didn't see Oliver on the back stairs?'' he asked.

''No. I was with Mitzy out by the elevator when Oliver showed up. I just assumed he'd come up the back stairs.''

''Could he have come up the elevator after Mitzy?'' Jack asked.

She shook her head. ''The elevator door was blocked just as he said with Mitzy's shopping bags. You're wondering about the extra key.''

''Could he have arrived *before* Mitzy, left his key in the elevator by accident, poisoned Peggy or at least found her body, then hid in the penthouse so that you and Mitzy only *thought* he'd come up the back stairs, but was actually there the whole time?''

''Could have, I suppose.''

Oliver was guilty of something. Jack would bet on that. But murder? ''I saw him look at you as if he expected you to say something when he was telling how he'd come up the stairs after you were already there.''

''I didn't notice.''

Jack definitely didn't believe that. He remembered thinking she was angry about something. But he let it go. For now. He reached over and shut off the tape recorder. ''Take the job. I need your help on this.''

Tempest stared at him, surprise and something he couldn't put his finger on in her gaze. "Aren't you afraid I'm too personally involved?"

He shook his head. "No more than I am."

She smiled at that. "I'll think about it."

It started to snow as he and Tempest left the café. Large, lacy flakes drifted lazily down from the darkness. The air felt cold, the snow icy against his face, and yet after she left him in front of the café, he walked around the small community of peak-roofed condos, art galleries, upscale restaurants and fancy shops.

The town had grown since he'd been gone. And changed. Once River's Edge had been little more than a playground for the affluent. But a resort needs workers. That's where people like he and Peggy and Tempest had come in. Their families had lived down the mountain in hurriedly thrown-up buildings along the highway and worked cheap just for the opportunity to ski on their days off or fish when the mayfly hatch was on or because they had no place else to go.

In the years he'd been gone, something had happened though. Not that people still didn't live in the flats down by the highway and drive old cars up to clean the condos and wait tables, but now there were smaller houses sprouting up, houses with real foundations and swing sets in the backyards, houses with real families who actually lived here year round and shopped at the pizza parlor, burger joint, service stations, working-class bars and video stores that had moved in among the fancier businesses. If River's Edge wasn't careful, it would turn into a real town one day.

Over it all stood the mountain that had prompted the resort town to sprout here in the first place. Even through the falling snow he could make out the lights of the grooming machines moving like caterpillars across the white slopes. Nearer, he could see the golf course—still buried under a foot of snow and crisscrossed with ski tracks, like a secret writing he'd never been able to decipher. This place had once been divided by those who skied and those who didn't. He hadn't skied.

As he stood in the silence of the falling snow he wondered what the hell he was doing. There were no answers for him here. Frannie had killed herself and taken whatever her reasons with her. He'd been a fool to think that anything of her was still here.

He walked through the snow to the motel along the highway where he was staying, telling himself he'd have to find a decent place to live if he was going to stay. On the way, he passed The Riverside and remembered Peggy's car, a new Ford Explorer, black and shiny. He still had the keys in his pocket.

He unlocked it and climbed behind the wheel. The seats were leather and the interior still had that brand-new smell. Wearing his winter gloves, he turned on the dome light and glanced around. No fast-food containers. No empty latte cups. Not even a scrap of paper. He opened the glove box. She hadn't had the car long enough to even throw old mail into it. He dug out the registration. It was in her name. No bank lien against it.

He climbed back out, locking the door after him, wondering what she'd paid for the car. More importantly, how she'd paid for the car.

He pulled out his cell phone and dialed Tempest's number. "Accept the job and meet me at Peggy's apartment," he said when she answered.

Silence. "Are you sure?"

"Yes." As sure as he was of anything. He understood her hesitation. He had mixed feelings about working with her as well. But he also thought she'd make one hell of an undersheriff. And he needed her help. She knew these people, maybe better than he did because even though she'd felt like an outcast in high school, she'd been one of them.

Silence. "Okay."

"By the way, she was driving a brand-new expensive SUV with leather seats and no lien against it."

"Maybe she has a rich boyfriend."

"My thought exactly."

FIVE

TEMPEST LET OUT a low whistle when Jack opened the door to Peggy Kane's apartment and they both stepped inside.

"Get a load of this," he said as he took in the place.

From the outside, the apartment house looked like something Oliver Sanders's secretary could afford in River's Edge. Not too cheap. But not too expensive, either.

Of course Peggy's clothing, her sophisticated look and her car didn't fit the profile. And not surprisingly, neither did the contents of the apartment.

"Holy cow," Tempest said as she moved through all the brand-new expensive furnishings. "Either this Girl Friday inherited big, is neck deep in debt or she's gotten herself a sugar daddy."

Jack agreed. "See what you can find, but keep your gloves on."

She nodded and he moved through the apartment, looking for something to explain Peggy's obviously recent windfall. Drugs. Signs of a benevolent boyfriend. A rich uncle's will.

They started in the kitchen. Jack searched the drawers, but found nothing more than over-the-counter diet pills. No large bags of drugs to be sold.

"Scary diet," Tempest said holding open the fridge door.

He could see that it held little more than bottled water and celery. Tempest dug through the freezer, pulling out several frost-encrusted Lean Cuisine meals and a half-eaten pint of frozen yogurt. Nothing more.

The cupboards were equally bare except for some rice cakes and large containers of vitamins.

"Where did she eat?" Tempest said going through Peggy's trash. The trash at least produced a couple of Chinese carry-out cartons. "Fried rice and chow mein, a girl meal," Tempest said and dropped the small white containers back into the can.

She stood with her hands on her hips, surveying the kitchen, dining room, living room. "There's no beer, no alcohol, no mix. If she had a boyfriend, he didn't come over here. They must have met someplace else."

Jack picked up the phone book, not surprised when it fell open to the restaurant section of a town forty miles away. Several of the more expensive dinner places had the numbers circled, the pages dog-eared. He held it out for Tempest to see.

She nodded. "Either she was a secret eater who took her love of food out of town or she had a boyfriend. Someone who didn't want to be seen with her."

"Maybe she didn't want to be seen with him."

Tempest shook her head. "No way. Not when he's footing the bill for all this fancy stuff. He'd be calling the shots. This guy's got something to hide."

Jack had to agree with her as he dug through the desk drawers. No record of any rich uncle or lottery winnings. Her last month's bill on her credit cards showed that she'd paid them off in full.

"It looks like she's only recently come into some money," he said, tossing the bills back into the drawer. He could hear Tempest in the bedroom. He followed the sound of her opening and closing dresser drawers.

"The drawers are full of new sexy lingerie," she said mugging a face. "Some of the price tags are still attached."

He opened the closet. It was packed with clothes, most with price tags still dangling from the sleeves. He moved to the night stand. Tempest went around the bed to the opposite one.

Next to the phone on the night stand, he found an address book. He thumbed through it, looking for a boyfriend. There were only a few names and numbers. Peggy didn't seem to have a lot of acquaintances, let alone friends. Not surprisingly, Oliver's cell phone, home and office numbers were listed, written in a big, bold script.

That's when he noticed the scratchpad, its corner caught under the phone. He pulled it out. Peggy Kane was a doodler. Hearts, flowers, stars. He turned the pad to read the words doodled around the edge, his breath catching as he saw what she'd written.

"Look at this," he said and passed it across the satin comforter to Tempest. Peggy had written three little words around the edge of the paper. Mrs. Peggy Sanders.

Tempest looked at the scratchpad for a moment, then handed him what she'd found in the opposite nightstand. A date book.

He flipped it open to January to find small neat notations. Dentist appointment 8:30 a.m. Pick up dry cleaning. Reschedule teeth cleaning appointment. Call landlord about leak in tub.

Spread among the mundane were small little notations: "O" at 8 at condo. "O" at Café Italiano. "O" weekend. "O" lunch.

He looked up at Tempest. She just nodded and said, "I don't think the 'O' stands for orgasm, but what do I know? Look at February first."

He moved to February. "'O' promised, Feb. 14." After that the days had been marked off with red "Xs" and exclamation points up to February 14.

"Valentine's Day," Jack said, thinking about the Valentine Peggy had clutched in her hand. When he'd checked the handwriting it had been hers. "She thought Oliver was going to leave his wife."

"You know, there is one other possibility," Tempest said. "That this love affair with Oliver was all in Peggy's head."

"Then who's been footing the bill for all this stuff?" He waved a hand at the loot packed in the apartment.

Tempest said nothing, just glanced around, her expression one of sorrow.

He looked down at the bright red circle Peggy had drawn around Feb. 14th. "Maybe Valentine's wasn't the day her lover planned to leave his wife. Maybe it was the day she and Oliver planned to kill Mitzy."

Tempest regarded him for a moment. "If that was the case, then what went wrong?"

Jack shrugged. "Maybe nothing. Maybe everything went just as Oliver planned it."

"You think he double-crossed Peggy?" she asked, not sounding in the least bit shocked by the idea.

"Oliver didn't seem very broken up over Peggy's death," Jack said. "If anything, he was probably relieved."

Tempest nodded. "Peggy had to have been putting pressure on him."

"So they cooked up a plan to get rid of Mitzy," Jack said.

Tempest was shaking her head. "Drowning her in the river was a plan. Poisoning the chocolates would only make them both look suspicious and bring about an investigation."

She had a point. "Also, it makes no sense for Peggy

to eat one of the poisoned chocolates. She didn't know they were poisoned. It's the only thing that makes any sense.''

Jack nodded. ''Unless she mixed up the boxes by mistake. But still, it just seems odd to me whether she knew about the poison or not, that she'd eat some of Mitzy's chocolates.''

Tempest seemed to give it some thought. ''After being forced to get all of that stuff for Oliver's wife, she was probably feeling pretty resentful and jealous. Maybe she decided she deserved what she knew Mitzy wasn't going to appreciate anyway.''

''You sound like you know the feeling.''

She smiled at that. ''I know what it feels like to get the short end of the stick. But then, so do you.'' Everyone knew about Jack being caught cheating on a test in his junior year. Few people knew the truth. That he'd gotten the blame when it had been Oliver, who'd had to take the class over, who'd been cheating. Of course, Oliver hadn't come forward to clear Jack's name. It had just added to the animosity between them.

''Do you think it's possible that Peggy came back just to seduce Oliver?'' He was only half joking. ''She lost all of that weight and if she really has always carried a torch for him....''

''That would make her awfully devious,'' she noted with a smile. ''And awfully bitter. It fits.''

''Nothing scars you quite like high school, does it?'' he said.

She shrugged. ''You get over it. Or you don't.''

He felt as if they hadn't changed, the bunch of them, just gotten older, their animosities toward each other now more deadly as adults.

''There was a time I would have taken great satisfaction in seeing Oliver fry for this murder,'' he had to admit.

"And no one would have blamed you."

"But now I'm a cop," Jack said. "I don't believe in personal revenge. Let the system dole out the justice."

She smiled. "That's big of you, considering sometimes the system screws up and justice isn't served."

"It's the best system we have," he said, watching her face. "Don't you think?"

She smiled and shrugged, but her look said hell-no and made him nervous. "You sound as if you think Oliver killed her."

"It certainly is shaping up that way, don't you think?"

She shrugged. "Who knows who the intended victim even was. Kind of clichéd, poisoning the chocolates though."

"What would you have done?"

"Something in the roses," she said. "One sniff and blam!"

"Except you wouldn't know who was going to smell the roses," he pointed out.

Her gaze met his. "That's just it, how did the killer know who was going to eat the chocolates?"

Good point. Especially since he didn't know who at the Sanderses' house wouldn't be able to resist the chocolate—except for Peggy.

"It's late," he said as he pocketed the date book. "I'll get a warrant to search Oliver's office first thing in the morning. Want to meet me there?"

She nodded and walked out of the apartment. He stood for a moment looking at all the expensive things Peggy had purchased, all the while believing her life was about to change for the better. It was depressing as hell.

JACK AND TEMPEST were waiting the next morning when Oliver walked into his office.

Oliver looked more than surprised. "What the hell do you want now?"

Jack handed him the warrant. "The lab found strychnine in the chocolate Peggy Kane ingested."

Oliver swore as he threw the warrant down on his desk. "What does that have to do with me?" He gave Tempest only a cursory glance as he shrugged out of his coat.

"You've already met the new undersheriff," Jack said.

"I didn't think you'd take the job," Oliver said. "I didn't think you'd be staying that long."

Tempest didn't comment.

Oliver turned to Jack. "I don't know how the poison got in the chocolates. But I can tell you one thing, there isn't any poison in my office."

Jack went around to the desk and tried the top drawer. It was locked. He looked up at Oliver who reluctantly pulled out his keys and threw them down on the desk top next to the warrant.

Jack picked up the keys without a word and opened each drawer, looking through the contents, not surprised when he found nothing of interest.

He glanced around the office. Oliver had gone into Peggy's office. He came back with what smelled like coffee in a glass mug. But from the looks of the tea-colored liquid, he didn't have a clue how to make his own coffee.

"Where's your safe?" Jack asked.

The question seemed to startle Oliver. He sloshed some of the coffee onto the carpet and let out an oath. His eyes moved to the oak liquor cabinet against the wall. He either wanted a drink badly or he'd forgotten something he wished he hadn't. "You'd better have a warrant to open that safe."

Jack motioned to the warrant still lying on the desk. "It includes all financial and personal records."

Oliver swore again. "You are determined to pin this on me, aren't you."

"The safe," Jack asked.

Tempest had moved over to the bar. She opened the cabinet, pushed aside a few bottles of booze and a wooden panel to expose the safe as if she'd known it was there.

"What's the combination?" Jack asked joining her.

"I'll open it," Oliver said and shoved them aside. It took him several tries to get the safe open. His hands were visibly shaking and Jack could see beads of sweat breaking out on his forehead and upper lip.

Jack stepped in quickly, stopping Oliver before he could remove anything from inside, the moment the door swung open. Tempest produced an evidence bag and began putting the papers he handed her inside it.

Oliver grabbed a bottle of bourbon and retreated behind his desk, his expression like death warmed over.

Jack dug through the safe, finding the usual stocks and bonds, insurance policies (five hundred thousand on both he and Mitzy), business papers dealing with his development plans and bank loans. He'd have Tempest go through all of it first because she had a head for numbers. While Jack didn't think they'd find a motive for murder in the papers, he could see that something in the safe was making Oliver very nervous.

He had almost emptied the safe when his fingers brushed a large manila envelope that had been pushed to the back.

He drew it out and held it up as he turned to look at Oliver. He could tell that whatever the man had to fear was inside the envelope. Jack opened it slowly, watching Oliver, expecting the worst. And yet he was still surprised by the contents.

A dozen black-and-white photos of a very young, very naked Mitzy Baxter, her barely pubescent body so pale it looked bleached, the poses awkward and embarrassed making them all the more unsavory. Strictly amateur night.

Jack dropped the snapshots on Oliver's desk. "Did you take these?"

"Good God no," Oliver said, not looking at either Jack or Tempest.

"Then who did?" Jack asked. Tempest was staring at the photos spilled across the desk and frowning.

Oliver poured a shot of bourbon into the weak coffee and took a drink. "I purchased the photos years ago from some hippie-type she'd taken up with one winter."

"Are you telling me this guy blackmailed you?"

He nodded solemnly. "I wish I'd destroyed them."

"Why didn't you?"

He shook his head and poured more bourbon into his mug. And it was only a little after eight in the morning.

"Does Mitzy know you have them?" Jack asked.

Oliver shook his head without looking up. "I never wanted her to know I even knew about them."

Jack closed the safe and went out to search Peggy's part of the office. It was obvious that Peggy had been very organized and a much better secretary from the looks of things than her boss had led him to believe.

Tempest followed him out and thumbed through the file cabinet without a word.

He thought he heard a sound coming from Oliver's office and stopped to listen. It sounded like crying.

He moved to the doorway and looked in to find Oliver with his head in his hands, the dirty photos of Mitzy spread like solitaire cards across the desk, his mug empty.

SIX

BACK AT the sheriff's department, Jack asked Tempest to look over the financial papers they'd confiscated from Oliver's office, then he went to his own office and closed the door.

For reasons he didn't want to delve into, the photos of Mitzy had made him think of Frannie. Her small, dark, girllike woman's body. So fragile. It had been a year since he'd buried her and a day hadn't gone by that he hadn't thought of her and agonized over why she'd left him the way she had.

There was a tap on his door. He motioned for Dobson to come in.

"Insurance policies?" he asked without preamble.

"Just the ones Mr. and Mrs. Sanders had on each other for five hundred thousand. As for alibis..." Dobson consulted his notebook. "Mrs. Sanders left work about eleven a.m. and didn't return. She had no showings on her schedule and couldn't be reached by cell phone. Not that that means much in this area."

"What about the candy shop?"

"The clerks there know Mrs. Sanders well, said she comes in a lot to buy candy for her receptionist and clients."

Jack raised a brow.

"The receptionist says Mrs. Sanders has never purchased her candy or any other gift," Dobson said, looking pleased with himself for anticipating the question. "The receptionist said Mrs. Sanders always keeps chocolate in her locked bottom drawer." Dobson nodded. "There were wrappers in the drawer from Sweet Things."

So she'd lied about chocolate. And she shopped at Sweet Things. That didn't mean she'd killed Peggy. But it definitely could have gotten her killed had she gotten into the chocolates before Peggy.

"Good job," he told Dobson. He noted that Mitzy had bought the candy for herself as cover, just as Tempest had said a woman might do. But it didn't prove she'd bought the extra box. "And Mr. Sanders?"

"No one saw him leave his office. He walked to work that morning, taking the trail between The Riverside and his office."

Jack nodded. "So there is little chance anyone would have seen him coming or going unless they'd been on the trail. See if you can find someone."

Dobson nodded. "Also no one remembers him shopping at Sweet Things, but they sold dozens of boxes of chocolates exactly like the one Mr. Sanders had Ms. Kane purchase."

Jack nodded, suspecting as much.

"I stopped by the bank like you asked." Dobson dropped several large manila envelopes on the table. "These are bank accounts for both Sanders and Peggy Kane, including canceled checks."

Dobson had the look of a man who'd just won the lottery. Or discovered oil in his backyard. "I saved the best for last. Peggy Kane only recently took out an insurance policy on herself. Five hundred thousand dollars. Guess who the beneficiary is?"

"Oliver Sanders," Tempest said, appearing in the doorway behind Dobson.

"Oh yeah!" Dobson said and smiled.

Jack motioned her in. "Thanks, Dobson. Good work. Let me know if you find anyone who can verify Oliver Sanders's whereabouts during the time in question. Any prints on that key that was in the elevator?"

Dobson shook his head. "Too smudged to get a clear latent."

Jack nodded, afraid that would be the case.

After the deputy left, Tempest gave him the items they'd taken from Oliver's safe. "Find anything interesting?" Jack asked.

She shook her head. "He was into all kinds of developments, a real wheeler-dealer, but nothing unusual or suspicious that I could find."

"Well, let's see if there's anything in the bank statements," he said as she took a chair across from him.

It didn't take but a few minutes to see a pattern—just not the one Jack had been expecting.

Mitzi had been making large withdrawals from her account for the last six months. A few days later that money had been showing up in Peggy Kane's account.

"Peggy was blackmailing Mitzy?" Jack asked, confused as all hell.

"Think it was the photos you found in the safe?" Tempest said.

"If so, what was Oliver doing with them then?"

She shrugged, eyes bright with interest. "I guess there is only one way to find out."

MITZY WAS SHOWING a three-million dollar log house near the ski hill, the receptionist at her office told them.

"At least she and Oliver weren't so distraught over

Peggy's death they couldn't work,'' Tempest commented as they drove up the mountain and parked in front of the massive house.

As they got out and went in, an older couple was climbing into a Suburban with out-of-state plates.

Mitzy seemed startled to see them on her turf. ''You aren't interested in a house, are you, Jack?'' She looked at him expectantly. More than likely she just wondered if he could afford this place. More to the point, if Frannie had left him enough, since Frannie had come from money, not him.

He didn't bite. ''Why was Peggy blackmailing you?''

''Peggy?'' Mitzy blinked and grabbed the back of one of the chairs at the breakfast bar for support. ''Peggy Kane?'' She paled, then flushed. ''Why, that bitch.''

Either she hadn't known who was blackmailing her. Or she was a damned good actress.

''What did she have on you?'' Jack asked.

Mitzy glanced at him, then at Tempest.

''Tempest is the new undersheriff,'' Jack qualified. ''If you'd rather, the three of us could discuss this at my office.''

Mitzy regarded him for a moment, then walked out to the redwood deck that ran the length of the house, dug around in her coat pocket and pulled out a pack of cigarettes. She lit one and took a long drag, letting the smoke out slowly as she stared down at the clutters of buildings that made up the town below. Jack and Tempest shot each other a look, then followed her outside.

It was cold, the sky dark with the promise of more snow, but the deck had been shoveled off. Jack figured that was Mitzy's doing. The place had better curb appeal without making clients trudge through the eight inches of new snow that had fallen the night before to get to the front door.

"My parents invested here before the ski hill went in," Mitzy said when they joined her. "This is my home. Other people have left, but I stayed." There was pride in her voice. "I've done what I've had to to survive here."

She finally looked at them. "And I've done well."

Obviously it pissed her off royally that she'd been sharing that money with a blackmailer. Especially Peggy Kane, her husband's secretary.

"What did Peggy have on you?" he asked again.

Mitzy took another long drag, stubbed out the cigarette and tossed it into the nearest snowbank. She let the smoke roll out. Her words fell hard as the granite countertops in the expensive kitchen behind them. "I met this photographer. He told me he thought I could be a model so he talked me into posing for a few shots."

Jack felt Tempest's gaze on him. "Nude photos?"

"What do you think?" Mitzy snapped. "It had been years, then about six months ago, I got an anonymous letter demanding money or the photos would end up on a Web page and everyone in River's Edge would have the address."

"What means did you use to pay?" Jack asked, already knowing where the money had ended up.

"A post office box in California," Mitzy said. "And yes, I tried to find out who had the box. It was just one of those blind address things." She turned to look at him. "You're positive it was Peggy?"

"The money was going from your account to hers within a matter of hours," he hedged.

"You probably think that I killed her now," Mitzy said. "Well, I wish to hell I had." With that, she turned and walked back to lock the house, before heading to her black Ford Explorer. Jack noted that the car was exactly like the one Peggy had bought for herself and wondered if Mitzy hadn't noticed as well.

SEVEN

BACK AT THE OFFICE, Jack didn't say a word as he dropped a sheet of paper on the interrogation room table in front of Oliver. The paper was a copy of the doodles from Peggy's scratchpad where she'd written "Mrs. Peggy Sanders" around the border a half dozen times.

Tempest sat and, at Jack's nod, reached over to hit the record button on the tape recorder.

Oliver watched her for a moment, then looked down at the piece of paper, and for the first time, seemed to really see it and what was written on it. He stiffened and sat back a little as if trying to distance himself from it and what was coming.

"It seems Peggy thought she was going to be the next Mrs. Sanders," Jack said. "Why is that?"

Oliver swallowed and slowly raised his gaze. "I guess it's no secret she was in love with me."

"Not anymore," Jack said. "Did you know Peggy kept a date book with all your clandestine dates in it, including your plans for Valentine's Day?"

Oliver shot a look at Tempest, then Jack. He dropped his face in his hands, his body jerking as he burst into racking sobs.

Jack pulled up a chair to wait. Tempest stared at a

spot on the wall over Oliver's head, seemingly unaffected by the display.

After a few moments, Oliver stopped sobbing, pulled out his handkerchief and wiped his eyes and nose with quick, angry swipes as if embarrassed.

"I was in love with her," Oliver said without looking at either of them. "Valentine's Day I was going to tell Mitzy I was leaving her. After my birthday, Peggy and I were going to blow this place and not look back."

"Kind of cold to tell your wife you're leaving her on Valentine's Day, isn't it?" Jack said.

"I couldn't keep lying to Mitzy, to myself. I couldn't keep…pretending." He looked to Jack as if he might understand. "Mitzy and I only married because it seemed like the thing to do. High school sweethearts and all that crap. Everyone kept saying we were so *perfect* for each other. Especially my parents. What could I do but marry her?"

Jack could see how Oliver might have gotten swept up in that. A lot of young couples did—and later regretted it. Probably the reason divorce rates were so high. It was hard to decide what to do with your life at eighteen—let alone who you wanted to spend the rest of it with.

"How long had you been having the affair?" Jack asked.

Oliver stared at the paper on the table, no doubt thinking it was all written down in the date book. "About six months."

"Is there any chance Mitzy found out?" Jack had to ask.

Oliver looked up in surprise. "No, I mean…you don't

think Mitzy...." He shook his head. "Mitzy can be a real bitch, but murder?"

"How do you think she'd have taken the news about you leaving?"

He shrugged and looked away. "I don't know. I thought she might be relieved, you know. She would have been pissed. At first. But she doesn't need me. She never has."

"And Peggy did?"

"Yeah." He looked as if he might cry again.

Jack still wasn't sure he believed the first breakdown, but he was one suspicious SOB and he knew it. "So who do you think poisoned Peggy?"

He wagged his head. "Maybe Peggy decided to take things into her own hands, you know—" he stopped as if horrified by the idea "—kill Mitzy, but then got confused or scared and accidentally mixed up the boxes of chocolates."

Jack loved the way Oliver was trying to make it look like Peggy killed herself—accidentally, of course. Tempest had a look of disgust on her face.

"Or maybe that was the plan all along?" she said to Oliver.

He looked confused.

"To kill Mitzy," she clarified. "You sent your secretary out to buy your wife Valentine's Day presents, why not send your secretary out to kill your wife?"

"What?" Oliver cried. "I didn't want to kill Mitzy. But who knows what Peggy might have been thinking."

"Yes, who knows," Jack agreed, as disgusted with Oliver as Tempest was by her expression.

Oliver was tearful again. "I didn't want to hurt either one of them."

"But Mitzy was bound to be hurt when you told her you were leaving her for another woman," Tempest noted. "Surely you didn't really think Mitzy was going to take it well."

Oliver shrugged. "I guess I just hoped..." He put his face in his hands again.

"Maybe Peggy didn't believe you would leave your wife," Tempest suggested.

"No." Oliver raised his head. "She knew I was going to tell Mitzy last night. That's what makes it all so awful."

"So what was the point of buying Mitzy all the expensive presents if you were dumping her?" Jack asked.

"Just keeping up the pretense one last time," Oliver said. "Everyone in this town knows us, knows when we sneeze. I wanted people to think Mitzy and I were just fine. I guess I wanted to spare her any humiliation, especially on Valentine's Day."

"But you were going to tell her you were leaving her," Jack said.

"Yeah, but no one would have had to have known," Oliver said as if it made perfect sense to him.

It did to Jack, too. "Until you'd left town. Then she would have been humiliated, but you wouldn't have been here or what would you care, right?"

Oliver looked at him. "You of all people know I've never been good at facing up to things."

No, Jack thought, remembering the cheating incident only too well.

"Peggy must have put the poison in the chocolates," Oliver said as if to himself.

"The thing is, Oliver, I don't believe Peggy mixed up the boxes of candy," Tempest said. "I've seen her work area and her files. She was too efficient, too methodical."

Oliver swallowed. "Well, then…" He shook his head. "I just can't believe it was Mitzy…unless she found out about us."

"How could she not?" Jack demanded. "I can't believe you could have had an affair in this small town without everyone knowing about it."

"I rented a condo in another town. We met there. Or went to dinner in other towns. Since we worked together, no one was the wiser."

Jack wondered about that. "You never met at the penthouse or her apartment?"

"Never." Oliver seemed to relax as if a great weight had been lifted from his shoulders. "Mitzy must have found out somehow. I'm glad it's all out in the open."

Jack glanced at Tempest, then dropped the bomb. "Maybe what Mitzy found out was that you were blackmailing her with those old photos in your safe and giving the money to your mistress."

Shock ran like a bolt of electricity through Oliver, leaving him pale and trembling. "Oh, Christ," he mumbled.

"You had the photos. Peggy had the money. The evidence is in the bank accounts," Jack said. "Mitzy withdrew it and Peggy put it in her account a couple of days later. Mitzy told us about the photos. The ones I found in your safe just this morning, so don't even try to deny it.''

Oliver slumped in his chair, shoulders hunched, and for a moment, Jack thought the man would cry again and the crying was getting tiresome. "It was Peggy."

"You're saying the blackmail was her idea?" Tempest asked. "She knew about the photos?"

Oliver shook his head. "Peggy thought the money was mine. She'd never had anything, you know? I just wanted to give her…something."

"In other words, she was demanding things?" Jack asked.

Oliver looked up, blinked, his eyes moist. "It wasn't like that. I *wanted* to give her things." He looked to Tempest as if he thought she might understand.

"Peggy *and* Mitzy were more than you could afford," Tempest guessed.

"I had no other choice but to get money from Mitzy," Oliver said irritably. "The hotel wasn't doing that well, I had money tied up in the new condo development and my mother was taking everything else. I just needed to hang in a few more weeks until my birthday."

"Couldn't you have taken money from your joint account?" Jack asked.

Oliver shook his head. "Mitzy had her own checking account. She put all her money into it and never let me touch a cent of it."

So that was it. Jack shook his head. Why did it always come down to money?

There was a tap at the door. Deputy Dobson stuck his head in, handed Tempest some papers and gave her a smile. The door closed.

Tempest looked down at the documents the deputy had given her, then said, "Is that why you took out an insurance policy on Peggy? Five hundred thousand dollars with you as the beneficiary." She looked up. "What was that, insurance just in case she should eat some poison chocolates?"

Jack was surprised. Oliver looked shocked.

"I don't know anything about an insurance policy." Oliver sat up, looking scared now. "I'm telling the truth. You have to believe me."

"You're saying Peggy did it all on her own?" Jack asked.

"She must have."

"Why would Peggy do that?" Tempest asked quietly.

"How should I know?" Oliver cried.

"Maybe she thought something was going to happen to her," Tempest suggested.

Oliver was sweating bullets. "I don't know. I mean, maybe she was worried things wouldn't go well with Mitzy when I told her. Maybe she thought Mitzy might…do something."

"Like kill her?" Jack asked. "So she wanted you to have some money?"

"Maybe." Even Oliver was finding that scenario hard to   swallow. "Maybe…she…meant…to…kill…herself."

"Or maybe," Tempest said, "Peggy was worried you might try to off her. The insurance money would make you look awfully suspicious. So would the date book in her apartment and the Valentine that was found clutched in her hand in your foyer."

It was obvious that this was the first Oliver had heard about the Valentine.

"Peggy had a valentine in her hand for you," Tempest said.

"Peggy knew I loved her. We were going to get married." He sounded shaken and not at all sure.

"What will you do now?" Tempest asked.

Oliver looked confused again.

"About leaving Mitzy?" she asked.

"I don't know." He seemed to give it some thought. "I guess I won't have to do anything if she's arrested for murder." The thought didn't sound like a new one.

"How would that make you feel, knowing that Mitzy killed the woman you loved?" Jack asked.

Oliver seemed at a loss for words.

"You never planned to marry Peggy, did you?" Jack snapped. "You planned to just take off once you got your money. You weren't just running out on Mitzy. You were going to run out on Peggy, too."

"No." The word had no conviction in it.

"You needed a clean break and you didn't want to have to pay anymore," Jack continued. "So you killed Peggy and now you're hoping to frame Mitzy for the murder."

"You're wrong," Oliver pleaded. "You just want to see me fry for this. That would make you both happy, wouldn't it?" He was looking at Tempest, looking afraid of her. And she was looking at him as if seeing him fry would definitely make her day.

Jack stared at the two of them for a moment, feeling incredibly tired. "Don't leave town," he said with a sigh as he snapped off the recorder and opened the interrogation room door to leave.

"*I'm* not going anywhere," Oliver said and was still looking at Tempest, implying maybe that she was going somewhere when Jack looked back at them.

He could hear Tempest coming behind him as he left the room. Once in his office, he turned to face her. "What's with you and Oliver?" he demanded.

She raised a brow, either at his tone or his question.

"He thinks we're both out to get him. I have my own reasons for disliking the ass, but what are yours?"

"My own and nothing to do with this case." She started to turn to leave, but he grabbed her arm. She froze and he quickly let go.

"You're not making this any easier," he said with a sigh.

"Oh, is that my job, to make things easier for you?" she asked.

They stood looking at each other.

"What do you want from me?" he demanded. "I'm sorry about the way I treated you in high school, I'm sorry I resented it when you tried to butt into my life with Frannie, all right?" Just saying her name made it feel as if she'd materialized and now stood with them, a small, dark, troubled apparition, the kind of woman in life who just naturally made a man like him protective of her.

"I was trying to help Frannie."

"Come on, you thought she made a mistake marrying me," he said.

"Marriage wasn't the answer to the problem," she snapped. "You just had to play the big man taking care of the little woman. You were so damned sure that by whisking her away from here, that you could save her. You were so sure that your love was enough that she couldn't possibly need for anything else.''

Her words hit like stones, too many of them striking their mark.

Tempest turned and started to leave his office, but stopped and swung back around to face him. ''I loved Frannie, too,'' she said, tears in her eyes. ''You weren't the only one who tried to save her. We just didn't know what the hell we were trying to save her from.''

''The rape,'' Jack said, his voice barely a whisper. ''I took her away from here so she wouldn't have to remember.''

''But she couldn't forget, Jack.''

Neither could he. He'd always remember the night he'd found Frannie, crumpled like a doll in the corner of their bedroom, her clothes torn, her body bruised and bloody, her eyes blank as darkness. Frannie had never been able to tell him what had happened. Never been able to tell anyone. The shock of the rape had left her with no memory of her attacker, the doctors said.

The sheriff at the time speculated Frannie had been raped by someone just passing through. A stranger. A lot of people hitchhiked through the state and Jack and Frannie had moved in together in a place only a block from the main highway.

Jack blamed himself. For them living so close to the highway because he didn't want them using Frannie's money. For him not being home that night because he'd been working for Otto Sanders and had been called out to fix some broken pipes at one of the condos. And Jack knew Tempest, Frannie's best friend, blamed him as well because she'd never thought he and Frannie belonged together in the first place.

Of course he'd taken Frannie as far away from River's Edge as possible after that. The doctor said she might never remember her attacker. Jack had always hoped she never would.

He looked at Tempest, wanting desperately to tell her how wrong she was about him and Frannie, to explain how hard he'd tried to help her. But the truth was, he *hadn't* saved Frannie and for some reason he'd never understood, she seemed as if she'd needed protecting long before the rape.

His cell phone rang. He cursed as he answered it.

"Sheriff?" Dobson said.

"Yeah."

"The bellhop at The Riverside says he has something important he needs to tell you. He gets off work in about fifteen minutes. He says he'll only talk to you. He seems a little…scared."

Jack looked up at Tempest. "Tell him we'll be right over."

EIGHT

THE BELLHOP was a young man with short spiky bleached blond hair, several small silver hoop earrings and a skier tan that gave him racoon eyes—his face deeply tanned except around his eyes from his ski goggles.

"I remembered something about Valentine's Day that I thought you might want to know," the bellhop said. "But first I have to know that I won't lose my job if I tell you."

That was a promise Jack wasn't sure he could keep. "Why don't you tell me what it is first. Anything you tell us will be strictly confidential." Jack figured he could get the kid a job somewhere in town if he got fired.

"I didn't think anything about it at the time, but someone went up the fire escape stairs to the penthouse," the bellhop said. "I noticed the door closing and since only the Sanderses have a key…. What was weird about that was at the same time someone was going up the elevator to the penthouse—and I'd just seen Mr. Sanders's secretary go up with a whole bunch of packages. I just figured Mrs. Sanders had taken the stairs and that they were at it again. But then Mrs. Sanders walked in not long after that."

"At it again?" Jack asked.

The young man blushed to the roots of his blond do. Obviously he'd been warned about discussing the Sanderses' personal problems. "Oh…ah…I mean—"

"They fight," Jack said. "Married couples do that. I need you to be honest with me. This is a murder investigation so we can't have any…confidences."

The bellhop nodded. "Oh, do they *fight*. They try to hide it, but I've noticed the way Mrs. Sanders gives him the evil eye and I've taken up breakfast before and caught her yelling at him when the elevator opens, before they know I'm there."

It didn't sound like the lovebirds had been doing a very good job of pretending. "So first you saw the secretary go up in the elevator?"

The bellhop nodded.

"Then someone went up the fire escape stairs. That requires a key, right?"

The young man nodded again.

Jack looked at Tempest. "Who has keys?"

"The same people who have keys to the penthouse elevator." That meant Oliver, Mitzy and Tempest, the house detective.

"Could it have been Mr. Sanders on the stairs?"

The bellhop shook his head. "I just saw movement, heard footfalls. But it couldn't have been Mr. Sanders. Because he was the one who went up the elevator."

"You saw him go up *before* Mrs. Sanders?" Jack asked in surprise. Finally, a witness who could put Oliver in the penthouse at the time of the murder.

"I just caught a glimpse of him, but there is no mistaking that cologne he wears, whew!"

Jack looked over at Tempest. She looked nervous. "So first the secretary goes up the elevator," he clarified. "Then how long after that does Mr. Sanders go up?"

"A few minutes. Five, maybe a little more," the bell-hop said. "At the same time someone went up the stairs."

"And Mrs. Sanders?" Jack asked.

"It had to be about ten minutes after the others," the young man said. "Maybe more. I was busy with a bus-load of skiers who came in."

"Would you do me a favor?" he asked the bellhop.

"Sure."

Jack motioned to the elevator. "I want to do a little experiment." He pulled the penthouse key from his pocket, the one he'd taken from Tempest the day before. Tempest and the bellhop followed him into the elevator. He inserted the key and they rose quickly to the pent-house where the door opened.

"Hello?" he called out. Mitzy was still at work as was Oliver, it appeared.

"Okay," Jack said. "Tempest, may I borrow your phone?" She handed him the department cell and he handed it to the bellhop. "Stand right here with the el-evator door open and when I call you on the phone, hang up then scream as loud and high-pitched as you can," he said to the young man. "May I borrow your pass key?"

The bellhop handed Jack his key.

Jack turned to Tempest. "Shall we?"

They took the fire escape exit down from the pent-house to the floor below. "Where exactly were you when you heard Mitzy scream?" he asked Tempest.

"Is this necessary?" she asked.

"I'm afraid so. Which room?"

She pointed down the hall to a room directly beneath

the penthouse and adjacent to the elevator. Jack used the passkey to get into the room, then he called the bellhop on his cell phone, asked him to scream and keep screaming until Jack called him back, then hung up.

He and Tempest stood in the middle of the room looking at each other for a long moment. Then Jack opened the door to the hallway and listened. He called the bellhop and told him he could stop screaming now and thanked him. Then Jack turned to Tempest.

"You didn't go up to the penthouse because you heard Mitzy scream," he said. "Why did you lie?"

She met his gaze. "I wasn't on the floor below the penthouse."

No kidding.

"I was on the fire escape stairs outside the penthouse."

He stared at her, waiting. Through the window he could see the February sky, cold and gray as if all the color had been washed from it.

"I thought I saw Oliver take the elevator up to the penthouse and I followed him since I knew Peggy had just gone up and Mitzy wasn't home," she said.

"You knew he was having an affair with Peggy?" Jack said.

She shook her head. "Ellie suspected her son was skimming money off the top of the hotel's proceeds."

"Was he?" Jack asked.

She nodded. "I figured he was gambling or just greedy. I thought he might be in on it with his secretary's help."

"When were you planning to tell me?" he asked. "Don't make me remind you that this is a murder investigation," he warned her, angry that she'd been hold-

ing out on him. Worse that she might somehow be involved more than he'd thought.

"Ever heard of client confidentiality?" she asked.

"But now you're the undersheriff."

"Yeah," she said, sounding like him. "So I just told
you. I had to okay it with my client, which I did just
this morning. I was going to tell you."

He let out a sigh. He would have preferred that she'd
told him before he figured it out himself. And why did
he feel like she was still holding out on him?

"Why does Oliver act so odd around you?" he asked.

"I would assume he's worried that I've found out
about the hotel books and plan to tell his mother," she
said with a shrug. "Ellie already knows, she just hasn't
done anything about it yet."

Maybe that was all there was to it.

"You didn't discover the affair between him and
Peggy when you were investigating Oliver?" he asked
again.

She shook her head. "Sure he had a lot of meetings
out of town, but I had a job here at the hotel and couldn't
follow him everywhere. But I would never have guessed
he was seeing Peggy. She seemed too…needy."

Jack nodded. "All we have is Oliver's word that they
were in love."

"Why would he lie about it?" Tempest asked in surprise.

He shook his head. "I don't know. Something just
feels…wrong about all of this."

Tempest said nothing as they left the hotel room. He
returned the key to the bellhop and retrieved her cell
phone.

They were walking back to the office when Jack saw
Ramsey pull up out front.

"I'm starved," the coroner said. "Can we discuss this over a late lunch?"

Nothing like talking about an autopsy over lunch, but Jack realized he hadn't eaten all day. "Sure. Tempest?"

They walked down to Dill's, a small sandwich shop, and sat at the back, although the place was empty that time of the day.

"Well?" Jack asked after watching Ramsey devour half of the sandwich special.

"Strychnine definitely is what killed her," he said between bites. "Found it in the stomach contents. Sent it to the lab and, bingo, there it was right in the chocolate she'd eaten and also in the creams spilled on the floor. But we knew that as soon as we found the strychnine in the chocolate creams."

Tempest looked up from her salad. "Only in the chocolate creams?"

Ramsey nodded. "Probably because they were the easiest ones to inject. Simple to do. Mix a little strychnine with water, use a hypodermic needle."

"Or maybe the killer knew who was partial to creams," Jack said, following up on Tempest's question. "How long before the poison killed her?" he asked, trying to calculate whether Oliver reached the penthouse before or after Peggy had died.

The coroner shrugged. "With strychnine poisoning the victim can't breathe so the cause can appear to be a stroke or choking. She would have gone rigid with convulsions, gasping for breath, maybe for as long as ten minutes, head thrown back, limbs stiff and extended. That would explain the strewn chocolates and the bites on her tongue. Within a minute, she would have turned blue."

Oliver would have seen it then, if not caused it. The

man had to be cold-blooded to watch his lover die like that.

Jack looked over at Tempest. She didn't seem bothered by this talk. She continued to eat her salad as if lost in thoughts of her own.

So there had been time for Oliver to go up to the penthouse before Peggy ate one of the chocolates. Maybe he'd even tempted her with the chocolates, watched her die, then hid until Mitzy came up. Tempest might have just missed him on the stairs.

"Strychnine, that's the stuff that's commonly used to poison gophers," Tempest said.

Ramsey nodded. "Historically. Still used in grain or pellets. Your killer would have needed the powder. Can't buy it except through a pharmacist and would have to have gotten it illegally. But I'll bet there's still some bags of the powdered strychnine around."

Killing gophers was almost a Montana sport. Either popping them with a .22 or poisoning them. Gophers dug holes that a horse could break a leg in so ranchers had always hated them. So did a lot of other land owners.

Tempest pushed her salad away. "Wouldn't a developer who owned land around here probably have strychnine?"

Ramsey nodded.

Jack knew what she was getting at. Oliver probably had some at his new condo development project. Jack dialed his office and sent Dobson to get a warrant to check.

Oliver now had not only opportunity and motive, but means if they could find strychnine on his property.

Jack thought he'd feel more satisfaction solving the murder and nailing Oliver. Instead, he felt as if it had been just a little too easy.

NINE

TEMPEST GOT a call just as they were leaving Dill's.

"I'm going to go help Dobson look for the strychnine," she said when she hung up.

"Call me when you find it."

She'd only nodded and taken off, appearing anxious to have this case over with. No more than he was.

He drove back to his office, going over the case in his head. What was he missing? Something. He kicked up the heater in his office, watched the first few flakes of snow begin to fall outside, then picked up the bank statements and canceled checks and went through them again, not sure what he was looking for.

It was almost dark when he found it. Mitzy had written a check to a George Callendar. Since she'd written a lot of checks for a lot of things, he hadn't caught it at first. It wasn't until he turned over the check, that he realized who George Callendar was. Callendar Investigations of Butte, Montana.

Mitzy had hired a private investigator.

Jack could only guess why. He hurriedly dialed the Butte number. George Callendar had gone home for the day. He tried his home number.

"Mitzy Sanders?" the older P.I. asked.

"From River's Edge," Jack repeated. "I'm the sheriff

up here and it's part of a murder investigation.'' Jack gave him a number to verify that fact.

George called him back a few minutes later. ''Sure, I remember the case.''

''I need to know why she hired you,'' Jack said.

''To confirm her suspicions that her husband was having an affair,'' George said as if that kind of case was all too common.

And Oliver thought he was being so sneaky.

''And?'' Jack asked.

''He was. With his secretary, a woman named Peggy Kane.''

Bingo. ''And you reported this to Mrs. Sanders?'' Jack asked, holding his breath. If Mitzy had known about Oliver's affair with Peggy—assuming Peggy had been the intended victim—well, that would definitely add a new dimension to the case. Mitzy would just as easily have access to any strychnine Oliver used to kill gophers on their properties.

George Callendar confirmed it. ''I gave her proof of the fact,'' George said like a man who knew his business.

''There was no doubt the two were having an affair and Mrs. Sanders was made aware of it?''

''That's right,'' the P.I. said.

Jack picked up the canceled check. So Mitzy had known—and for some time now. Plenty of time to plan a murder.

''There was another woman, too,'' the P.I. said. Jack could hear him digging in his files.

''Another woman?'' Jack heard himself echo. ''Oliver was having an affair with two women?''

''No, not an affair. This relationship was more…confrontational. Possibly an old girlfriend? Just thought I'd mention it in case it's important to your investigation. I told Mrs. Sanders, but she didn't seem interested. Just a minute, let me find her name. It was an unusual name...here it is..." But Jack knew before George said, "...Tempest Bailey. She was employed as the house detective at The Riverside and I believe she worked for Mr. Sanders. But their meetings were clandestine and didn't appear to be employer-employee related and quite tumultuous from what I saw."

"But Mrs. Sanders wasn't interested in that part?" Jack asked.

"No. I think her mind was more on the affair and possibly the meetings between Bailey and Mr. Sanders were hotel business related. Hard to say. But I was curious."

Yes, Jack thought. So was he. He thanked the P.I. and hung up, then started to call Tempest, but changed his mind. He should be able to find her easy enough. He pulled on his coat. The phone rang. He picked it up.

"I found the gopher poison, straight strychnine," Dobson said. "A bag of it was at the back of a top shelf of an old shed owned by the Sanderses. The shed lock was broken, but it appeared to have been broken for some time."

"So anyone could have gotten into the shed," Jack said.

"Looks that way."

"Bring it in as evidence. Have Tempest document where it was found."

"Ms. Bailey?" Dobson asked.

"Yes, she left to meet you right after you called her," Jack said.

"I didn't call her. I haven't seen her since this morning."

"I must have misunderstood," he said and hung up.

It had started to snow hard again. A wind drove the flakes into him at a slant, the ice crystals as biting as the cold. He remembered another night like this. The night he'd stood Tempest up for the prom and hooked up instead with Mitzy for the first time. The memory didn't bode well, he thought, as he drove through town toward the condo where Tempest lived. He could see the lights shining from the windows as he neared. Her four-wheel drive was parked out front, enough snow on the hood to make it appear it hadn't been driven for a while.

But as he slid into a parking spot a few vehicles down, the lights in her condo went out. He cut the engine, shut off his headlights and slid down in his seat.

She came out of the condo alone. He thought she'd head for her car. Instead, she took off on foot, going south toward The Riverside hotel.

He waited until she'd passed, then got out of his car and followed her at a safe distance through the falling snow. She had bundled up for the storm and walked quickly as if she knew exactly where she was headed and why.

He passed a stand of pines, the trees breaking the wind, increasing visibility. He could see her ahead, as dark as the fringe of cold pines etched against the snowy skyline. The air seemed to grow colder, the wind stronger. He bent his head to the snowstorm, staying back as far as he dared, but determined not to let her out of his sight.

She entered the side door of The Riverside and he had to run to catch up, afraid he'd lose her once she got inside. He'd barely cleared the door, when he caught a glimpse of her disappearing through another door. This one he realized led down to the basement and the boiler room. What the hell was she going down there for?

With growing anxiety, he hurried after her, catching the door before it could automatically lock behind her. Quickly he stepped through and pulled the door closed with a click he was afraid Tempest would be listening for.

He could hear her footfalls on the concrete steps. Cautiously, he followed her down. She hadn't turned on more lights. Dim bulbs provided a bare minimum of illumination, no doubt to save energy.

He could hear the scuff of footfalls over the sound of the steam heat belching from the boilers. She was moving through the dark shadows of the large water tanks. He tried to stay with her, hoping she couldn't hear him behind her.

It took him a moment to realize the sound of her footsteps had ceased.

He stopped walking but too late. She came out of the darkness from behind one of the tanks, stepping out in front of him, her weapon drawn.

"Easy," he said quickly, palms up. "It's me." He expected her to put her piece away, hoped she would, hoped she'd then explain why she'd lied about meeting Dobson and what she was doing down here.

When she didn't, he felt his heart drop. Until that moment, he hadn't realized how afraid he was that she was the murderer.

"What are you doing here?" she whispered.

"That's exactly what I wanted to ask you?"

She motioned for him to keep quiet, and glanced behind him as if she suspected they weren't alone as she lowered her weapon. "Oliver left me a message to meet him down here," she said in a whisper. "He said he wanted to tell me the truth about Peggy's murder, that he couldn't live with the horrible things he'd done."

"And you believed him! Why would you agree to meet him here of all places?" Jack demanded. "Especially knowing he might have already killed at least one person?"

She met his gaze, hers steely. "I know perfectly well what Oliver is capable of." But she seemed jumpy.

Jack heard something. A creak. Then another. He drew his weapon and motioned for Tempest to follow as he stepped around the large water tank off to his right, moving in the direction he thought the sound had come from.

At first he couldn't see anything. Then he saw the shadow silhouetted on the back wall. "Oh God," Tempest cried when she saw the hanging figure.

"Holy shit," Jack said and lurched around the tank to where Oliver Sanders's body dangled from a makeshift noose. "Christ, he hanged himself." The rope creaked again from the weight of the body. He started to reach to pull the body down even though it was plainly too late for Oliver. He'd been hanging there for some time.

"No, don't touch him," Tempest said, grabbing Jack's arm. She still had her weapon drawn. "Don't touch the crime scene," she said, pointing the gun at him again.

"What the hell?" he said, trying to keep his voice calm while his heart drummed in his chest and he looked at the weapon she had pointed at him again. "What's going on?"

"We both know Oliver didn't have the guts to kill himself," she said.

"You think I killed him?"

"Someone did," she said, pulling out her flashlight to shine the beam at Oliver. "Look at his neck," she said in horror.

He followed the beam of her flashlight. Oliver had clawed at the noose and his neck, tearing deep gouges in his throat as he'd desperately tried to free himself.

"He could have changed his mind at the last minute," Jack said.

"Then why didn't he just stand up on the wooden box? He could have reached it without any trouble."

Jack felt a chill. Tempest was right. The box was close enough so that Oliver could have drawn it closer with his feet and stood up.

Tempest shone the light on the concrete floor. There were drag marks. First where the box had been pulled over under the beam and the noose. Then where the box had been pulled back—and then slid over again, the scrapes fresh and not the same as the first.

Jack swore and looked over at her. "You're right, he didn't hang himself." Then he realized that Tempest was again holding her weapon on him. "Come on, why would I want to kill Oliver? Not all the crap from high school. You can't believe that I'd kill a man over that petty stuff."

She shook her head. "Frannie must have told you."

His breath caught in his throat. "Frannie must have told me what?" he asked, his entire body suddenly weak with fear.

Tempest's hands were shaking and she looked scared. "Drop your weapon," she said, pocketing the flashlight to take her own weapon in both hands. "Please, Jack, drop the gun."

He did, afraid she wouldn't tell him otherwise. "What is it you think Frannie told me?" She swallowed, keeping the weapon aimed at his heart, searching his face as if she could read the truth there.

He wanted to take the weapon from her and shake the words from her. "For God's sake, Tempest, tell me."

The rope creaked again. Another boiler cut on. "Frannie called me the day she…died," Tempest said slowly, still watching him closely. "She remembered."

Jack felt his legs go weak beneath him. He realized he was shaking his head as he fought to stay on his feet. "No."

Tempest nodded.

He closed his eyes, swaying under the weight of it.

"That's why Frannie blocked it from her memory," she said. "Because her attacker was Oliver."

He was still shaking his head, not wanting to believe it, his eyes squeezed shut. When the sheriff's job had opened up, he'd jumped at it, believing it was fate. As sheriff he could look into Frannie's case, maybe find some answers, but not really expecting much. He'd never dreamed—

"It's true, Jack," Tempest said more softly. "I tried to help Frannie. I swear I did. I told her I'd kill the son of a bitch for her. When I hung up, I thought she was all right. I never dreamed she'd—" Tempest started crying. "If she'd have been here in River's Edge, I could have gone to her. I could have done something—" She was crying hard, angry sounding sobs. "If only I'd been able to stop Oliver…before he hurt Frannie, too."

Jack opened his eyes. "He—"

She nodded through her tears.

"But you didn't turn him in?"

"I went to the sheriff," she said angrily. "You remember who was sheriff then, don't you, Jack? A good friend of Otto Sanders. He called me a liar and a lot of other things and threw me out of his office. I didn't know who else to turn to. There'd already been so much scandal in my family.... That's when that rumor started going around school that I was a slut and did it with the entire football team.''

Jack shook his head, too sick to speak for a moment. Now he understood why she'd gone into law enforcement. Why she'd come back here. Not just to torment Oliver with what she knew, but to make sure no other girl would have to go through what she did. It also explained what he'd seen between her and Oliver. Oliver's fear. Tempest's anger. And the meetings the P.I. had witnessed.

''I'm sorry. You told Oliver you knew?''

She nodded, getting control of herself again. ''I wanted to make him suffer like Frannie had all these years, not knowing what I was going to do to him. Can you believe Frannie blamed herself? Oliver told her she'd *made* him rape her. At least I didn't fall for that.''

Jack saw now how easy it had been for Oliver to get to Frannie that night. Otto had sent Jack up to fix those broken pipes. Oliver had to have known Frannie would be alone. Oliver had gotten away with it once, he must have thought he could get away with it again. And he had.

He looked up at the body hanging from the beam, wondering what he'd have done if he'd known about this before and what he would have done if he'd found Oliver before someone else had.

''Oliver hurt Frannie because of me,'' he said, the words coming hard. This was about the competition between the two of them. Good God.

''That's exactly why Frannie didn't want to tell you.

She knew you'd blame yourself, just as she blamed herself," Tempest said.

"I'm so sorry," he said to Tempest, to Frannie wherever she was.

Tempest shook her head. "Oliver is to blame, not us," she said angrily. "That's what I couldn't get Frannie to understand. I hope you're smarter than that."

He stared at her.

Tempest studied him for a moment, then sheathed her weapon. "I was so afraid—"

He nodded. "We both had good reason to kill Oliver. But we didn't."

"No," she said.

"I think we'd better call in our crime team and find Mitzy," he said. "She knew about Oliver and Peggy. She's known for several weeks."

"But she couldn't have done this by herself," Tempest said, glancing again at Oliver's body.

"No," Jack agreed. "She would need help." Nor would it be easy to prove. If he knew Mitzy, she would have covered her tracks well.

TEN

MITZY DIDN'T seem surprised to see Jack. In fact, she jumped up from the couch and rushed toward him, stopping just short, her gaze searching his face.

"Oh, Jack," she said, her hand on her heart, tears filling her eyes. "It's about Oliver, isn't it? I just knew it. I've been so worried. When he left here—he was talking so crazy! I called Randall and we tried to find him...."

Jack looked past her to Randall Garrison, Oliver's attorney. It was clear what Mitzy would see in the guy. She'd look good on his arm and Mitzy had always cared about appearances.

"Please, Jack, tell me Oliver's not..."

"Oliver's dead," Jack said.

She burst into tears and turned to Randall. He put his arm around her and tried to console her.

"He was murdered," Jack said.

Mitzy stopped crying and jerked her head up in surprise.

Jack began to read them their rights. "...for the murders of Peggy Kane and Oliver Sanders," he finished.

Mitzy shook her head in disbelief. "Jack, you know me! You can't really believe that I killed my own husband."

"Yes, I do know you, Mitzy. That's why I should

have figured it out a lot sooner. The bellhop thought he saw Oliver going up the elevator not long after Peggy because of the cologne Oliver wore, but it was Randall. They wear the same brand, dress alike.'' He smiled at Mitzy. ''I'm sure that was your doing. And Randall and Oliver looked enough like each other even if the bellhop had seen him, he'd have sworn it was Oliver.''

''Don't say anything,'' Randall warned her.

''We know you bought the chocolate,'' Jack continued as if the attorney hadn't spoken. Jack remembered on the way here that he'd seen Randall Garrison's name on the list of people who purchased the heart-shaped Valentine's Day boxes, but hadn't thought anything about it at the time.

''We know you bought two boxes. One, obviously to poison, and the other box…'' he motioned to the coffee table finding it hard to believe what he was seeing ''…to celebrate your victory.'' Mitzy did love to flaunt her successes.

There on the glass coffee table was a big heart-shaped box of chocolates identical to the one that had killed Peggy Kane just the day before—open and partially empty.

Jack shook his head, remembering what Oliver had said about never eating chocolate again. But Mitzy had no reason to fear a few chocolate creams—other than what they'd do to her hips.

''I can see how you manipulated Oliver to make him look guilty and make his suicide almost convincing,'' Jack said. ''I have to hand it to you, Mitzy, you're good. But how did you get Peggy to eat the chocolates?'' he asked conversationally.

''Mitzy—'' her lawyer/lover tried to warn, but she waved him off.

She smiled at Jack, no doubt figuring it would be his word against hers. "That was the easy part, Jack. I knew her weakness. I knew once those chocolates were opened and one was missing, she wouldn't be able to help herself. That's what killed her. Not her weakness for chocolates so much as her weakness for *my* chocolates."

"And what was Oliver's weakness?" Jack asked.

"Shut up," Randall hissed at her. "You've already said too much."

But Mitzy was dying for Jack to know how clever she'd been. "Oliver had soooo many weaknesses. He was always leaving his elevator key lying around. It was easy to pocket it, give it to Randall and make it look like it had been Oliver who'd switched the chocolates that killed Peggy."

"Mitzy!" Randall said through gritted teeth.

But she didn't seem to hear him. "I followed Peggy around town as she bought my Valentine's presents because I knew Oliver would send her out to do his dirty work, and I knew she couldn't resist taking a look around the penthouse. It was so-o-o easy. Randall wouldn't have been noticed when he came right back down by elevator. The desk clerk and bellhop had been too occupied with the busload of Minnesotans."

"But getting Oliver down to the boiler room, that must have taken something," Jack said.

"Another of Oliver's weakness," Mitzy crowed. "Women he couldn't have. I just sent him a note that he thought was from Tempest to meet him in the boiler room."

So Mitzy thought Oliver had been pursuing Tempest. Jack didn't correct her.

"You must have hit Oliver with something," Jack

said. "I can't imagine him climbing up on the box and putting the noose around his neck."

She laughed at the image. "Randall had to hit him with a wrench. Unfortunately, Oliver regained consciousness before he could strangle to death." She pretended dismay. "It was downright ugly to watch."

"I'll just bet. But why did you do it?" Jack asked.

"I figured once Oliver was dead, that would be the end of the investigation," Mitzy said. "You know, tie up all those loose ends."

Randall had sat down, his hand over his face.

"I meant, why did you kill Peggy? Why not just let Oliver take off with her?"

Mitzy looked shocked. "That bastard thought he could leave me for someone like...Peggy?" Mitzy sneered. "I'd spend the rest of my life in prison before I'd let him leave me for *her*."

"Be careful what you wish for," Randall said.

"Don't worry, darling," she replied sweetly. "Jack can't prove anything. It would just be my word against his and I'm still a Sanders and the name carries a lot of weight in these parts. Jack can't prove a thing or he would have brought his *under*sheriff and those two cute deputies of his."

"Oh, but I did, Mitzy. Tempest? Deputy Reed?"

Tempest stepped out, the tape recorder in her hand, Deputy Reed behind her. "Got it all on tape, including you reading them their rights," Tempest said to him.

Mitzy looked as if she'd been slapped.

"I knew your weakness, too, Mitzy," Jack said to her. "You just couldn't stand the thought that you'd pulled this whole thing off and no one might ever know just how amazing you were."

"I told you to shut up," Randall said. "I want an

attorney. None of this was my idea. It was all hers and I'll testify to it,'' he said, glaring at Mitzy.

"Why, you bastard—after everything I've done for you." Mitzy lunged at him, but Jack grabbed her wrist before her hand could reach its mark. He snapped a pair of cuffs on her as Tempest stepped in to cuff Randall.

Deputy Reed took the two into custody, leaving Jack and Tempest alone in the penthouse.

"I suppose River's Edge will be looking for a new sheriff now," she said studying the chocolates in the heart-shaped box on the coffee table.

At that moment, he realized that he'd never planned to stay. That's why he hadn't bothered to look for a place to live other than the motel.

He watched Tempest reach down to pick up a chocolate cream from Mitzy's box of Valentine's Day candy. Maybe he could stay around for a while. It wasn't like he had to be somewhere else. And no matter where he went, a part of Frannie would always be with him.

"I don't know," he said. "You and I make a pretty good team. And I've always wanted to learn to ski. Maybe it's not too late."

"Just my luck," Tempest said as she popped the chocolate cream into her mouth, her lips closing around it, her eyes fluttering shut. She let out a long satisfied sigh and smiled.

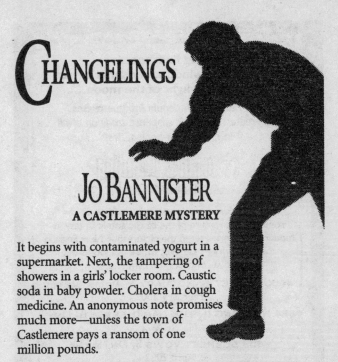

CHANGELINGS

JO BANNISTER
A CASTLEMERE MYSTERY

It begins with contaminated yogurt in a supermarket. Next, the tampering of showers in a girls' locker room. Caustic soda in baby powder. Cholera in cough medicine. An anonymous note promises much more—unless the town of Castlemere pays a ransom of one million pounds.

Superintendent Frank Shapiro, recovering from a bullet wound, has been cleared for desk duty. But with Sergeant Cal Donovan on holiday cruising the Castlemere Canal, he must rely on Inspector Liz Graham as hysteria rises.

The situation worsens when the detectives learn Donovan's abandoned boat has been found—and that the volatile sergeant is believed dead by the hand of the blackmailer....

Available February 2002 at your favorite retail outlet.

WJB410

**Creaking floorboards...
the whistling wind...an enigmatic man
and only the light of the moon....**

*This February Harlequin Intrigue revises
the greatest romantic suspense tradition of all
in a new four-book series!*

Moriah's Landing
A Modern Gothic

Join your favorite authors as they recapture the
romance and rapture of the classic gothic fantasy in
modern-day stories set in the picturesque New England
town of Moriah's Landing, where evil looms but
love conquers the darkness.

#650 SECRET SANCTUARY by Amanda Stevens
February 2002

#654 HOWLING IN THE DARKNESS by B.J. Daniels
March 2002

#658 SCARLET VOWS by Dani Sinclair
April 2002

#662 BEHIND THE VEIL by Joanna Wayne
May 2002

from

HARLEQUIN®
INTRIGUE®

HARLEQUIN®
Makes any time special ®

*Available at your
favorite retail outlet.*

Silhouette®

INTIMATE MOMENTS™

Where Texas society reigns supreme—and appearances are everything!

When a bomb rips through the historic
Lone Star Country Club, a mystery
begins in Mission Creek....

Available February 2002
ONCE A FATHER (IM #1132)
by Marie Ferrarella
A lonely firefighter and a warmhearted doctor fall in love while
trying to help a five-year-old boy orphaned by the bombing.

Available March 2002
IN THE LINE OF FIRE (IM #1138)
by Beverly Bird
Can a lady cop on the bombing task force and a sexy ex-con stop
fighting long enough to realize they're crazy about each other?

Available April 2002
MOMENT OF TRUTH (IM #1143)
by Maggie Price
A bomb tech returns home to Mission Creek and discovers that an
old flame has been keeping a secret from him....

And be sure not to miss the Silhouette anthology

Lone Star Country Club: The Debutantes

Available in May 2002

Available at your favorite retail outlet.

Where love comes alive™

THE PUMPKIN SEED MASSACRE

Native American psychologist Ben Pecos has returned to New Mexico as an intern with the Indian Health Service. Still struggling with the demons of his past, he is plunged into the nightmare rampage of a mysterious virus that is killing the residents of the pueblo, including his own grandmother.

One of the victims, the powerful tribal governor, opposed the construction of a proposed gambling casino on pueblo land. Ben suspects his murder was premeditated—but that doesn't explain the insidious killer now stalking the innocent.

> "...great plot...a gripping novel."
> —Tony Hillerman

Available February 2002 at your favorite retail outlet.

SUSAN SLATER
A BEN PECOS MYSTERY

MYSTERY
™ **WORLDWIDE LIBRARY** ®

WSS411